Multiplarity

Omniphage – Selenaphiles – Micasians

Multiplarity

Omniphage – Selenaphiles – Micasians

Written by Anthony Stevens

Edited by Elise O'Loughlin
and
Stephanie McGrath

Cover art by John Picha
Cover layout by Anthony Stevens

Multiplarity

Omniphage – Selenaphiles – Micasians

Copyright 2016-2018

First Printing by Post Orbital Library: 2018

ISBN-13: 978-0-9885488-4-6

Discover other titles by Anthony Stevens at http://postorbitallibrary.com

Dedication

This novel owes a great deal to support and input from many fascinating people. Among them are My lovely wife, Brenda, Elise O'Loughlin, a cop called Kirk, Stephanie Burke, Stephanie McGrath, a cop called Bryan, an exotic dancer called Wendy, a gamer called Evan, a scientist called Sarah, and Kris, the bookseller.

Thank you for your ongoing patience and support!

Book One: Omniphage

Uninteresting Times

A blacktop ribbon disappeared into the distance between rows of waist-high corn while a distant rumble grew louder and coalesced into a lime-green sports car. Frantically waving cornstalks several yards behind were visual proof of its hundred mile per hour passage.

This farmyard was like hundreds of others. It held a large barn, several small storage sheds, machinery shop, and a sprawling nineteen fifties style ranch home of burnt brick with a windbreak wall of evergreens on the north side.

The bilious green of the '69 AMX seemed out of place as it rolled up the driveway and rumbled for a moment alongside the well-worked pickup.

"Dammit Victoria!" Mrs. Veski's voice echoed through the kitchen and out the back door as she moved onto the back steps. ."Yer gonna kill yerself with one of those damn cars yet."

"Not today Mom, I'm looking forward to some of your pie and ice cream." Tall and slender, the woman climbing out of the vintage hot rod was good-looking in an average way. "Where's Dad?" she asked as she hugged the buxom woman.

"He's back in the shop workin' on some ol' El Camino."

She walked around to the garage-cum-shop under the old barn and could see the back of a classic Chevy pickup sticking out. "Yo! Dad! Where are ya?"

"In here Vicki!" He hollered from in front of the pickup.

She gave him a hug and pointed at the pickup. "Where'd ya get this?"

"You remember the Kozio boys over near Gary?"

She nodded.

"Well, one of them bought this new in '62 and ran it at US30 Drag strip for a coupla seasons. When he got beat a few times, he put it up on stands in the garage. He was going to put a new engine in it later on."

"What's it got now?"

"Well now, he got real busy and kinda forgot about it for a few years and never did anything else with it." He pointed under the hood. "That's a stock 409 with a factory tri-power set-up!"

"You've got to be kidding! I didn't know Chevy even made a triple carburetor manifold."

"That just goes to show they don't teach ya everything at college. Anyway, old man Kozio got tired of tripping over this thing last month and I bought it off of him for five grand. Take a look. I buffed out the paint, only 28,000 original miles, seat fabric is intact, and all the instruments work."

"This is a real classic, isn't it Dad?"

"I'm going to put this one on the show circuit it's so damn clean. In a year or two somebody's going to offer me fifty or sixty grand and I'll let him talk me into it."

"How about a ride?"

"Not now, I'm still tweaking those carbs. In a coupla weeks, if you've got some time. I'll let you take it to the lab and impress all those other doctors. Speaking of which- what's the latest on that nanite project you got the grant for?"

"It's progressing really well. I think we solved the rejection problem finally and this should allow us to adapt the new rhino-virus to anyone's blood type."

"Well now, what do you think will be the outcome?"

"If all goes well, we should be able to show a targeted destruction of cancerous cells within the year. If there are no long-term side-effects, we could have a commercial cure for most types of cancer within five years. Oh, and by the way, don't tell anyone about this. We don't want to raise hopes until we've got all the bugs worked out."

"I understand, baby." He stopped and listened for a second to his wife's voice over the intercom.

"You two better come and get dinner before I feed it to the dog." Her voice was laughing. "... and Victoria, I expect you and your father to wash up first!"

Wakeup Call

Donald Samuelson was face-down, naked, on the waterbed. His wife Marsha, also naked, was astride him and slowly rubbing oil into his tired shoulders.

"Uhh... that feels great." He muttered.

"Shhhsss... " She leaned forward rubbed her breasts on his back and whispered in his ear. "Just relax and let me work these knots out."

At fifty-five he was in pretty good shape. He jogged when he got the chance and watched his diet. Marsha was forty-eight and his wife of thirty years. She was slightly overweight but carried it in the right proportions.

When she finished the massage, she climbed off, he rolled over and she started on the front. In a few minutes, she mounted him and they were furiously thrusting when the phone rang.

She leaned carefully over and lifted the receiver from the night stand. "This better be good!" She warned the caller in a husky voice.

"This is Dr. Witham. I'm sorry to disturb your Sunday afternoon Mrs. Samuelson, but I've got to speak with your husband as soon as possible."

She handed him the phone. "John Witham."

"What is it John?"

"You know that batch of test rats we injected Friday night?"

"What's the matter with them?"

"That's just it. There's nothing the matter with them. I came in this morning to check things out and Kathi was examining one of them. I asked her why the Sunday work and she pointed to this particular rat's medical record."

Marsha grasped a breast in each hand and presented them as she slowly moved her hips.

Her husband moved in response to her eroticism.

"Can you speed this up? I really am very... uh... busy right now..."

"Just let me finish. The rat she was examining had been written up as having several major, visible tumors and a general bad skin condition. We didn't think it would live until the end of summer. When she checked on it this morning it looked like a six-month old house pet. There were no traces of any disease."

"Did you call me to tell me some of our records have been tampered with?"

"Not that simple Don. I thought it was a paperwork error too. Then we started to check the rest of the lab. Get this. Every one of the rats we injected with that last batch on Friday was the same. They all appear to be in perfect health. And something else interesting, I found every cage was filthy and bloody. It looked like they had been torn apart in there. The food and water was almost gone in each cage too."

"Do you think we've been sabotaged by some animal-rights group?"

"I don't think so. Nothing else has been bothered and all the alarms seem to be working. I really think you should see this, Don. Besides, several of the test animals had video tapes running on them. I know it's Sunday afternoon, but this looks like we may have something really unusual."

"Okay, okay, I'll be down in an hour or so. Don't touch anything else until I get there."

He handed the receiver to Marsha and, as she stretched over him to hang it up, he grabbed her breasts and stuck the nearest nipple in his mouth. She arched, threw her head back and moaned low.

Hope Glimmers

"Hi Kathi, John. What've we got here?" Dr. Samuelson inquired of his team mates as he pulled on his lab coat.

"Come over here Doctor and take a look at this video from yesterday."

"Good afternoon, Don. You are not going to believe this tape. I've watched it three times with Kathi and I still can't believe it's not some Hollywood special effect."

"Go ahead Kathi, let's see what we've got."

Kathi pressed "play" then the "fast-forward" button. "If you'll watch the timer, you'll see this tape starts just after we injected this batch with the new nanite group.

The accelerated movements of the rat slowed down as it appeared to go to sleep. In a few moments, it started to twitch and curl into a fetal position, almost as if it were in pain. It still appeared to be unconscious though. Fresh, shiny fur started to push out all over and the exposed tumors shriveled up and fell off like old scabs. It sneezed several times and clots of blood containing small chunks of tissue were expelled. Its urine and feces also showed large amounts of blood. After about ten minutes, the small animal looked as if it had lost a third of its body weight but was in otherwise much better condition than when the tape had started. Waking up, the rat shook itself several times and staggered over to the watering tube where it drank for a long time. The food tray was the next target and it ate until her belly was distended. Obviously uncomfortable, it wandered around the cage for a few minutes, regurgitated most of the meal, then went back to drinking and eating.

She pressed the off button and stood with her arms folded.

Dr. Samuelson sat quietly for a few moments staring at the blank screen. "Have you examined that rat?"

"Only superficially. Before I saw that tape I gave it a quick exam and decided, like you had suggested, that somebody was screwing around with our experiment. I couldn't understand why someone would go to so much trouble though. I figured the tape would show at the very least, when the animal was switched." She shook her head. "Boy, was I surprised. That's when I called in Dr. Witham to verify the rest of these. We've been here for almost seven hours going over the other two tapes that were running. The one rat died after going through about the same stages as the other two. We wanted to wait until you were here before we went any further.

"Thanks for calling me. You two have done well. Let's get a cup of coffee and examine each of the rest of this batch. Oh, and by the way, I don't think I need to remind you two of the obvious need for secrecy until we can confirm these findings. This still might turn out to be a very elaborate practical joke some unfunny colleague is playing on us."

Discovery

"We've been testing batch 471 for the past ten days." Dr. Samuelson looked around the conference table at his staff. "I think we're all in agreement as to the effects if not the exact mechanism this strain is using." He paused.

"Anyone want to clarify a few points for me?" Bob Lorraine, their computer simulation guru and physicist, spoke up. "I know I helped design these little fellows, but I thought they just targeted cancerous cells. From what I've heard over the last few days they seem to cure everything from Leukemia to athlete's foot. What gives?"

"It's really rather simple when you look at it." Vicki started. "Excuse me Don, but I think I've got a pretty good handle on what's going on here."

"Go ahead Vicki. Maybe you can help clarify it for the rest of us."

"Well, the way I see it, the nanites grown in batch 471 are completely neutral when we produce them. They are small semi-biological engines with a missing component. This component matches the human DNA double-helix perfectly. It has already been structured with the basic healthy DNA pattern. All the so-called junk DNA along with markers for things like sex, eye-color, and hair color are in place, but need to be filled. When they come in contact with a sample of DNA that matches this basic pattern, they grab it, incorporate it into their own structure and begin looking for more. If there are conflicts that match known genetic diseases, it replaces them with a neutral marker. Whenever that particular nanite runs into another cell, it checks for a DNA match. If it matches, nothing happens and it moves on; if it doesn't match, the nanite attempts to rebuild the cell's DNA to match the pattern its holding. This process either completely rejuvenates the cell on the molecular level or it destroys it."

Dr. John Witham spoke up. "Excuse me, but I think we're all beating around the bush because we don't want to say what we're really thinking."

"And what's that John?" Don could always count on his mentor shaking things up a bit.

"Very easy... we've have stumbled onto the proverbial "Fountain of Youth" and you're all a little hesitant."

"Whoa now!" Bob cut in. "I think we're getting a little ahead of ourselves here. After all we're talking about a small sample and a few test..."

John interrupted him. "You've tested it on over sixty terminally-ill rodents, a dozen guinea pigs and three sick old alley cats that Vicki brought in from her dad's farm. Out of all those you lost one cat and three rats who were so far gone to begin with that they probably wouldn't have lasted the night." He took a sip of water and they waited for him to go on. "Correct me if I'm wrong, but it seems to me that if any patient is well enough to withstand the loss of ten to fifteen percent of their body weight, they'll end up with a brand-new, healthy-in-every-way body within a few hours of treatment."

"This is potentially very explosive." Don began.

"HA! That's an understatement if I ever heard one."

Don gave him a pained look and continued. "Let's keep a tight wrap on this until we get some more information. Vicki, can you arrange to get us some larger farm animals to test this on?"

"I'll have to be careful. My folks are cool, but they have a very healthy farm. If I ask the neighbors to bring in all their sick critters, they're going to start asking questions."

"We can't afford that right now. Let's take it real easy until we've gotten some more tests documented and a few more species confirmed." He stood up. "Bob, how much 471 do we have left?"

"Enough of the serum-base for about fifty rodent tests. Oh and while I'm on the subject. I would like to propose another test."

"What's that?"

"The nanites are grown and injected in a serum medium of course. I was wondering if the first-stage serum and liquid by-products could be drained and provide us with a stable, crystalline compound that we could store without refrigeration. The computer simulations I've run in the last few days seem to indicate it would work and they would go into emulsion almost immediately when exposed to whole blood."

"That would greatly simplify storage and transport, go ahead and take half of batch 471-F and experiment with that. If it works the same over the next week or so, then we'll take it from there. Good work Bob." Don opened the conference door. "Everyone agreed?"

They all nodded and went back to work.

Deathly Scared

"Sit down Mrs. Samuelson." The doctor pointed toward a chair. He sat on the corner of his desk, crossed his arms and sighed. "I'm afraid I've got some bad news for you. That lump you felt isn't alone. The scan showed several smaller tumors in both breasts. At this point, I'm afraid I must recommend a radical mastectomy. You'll be checking into the hospital on Monday." He placed his hand on her shoulder as she sat staring out the window. Her face was ashen with fear. "Have you told your husband yet?"

"No." Her voice was soft, controlled. "He's been very busy at work these last few weeks. I told him it was just a routine check-up."

"Do you want me to see him this afternoon...?"

"No. That's all right. I'll tell him tonight and he can make arrangements to be with me on Monday." She looked at him with tears in her eyes. "Doctor... Do you think... That is... What are my chances?"

"If we get all the major tumors in the breast area, we may be able to arrest the ones in the lymphatic system through radiation and chemotherapy. We have had some very high survival rates in this area." He tried to be positive.

***

"This is crazy! Have you lost your mind? I can think of at least a half-dozen federal laws that would be violated." Dr. Samuelson stared around the table.

Vicki pleaded. "Don, listen to me. If Marsha signs a complete set of release papers and you get her doctor to give you a written diagnosis of terminal cancer, then we may be able to save her life with 471-G."

"...or kill her within days!" A mixture of emotions played across his continence. He covered his face with his hands for a moment then laid them flat on the table. His expression was cold and distant as he looked at his colleagues. "I love my wife more than anything in the world... but we cannot use her for a guinea pig. We have no way of knowing what sort of side effects this may have. It's way too soon for a human volunteer... and the FDA won't even..."

Dr. Witham waved him to silence. "A thorough testing schedule will take five to eight years when the FDA hears of what we've got. You and I both know Marsha has six, maybe ten months."

Don looked at each face for a few seconds. "You understand that this will probably put all of our careers in jeopardy? We might even end up in prison."

Dr. Witham smiled. "My career is almost over anyhow."

Kathi shrugged and nodded.

Bob Loraine was frowning until he realized everyone was expecting an answer. "What th' hell! I can always take that around-the-world cruise on my sailboat if the shit hits the fan. You guys can help me handle lines."

Vicki spoke last. "None of us can stand by and watch Marsha die when we may be able to save her. John is right. If the FDA doesn't slap a lid on this, think what the lobbyists representing the drug companies will be up to. Don, Marsha can't wait."

Bob spoke up. "Classes start in three weeks. The board of regents is going to want to see you before then for an update on the research." He laughed. "Boy! Are they going to get their money's worth this time."

Don took a deep breath, let it out, and stood up. "Okay. I'll ask her if she wants to be the first human volunteer."

Dr. Witham stood up. "You all know I have a cabin in the mountains. There is a clinic nearby where I've donated quite a bit of time and money. I'll arrange for a room for Marsha and afterwards she can recuperate up in the woods. It may be a little cramped, but we can take turns looking out for her. There shouldn't be any problem with security leaks this way."

After the others left the room Vicki noticed a concerned look on the elder surgeon. "Don't worry, John. My intuition tells me this is going to work."

He gave her a lopsided smile. "She's a strong woman. I'm more worried about long-term results."

"We've seen none in any of the test animals."

"I don't mean her individual case. I mean the impact this could have. This single, rather economical treatment could cure every known disease within a few years."

"Overpopulation could be a problem if it was used indiscriminately... but I don't think..." She stopped.

His smile broadened. "You thought of it too, didn't you? Who decides? Who gets treated and who is left to die?

"Federal controls..."

"Hah! There isn't a government in the world that can stop ten percent of their population from smoking marijuana. What makes you think they could put a cap on the ultimate cure? Hell if they tried, their own office staff would lynch them."

She continued, looking for excuses. "You need a modern lab first and... yeah, I know, they have excellent labs for making several dozen illicit drugs. You're right. Well? What can we do? We can't just forget about it and let Marsha die while we look for answers to questions people have been wrestling with for a very long time already."

"I'm just a semi-retired surgeon; not a philosopher, nor a politician." The smile slowly left his face. "I am scared though. This discovery probably means the end of our society." He stared at a painting on the wall. "I only hope we like what comes next."

"Remember that old Chinese curse?"

"Huh?"

"May you live in interesting times."

He nodded, still not smiling.

Life Renewed

The following Friday afternoon, two SUVs and a minivan left the lab parking lot. Once on the interstate, a low-slung, orange pickup pulled up behind.

"Lab One, this is Lab Four. Everything okay?"

"Everything went well on our end, Lab Four. Where did you get that thing? It is bound to attract attention."

"That's the idea. People will be distracted by and remember my Dad's bright orange El Camino with camping supplies in the back. They are not going to remember a couple of modern SUVs parked alongside it."

It was later that night, when the little caravan slowly wound up the gravel driveway to a large log cabin.

"Vicki, you can park that thing in the machinery shed, alongside my tractor. Unpacking can wait until morning. I called up and had the caretaker put fresh linens on all the beds, including the guest room over the garage. Right now, I think we could all use some sleep."

A muttered chorus of agreements followed him up the steps and into the great room.

"Wow! Nice digs, Doc."

"Thanks! Don, you and Marsha take my suite off the kitchen. It will be a good recovery room. I'll take the guest room downstairs. Kathi and Vicki get one bedroom upstairs and Bob gets the other. Oh, and don't be surprised if you see a young fellow poking around outside tomorrow. That's Mark Brownam; our caretaker. I told him there would be guests for a couple of weeks."

Free Will

The clock on the wall of the private clinic showed eight in the morning.

"Give us a moment alone, please."

They nodded and went to wait in the hall.

"Darling. Are you absolutely sure you want to go ahead with this?"

Her voice was soft, but firm... "We've been over it a dozen times and I know the risks. All I ask is that you stay with me no matter how it resolves. Now get the team back in here and let's get this over with."

He held and kissed her for a moment, then opened the door. "Let's do it."

Doc Witham inserted the syringe half full of white powder into the IV shunt. Slowly, he opened it and allowed it to fill with bright red blood. As it mixed, the powder instantly went into solution. He paused for a moment once it was full, then slowly depressed the plunger until it was empty.

They were all watching as her arm muscles started to tighten. "Oooh... I can tell this isn't going to be fun." She winced and clenched her hands. "I can feel something moving up my arm and it's burning and itching at the same time... " She gritted her teeth, arched her back and let out a low moan. "Damnit! This is really starting to hurt now. Shit! Shit!" Suddenly, she let out a deep moan and clutched her arms to her chest. She started to convulse, but they held her down. Her eyes went wide and she screamed in agony for only a moment and then passed out. Her body continued twitching once in a while, but the convulsions were over.

Aside from some minor irregularities in physical symptoms over the next few hours, she seemed to be in a coma. As her bowls and bladder spontaneously emptied, the two doctors collected it as specimens and carefully cleaned her up. Each member of the team took two hours at a turn watching her, while the others remained nearby.

A little after two in the morning, Marsha moaned softly. Vicki leaned close. "Marsha. How do you feel?"

She blinked several times in the dim light and focused on her nurse. "Like I've been run over with a tractor. What do I look like?"

"You look tired and you have lost some weight, as we expected. You also have a pair of black eyes, but I expect they will clear up shortly. Want something to drink?"

"God, yes! I'm parched and famished too. How long was I out?"

"About eighteen hours. You've had a few nightmares, but this is the first time you've been coherent."

"Damn! I stink! I can smell myself. Let me at the bathroom."

Vicki smiled. "I just paged Don and John and..."

The door burst open as the two physicians ran in.

"Hon! You're awake!" His relief evident, Don leaned in close to give her a kiss."

"No!" She pushed him back. "I need to use the bathroom, NOW!"

He helped her and although weak and a bit unsteady, she made it to the bath while Vicki opened a sports bottle of distilled water.

The next afternoon, she was taken out in a wheelchair and they returned to the cabin. She was more than thirty pounds lighter and her hair was falling out. She complained of itching and where ever she had an old scar or skin flaw, it was flaking off and only fresh, smooth, pink flesh was underneath. She had a ravenous appetite and there was still blood and wasted pieces of flesh in her stool and urine.

Four days later, she was almost bald and had flawless skin. The black eyes and other bruising had long faded away and she seemed much stronger and physically stable.

Another couple of days, she had a short crop of auburn hair, the same shade she had as a teenager and was starting to put on weight. She also felt more energetic than she had in years and started an exercise program that included dance, yoga, and running on the trails around the cabin.

One week to the day, they returned to the clinic and put her through a series of diagnostics, including an MRI. All traces of the tumors were gone. Aside from some tooth aches, she was in perfect health and had the body of a teenage athlete.

Unanswered Questions

"Hi there. Got a few minutes, Nicholas?"

"Donald! Of course. I was going to call you this week. What's this I hear about your lab being left in the hands of a few interns for the last ten days?"

"That's why I'm here, Nicholas. We need to talk."

The Dean narrowed his eyes at the expression on his old friend's face. "Is something wrong, Don?"

"Yes and no... That's why I asked you to meet me here at my place instead of your office."

"You're being cryptic and that always makes me nervous. I thought you were making some good progress? Did something go wrong?"

Over the next hour, Donald explained the events of the last few weeks. The Dean asked a few questions, stared at the photographs and charts and watched a few video clips. Finally, he just sat and let it sink in for a few minutes while Don sipped his drink and said nothing.

"The more I think of this, the more is scares the hell out of me."

"Join the club. We've been batting the consequences around for the last week and so far, have got nothing but more questions. I knew I had to give you a report, but we all realized we needed to get some help in how to spin it so that it doesn't totally destabilize the entire economy."

"As you well know, more than two-thirds of our budget is derived from grants from two major pharmaceutical companies. When word of this gets out, they will be bankrupt within a year."

"Believe me, we have been thinking the same thing. We keep coming back to the idea of sharing the data with all of our major contributors and the FDA and allowing them to simultaneously test in controlled environments while they prepare the market." He took another sip of his drink. "But we're not economists, nor philosophers. There are going to be a lot of questions for which we're not going to have answers. The way I see it, the lab can be left in caretaker mode for another month or so. Nobody will ask too many questions there. The hard part is going to be keeping a lid on this until we can come up with some answers. My team is okay for now... But I know that sooner or later, somebody is going to slip."

"I have an idea. Everybody is going to be back on campus next Monday, right?"

"Except for my wife, yes. She's going to lay low for another few weeks and if needed, we can tell people that she has been to a special clinic for a face lift. That should give us a few more months."

"Agreed. I'm going to talk to the economist, Madeline Squire and George Englesheart..."

"Englesheart" The name is familiar, but I don't recall..."

"He's the English fellow that took over the philosophy department this past spring. You'll like him."

"Ah yes. I recall seeing him at graduation, but didn't get a chance to chat. Madeline is a good choice too. She can give us an idea of how this will effect the balance of trade."

Burning Times

"Well, it's about time you got home. What kept you at the university so late, dear?"

"Sorry, Hon, but we've a bit of a crisis brewing and I really have to stay on top of it. Things are going to get really interesting in the next few months." He hung up his jacket, loosened his tie and accepted a drink from his wife.

"Well, we had a marvelous prayer meeting tonight and the new minister is just so excited about being called to serve in a college town. There is so much sin to confront on a daily basis, that he's just not sure where to start. What do you think, dear?"

"You already know my answer on that issue, Hon. Anyone that bent on finding sin is going to find it first, on their own doorstep. 'Let he who is without sin... etc.' You know what I mean."

"Well, I'm sure you've each got a point. We'll have to all sit down, together some evening."

With his face turned away, Dean Blackstone rolled his eyes and whispered fervently, "Please Lord. Deliver me from your followers."

"What's that, dear?"

"Nothing, Hon... nothing at all." He arranged his face in a smile and turned back toward her. "While we're on the subject of meetings, I'm going to have Dr. Samuelson and his team over for some meetings in the next couple of weeks. We're going to be going over some things relating to this coming year's funding and staff allocations. It's all part of heading off that impeding crisis I mentioned earlier."

"Oh dear! I must get the service in to clean the living and dining room then. How many should I tell the caterer to expect?"

"Oh no, please no caterers or extra effort. This is not going to be a black tie affair. We're just going to meet in the basement and brainstorm some things. I'll be setting up for a series of multimedia presentations. I really do want to keep this as low key as possible."

Joan Blackstone didn't seem to think much of this manner of entertaining, but she knew when not to argue with her husband. Perhaps she would be able to talk to some of the lab team afterwards. It was a sure thing that some of them could stand to hear a bit of the Lord's word.

Difficult Answers

"Well, I'm really glad you brought me in on this, Nicholas. Dr. Samuelson and his team are correct in that we've got to keep a lid on the situation for the near-term. We owe it to our sponsors to give the FDA time to test this Omniphage and for them to gear up for large-scale release. What's your take on it, George?"

"Oh, I agree that this will have a destabilizing influence, but to be honest, I don't think the repercussions will be as bad as you think. There have been a great many lifestyle-changing technologies over the centuries and humans do seem to adapt." He waved his hand dismissively. "Oh, there will be a few problems, perhaps even some civil disorder, but I think that overall, this will be just another wonderful moment for science. Just how long before you think the FDA testing and clearance process will release this for general usage?"

"General usage? Are you mad, man!" Madeline was honestly shocked. "Do you have any idea what this really means? If there are no major problems, then this is the proverbial fountain of youth. Death, as we know it, will no longer be an accepted part of growing older. I've not done the math yet, but if this goes into general use, we can expect the world wide population to double in the next five to seven years. Our food, water and housing resources just won't handle that. It is more than possible that the entire world could be at war in the next couple of years."

"Well, if you're not going to make it available for general usage, who is going to decide who lives and who dies? Now that becomes a very sticky ethical question that I'm not sure I would even want to discuss, much less suggest an answer for."

Don Samuelson waved them to silence. "Please, friends... let's not bicker among ourselves. These are the same sort of arguments my team has been considering. With your support, Nicholas..." He nodded at the Dean. "I suggest we assign our lab to other uses for this Fall quarter. I've already arranged for a place in the country where my team and I can set up some more studies. In the meantime, we're putting together a presentation package including samples. Once we are finished, Dean Blackstone is going to arrange a dog and pony show with our sponsors and the FDA. Each of them will get one of the packages and it will be up to them to sort out when and were it is approved and released.

    ***

Joan closed the door as the last of their guests were pulling out of the driveway. "Dear? I am a bit concerned."

"About what, Hon?"

"Well, I know it's none of my business, but I couldn't help but overhear some of your discussion. Is it true that Don has found a cure-all drug?"

"Well, it does appear that way. So far though, they hadn't told anyone outside their team about this. It is still too new and we haven't all the data yet."

"Well, Marsha was dying of cancer, wasn't she? And it brought her back from the edge of the grave. I would call that a miracle. I'll bet she gave thanks to the Lord for her recovery." She paused. "Why are you smiling?"

"Because I seriously doubt she gave thanks as she is agnostic."

"Oh my goodness! That's terrible. Why was she saved then?" Her brows furrowed as another thought crossed her mind. "Will this drug work on a dead body?"

"Huh? What do you mean?"

"Just that... if somebody is killed in a car crash and you pump this drug into their body... will they rise once more?"

"Oh don't be silly. Of course not. It will only work if your heart is pumping and moving the nanites through your entire body so they can repair things."

Joan smiled and headed for bed. There would be time enough in the morning to get Reverend Barstow's opinion on this. She was sure the Lord spoke through him and it would all be so very clear then.

Righteous Mob

"And he was positive that this could not raise the dead, but merely heal the living?"

"Oh yes, Reverend. He was adamant on that. I was almost hoping that this was a sign that the Christ has risen, but it was false hope."

"Well, you were half right, my child. It is a sign. But not the sort of sign that God-fearing Christians like ourselves want. If I recall correctly, one of the signs of the devil incarnate, is that he can perform some false miracles since he was once a beloved angel of the Lord. But the one thing he cannot do is raise the dead. That power is reserved only to Christ, Almighty!" His resonant voice had gone up both in volume and pitch as the power of his convictions washed over them both.

It was Wednesday evening and his usual flock of devout Christians filled about a third of the seats in his small church. He had hoped for more, but he thought this would be enough to spread the warning. He was a patient man. If he was careful in his delivery, his star would soon shine very bright indeed. Since he didn't want to give the enemy time to mount a counter-campaign, he had suggested that Joan remain home for the next few Wednesday nights, in order to gather more information so they might know more about this evil. She didn't realize he wanted to make sure the information flow was one-way and her husband would have no idea he was about to become very famous as the Antichrist. He held up his hands and the murmuring from the pews grew silent.

"Brothers and Sisters... Tonight, we are going to contemplate the public face of evil. And you better believe that evil walks among us, even as we speak. Some of this is the usual, petty evil that we see every day. The shoplifter, the liar at work, the whore on a street corner... or movie poster. Some of it is deeper and not so obvious because it hides under the guise of doing good for all humanity." He paused to savor the moment. "One of my flock has brought me word of a terrible evil that is about to be released among us. Brother, would you please dim the lights so we can see some of these images on the laptop on that table, over there? Thank you..."

When his sermon was over and the prayer meeting ended, he pulled aside a couple of the strong, young fellows. "Tell me, boys... if it really comes down to it, are you on the Lord's side, standing tall and proud to protest this evil?"

They nodded and asked what he had in mind.

"Well, I have heard that they are going to be scheduling another meeting of their terrible coven and as soon as I know when and where, we can throw open their doors to allow God's light to scatter them like roaches. If we expose their evil for what it is, they will be forced to close down that abomination of a lab and we can lock up those devil worshipers."

"Don't worry, Reverend... We're with ya!"

The Reverend Barstow was pleased, because he knew the lad was a journalism student and his father was an editor for one of the sensationalist rags one sees in supermarket checkout stands.

Tabloid Truths

The caller ID showed Vicki.

"Don? I thought we had agreed to keep a lid on this?"

"Yes. Of course, why?"

"Well, as we speak, there is a reporter saying she has an appointment with you to discuss the fountain of youth drug. And to make matters worse, she brought a camera crew with her."

"I don't recall authorizing any sort of interview, but I will try to defuse this as quickly as possible. Tell her, I'll be right there."

As he pulled into his parking place, a half-dozen people approached. Two of them carrying cameras and others with hand-held recorders.

"Dr. Samuleson? My name is Dorothy Meyers with "Basic Truth" magazine. I understand you're in charge of the fountain of youth project?"

"Pleased to meet you, Miss Meyers. But to be honest, I'm not sure what you are talking about. This is a genetics research lab and we have had an interesting summer, but there is nothing ready for public release as of yet."

"What about these images then? How do you explain a human experiment that restored your wife's youth and vitality after she was diagnosed with terminal cancer?" She held up a clipboard with images from their lab notes.

"Where did you get these? They were to be part of a report that will be published in a medical journal."

We cannot disclose our sources, but you don't deny these are images of your wife, undergoing a groundbreaking procedure with a new drug?"

He moved to go around her, towards the side door to the lab. "I have no comment on research that has not been authorized for release."

She stepped in front of him and the cameraman blocked him from the other side. "But surely the release of these images proves that you have a fountain of youth drug. I was discussing this with some members of the University Board of Regents and they haven't heard much from the lab during these long summer months. School is going to start in another week. The administrators wanted to know what has been going on and why haven't they been appraised of your findings."

"You are dealing with stolen data and we will prosecute the thief. I said no comment and I meant it. Now get out of my way." He pushed the cameraman to one side and smiled at the campus security guard. "Please keep these people out of the lab. It is a secure area and they cannot enter."

"You can't keep us out forever, Dr. The public has a right to know what sort of drugs you are creating in there." As he entered the building, she turned back to the camera. "There you have it, folks. Just another case of trying to hide the truth. Don't worry, though. We will not be deterred so easily. In the meantime, let's get some feedback from some of the concerned bystanders... You sir, what is your name and what do you have to say about all this?"

"I'm Reverend Rod Barstow and we had heard of a so-called miracle just this morning. I must admit that I am very concerned, however."

"Why is that, Reverend?"

"Well, it has been said that the devil himself is capable of healing, but that only the Lord, our God Almighty, can raise the dead. It is my understanding that Mrs. Samuelson was terminally ill with cancer and this miraculous drug appears to have restored her youth and vitality. Since they appear to want to keep this secret, I'm worried about what side effects they may be hiding."

"What do you mean by side effects?"

"As we all know, there is always some cost for everything. Sometimes the cost is not obvious. If this truly restored her as the images you have and those secret reports seem to show, then what did she give up to gain it? As a man of the cloth, I'm naturally most concerned for her soul."

"Are you saying this might be the work of the devil, Reverend?"

"We shall have to see how forthcoming they are with the

information and how much of this are they going to devote to the Lord's work."

Inside the lab, Don closed the door and hollered. "Vicki! Kathi! Bob! You three in my office in twenty minutes. The rest of you, do a safe shut down of whatever you're working on and get out of here. Take the north door and do not talk to the media! Oh! And Bob... Make sure you lock up behind everyone before you come to my office."

***

"Okay. We're here. What's going on, Don?" Vicki closed the door as Bob followed Kathi into his office.

"We've got some serious problems. Somebody got a copy of Marsha's test files, including the images, and gave it to some TV reporter. I just got ambushed in the South lot by a news crew."

"Damn! Who in the world...?"

"Never mind who! Right now, the important thing is what we're going to do about it. I just got off the phone with Nicholas and he agrees that we had better lay real low until we can get a handle on things. That means this lab is shutting down as of now. Whatever records you have on OmniPhage are to be boxed up tonight and I'll see about getting some secure transportation. By tomorrow morning, I want us to be on our way up to the cabin. You had better call anyone that expects to see you in the next few days and tell them you're taking a sabbatical prior to classes."

Vicki's cellphone chirped. "Yes? Okay, hold on a moment." She looked at Don. "Marty needs to get back in the lab, he was in such a hurry to get out that he missed a notebook." She paused thoughtfully... "You know, he's a strong fellow and we are going to have a lot of boxes tonight. Want me to ask him to help?"

"If you're sure he can keep his mouth shut and not ask questions, yeah. While you guys start to pack, I'm going to call Dean Blackstone and see if we can round up some more labor."

"What about the latest run of OmniPhage? We were gearing up for some large scale tests and to provide samples for our sponsors. There is almost a kilo in the desiccator right now."

"My wife seemed to do well with a single gram, so let's break them down into hundred gram packages... And while you're at it, have Marty grab some cases of syringes and sterile wipes from storage and load some into each of our cars." He picked up the phone. "Nicholas? Don here. Yeah. I know, I know. We're on it as fast as we can. Can you make sure we have a couple of the college cops to cover us for a moving party?"

Joan Blackstone was furious but didn't show it. How could her loving husband be involved with these people? The good Reverend Barstow had as much as stated that they were doing the devil's work. They were ignoring her, so she stepped out to the garage and used her cellphone to apprise him of this horrible situation.

    ***

By midnight, with Clare and John Witham's help, they had Vicki's El Camino loaded with boxes of papers that were tightly tied down with a blue plastic tarp. Sealed plastic tubs of supplies and other file boxes filled the back of the Nicholas Blackstone's Escalade, Don's Hummer, Kathi Long and Bob Lorraine's minivan and Madeline Squire's Jeep. They were all lined up at the loading dock door of the lab.

"George! What are you doing here? Nicholas told me you had something to take care of and I wasn't sure we'd see you."

"Sorry, I'm late, but I have something for each of you. I had to stop by the local computer store and pick up a handful of these new, high-capacity thumb drives. You will recall, the last couple of days I've been going over the data files and was putting together a presentation?"

"Yes..."

"Well, I put together the full presentation along with the lab directions for making OmniPhage, made a single tarball out of the whole thing and copied it to each of these little jewels." He held up a handful of thumb drives on lanyards. "There is one for each of us. My idea of a safety precaution."

Suddenly, Dean Blackstone's phone rang. "Hello? What's that, Hon? He wants to talk to me? But it's after midnight... What? What do you mean, he's here?" He paused... as the enormity of her treachery sank in. "Uh.. hold on a moment... Yeah, I'll come to the front and meet with him. Give me a minute, though."

"What's going on, Nicholas?"

His face was white with fury as he took a moment to collect himself. "My wife! That... bitch... was... our... leak." He took another deep breath; fighting for control. "She's out front, right now... with Reverend Barstow in tow."

"Now what?" Kathi asked quietly.

"Get in your cars, lock the doors and I'll get the gate. If we're lucky, they won't see us until we are turning onto the street.

Break Away

As the gate opened, Don's Hummer was in front, Nicholas, Clare and John followed in his Escalade, Kathi and Bob were close behind, in the minivan, Vicki's El Camino was next, and Madeline came up the rear, in the Jeep.

The chain link gate to the parking garage was on an alley shared by several other university buildings. When the Hummer approached the stop sign for the main street, Don slammed on the brakes and leaned on his horn to avoid hitting several men with flashlights.

"Stop! In the name of the Lord, Stop now!" All three of the men appeared drunk and at least one was carrying a shotgun. He waved back towards the front door and hollered. "They're over here!!! They're trying to sneak out like you said. We got 'em!"

Don honked again and drove slowly forward, pushing the drunk out of the way so that there was room for the other cars to cut over the curb along side him.

As he passed, Nicholas glanced down the sidewalk and saw another dozen or so in a crowd, with his wife and the Reverend in the lead. "Damn that woman," he muttered under his breath as he leaned on the horn scaring one of the drunks who was trying to block them.

That one jumped back a few inches, then raised his flashlight threateningly.

"Stop them! Stop them before they escape with that devil's brew!"

Suddenly, the shotgun went off and the passenger window of the Hummer disappeared. George jerked and fell over the console. Don felt glass shards and something metallic on the side of his face. He jerked the wheel to one side and punched the gas just as Madeline's jeep pulled alongside.

Barely a car length ahead, he glanced in the rear view mirror and saw the fellow raise the shotgun and crank off another round. The Jeep windshield shattered, Madeline swerved, jumped the curb and rammed the corner of the lab. Don saw the drunk struggling to chamber another round and, not considering the consequences, slammed on his brakes, threw the Hummer in reverse and, tires squealing loudly, backed over him.

"Get in!" He hollered at Madeline as he saw her stumbling from the wreck, bleeding.

She jumped in the back and as soon as he could, he accelerated up the street, leaving the screaming crowd behind. "Where the hell is campus security now that we need them?"

After a few blocks and two quick turns, there didn't seem to be anyone following them. They all slowed to the speed limit and headed for the interstate.

"Don? What about George?

He glanced at his friend and didn't answer for a moment. "There's nothing we can do for him now and if we stop for any reason, we'll all end up in jail at least overnight and those fundamentalist assholes will have the media behind them. Right now, our only chance is to go into hiding until we can get our story out and stay clear of jail." He glanced in the mirror. "Are you okay?"

"I'm fine. Just a bit shook up and not used to driving around with a corpse." She didn't tell him her arm was broken and she was having trouble focusing. "What about you? You're bleeding, it looks like."

"It's nothing... just some minor cuts from the glass. Get the others on the phone and see if anyone else is hurt."

Running Times

Mark Brownam met them at the cabin door. "Looks ta me like you guys really kicked over a hornet's nest. You're all over the TV news. Soon as I saw the pics of that fire on campus, I figgered y'all would be here." He was half-smiling until the bloody faces and limping figures moved into the porch light. Then he grew dead serious as he hollered over his shoulder. "Cheryl! Boil some water and clear the table. We got some wounded!"

John Witham shook his hand and asked, "What have they been saying about us?"

"Well, right now, there are bulletins out for you on all the networks. One channel says you're all a bunch of devil-worshiper's that drove through a crowd of peaceful protesters and actually backed up to drive over a man who was trying to get away. The other networks say you set fire to the lab building in order to destroy evidence of your illegal research. In all cases, the FBI has been called in and they say you are to be considered part of a science 'cult' that may have gone awry."

"Damn! That didn't take long, did it?"

Clare Witham interrupted them at that point. "It probably should not surprise you that both Nicholas and Madeline are hurt much worse than they had reported. She's got a concussion, a broken arm, at least a couple of broken ribs and who knows what internal injuries. He's got a mild concussion, a couple of shotgun pellets in his shoulder and glass shards in the side of his head. They are both really groggy right now and they should be in a hospital."

"Hey! You guys! Come in here and watch this. I don't believe it!"

They spent the next half hour watching a special news broadcast showing the burning lab and a huge mob of fundamentalists, greens, and some other publicity hounds as they described a running battle where the crazy scientists had shot, run into, and driven over peaceful church folk that only wanted to ask a few questions. The Reverend Barstow was in every other frame, firing up his righteous indignation. Interviews with people in the street in several nearby communities showed that people were really scared and several other bible-belt preachers were telling their flocks that the devil may very well have risen, gathered the generals for his army and was, even now, getting ready to rain terror on the children of men.

"Don?"

"Yes, Clare?"

"I'm really concerned about Nicholas and Maddy. They are slipping fast but neither wants to go to the hospital in town. Will you talk to them?"

"You two need medical help that we can't provide. Let me drive you down..."

"No!" They echoed.

Nicholas half-smiled. "If we turn ourselves in, we will all be in jail shortly. We need time for all this hysteria to die down so that we can tell the real story in a calm and rational manner."

"What about OmniPhage?" Madeline suggested. "Clare has already set my arm and a dose of OmniPhage for each of us, would put us both in the peak of health in a day or so."

"Oh my God! Look! Some of those fools are vandalizing the other bio-science labs and the Governor has called in the National Guard! Look! That's Dr. Napta they're dragging out of the... Oh no!" Her voice died out as they watched in horror as the mob beat the researcher with tire irons and bats. The police carried away a limp figure.

Don turned to his wounded friends. "You two realize that you will be out of it for at least a day or so, right?"

"Yes, but we'll be in much better shape to deal with all this if we're healthy. Do it. Just do it." He looked at Madeline.

"Yes. Just do it and get it over with."

They prepared a couple of syringes and Clare administered each one, while the rest of the team watched. In a few moments, the wounded couple were stretched out on a bed, deep in coma.

"Well, that's it for now. Everybody take turns grabbing showers and find a place to crash. I'm going to wake everyone at nine for a conference." Don turned to Kathi and Bob. "If you two will help me, let's go out and park all the cars in position to leave if we must.

No Options

"Okay. I know that a few hour's isn't much sleep, but we don't have a lot of time. I figure it's only a matter of hours, or days at the most, before the police will be coming up this driveway. From what I've seen on the TV this morning, we only have a couple of options." Don held up a finger. "One is that we contact the police and turn ourselves in and let the truth be known."

"Yeah, right!" Kathi spoke up. "Bob and I have been watching the idiot box and so far, two other researchers are dead, a dozen pre-med and biology major students have been beaten up and only a few people are in jail for it. The media is making us out to be the bad guys. I have no desire to spend any time at all in jail for something I didn't do."

Most of the heads bobbed in agreement as Don added, "I understand, but I just wanted to present options and then we can make some rational decisions. The other thing is to try to scatter and just lay low while only one of us goes to the police."

"But we're not crooks and regardless of how easy the movies make it look, hiding while on the run can't be a picnic. Why not just stay here?"

"Because this address and location is known to several people at the university and a search of public records will tell the police where we probably are... I'm thinking that with the FBI involved, we have another day at most. If we are going to be proactive, then we need to make a decision in the next couple of hours."

Bob spoke up. "I'm with Kathi. We have some friends scattered around that we can visit. They are the quiet type that won't say anything. I'm going to check out the van and head out of here in the next few minutes. Here..." He handed Don a card. "That's one of my private email accounts. I will open a new one in a couple of days on a foreign server and give everybody here access to it. We can stay in touch that way, no matter where we are."

"Well, keep in mind that all of our vehicles are known and the license numbers are probably on cop car dashboards right now."

"That's no problem, Don." Mark spoke up. "Vicki has that ugly old hot rod of hers in the shed. Nobody this side of Indiana knows about it. I've got a Taurus station wagon that is a bit rusty, but runs real good. I'll trade it for that minivan if you two are willing. That makes two clean cars that nobody will notice."

"Okay. That's Vicki, Kathi and Bob. I'll stay here with our two patients What about you and Clare, John?"

"We're okay. I've got an '85 Dodge pickup with a camper on the back that I've been using around here. It's been rebuilt and runs good. I'll toss in our camping gear and some supplies and we can be out of here in the next hour or so."

"Marsha?" Don turned to his now-gorgeous young wife. "How are you feeling? Want to hit the road with these bums until this all sorts itself out?"

She hugged him. "And just where the hell do you think I should go without you, eh?" I'll stay and help you nurse those two in the next room."

He smiled, kissed her and turned to the caretaker and his wife. "Mark, Cheryl... I think you guys need to grab whatever you might think useful from here and high-tail it back to your place. If you're not here when the cops arrive, you can always claim to just be neighbors."

"Sounds good to me, Don."

"Oh... and one other thing... here... " He opens a backpack and pulls out a sealed bag of OmniPhage and a box of syringes. "You watched how it's done. There are approximately a hundred doses here. It hasn't had a lot of testing yet, but it does appear to cure damn near anything. I would hide it very carefully, because it just might be worth a great deal one of these days."

"Does it have to be refrigerated?"

"No. Just kept perfectly dry, sterile and out of direct sunlight until you're ready to use it."

Mark took it, nodded, and headed for the door, wishing everyone good luck.

"Okay everyone... as soon as you roll out of here, you need to split up. Do not tell us where you're going. Just go in opposite directions, and as soon as you see an ATM machine, park out of sight of the camera and withdraw as much cash as your cards will allow. Once you have the cash, drive a few miles in one direction, then take some side roads to change directions and you're on your own. For the next couple of days, lay low, then find an open wireless access point and check the email link that Bob Lorraine has given us. It will be awhile before anyone figures out what it is being used for and in the meantime, we can all use encryption to keep messages private."

"Don! Gang! Come here! Check this out!" Bob looked scared. "I was checking my usual news feeds and found this posted just a few minutes ago."

Washington Poster – Current News Feed
FBI Claims Dangerous New Drug!

FBI representatives announced today, that an alleged new 'fountain of youth' drug that was the root of a major riot at TriState College last night, is actually a deadly dangerous concoction that only appears to work miracles by making people 'feel' younger. They warn that the so called scientists involved in the murderous assault on a peaceful church group, were responding to threats to unveil their illicit drug lab, cleverly hidden under the guise of legitimate research.

The university regents and the legal representatives have gone on record saying they were unaware of any illegal activities, but since both Dean Nicholas Blackstone and the department head, Dr. Donald Samuelson and his wife Marsha Samuelson are among those wanted for questioning, a full investigation is underway.

Particularly critical testimony by Joan Blackstone indicates she has been greatly concerned about illicit drug activities for some time now and has been consulting with her religious adviser. She was among the crowd attacked by the ivy league drug lords, last night.

The running gun battle and car crash they instigated, may have backfired however, as one or more of them might have been wounded. Forensic evidence has revealed a great deal of blood from at least two people.

The following individuals are wanted for questioning by the FBI. If you see any of them, please do not approach them as they may be armed and dangerous.

Dr. Nicholas Blackstone [picture]
Dr. Donald Samuelson [picture]
Marsha Samuelson [picture]
Dr. John Witham [picture]
Clare Witham [picture]

Victoria Veski [picture]
Dr. George Englesheart [picture]
Dr. Madeline Squire [picture]
Kathi Long [picture]
Robert Lorraine [picture]
Contact your local law enforcement agency or dial 911 to report any sightings. Do not attempt to apprehend these dangerous individuals yourself.

Until further research is accomplished, any samples of this new drug, street-named OmniPhage, are to be considered contraband. FBI researchers have classified it as a member of stimulates similar to cocaine and have labeled OmniPhage a Federally Controlled Substance.

"Well, that cuts it. We're now officially drug runners."

"Yeah, that didn't take long to spin the wrong way." Clare's voice was soft.

Don shook himself. "You guys better get packed and get rolling. I have a funny feeling Marsha and I will have to stick around and answer questions. If our two sleeping beauties wake up in time, they can split too. Otherwise, we'll just have to let the evidence speak for itself."

"What about Dr. Englesheart?"

"We wrapped his body in plastic last night and taped up the side window of the Hummer. That will keep until you guys are gone and we call the FBI and surrender."

A little over an hour later, amid tearful hugs and good byes, an old blue pickup, a rusty gray station wagon, and a bilious green hot rod wound down the gravel drive.

Arm in arm, Don and Marsha went back inside to care for their patients and watch the news. Behind the machinery shed, flies were gathering around the bloody Hummer.

Hotrod Run

Once more, Vicki took the rear slot since her car was the most memorable. When they got to the interstate, the blue pickup with John and Clare headed east. She followed her friends in the gray wagon as they headed west. Knowing her folks would be worried, when they pulled over at a truck stop for gas, she paid cash for a disposable cell phone.

As she was getting into her car, she saw Bob and Kathi, carrying their backpacks and waving.

"What th' hell? I thought we were going to ignore each other from here on out?"

"Sorry, but some asshole in a dually pickup just backed into the wagon and trashed the front end. We told him we had to call our folks, since it was their car. He's on the phone to his insurance company right now."

"Damn! Get in quick and let's hope nobody is paying attention."

With Bob sitting on a backpack and Kathi riding shotgun, they made a hasty exit. Several miles up the road, Vicki took to a back road.

"Are we going in a particular direction?"

"Uh huh. First we're heading north along these farm roads. The trees will tend to hide us from overhead and most of these country folk wouldn't give a damn about another old hot rod. Also, I used to date a fellow up here a ways."

"Can you trust him not to blow our cover?"

"Not for a moment. But I also know he and his dad kept this little fishing shack down by the river and they only use it on holidays. Since he's in school out on the coast now and his dad's got a business to run, there's a real good chance we will have at least one night of peace and quiet. While I repaint this thing."

"Repaint?"

"Yeah. Although this is a classic in the original factory colors, it has already been painted once, when I was restoring it last year. After this is all over, I can paint it again, but right now, this green is way too bright and attention-getting. I'm thinking a coat of gray primer and some duct tape here and there will make it look like a different car."

The cabin was really crude, but dry. It was obvious from the dust and cobwebs that it hadn't been used in a while.

"You two grab a shower, wash your clothes in the sink, hang them to dry and then see what you can find for dinner. We're going to be leaving early tomorrow." She grabbed a roll of masking tape and some newspaper and started to mask off the chrome and windows. Two hours later, it was almost dark and she was hot and sweaty. The brilliant coupe had been transformed into a credible rat rod.

As soon as she opened the door, she smiled at the smell of fried chicken. "Oh my gawd! Where did you find that?"

Kathi grinned. "The last time we got gas at that stop-n-rob, I saw fryers on sale. I just figured since you had that cooler in the back of the car, a bag of ice would keep them at least overnight. I knew we'd have to stop sooner or later and fried chicken, a can of corn and some baked potatoes is a good, hearty meal."

"Well, my earlier plans included that loaf of bread and some peanut butter. I'm glad you're ahead of the curve."

Bob grinned while chewing, swallowed and asked, "We going to camp here awhile?"

"Nope. I expect the ex or his dad would show up here in a couple of days and I don't mind them thinking some bums stopped in for a bit, but I would rather they not know it was us."

"Okay. That makes sense. Any idea where we can head from here?"

"Yeah. My family has some old friends that own several large farms about four more hours west of here. I'm sure they wouldn't say anything and would be happy to let me stash this crate in one of their barns. A short hike through the woods will take us to an old hunting camp. My folks can keep us updated on what is happening and sneak some supplies every couple of days.

Police Presence

Nicholas Blackstone and Madeline Squire woke up within minutes of each other. They were a bit weak, very thirsty and ravenously hungry. Don and Marsha took care to reassure them that only a day had passed, everyone else had gotten away safely and nobody had come snooping around.

A couple of hours later, the four of them were showered, in fresh clothing and sitting down to dinner when they heard the crunch of driveway gravel.

"Oh well. It was fun while it lasted." Marsha sighed.

Don stepped out on the porch. "Good evening, Deputy."

"Good evening, Dr. Samuelson. I hear that you're a wanted man. Care to tell me what that's all about?"

"If you want to hear the whole tale, sure. Pull up a chair. Care for a cup of coffee while I fill you in?"

"Don't mind if I..." His eyes landed on Marsha, standing in the doorway. "Oh, I see you have company. Is this one of your students?"

Don chuckled and Marsha smiled. She was wearing a thin sun dress that showed more thigh than it hid. "Oh come on now, Bryan. I remember when you were still a cadet and helping clean the station. Don't recognize me, do you?"

His brow furrowed and then it dawned on him. "Oh... my... God...

Mrs. Samuelson? Is that you?"

She struck a pose and grinned. "In the flesh. How do you like my new body?" She wiggled suggestively and Don just shook his head and continued to smile at the officer's confusion.

He stared for a moment, then took a seat next to Don. "I think I will take a cup of coffee. This looks like it might be an interesting conversation."

Less than an hour later, he had the gist of the tale and was shaking his head. "Damn! You sure have stirred up a hornet's nest with this. I can see why the big money people are running scared. I don't see why you're still sitting here, wasting time, chatting with me though. I'd like to think I'm an old friend, but if I get orders to arrest you guys, I've a family to look out for, and I will do my job. Right now, I've an excuse that I didn't think it was the same folks. But that ain't gonna last long."

"Well, Nicholas and Maddy are still pretty weak. And to be honest, I don't think that running will accomplish much. I'd much rather get the truth out there."

"Speak for yourself, Don. I don't think they're going to give us much of a chance to tell the truth. Let's get out of here while we have the chance."

Two young people in robes stepped onto the porch and once more, Bryan did a double-take. "Dr. Blackstone? Is that you?"

He stuck out his hand. "Right the first time, Bryan. Good to see you again." He turned to Don. "I hate to say it, but I agree with your wife, Don. I think you should leave now, while you have the chance. Maddy and I are enough to get the word out and when the hubbub dies down, we'll email you."

Don stared at his old friend for a moment, then nodded. "Okay. I do have a lovely young bride to consider." He grinned at Marsha and she blew him a kiss back. "What are we going to go in though? I don't have another ride here, except..." His eyes got a faraway look. "That's it! Get your back pack, Marsha and I'll grab mine. We gotta pack light." He turned to the Deputy. "Bryan .Thank you for giving us a chance. But now is the time for you to get scarce. It wouldn't do for them to think you were part of all this."

As the good ol' boy headed down the drive, Nicholas asked, "What have you in mind, Don?"

"I almost forgot. Remember I was taking flying lessons awhile back?"

"Yeah, but you got busy with the project and..."

"But not too busy to pick up a good deal on a two-place sports craft. It's parked at that grass field a couple of miles down the road. It will only take a few minutes to gas it up and do a preflight. There is no radio tower there before seven in the morning and we can have it ready at dawn. Marsha and I can be a couple of hundred miles away in a few hours. Two, maybe three gas hops and we're in Canada."

The sun was just peeking over the mountains when the ultralight Rotax engine carried them out of the valley.

Two hours later, a caravan of black SUVs and marked police cars pulled up to the house. When the cops found the blasted and bloody Hummer behind the machinery shed, they arrested the two young people sitting on the porch. Instead of taking them to the local jail, they were rushed to the county airport, where they boarded a corporate jet. Somewhere over the Atlantic, they were informed that they were being charged with the manufacturing and distribution of a controlled substance in order to finance terrorist activities. They were going to be held as 'enemy combatants' and would not have access to either an attorney or, God forbid, the news media.

Furry Run

The elderly couple were scared. It was after ten and a dense fog was already filling the run, hollows and swampy areas around the run down motel.

"Sooner or later, they are going to realize who we are and try to collect the reward."

"Agreed..." Her husband nodded. "I think it is time we tried our little experiment. I don't know about you, but I'm way too old for running and our options are just too limited now."

She gave him a wry smile and a hug. "Hey, OmniPhage worked well for everyone else, this is just our turn."

The colorful neon beer advertisement caused some odd shadows, and a furtive movement on the sidewalk caught his eye. He squinted at it for a moment, then realized it was the resident calico cat with a still wiggling mouse. Smiling, he closed the blind, pulled the drapes and hung the do not disturb sign on the door. He missed the part where the mommy cat ran around the cottage and took her secret entrance to a hiding hole, behind the antique tub. Their rundown cabin hadn't been used in many months.

"Where is it?

"Here." She opened a large purse and pulled out a decorative tampon case. Inside, there were two sealed syringes and a dark glass vial. She laid a sheet of tin foil on the dresser and carefully opened each of the syringes. The vial revealed a yellowish crystalline powder which she very carefully measured and divided into two piles.

"I need to take a leak before we do this." He opened the bathroom door and the startled cat ran between his legs. When the poor feline saw Clare, blocking her way, she jumped on top of the dresser. This gave the mouse a scant second to break free and run for it's life. It ran beside the tin foil, dove off the table and under the bed. The cat was a half second behind as the man spun around.

Clare wrapped her arms around the precious drugs and ducked her head as the half-wild mommy cat sailed over her head and under the bed.

"John! Get the door and get them out of here!" There was a note of panic to her voice.

He opened the door and lifted the bed spread, towel handy, ready to smack either beast away. He need not have bothered as the cat had already recaptured her prey and as soon as she saw the open door, made a beeline for the parking lot. He closed and locked the door again. "Are you okay?"

"Yeah... no problem. Just scared the hell out of me though."

"What about the OmniPhage?"

She carefully examined the two syringes and the small pile of power. "We got lucky on that one. They missed it all."

What neither of them realized was that a few hairs from the mouse had landed on one side of the pile and a single cat hair had blown into the open end of a syringe.

Still rattled, she carefully filled each syringe and resealed them.

"John..."

"Yes, hon?"

"I love you."

"I love you too." He took her in his arms and kissed her.

He watched her proudly as, with skill born of years of nursing practice, she slid the needle into his vein. Gently, she pulled back on the syringe and the powder dissolved on contact with the warm blood. She knew that working on the molecular level, the OmniPhage nanites had already read his DNA and were ready to start their work. Slowly, she pressed the piston, pushing the blood and its nanite payload back into his vein.

Clare repeated the process on herself; using the other syringe. After replacing the syringes in their case for disposal later, she stretched out alongside her husband.

"It's just as they described. I can feel it tingling, almost a burning sensation moving around my body. Not really that painful, but not comfortable, either."

He didn't answer. As expected, he had slipped into the first-stage coma. She wiped a single tear and joined him a moment later.

Katte & Mohse

As programmed, the OmniPhage nanites had absorbed any DNA samples given them. The great majority were human, thus only a few items from the animal samples were used. Since there are large segments of 'filler' programming in human DNA, the very limited OmniPhage programming decided the extra samples were handy for filling in the blanks. Over the next few hours, the nanites replicated themselves millions of times and found their way into every cell served by the bloodstream. The immune system was first modified to ignore the nanites themselves and then it was boosted to teenage levels. Hidden tumors that couldn't be adjusted back to healthy tissue were broken down and passed to the urinary tract and bowels.

After waking from their coma, they kept the do not disturb sign in place for the next couple of days. The pile of MREs, frozen dinners, bottled water and sports drinks rapidly shrank as their bodies cried out for material to rebuild.

In the pre-dawn hours of the third day, she whispered to him. "You're awake too, aren't you?"

"Yes." His voice sounded strange... softer than normal and yet with an edge of hysteria.

"What's wrong, hon?" She was straining to keep her voice calm.

"There must have been something wrong with that batch."

Instantly wide awake, she struggled to maintain her calm. "Why? What are you experiencing?"

He stopped her hand from the turning on the light. It felt strange on hers. "Don't you feel different?"

"Well, now that you mention it, yeah... I do feel as if I need a shave. I don't recall having this much body hair when I was a kid. What about you?"

"I have been watching you sleep in the moonlight, love. There have been some drastic changes in both of us. Please don't be shocked when you turn on the light."

She did and gasped in disbelief. Although naked, they were both covered in a very short, soft fur. Her husband was also very obviously female and had the features of a cat, complete with large ears that had moved up the side of his head and were pointed and tufted.

She hurried over to the dresser and the mirror showed her ears were thinner, wider and rounded. They also appeared to have moved up from their normal locations.

"It must have been those critters that we chased out of here the first night."

He continued, with only a slight trembling in his voice. "I woke a few minutes ago and thought I was in some weird dream. Then I realized that even with the dim light in the room, I could see you clearly. I don't feel bad... as a matter of fact, I feel better than I have in years. But when I felt..." His voice faded.

"We only rented the cabin for four days. The manager is going to come for another payment tomorrow. We can't let him see us like this." She was looking at herself in the bathroom door mirror. "Ohmigod!"

He looked up. "What is it?"

She turned and showed him where her spine was extending to form the stump of a tail. He reached around and realized he had a short nub as well. With a wry smile, he said, "Looks like our metamorphosis isn't quite finished."

After standing and posing in front of the mirror for a few moments, the new catwoman sighed and turned to her mate. "Well, if I'm going to be female, I must admit this is a pretty hot body. What do you think, hon?"

She smiled, then broke down into a giggle.

"Why? What did I say?"

She caught her breath, put her hands on the tall cat's shoulders and pulled her closer, grinning up at her. "It just occurred to me that cats eat mice. Are you going to eat me, love?"

Coping Mechanisms

They spent the morning making love, took turns washing each other in the shower and slept until late afternoon. They tipped off the restaurant staff that they were working on some costumes for a movie and the delivery guy was suitably impressed with their makeup.

After brushing her new fangs, she cracked the blind to see the evening fog rolling in. "They've probably found out we're not going back to the lab by now and have traces on our credit cards. I'm really glad I had the old pickup licensed here in West Virginia instead of back in Maryland. I hated to leave the SUV at that abandoned gas station, but they'll realize it's out of gas and think we walked back to the interstate and hitchhiked. It will take some reviewing of school records to find our cabin address and by then, we need to be gone from this area. We don't dare let the motel manager or maid see us now, so I think our best bet is to take off tonight and lay low for awhile. We've still enough cash for a couple of weeks."

"Well, we're not exactly built for hiding right now, are we love? A six foot kitty and five foot mouse are going to attract just a little attention, I would think."

"Wait a minute." She paused, brows furrowed in concentration. "This is Sunday night, right?"

"Yeah, so?"

"There was a large carnival at the county fairgrounds about ten miles back, correct? If this was their last weekend, then they are packing up tonight and by noon tomorrow, they'll be out of town and on the road. Carnies are used to weird folk. We'll just tell them that we're lesbian furries and have had a lot of cosmetic surgery. I'll bet we can get a job and run with them for awhile."

The mouse nodded. "But what about social security cards and driver's licenses and names? The feds are going to be looking for anyone without the proper documents."

"True, but only for another few weeks. The OmniPhage formula has been posted to hundreds of websites. They cannot keep the lid on it for too long. Inside of a week, there are going to be a dozen labs making batches and in a few months, we will just be noise on the curve. Their own agents are going to want some for themselves and their families. We're heading into a period of anarchy. All we have to do is stay out of jail for a month or so and there will be too many others like us."

She grinned at him. "I really don't think there will be too many human cat and mouse hybrids. But it does sound as if a carnival would be good cover for a couple of freaks like us. I even thought of names for us." She held up the pad she had been marking. "I took my immigrant grandfather's surname and added our two new first names. What do you think?"

The cat read the names several times, then let a wide grin as she mouthed their new names... Katte and Mohse Voncoven.

"We can tell them we were married in a lesbian ceremony up north and some religious zealots burned us out. We lost all our documentation in the fire and have been on the run since then. We're strong and healthy and there isn't too much you can't do with machinery and I'm a pretty good cook..."

His grin broadened, "Okay! Okay... you've got me convinced, Mohse. Tonight, we run away and join the circus!"

Carnival Ride

It was late and the carnival manager didn't want any part of them. He frankly didn't believe their story and although he said he wouldn't turn them in, he had no use for cops of any kind, he wasn't going to give them jobs. "There is way too much attention paid to my hiring habits and paperwork in every damn town the show works. Cops are always looking for folks on the run and I can't afford to get involved."

They thanked him and turned to go.

"Of course..." He pointed to a pile of posters. "If someone was to steal a bunch of those posters and the two magnetic signs while my back was turned, I would probably not even notice it for a week or so." He grinned and turned to open a file cabinet and looked busy for a moment.

They grabbed the posters and signs and headed out to their old Dodge pickup with a camper back. The two magnetic signs stuck well to the steel doors and some duck tape attached a poster to the inside of the rear topper.

"If I read that old guy right, we'll just sleep here tonight and when they leave tomorrow, we'll just join the caravan. We're not working for him, but it will look like we're part of their team." That should get us out of town at least."

Mohse nodded. "Well, we're going to need money in a week or so. Gas alone is going to eat up the cash reserves."

Katte hugged her. "Don't worry, love. We've got this far, I'm sure something will come up."

   ***

Two days later, the caravan pulled into a small fairground on a bluff, overlooking a winding river and an old town. Bon Rivage had started as a trading post near a wide spot in the river. A small dam provided power for a textile mill that supplemented a few lumbering and railroad jobs. When the dam broke, back in the 50s, the mill closed and the railroad wasn't really profitable any more. It was a dying town.

Katte saw the manager of the circus. "Hey there. I was wondering if I could be of any help."

"Actually, I was just coming to find you two. This town is pretty much as far into the sticks as you can get. The only reason we play it, is because there are a couple of nearby communities that treat the weekend as part of their celebration." He paused to look around. "If you go south on that road, you'll come to a National Guard base about ten miles north of the city. If you go the other way, you've about twenty miles of nothin' but woods and hills 'til you cross over the state line. There's an interstate a few miles after that and a State Police barracks at the intersection." He turned and pointed to the road on which the circus had arrived. "If you continue on that, you come to another of these old mill towns, but that one still has a furniture manufacturing plant and more cops than you can shake a stick at. They don't like us there."

"Thanks for the tips. Any suggestions?"

"Well, you two are pretty cute in a kinky kinda way... If ya don' mind me sayin' so."

"Yeah, thanks, your point?"

He stared at Katte for a few moments. "Please don't take this the wrong way; I'm just trying to help out. I know you are on the run from something and I really don't want to know why. I also know that you're goin' ta be runnin' out of money sooner or later." He pointed towards the road heading towards the city. "If you drive to the edge of town, you'll see a bar up on the hill that advertises topless dancers. I know the manager and he's a pretty good fella. If you want to earn cash on the side with no questions asked, tell him I sent ya. In any event, when we leave here, you'll not be able to come along. Our next gig is at the state fairgrounds and that is the other side of the city."

"Thanks." Katte handed him a small nylon pouch.

"What's this?" He peeled open the velcro and stared at the syringes and vial within. "Hey! I don't do fuckin' drugs..."

"That isn't a drug. Have you been following the news? It's OmniPhage."

"That stuff that the gov'mint says will kill ya?"

"Do I look dead?"

"Well, nothin' personal, but I don't want to look like a cat or a mouse."

She smiled ruefully, "Well, that was a mistake. Look up the instructions on the web and there is enough in the vial for four doses. Right now, it's worth a fortune. In another six months, it will be on the streets, but not in as perfect a quality as that."

"So that explains why you're on the run. You two are some of them scientists that created this stuff."

Katte shrugged. "Keep in mind, it takes about three days to fix anything that ails you. But keep it perfectly sterile. Some feline and rodent hair got into our batch by accident and that is why Mohse and I look like we do. That vial is perfectly sterile right now."

He put it into an inner jacket pocket and smiled. "This will cure my arthritis, won't it?"

Katte just smiled and nodded. "Thanks again."

Dance Money

"Here's how it works. You pay me ten bucks a night for the privilege of working here. That way, according to state law, you're not an employee, you're a paying customer. That means I only have to determine that you're over eighteen."

"How do we make money then?"

"You dance and collect tips. On a busy weekend night, you can make two hunnert bucks, easy. On slow nights, you might barely make twenty, but with your exotic looks... I have a funny feeling you'll do okay."

"When can I start?" Mohse asks.

Katte interrupts. "When can we start, that is?"

He put out his cigarette and nodded at the clock. "Today, we're open from noon to midnight. You can start now, if you want."

Alone in the dressing room, Mohse turned to her mate. "Are you sure you want to do this? You know I love to dance and dress slutty, but you've only been female less than a week."

"I dunno love, but I'm thinking of all that time we spent with the Rocky Horror cast during post grad and I really am kinda lookin' forward to strippin' for a livin'." He grinned wickedly at her. "Besides, why should you have all the fun?"

The first night was rough. They each made about twenty five dollars, but were exhausted and really fed up with second-hand smoke and rude drunks.

"Do you believe that asshole with the green tie? I had all I could do to keep his hands off me. I'm glad the bouncer finally gave him a little talking to... and what was worse, when I was thanking him later, he copped a feel himself."

Mohse just shook her head, "Yeah, I know exactly what you mean. After all, it's been happening to me since I was about fourteen."

Katte thought about that for a bit. "I never really thought about it that way. I guess most pretty women put up with this a lot, eh?"

"Don't worry, love. You'll get used to it. Anyway, I want to talk to Janelle tomorrow. Did you see her work that brass pole? I thought she was going to kill herself, but the guys were just lappin' it up."

"That just may be a great idea for you Mohse, but I'm going to stay on the ground, thank you. I'm sure I can come up with a routine of my own."

"Well, one thing is for sure, we need to practice a lot more and develop some routines. All the other girls had something worked out and the novelty of our exotic looks is going to wear off in a few days. Right now, I just want a hot bath and some time cuddling with my favorite kitty."

Pole Monkey

"If I teach you my moves, yer gonna be getting' my tips. What's in it for me?"

"I thought of that, Janelle. If you teach me the basics of how to work the pole, I'll give you one half of my tips for the next month. Besides, you are so good, I know I'll never be that hot."

"Yeah... there ya go with the flattery. Make it ninety days of half tips."

"How about sixty days and you also help Katte an' me put together an act."

"An act? Hhhmmm... Now that sounds like it just might be fun. But only if I am part of it. Room for three, okay?"

"Okay. You got a deal." They all shook on it.

She grinned. "I've had an idea for a routine that I've been waiting for someone to try it with... Since I'm not working tomorrow, hubby and me will be driving down to the city and stopping off in a surplus shop. I'll need your sizes. Part of the reason you're not getting decent tips is because old worn out heels, bra and panties just don't count as a costume."

"Well, we've had some hard times recently..."

"Save it. We've all had hard luck and I don't really care. I just want to get you two dressed up and dancing better, so I can get some more cash in hand." She took a drink and continued. "Oh, and one more thing. You better stay out of town during the day. There's a preacher down there that is convinced the end is near and you two are just weird enough to end up on his shit list."

"Thanks for the tip, but we are going to need a place to crash. We can only afford the motel for another couple of days."

"I dunno... there's somethin' 'bout you, Katte. You know anything 'bout cars?"

"Well, I rebuilt the slant six in our truck last year and all the body and electrical work on it is mine. Mohse stitched up the interior and seats. Why?"

"You mind working part-time for room an' board?"

"Not at all; what do you have in mind?"

"Well, my husband Brendhan has a little shop up towards the interstate and our place is out back. I've an old trailer behind the house and if you will help him around the shop, I'm sure we can work out something you can afford on the trailer. That is, if you don't mind hangin' out with some rednecks like us."

Mohse piped up. "That sounds great, Janelle. Doesn't it, hon? Can we take a look in the morning?"

Grease Monkey

"Brendhan, this is Katte and Mohse Voncoven. They're going to take a look at the trailer. Katte did the work on their truck."

He shook hands, "Katte, is it then. Well, I'm sure you've heard all the jokes, so I'll just stick to business. What sort of work did you do on your truck?"

She told him in some detail and he occasionally stopped to ask questions. After a few minutes, he stopped her. "Janelle tells me you might like to swap some time in the shop for rent. That true?"

"Yes sir. We're way short of cash right now and I don't mind helpin' out if I can."

"Well, if we just do a straight swap, then there's no paperwork and no taxes to worry 'bout. That work for you, I assume?"

They both nodded.

The trailer was a thirty year old aluminum bodied model that was being used for storing some spare parts and used tires for the garage. The bed room was dusty and full of spider webs, but it appeared dry.

Janelle was apologetic, "I'm sorry it's so messy, but I'll be happy to give y'all a hand cleanin' it up."

"Don't worry, Janelle. Just give me a couple of days before I have to help at the shop and we'll have this place lookin' like new in no time."

"Oh, and Brendhan told me to suggest that you don't clean up the outside and park your truck in back all the time."

"Oh? Why?"

"Well, we both seen the TV news the other night and know that the FBI is lookin' for a pair of mad scientists that were involved with that new killer drug. They said they were elderly folk and they described that old truck of yours. The license number matched. I hope you realize we can't have any killer drugs around here, but I'm sure ya know that. Don't ya?"

Mohse looked at her mate and shrugged. "First Janelle, thank you for trusting us. Secondly, you're right, we are those scientists, but there is no killer drug. On the contrary, it is something that scares the government even more than poison. It's a drug that can heal any illness and restore youth. It rebuilds your own DNA and repairs damaged cells in your body."

Mohse continues the explanation. "They are after us because they wanted to slap a lid on it so that only rich politicians would have access to it. The drug companies and medical firms are running scared because their time has come. They will all be out of business in a few years."

"Is that what happened to you two? This Omnithing?"

"OmniPhage. This isn't how it normally works. We accidentally took a bad batch that had been contaminated with cat and mouse hair. Perhaps we can fix it later, but for now, the powers that be are really pissed at us 'cause our whole team published the formulas for making OmniPhage on the web."

"We figured it was sumpin' like that. Never had much use for the feds 'round here anyway. If you two keep your truck outta site for awhile, you can ride to the club with me and hubby has a service truck that all the cops around here know and they won't bother ya."

"We hate to put you to too much risk getting' involved an' all..."

"Hey, don't worry 'bout it. I can use the extra tip money from turnin' Mohse here into a pole monkey and the shop can use an extra grease monkey to give Brendhan some time off once in a while."

Constitutional Rights

The cities were having a hard time of it. Once the first few illegal batches of OmniPhage hit the streets, pharmaceutical stocks plummeted. As people started to realize the spin off effects on both medical and life insurance firms, the same thing happened. Wall Street was gripped in a panic unseen since 1929.

Citing various health risks associated with uncontrolled production, the federal government classified OmniPhage as a dangerous drug and banned all use, except for licensed 'testing' facilities and the FDA.

Brendhan was grinning. "Hey! You guys aren't alone anymore." He was waving a paper.

Katte looked up from the engine with a curious expression. "What are you talking about?"

"It says here that a bunch of old folks in a group home tried some OmniPhage that had been contaminated with cat hair, just like you. The whole lot of 'em, more than two dozen, are now kitty folk. One of their relatives stopped by for a visit, found them all in a coma and called 911. When the EMTs saw what was going on, they notified the cops and the whole lot of 'em are in custody now."

"What are they charged with?"

"Actually, they are being held 'for their own good' according to this. The feds are saying this is an excellent example of how terribly dangerous this horrible drug really is and that these folk are no longer human, therefore they have no rights under the constitution."

"Damn! I didn't think it would get this bad. It's only a matter of time until someone mentions seeing us around here and puts two and two together."

"Don't be so fast there, kitten. The last few weeks, you two have more than pulled your own weight and I have a funny feeling we're all going to be needing friends we can count on. For the near future, why don't you keep a low profile during the day? I'll cover all the public stuff up here and stuff I need a hand with, we'll pull into the shed behind your trailer."

"But what about the club? We're both on stage at least five nights a week..."

"So, you're a couple of them furry weirdos that had some plastic surgery and like to dance nekkid? So what? Nobody that knows ya 'round here is gonna give a crap and them that don't, will just think it's part of the act."

"I'm just worried that they're gonna lock us up and use the excitement to get away with running tests on us until they get bored and then just letting us disappear."

"You know how to use a gun?"

"I've shot a rifle a few times, but that was when I was a kid. Why?"

He motioned for Katte to follow and went into their house. "Here..." He opened the dark green closet safe and handed her a pistol and a pair of magazines. "This is a basic semi-automatic handgun and this is how you check to see if it is loaded..."

After going through a box of ammo, getting used to it, Katte and Brendhan were relaxing in the late afternoon light when Jannelle and Mohse got back from the weekly grocery run. They looked tired and angry.

"That sanctimonious sonuvvabitch..." Jannelle started.

"Which one?"

"Remember that hell fire and brimstone preacher on the north side? Well, the Reverend Patrick Davis and some of his flock were in the grocery store and the moment he laid eyes on Mohse, he accused her of being marked as an inhuman spawn of the devil and not fit to share the town with God-fearin' folk. He had the crowd worked up pretty good and they even tried to follow us. The damn store manager asked her not to come in again, until she had 'taken care of her condition'."

"Follow you?"

"Don't worry, we got out of there pretty quick, but you know it's only a matter of time before we hear from them again. That asshole just has to have something to go on about and he's sure to bring attention."

Mohse looked like she had been crying. "Well, looks like we're gonna have to leave town. We sure can't stay here and bring any more trouble on you guys."

Brendhan interrupted her. "No! I have a better idea. The whole country is upset about OmniPhage so there really isn't anyplace else for you to go since you look like you do. How about the hunting camp?" He looked at Jannelle. "You remember the place up in the woods that your dad, brothers and I rebuilt a few years ago? Nobody but family will be up there and it can sleep eight. We'll send 'em up with some supplies and when things cool off a bit, they can come on back down."

Katte looks worried. "Where is this camp and what are we going to do for a living while up there?"

"Well, you'll need no money for the time being as it's pretty primitive. But you can just come into town after dark and work out at the club. We can put some of that solar film on your truck windows and after dark, nobody will be able to see who's driving. The preacher knows better than to show up there, 'cause the last time he tried it, half his damn congregation found their tires flat the next day."

Battle Lines

The act was a success! Jannelle had picked up an old fedora and a trench coat at a thrift shop. A few minutes with a hobby knife and it fit over Katte's ears just fine. A realistic water pistol, an ornamental security guard badge, and a bit of choreography, and Katte became a film noir detective. Jannelle's outfit made her an evil madam and Mohse was the call girl with the heart of gold that falls for the crazy detective. There were actually three parts to the script and each one was a two-song set for dancing. If the club patrons wanted to see the whole thing, they had to stick around for at least three hours. This meant more drinks and tips for all the dancers and they were really popular.

Too popular, perhaps. Six months after OmniPhage, the economy had all but collapsed and all the major metro areas had been locked down under martial law. Refugees from the cities, mostly big-money types whose financial house of cards had collapsed around them, drifted into town. Some adapted and some moved on. For some reason, the little biker bar on the hill became a haven for a wide range of men and a few women, trying to forget their problems.

One night, the club was packed with a few military men, some bikers, the usual truckers, and a handful of dour-faced men in the back to which no one was paying much attention. After the first set, the preacher and a couple of deacons nodded to each other and left.

Local regulations dictated that all establishments serving alcohol must close by two o'clock in the morning. By two thirty, the manager, bouncer, both bartenders and the six dancers were ready to lock up.

"Charlie? Everybody clear of the parking lot?" Joe the manager queried.

The bulky bouncer who had just walked through the door nodded. "Okay girls. Y'all go get some sleep. Charlie and I will lock up."

A chorus of g'nights echoed in the empty club as bartenders and dancers headed for their cars.

"Hold it right there, freak!" The voice came from the corner of the building.

"What the hell? We're closed. Go home!"

They realized the parking lot had several cars that weren't there a few minutes ago.

"Don't worry, we already caught your disgusting show. That's why we're here... to clean up this cesspit."

Mohse recognized the voice almost as soon as the figure stepped from the shadows. "That's the preacher I told you about." Katte nodded, but kept her eyes on the the preacher and the two men, fanning out to either side of him. They both carried baseball bats.

Two of the other dancers turned and started for their cars, but stopped when they saw more men coming out from behind the parked vehicles.

A crunch of gravel warned Katte and she glanced over her shoulder to see five more zealots with a mix of pistols, hunting rifles and trucker flashlights. "What do you want?" She asked, stalling for time.

"Well, you and the other damned freak are going into cages in the back of Brother Steven's pickup and then you'll be delivered to the authorities in charge of dangerous animals and drug dealers. The rest of these whores will be escorted out of our town so that it will be safe for God-fearing folk by morning."

"We've done nothing wrong. You don't have the right..."

Spittle sprayed as he screamed in righteous indignation. "I have every right and a responsibility to rid my community of abominations like you!" He held a large crucifix in front of him and ordered his flock. "Get them! In the Lord's name, get them now and rid ourselves of these freaks!"

Bloody Bar

A bright flash and an explosion ripped the night and all eyes turned to the club owner, standing in the entrance with a Mossberg 12 gauge leveled at the preacher. The barrel was still smoking from his warning shot. "You and your boys better get the fuck out of here, Preacher."

He didn't bat an eye, "You're out gunned, Charlie." He nodded at his well-armed and nervous companions. "You shoot me and they'll kill you before you can jack another round. Go inside and shut up, we only want these freaks and abominations."

"Yeah, and if I let you take 'em, in a week or so, you'll be back for me and the rest of the girls. Just to satisfy your asinine holier than thou attitude. For the last time, get the fuck out of here before someone gets hurt."

They stared at each other for a long moment, then the preacher smiled. "He may be a damned sinner boys, but he doesn't have the balls to kill someone in cold blood."

"But I do." The calm voice intruded."

Preacher slowly turned and saw the bouncer, Joe, standing behind his pickup with both hands wrapped around a large pistol.

"The first man to touch one of those girls gets two bullets in the gut. I have eighteen rounds and qualify on the sheriff's range once a month. Nine of you will be bleeding out before you can get both me and Charlie."

One of the zealots with a rifle warned, "Watch out! That damn cat has a pistol in a shoulder holster."

"Never mind that, Pete." The preacher sneered. "That's just a water pistol she uses in their obscene gyrations on stage. No telling where it's been."

Suddenly, the rifleman sneezed and a single shot rang out. Katte stumbled to one side and Mohse dropped with her. Almost on top of the sound, Joe's weapon barked twice and Pete dropped the rifle and tumbled back, clutching his stomach.

The preacher dropped to one knee and grabbed the fallen rifle. "Die you filthy perversions!" He screamed as he swung it towards the girls.

Katte's handgun barked once and the rifle was once more ownerless. "I use a water pistol on stage, but I carry the real thing."

As the echoes faded away, so did the rest of the mob. Without a word, they ran for the shadows and moments later, the parking lot echoed with the sounds of several cars throwing gravel as they raced for safety.

Charlie slowly approached the two wounded men as Joe kept an eye peeled for stragglers. He picked up the rifle and unloaded it. "You two okay?"

"Katte is hurt!"

"Naw... I'll be fine. The bullet just skinned my shoulder. Some first aid cream and a good night's sleep and I'll be ready to go. What about them, though?"

Pete was folded into a fetal ball and whimpering in pain. Charlie pried his arms up and saw the gushing blood from a gut wound. "Keep pressure on it and we'll get you some help."

The preacher's wound was higher on the chest and pumping slowly. His breath was labored and wheezing and pink blood trickled from the corner of his mouth.

Charlie stepped over to the girls and bent close. "I saw stuff like this in Kuwait... I don't think either one of them will make it to the ER. If we call 911 right now, it will be at least twenty minutes before the ambulance arrives and another twenty to get them to the ER. They are both going to bleed out in the next fifteen minutes or so. Anybody have any better ideas, better speak up quick."

Katte shook herself. "Get them inside on the bar. Boil a pot of water and get me a bundle of clean bar towels. Mohse and I can work on them if you guys keep us supplied."

"You know some medicine?"

"Before... Well, just before... I used to be a surgeon and was in charge of a biomedical research lab. Mohse was a nurse. It's been awhile, but I think we can stabilize them if we can keep them alive for a little longer."

"What about your shoulder?"

She smiled at her mate. "I told you it's just a scratch. Now let's get these two inside and you and I can scrub up and put on some of the nitrile gloves from a fresh box. Right now, I'm going to get the bugout first aid kit from our truck."

Country Law

Fifteen minutes later, two sheriff's cars and the shift commander scattered gravel in the parking lot as they slid to a stop. Joe saw them on the security cameras and met them at the door.

"Howdy Sheriff. I guess you got an earful from those bible-thumpers, didn't ya?"

"They said the preacher and Pete are dead in the middle of the parking lot. I don't see any bodies, so I'm guessing that is an exaggeration. Where are they?"

"Inside. But before you go in, you need to know they're in surgery right now."

"Surgery? What the fuck do you mean, surgery? This is a damn strip joint, not a... And just who the hell is working on them?"

"Katte used to be a surgeon and Mohse was a nurse. Charlie and I figured Pete and the preacher as goners for sure, but they said they could stabilize them until the ambulance arrives. Which reminds me, is it coming?"

"Yeah, we just heard they are leaving the hospital. It was working a crash out on highway 220. It may be a half hour with the fog though."

"Well, right now, Charlie is helping and they appear to be keeping them alive. They had a full field surgical kit in the truck and another bag full of drugs. You know I was in the first Gulf War and I've seen medics at work. Those two girls are pros. Even though those two scumbags tried to kill them, they are doing a helluva job keeping them alive."

"Well, that will go well for them in court."

"What court? What the hell you gonna charge them with?"

"The way I heard it, them church folk were just up here for a peaceful protest and those freaks opened fire on them."

"I thought the bible thumpers would say something like that. It's a good thing I had all them security cameras installed last year. I have audio and video of the whole damn thing and it is backed up both here and on my web server. I'll see to it you have a full copy, including everything up to the ambulance leaving. Your brother shot that mousy girl first and they just defended themselves."

"I love it when I'm saved a lot of work." The old cop gave a wry smile. "Boys, you keep a watch out here and I'll check inside."

Inside, all the lights were on and the two patients were stretched out on the bar. Katte and Mohse were washing their hands and Mohse spoke first. "Are the EMTs here yet? These two are barely holding in there and we don't have any blood to replace what they've lost."

Before the sheriff could reply, a voice came over the radio and a moment later, he was shaking his head. "More damn bad news. The ambulance just got t-boned by a drunk. It looks like we're going to have to call two ambulances from the city and that will take at least an hour. Will these two last that long?"

Katte shook her head. "Pete might. We have him sewn up enough to keep from bleeding out any more... but it will be close. I am not sure the preacher will make it more than another half hour though. Not only has he lost a lot of blood, but there is some buildup in his lung. Even in a perfect ER right now, I'm not sure I could save him."

"Well, you need to do all you can, because he has a small but very mean and vocal following in town. If he dies up here after you worked on him, I can pretty well guarantee you'll be lynched the minute I turn my back."

Charlie spoke up. "What about OmniPhage?"

Mohse turned to her mate. "Katte, honey... it is possible."

Katte said nothing. Just stared at the slender form of the preacher.

"I've heard the TV propaganda and read the official reports, but I take it you two have first-hand experience. What exactly does this OmniPhage do?"

Katte's voice was soft. "It repairs your body. Every part of it. But it may be too late for him. He's skinny and has already lost a lot of blood. We have the surgical supplies and some first aid meds, but no blood or plasma..."

"Use me then, doc." The sheriff was serious. "After all, Patrick is my brother and even though I know he can be a sanctimonious asshole, he's still family. That's how come I know we have the same blood type. When I was in that wreck a few years back, he donated some blood for me. I'm just returning the favor."

"That just might work after all, honey." Mohse was looking at Katte. "With a whole blood transfusion and a dose of 'phage, he might pull through."

"I think you're right. Officer, tell your men not to disturb us and then get up on the bar at his head. Mohse, rig the IV."

Unstable Truce

The deep fog was fading in the first pale light of false dawn when the preacher's wife arrived in an SUV. "Where is he? What have these heathens done to him?"

"He's inside, recovering and needs some peace and quiet for a little longer. You need to sit down and let me explain."

"You can start by explaining why these... people... aren't in jail right now for attacking my husband. And why in God's name isn't he on his way to the hospital right now? I heard he was shot. At first, they said he was dead, but your deputy told me he was only wounded."

The sheriff grabbed her by the elbow as she tried to brush past him. "Now you stop right there, Anita! These 'people' as you call them, saved your husband's life, even at the risk of their own, and he is the one that started all this bullshit. We have him and half the drunken fools from his church on videotape. They shot and wounded Mohse, and your husband tried to finish the job. Charlie, Joe, and Katte only defended themselves."

After explaining the rest and answering a few questions. She seemed a bit calmer and he escorted her into the bar.

Pete and Preacher were still laying on the bar. Mohse was wiping her attacker's brow with a damp cloth and Katte was checking his blood pressure.

"What are you doing to him?" Her voice gave a hint to barely controlled fear.

"We saved his life. Who are you?"

"Mohse, this is Anita Davis, her husband is Reverend Patrick Davis."

She stood, staring down at her husband, her lips trembling. "Where was he shot?"

"Two wounds, one in the upper right shoulder and one a bit above and to the right of his heart. Fortunately, they both missed major arteries, although the one did puncture his lung. He lost a lot of blood, but a transfusion from his brother helped us to stabilize him."

"I... I don't see any stitches or the wound. You did surgery here, in this place?" She glanced around in distaste.

Mohse looked at the sheriff and he shrugged.

Anita noticed her pause and the look. "What did you do to him?"

Katte stepped forward. "We did the only thing we could to save his life. I used to be a surgeon. I did my internship in a major emergency care center as well as time as a medic in the military. If we had tried normal surgery, he never would have made it. As it is, he will be healthy as a horse in three days."

"What... did... you... do... ?"

"We treated both your husband and Pete with OmniPhage. It is repairing their bodies right now. The wounds have already closed up and they are no longer losing blood. Their vital signs are stable and they should be good as new in the next few days."

"OmniPhage? That killer drug... That makes monsters like you?"

Katte took a moment to control her temper. "It is not a killer drug. It is the ultimate lifesaver. These two got sterile batches, so they are not going to look like us."

She wiped her husband's brow. "When will he wake up?"

"He will be in a coma for about a day, then wake up feeling very weak, tired, hungry, and thirsty. Be ready to give him all the food and water he wants. Whatever sort of food he normally eats and plain water or fruit juices. No alcohol of any kind for at least three days.

"And then...?"

"He'll be his old self, except he's going to look and feel like a teenager again. Since it's now Saturday morning, I'd say he's going to miss Sunday services, but he'll be up and about Monday and should have all his strength back in time to preach his Wednesday evening gathering."

"Can he be moved?"

"Just be careful not to jostle him too much, but yeah... he isn't in any pain right now and will remain in a coma for at least another twelve hours. You can take him home and just keep an eye on him."

The sheriff spoke up. "Pete lives alone, I'll take him to my place. My wife and I will see that he is taken care of for the next few days, then he can scurry back to his cabin. My deputy will stop by and feed and water his huntin' dogs."

A few minutes later, Anita closed the sliding van door, got in and started the engine. She stopped and rolled down the window. "Sheriff?"

"Yeah, Anita?"

"Thanks... and..." She looked at the two furry strippers. "And you too. I won't pretend I like you or what you do... but I thank you for saving his life." Without waiting for a reply, she drove off, one of the deputies leading the way. They could see the red and blue lights flickering among the trees heading back to town.

High Times

They landed at yet another grass field and taxied up to the gas pumps. "Here's the cash, Marsha. You fill it and I'll check on some things. If anyone asks, we're just on a checkup run and will be circling back home, tomorrow."

"Got it. But first, I'm hitting the ladies room. Then, I'll pump the dang gas."

While wolfing down burgers and drinks at the FBO cafe, Don filled her in on a change of plans. "The newspaper already has our pictures. They'll never recognize you, but even with a three day growth, I'm easy to spot. I don't think we'd make it into Canada without being forced down."

"Okay. Where to else then?"

"I'm thinking they will expect us to head that way and I'm sure some people probably saw us taking off and flying north. So my idea is to leave here the same way, but as soon as we're out of sight of the airport, we turn southeast."

"Why southeast?"

"Because they won't expect us to head back towards the campus. You recall that failed development project in the next valley over? There are some empty sides streets with nothing but weeds? Well, I think I can get us there by nightfall. Hide the plane under some trees, walk to the road and then hitchhike out to the truck stop on the interstate. Then, see if some trucker wants to help out an old man and his daughter. Especially, if she's as cute as you."

"Any final destination in mind?"

"Yeah. A small town on the coast, near Tampa. A fellow I knew back in high school by the name of Tony Grenelli, settled there and we had a few drinks last year. He and his wife, Annette run a little tavern near Ybor City. Good folk. Very low-key types.

Times A'Changin'

The cross town expressway was an elevated affair that insulated the commuters from the warehouses, shipbuilders, railroads, and docks. Huddled under and nearby were gentleman's clubs, auto repair shops, self-storage warehouses, and many boarded-up buildings. Two blocks farther, lovely old homes that were in a sad state of disrepair because the city had gone in a different direction, and times are tight.

Footsore, dirty from three days on the road, and bone-tired, Don and Marsha had been walking since early morning. They turned the corner and stopped.

"Well, that doesn't look good."

She looked up to the three-story office building ahead of them. The top two floors had been boarded up and there were smoke marks above each window. The main lobby doors were chained and locked. Only the corner restaurant seemed to be open. The sign read, Schoonerville Pub.

"That your friend's place?"

"Yeah, but when I was here last, the offices were all open and that place was thriving. Look at the warehouse on the other side. It looks like a fire started there and jumped the alley." He shook his head, slowly. "Well, no sense standing out here in this heat. Let's see if he's still there. Either he'll give us a hand or turn us in. Either way, I'm way too tired to walk any further." He smiled at Marsha. "You want to wait out here and let me scope it out?"

She looked around at some of the bums, watching them from the shade. "Are you crazy? In this neighborhood? I feel like a mouse in a room full of cats. I'm going where you go."

Schoonerville Cafe

The woman behind the counter smiled as they walked in. "Sit anywhere you like, folks. What can I get you to drink?"

"Two sweet ice teas, if you will, please."

"Comin' right up." She hurried over to the stainless cooler and filled glasses from a plastic pitcher.

Placing their drinks in front of them, she waved towards the blackboard. "Specials are up there, unless you want to see the menu." Then she paused for a moment... staring at Don. "Say, do I know... Don? Is that you?"

He smiled and nodded. "Hi there, Annette. Is Tony around?"

"He's in the kitchen. I'll go get him." She turned and then stopped, glancing at the door. "You know. We get a few cops in here on a regular basis. You might want to step into the back, yourselves."

"Thanks, Annette. You're a doll."

"Just make sure we don't regret it, Mister." She warned as they took their teas through the swinging doors.

The cook was wiping a cutting board and started to challenge them for entering his domain. Then he recognized his old schoolmate. "Don! I was wondering if I was going to see you. Come on back and sit down." He hugged his friend and pumped his hand in greeting. "Now who is the lovely lady and why is she hanging out with such a hardened criminal as you?"

"This is Annie. If anyone asks, she's my daughter. And my name is Dan for now. I take it you've been following the news?"

"Oh yeah. You two are on the most-wanted list and you've been accused of everything except molesting the White House poodle. What's this about a killer drug that sucks your soul and makes you the helpless pawn of terrorists?"

"Well, to start off, it's not a killer drug. That's the main problem. It's much worse than that."

His friend stepped back. "Worse? What do you mean?"

"Annie. Tell the nice man how old you are."

She grinned mischievously and stated simply, "I'm forty-seven."

His eyes widened at this confession. "Bullshit! You're no more than twenty four or maybe twenty eight at the latest..." Pausing, he thought for a moment. "You mean that earlier crap they were spouting about a fountain of youth drug is for real? Then that means this is..."

"Yep. Four days ago, Annie was known as Marsha, my wife. She was the very first one that we treated with OmniPhage. That was a couple of months back. She was dying of cancer."

"Well why are they spouting all this crap about killer drugs, etc?"

"They are trying to keep a lid on this so the major drug companies, hospital supplies, etc. don't all go out of business. You know how big money people work. The powers that be are running really scared right now and we need to lay low until the truth can get out."

"No shit." He pointed up. "Did you see what is above me right now?"

"The fire? Yeah... what happened?"

"Well, Annette and I dumped everything we had into this building three years ago. I had an insurance firm leasing the two floors above us and this was a thriving little coffee shop. The old folks that had it retired and gave us a good deal. We also own that parking garage on the other side."

"Sounds like you had a real sweet deal. What happened?"

"Yeah, it was sweet. Then, some crack heads built a lab in the back of that warehouse next door. When the cops raided the place, it caught fire and spread to the insurance offices. The fire company put it out before it had spread too far, but all the broken glass and gazillion gallons of water finished trashing the place, including this restaurant. Fortunately, my insurance company took care of drying out and rebuilding my little corner, but the offices upstairs are still a mess."

"Why hasn't the insurance company rebuilt and moved back in?"

"They were a branch office of a firm based in Boston. After being smacked pretty bad in the last couple of hurricanes to hit Florida, they used this as an excuse to pull out of the state. It was cheaper for them to just pay me a lump sum and cancel the lease. It was good enough money to keep me afloat here and by running the place ourselves, Annette and I can pay the bills for now. But we can't afford to remodel upstairs and none of the big businesses want to move to this part of town."

"Well, for what it's worth, if you can let us crash in a dry spot, we'll be happy to give you a hand. I'm going to have to find some day labor job anyway, 'cause our cash is running low, too."

Tony thought for a few moments. "There is a room on the third floor, between the elevator and stairwell that used to be the maintenance office. It has a skylight, some closets and a washroom. We can clean that out and it won't attract attention. Will that work for the time being?"

"Sounds good. After I get rested up, maybe I can get a cash job as a deckhand?"

"That would probably work. But aren't you a bit old for that kind of hard labor?"

Don grinned. "As soon as we're sure of a place to crash for a couple of days, I'm going to take a shot of OmniPhage." He hugged his wife. "And then I'll be able to keep up with this little minx I married."

Garage Sale

"Say, Tony... I have an idea." The rejuvenated Dr. Samuelson was helping to clean the back room.

"Oh?"

"Yeah... you know that parking garage is empty or near so. With the real estate market so damn depressed now, you're not going to sell it anytime soon. Have you thought of using it as a flea market?"

"A flea market? Who would come down here for a flea market?"

"Well, each weekend, I see lots and lots of garage and front porch sales around here... And it occurred to me that having a central spot with good parking might be a nice idea. That garage is four stories and if you left the lower two as parking and made the third and top floors as sale areas, it might just draw some money in from outside the area."

"Well, I don't have the time to run something like that since Annette and I are the only staff for the cafe. How's this for an idea? You and Marsha set it up and run it. Then, split the profits. It can't hurt and it just might bring in a little spare cash."

The next few days, Don picked up the debris scattered around the parking garage and had the elevator serviced. Working on a borrowed laptop, Marsha printed some posters and vendor guidelines for the Flea Market. A simple steel cash box along with a folding table and four plastic lawn chairs completed their 'office'.

By Saturday morning, every grocery store, hair salon, barbershop, hardware store, church, and school with a bulletin board within five miles had a small poster advertising the "Flea Market". A simple, spray-painted "Flea Market – 7am to 3pm – Sat & Sun" sign was hung over the parking lot entrance.

They only charged $10 a day, per parking space. The vendors could bring in their own tables if they wished, otherwise, just lay their wares on the concrete. Spaces were first-come, first-serve. But if you wanted to reserve the same space from week to week, you had to pay thirty five dollars for a month in advance.

The first turnout was dismal, as might be expected, but as word got out more vendors as well as customers started to show up.

Each floor had two hundred and forty spaces and by the third weekend, he had several vendors ask about permanent spaces they could close off and install electrical outlets."

On the morning of their fourth weekend, they had another visitor. A local cop pulled into the garage and took a walk around the area. He stopped at their makeshift office and asked who was in charge.

"That would be me, Officer." He stuck out his hand. "Dan Samuels and this is my wife, Annie. What can we do for you?"

"Pleased to meet you, Mr. Samuels." He nodded at Annie. "Can I see your business license?"

Dan looked chagrined. "Since this is already licensed as a public parking garage, I didn't think we needed one, Officer Roberts."

"Well, the city rather frowns on flea markets because it conflicts with the regular merchants and mall stores. Since you're almost ready to close today, I'll cut you some slack. But by next weekend, you'll need the proper documentation, understand?"

"Yes sir. Thank you and we'll find out what we need to do to get the proper papers."

"To be honest, I doubt they'll go for it... For the reasons I've already mentioned. But if you want to avoid any hassles, there are some things you'll have to address up front."

"Oh? Like what, for instance?"

"Well, you're going to have to have working public restrooms on each sales floor, as well as insurance docs available with your business license. You better read up on the fire marshal's codes as well. Once this place gets going, I think you're going to want permanent booths and that will require careful attention to clearances for wheel chairs, etc."

"Good points. Thanks, Officer Roberts."

"You're welcome. Oh, this is my partner..." He introduced a slender blond woman in uniform. "Officer Barbi Behr is usually patrolling this area with me.

"Pleased to meet you, Officer Behr."

"Pleased to meet you, too. Actually, I'm hoping you can talk them into a permit. This place is more than ten blocks from the nearest real shopping center and the mall is about five miles away. It might help give this neighborhood a boost up if you can make this work."

The older cop looked Dan and Annie over and commented, "It's good to see some young folk take an interest in this part of town and try to bring in some real business. I can see from what you've done so far, that you're not afraid of a little work. Good luck, ya hear?" With a wave and a smile, the two officers head back downstairs.

When they were out of sight, Marsha turned to her husband. "Annie? You couldn't come up with a better name than that?"

Don shrugged. "Hey! It was off the cuff and besides... I'm not sure we actually put too much over on the old guy. I don't think either one of them really believed us. On the other hand, I do think they are willing to let things go for a bit." He glanced around at the handful of stalls and couple of dozen customers, cruising the aisle. "Let's see what Tony says tonight."

That night, after helping close down and clean up the cafe, they each grabbed a beer and sat down with Tony and Annette.

"You're lucky it was Bob and Barbi. They are two of the good cops in this area. He's right though. You're going to have a hard sell at City Hall with all the big mall merchants trying to keep flea markets out of the area." Tony took a sip of his drink. "There is something that might work in your favor, however. About six blocks from here, there's a big old brick place that's owned by an attorney that is a member of the city council. He's been fighting for a redevelopment project for this neighborhood for a long time. If you can get him behind you, then they'll have to issue a license."

Redevelopment District

"Charles Dunning. Good to meet you Mister Samuels. What can I do for you, today?"

"Thank you for meeting us on such short notice, Sir. My wife and I have a proposal to help with the redevelopment of our neighborhood."

They had the proper paperwork the following week, with the understanding that it was all in Tony and Annette's name. Don cleaned out, tested and reopened all the bathrooms and they arranged with electricians to run outlets to each of the proposed permanent booths. The city had put aside some budget money for redevelopment in that area, but nobody had claimed it. So Charlie had Tony and Annette address a public council meeting and show off some pretty plans and charts and the council gave them a twenty thousand dollar grant to help jump start the business. The only caveat is that they had also to provide some sort of cultural venue.

All the hoopla over OmniPhage seemed to have died down, as government sources claimed it was a dangerous drug and classed it with crack cocaine. The folks around Tampa just sort of let the news slide by them. This sounded way too much like a snowbird problem to them.

A couple of months later, they had traded a local artist a year's booth space, in exchange for several, large, colorful signs proclaiming the 'Lazy Fair'. One end of the third floor had been closed off and made into a small stage with lighting, seats, dressing rooms, and a snack bar. All the drinks and foodstuffs were prepared at the Schoonerville Cafe, of course. Local bands and choral groups were welcome to use the stage for an hour at a time, all weekend. It was part of the cultural support program they had agreed to implement. A local theater group was signed up to teach acting classes and have rehearsals twice a week, with one weekend a month scheduled for a performance. Three mornings a week, a tai-chi class was held on the open, fourth floor. As business grew and parking became tight, they started charging $2 to park in the garage and that included entrance to the Lazy Fair. One half of the parking gate receipts was given to a series of local churches and other charities in a round-robin manner.

Plans were well underway to close in the entire third floor and make it locked, permanent booths while keeping the fourth floor open for people to spread their tarps and sell what they brought. The closed and air conditioned booths were payable in advance and went for $500 a month. The waiting list had already been filled. The Schoonerville Cafe was filled to overflowing on the weekends and they had to hire some extra help. It was too good to last.

"Hey Dan! Did you see the news this morning?"

"No, what's up?"

He looked around to make sure nobody was in earshot. "Looks like that OmniPhage isn't as harmless as you thought. We have a whole nursing home full of cat people."

"What? Where? How?"

"It said that there was a retired chemist in some nursing home up in Ohio that was visiting with his grandkids and they showed him a set of instructions they had gotten of the internet for OmniPhage. He looked it over and figured it wouldn't be that hard to make a batch. When he turned their fifteen year old dog into an overgrown puppy overnight, he was convinced the government was spreading fear, uncertainty and doubt to protect pharmaceutical firms."

"Well, he's right there. But what's this about cat people?"

"He made up a larger batch and took it back to the nursing home with him. The following night, he gave it to all his friends as well as himself. When the police and camera crews arrived the next morning, most of them were in a coma and all of them had fur, claws, whiskers, etc... of cats. The government has all the old folks as well as all their support doctors, nurses and orderlies in custody and in isolation so they don't infect the rest of the area."

"Infect? What the hell! There is no infection! It's nothing but a powder that must go into solution with your blood first and then be injected."

"Hey! Calm down! I'm just the messenger, here."

"Sorry. But it's bad enough we have to be on the run here, without all that extra misinformation being fed to the masses by Washington."

Culligan's CatBoat

The downtown skyscrapers were beautiful in the last rays of the sunset and it was hard to tell when full darkness had taken over because of all the pretty neon and streetlights. This was the pretty, the good stuff, the fine coastal Florida lifestyle that was created for those who could afford it.

A nicely-dressed, eldery black man sat on the porch of a three-story walkup. He was talking to a very young, pale, and scrawny hooker. Several bombed-out tenements were further down the street and the Schoonover Cafe sign was blinking a block away.

"... and then I bought this place with the money from the car-wash and the rent from those apartments up on 30th street."

"Tha's real intrestin' Mistah Webster... but... ya know ah gal's gotta make a little money before she can go on investin' in property an the like."

"Yeah. I know what you mean girl. I still wish you'd find some other way of making a living. Those streets are just not safe these days."

"Now don't you start at me. Ah gotta go now."

He smiled and waved her on. "Okay. Okay. Goodnight and you be careful now."

Plastic platforms clacking on the hot sidewalk, she practiced her strut... exaggerating her swaying hips, hoping to catch the eye of some executive, taking the long way back to his safe place in the suburbs. She turned the next corner, heading towards the docks. The owners didn't tolerate hooking in their strip clubs, but they didn't mind if you hung around outside, just to give their places a bit of color.

As she strutted, she could see where the downtown skyscrapers quickly gave way to the smaller two to four story buildings. The graffiti, blowing trash and doors covered in unpainted and peeling plywood were just some of the signs that she might have been in the wrong neighborhood.

***

Inside one of the clubs, a pair of sweaty breasts were moving to a hot rock piece. Dawn finished her dance, picked up her lingerie and tossed it to the DJ for safekeeping. Then, wearing little more than platform heels and a smile, she moved among the crowd, kissing cheeks and getting dollar bills tucked into her garter. It wasn't much of a crowd, but it looked like she would be able to stay ahead of the bills for now.

"Thanks lover... Hi Jack, howya doin'? The pretty dancer moved on to the next table. "Hello. Would you like to contribute to my dance?" Another dollar; another kiss on a forehead... "Thanks."

The Club had just a few regulars hanging out and the music was starting again as another girl began gyrating on stage. Dawn finished moving through the crowd and headed back to the dressing room.

Wendy glanced around, then spoke to her friend. "Nice crowd tonight. They don't seem to be too drunk and they like to spend money."

"Yea, I know what ya mean." The smoke in there is killer right now though! I could really use a breath of fresh air."

"That sounds like a great idea. But the boss'll give us hell if we try to leave early."

Dawn shook her head. "I'm making way too much money to leave early tonight. Why don't we slip out the back door and sit in Jim's boat for few minutes. Nobody will miss us until your next set is due and..."

"... and I'm not due up for at least another hour."

"Great! Let's go!"

The girls slipped out the back door wearing only heels, g-strings and shorty dressing gowns. They took off their heels, climbed down onto the bow of the small cabin cruiser and stretched out on a couple of cushions. They were hidden from view of the bar by the cabin.

"Wow! That rain cleared up some of the smog. Look at all the stars!"

"Yeah that's pretty, but it ain't nothin' like what you can see when you're really out to sea and away from all the light-pollution."

"Yeah... but I... Shhh! Someone's coming!"

They knelt and peeked over the cabin top as a local cop walked past them and out to end of the pier. A small-time dealer followed him out and they start arguing in low tones. The cop suddenly gut-punched the punk, grabbed some chain and tied it in a knot around the victim's neck. The hapless dealer was gagging and making faces while struggling to free himself.

The girls kept low, behind the gunwale and Dawn whispered. "I know him. That's Steve Palmer. Mean sucker, isn't he?"

The gulf breeze pulled the cop's mean voice to them. "I've warned you about stealing boat supplies before Eddy. Here you go, stealing an anchor and chain." Palmer shook his head in mock dismay. "Oh well, I guess I'll have to arrest you... but wait. Maybe I should give you chance to escape. You know... just for old time's sake?"

The punk tried to smile and nod agreement. Without warning, Steve grabbed the heavy anchor and heaved it off the dock. The chain snapped taunt and yanked the punk into the dark water. The sharp crack of broken bone was hidden by the follow up splash. Dawn let out a squeal and Wendy clapped a hand across her mouth. Too late. Steve spun around and pulled his gun.

"Who's there?" He was squinting into the light from the bar. "I heard you." Suddenly he spotted the girls, smiled wickedly and took aim. "Nobody's gonna miss a couple of whores..."

With a squeal of salt-rusted hinges, the bar door opened and the manager looked out.

"Where th' hell... Oh! Hi Steve! Have you seen a couple of my dancers out here... Hey! What's with the gun?"

"I thought I heard some noise and I was just checking things out." He smiled at the terrified girls." You can never be too careful you know. Go on in and let me finish my job."

"OKAY! Sure! Catch ya later!"

Palmer watched the door close, then he jumped down, into the boat and brought his gun back up. Wendy threw one of her shoes and when he ducked, she grabbed his gun, twisted and folded his wrist back at an impossible angle. He grunted in pain and she followed through and pulled him face down onto the bow. She forced his forearm down hard on a piling and he dropped his gun into the water.

Grunting again at the pain, he kicked back and tried to struggle.

Through gritted teeth, Wendy told her friend to, "Jump! Quick!" then kicked him hard in the armpit and followed Dawn over the side. They both swim rapidly off into the darkness. Steve grabbed the backup revolver from his ankle holster and it caught on his trouser leg and discharged, shooting him in his own foot.

     ***

Krong Thip were working on a song on the Catboat stage and there were maybe a dozen people in a room meant for a hundred when, Wendy and Dawn came running in the side door.

"Jorge! Where's the Captain... or DJ? We need help man."

Jorge was smiling at the two dripping wet girls in nothing but g-strings and traces of oil-slick. "Take it easy you two. Who is chasing you? And why?"

Wendy was trying to wring some water out of her hair and the barkeep took a breath as if to say something until Jorge growled at him.

"We just saw Steve Palmer murder someone... and he saw us."

Dawn broke in, "...and he tried to shoot us. We've got to hide until we can talk to the police."

"Whadya mean 'Tell the police?' For Pete's sake he is the Police. We've got to think this over."

Jorge pointed towards the back stairs of the Catboat. "DJ and Cardinal are upstairs in DJ's apartment. They said they didn't want to be disturbed for a few hours sleep, but I'm sure they won't mind seeing you two. Go on up. Don't worry." He winked. "Nobody here has seen the pair of you this evening."

At the top of the stairs, they knocked quickly on the door and, still scared, they stepped inside the lavish suite.

The first thing they saw was a pretty pair of feet wearing dark stockings and spike heels. Then, they focused on legs, naked buttocks and a garter belt. This assembly was draped over a black, hairy-legged lap. The sharp final smack of a large hand was punctuated by a feminine squeal of pain and pleasure.

DJ was in drag. Cardinal jumped up and dumped his embarrassed and semi-nude lover on the floor.

"What th' bloody hell is going on! Get out of here!" He was waving his arms at the girls and advancing on them.

Recovering her voice, Wendy pleaded, "Hey. We're sorry... okay? We didn't plan to drop in like this."

DJ jumped up and grabbed the captain's arm. "Wait a minute Card. DeeDee, Dawn... Look at you two. You're filthy... and wet too!" He ran a fingertip down a greasy arm. "Yuk! Where have you been?"

Still angry, Card squinted and realized something was really wrong. "This better be good."

Wendy was clutching herself and starting to shiver. "We just saw Steve Palmer murder someone... and he saw us and tried to kill us."

Dawn broke in. "It was that scummy little coke dealer that came by last month.

"You mean Eddy Watkins?"

"That's him. He's under Ted's pier right now. Steve almost shot us. DeeDee saved both our skins with some karate stuff. By the way..." She looked at her friend. "How'd you do that? Can you teach me?"

"Sure, if we live long enough." She looked pleadingly at DJ and the Cardinal. "What we need now is a place to hide until we can figure out how to get out of this."

"Did Steve Palmer see you come in here?"

"No! We swam under the boat across from him and were in the shadows all the way. I caught my breath and heard him shouting and cussing about something. We swam all the way over here and climbed up the ladder at the end of your dock."

"Hey, listen... could we have a blanket or something? I'm freezing."

DJ waved them both towards the bath. "Not as dirty as you two are. Card will take care of everything. You both need a good hot bath and then you can have some of my things to wear."

The Cardinal grabbed a shirt and headed towards the door. "That's right. You two stay right here tonight. I'll make sure the cops are looking someplace else."

DJ opened the bathroom door. "Come on now ladies. My carpet doesn't need an oil change."

As the two girls pass him, Dawn paused and smiled. "Hey DJ..."

"Yes love?"

She smiled wickedly. "Just for the record... you have a great ass."

He grinned at the compliment. "Thanks love. I'll be back in a moment with some things for you ladies to wear."

Dock Cops

Detective George Melendez heard that an officer had been shot and rushed over to the emergency room. When he parked just past the door, Steve Palmer pulled up and rammed his car from behind.

"Palmer! What in Sam Hill do you think you're doing?"

"I've just been shot!"

"Where? Who?"

As the orderly loaded him onto a stretcher, "Down on the docks. I saw a couple of whores jump Eddy Watkins and throw him off the dock. I tried to stop them and one of them pulled a gun on me. I took cover and returned fire. She hit me in the foot and the two of them took off."

"You had your radio. Why didn't you call for an ambulance? You could have bled to death on the way over."

The ER doctor interrupted them. "This can wait a few minutes. I have a patient to take care of." He turned to Steve. "You lay still and shut up until I have a look at this foot."

The doctor carefully cut the laces and side of Steve's shoe and pulled it away. Steve grimaced and gritted his teeth at the pain. Something fell out of the shoe and onto the table.

George bent over and looked at it. "I'll be damned. Looks like you've got some evidence there. Nurse, pick up that bullet and put it into a specimen bag."

"I thought that thing would have gone clean through. It will make a nice souvenir."

"Not so fast Officer Palmer." The detective took it from the nurse. "This needs to go to the lab. You should know that ballistics will help us find who shot you. Hmmm... interesting. He looked closely at the bullet. This is a thirty-eight. I'm surprised that a whore would be carrying a gun so large. They don't fit in a purse that well. Who was it? Did you get a good look?"

"It was DeeDee and Dawn. You know. They both work at the Ribald Raccoon when they're not turnin' tricks."

The grizzled detective got a real thoughtful look on his face. "Yeah, I know who you mean. Are you sure? Those two have always been pretty clean girls. I thought..."

"Listen George, you're not down on the docks every night the way I am. Those two have been turning tricks, mugging every other one, and selling crack for the past two months. They've gotten a taste for the fast lane and don't want off. You better tell everybody that they're armed and nasty. If they argue, shoot 'em."

Disbelief was growing on the older detective's face. "I think that's up to the Chief to decide. What's the verdict Doc? Is he gonna make it?"

"This foot is going to be real sore for a few weeks, but there were no bones broken. I'll clean and sew it up and this man will be out of here in a little while."

"In that case, I'm going to see if I can round up your two attackers and save our fair city from this terrible crime spree. Call when you're ready to go and Sarge will send a marked unit to take you home. I'll arrange for a tow for our two vehicles."

All the News

Samantha "Sam" Wilson was the hottest TV news hound in three states. She was talkative, petite, gorgeous, blond, self-centered, career-minded, thirty two years old, and had just about given up hopes of finding a mate that would put up with her work-schedule. While getting dressed to cover the costume ball at Captain Culligan's Catboat, she was browbeating Kevin as usual about camera angles, lighting etc... all things he was already well aware of as a seasoned professional.

With his muscle builder physique, martial arts training and slight southern accent everyone wondered why he continued to stick around the small city station when he could be making more money on the coast. The answer is that he loved Sam even though she didn't realize it yet. He has always appeared slow but was really very careful and thoughtful. He just tells his friends that, "She's just working off steam and "puttin' on airs."

Unfortunately, Kevin was just another piece of technical equipment to her. She didn't realize or really care, that her casual display of semi-nudity was a painful tease to her long-suffering, but loyal cameraman.

"Com'n Kevin! Grab your gear and let's get this show on the road. It looks like the after ten crowd is already gathering at the Catboat."

"You got it, boss." He climbed out of the van and slung the SteadyCam Jr. into its harness. "Ready to roll."

Heels clicking, she crossed the parking lot, down the wide metal gangway and stopped in front of the entrance. "Hand me the mike, grab a ten second harbor shot, then pan over to me."

He switched on the microphone, spoke into it and watched the VU meter jump and handed it to her. Then, he chose some really bright neon down the block, focused and realized it was the Ribald Raccoon topless club, so he moved slightly and started recording.

He panned slowly over the nearby restaurants, piers, boats and, exactly ten seconds later, focused on the lady in the red suit.

"Good evening! This is Sam Wilson with WTPA and I'm coming to you from the hottest club in town, Captain Culligan's Catboat! You don't want to miss this one, folks. We'll be right back." She continued to smile at the camera for another ten seconds then drew her finger over her throat in the classic 'cut' sign.

"Okay. Now let's see if we can find the owner. He's supposed to be around tonight."

Once inside, they were assaulted by a strong Techno beat with some odd Asian strings overlaying it. They worked their way through the crowd to the bar, and caught the bartender's eye. "We're looking for Captain Louis Culligan."

"He's taking care of some business in the office. I'll tell him you're here."

"Kevin. Get some stock footage of that band. Notice how they all look alike?"

"Yeah, that's Krong Thip. They're pretty good. I've got their first CD at home."

"Krong Thip? What kinda name is that?"

"Dunno. Maybe you should interview them?"

"Yeah. Might be a good filler piece. We'll see how long this one runs."

A fellow looking like Ernest Hemmingway, came out of the office and smiled at them. "Miss Wilson? I'm Captain Culligan. Where do you want to do this?"

"Right here is fine, Captain." She waved vaguely around them.

He pulled out a pair of bar stools, offered her one, then took the other for himself. Sam smiled, and introduced them.

"This is my cameraman, Kevin O'Conner... Kevin, Captain Louis Culligan." They shook hands. "Kevin, please grab ten seconds of Krong Thip, then pan over to us." She turned to the Captain. "Sir, when he points the camera at me, I'll introduce us and then go right into the interview... Okay?"

He nodded and a few moments later, the camera swung slowly around to focus on Samantha.

"Good evening and welcome to Captain Culligans Catboat. The band behind us is called Krong Thip and we're planning an in-depth interview with this amazing group, in a little while. Right now, I'm with the illustrious owner of the Catboat club... none other than Captain Louis Culligan himself." The camera lens widens to include them both. "Thank you for sitting down with us this evening, Captain."

"The pleasure is all mine, Sam. And please call me Louis. No need in being formal here at the bar."

"Wonderful, Louis. So, tell me a bit about yourself. Where do you come from and why have you converted an old dredging barge into one of the hottest night spots in Tampa?"

"Well Sam, I'm of mixed Cajun and Irish ancestry and both my grandfathers and my father were fisherman. My great grandfather actually sailed clipper ships around the Horn back at the end of the 19th century. I worked hard and managed to get a sea tug awhile back and made some pretty good money towing things around for oil companies."

"I'm not an expert on ships, but I don't think the Catboat is a seagoing tugboat."

"Very observant, Sam. And of course, you're right. This barge has been through four incarnations." He ticked them off on his fingers. "First, it was a heavy dredge used to clear a harbor and inlet in a small, Latin American country called Perritofeo. They had a revolution and the new government confiscated it. When the machinery broke down, they sold the parts for scrap and rebuilt the inside as a portable troop barracks. When their new navy base was finished, they sold the barge to a corrupt politician who remodeled it into a house of ill repute. The

Perritofeo government purchased a couple of decommissioned minesweepers from the US Navy and they hired me to tow them down to their base. The first delivery went well and they paid promptly. The second delivery also went well, but then, they told me they hadn't any funds left in the treasury to pay me. Instead, they said they would give me the Catboat as well as this pier and warehouse that had been used to store military supplies prior to being shipped south. Since it looked like another revolution was brewing and we could hear almost continuous gunfire up and down the docks, I reluctantly agreed. They cleared the girls off and helped us to hook it up and, as we were pulling out of the harbor, our tug was strafed with machine gun fire."

"Oh my goodness. Were there any casualties?"

"One of my crew was seriously wounded and our Coast Guard picked him up as soon as we entered territorial waters. Fortunately, that was our only human casualty."

"Only human? What other casualty did you experience?"

"Well, we were pushing the engines so hard getting out of there and in trying to get back to within range of a hospital, that by the time I had the Catboat tied up here, my tug was shot. The crooks down in Perritofeo had shown me pictures and invoices of a warehouse full of building materials and machinery and I hadn't had the time to double check. When we arrived and I unlocked the door, there were a few rusted out containers and piles of wooden pallets. My first thought was to sell the Catboat as a private residence, rebuild the tug and go back to sea. Then, I realized I was kinda tired of getting shot at and Tampa is my home port. So my only real choice was to sell the tug for enough to pay off my crew and turn the Catboat into a night club. I think it was the right decision, what about you, Sam?"

"Oh yes! You have done wonders with it."

"I can't take all the credit though. My business partner is DJ Zachariah and he's the artist that helped design the interior, lighting, and sound systems, and he also keeps it all going. I'm just here to add some seagoing 'flavor' to the place. Oh! And by the way, he also discovered Krong Thip."

She thanked him, wrapped up the interview and they moved over to the side of the dance floor, next to a DJ booth. When the band announced a break, they were there to interview them.

As each member stepped down from the stage, Sam and Kevin realized that not only were they dressed exactly alike, but that they also looked alike as well. The band quickly agreed to an interview and pulled up chairs in a semi circle with Sam in the middle.

When they were all in position, Kevin said... "I'll use some of your earlier concert footage as lead in here... right now, you're on in five, four, three... he held up two fingers, then one, then points at Sam.

"Hello again! This is Sam Wilson coming to you from the dance floor of Captain Culligan's Catboat. I'm sitting here with the newest band sensation in town. You heard a little of their music earlier. Now let's get some more info. What is your name?"

"My name is Krong Thip."

"So this is your band then?"

"Yes. We are all Krong Thip. We have no individual identities when playing."

She turned to the young lady on the other side of herself. "I heard you sing. You have a great voice. What is your name?"

"My name is Krong Thip."

She looked confused for a moment. "But... I though he was..."

"As he said... We are all Krong Thip. We have no individual identities when playing."

"Oh, now I think I understand. You all want to use the same name while performing. Well, what can you tell me about yourselves?"

"The music is what is important, not our individual egos."

"I understand you have an album out now. Can you tell me about it?"

"You can login to our website and download a couple of sample tracks as well as purchase the CD. You can also track our latest project."

"Tell our viewers about your latest project, please."

"Krong Thip is proud to be collaborating with The Cardinal, Wendy Miller, and Dawn Smith on a Techno-Industrial Opera based on Hamlet. We hope you'll visit us this winter for the premier?"

"There's nothing I'd like more, Sir. Where are you playing next?"

"This coming weekend, we're going to be giving a free concert starting at noon, down at the Lazy Fair Flea Market. It's just a few blocks from here."

"Sounds great. Well, we're out of time now. Thank you and good luck!"

"Thank you."

Daddy Judge

"Dad?"

"Dawn? Is that you? What's the matter?"

"I hated to wake you Dad; but Wendy and I are in a pickle and we need to see you as soon as you can get down here."

"You mean your place?"

"No. Please don't go near there or the club and do not tell anyone where we are... please!"

"What have you done now? If you're in trouble with the law, it might be better if I send our attorney..."

"No! Please Dad... Listen... We saw a cop murder someone tonight and he saw us. You're the only one I can think of that will listen and not just try to lock us up. Please, just hear our side of it and if you think we need to go in, we will."

"Where are you?"

"Down at Captain Culligan's, in DJ's suite."

"Okay. I'll be there in about forty five minutes. Stay put and don't say anything to anyone until I get there."

"Thanks, Dad!"

"Don't thank me until we sort this out." He hung up.

The woman alongside him was short, well-padded and speaking with the southern Texas accent of her youth. "Robert? What has Dawn gotten herself into now?"

"Her and her room mate witnessed a murder and they are too scared to go to the cops. Sarah, I need to head down to the Catboat. That's where they're hiding for the moment."

She hopped out of bed and started dressing. "I'm going with you, Robert."

    ***

The girls took turns telling their tale while Judge Robert Smith and Sarah Culligan alternated questions.

"Okay. I think we have enough. Let me make a call." He checked a number in his cell phone, dialed it and a moment later... "George? Good evening. I'm glad I caught you on shift... Yeah... Tell you what.... I need you to bring a recorder down to the Catboat. What? You're already nearby? Ah... I see... Well, get over here as soon as you can and I'll talk to the Chief about authorizing some overtime. Yeah... see ya soon."

He turned back to the women. "Well, Steve Palmer is in the ER right now with a bullet hole in his foot. He claims you guys shot him when he caught you rolling some crack dealer. George will be over in a few minutes. Once he hears your stories, I think he will help me spearhead an internal affairs investigation."

"Do you think it will help clear us?"

"I think so. I've suspected the Palmers of something underhanded for awhile now and Detective George Melendez agrees with me. This could be just what we need to put an end to their criminal careers."

The door opened and Captain Culligan entered. He smiled assuredly at everyone. "Hello Sarah. How are you doing?"

"Doing great, Louis. It appears as if you've had a busy evening. The bar looked pretty full and I saw a news van pull away a few minutes ago."

He smiled wryly. "Yeah. I love the free publicity, but I was glad to see the media leave before they spotted the rest of you guys." His phone buzzed. "Hello? Hold on..." He muted it and turned to the Judge. "Did you ask for a cop by the name of Melendez?"

"Yeah, he's one of the good guys."

"Send him up." He shut off the cell phone and a moment later, Detective Melendez knocked and walked in.

"Good morning, Your Honor. I'm glad to see the girls are safe, but have they told you what happened?"

"Yes. And you need to hear it too. Wendy, Dawn... tell him everything you just told me."

***

Before they were finished, he was smiling. "We got him, Your Honor. We got him dead to rights. I have the bullet that came out of his foot. He tried to get it from me, but I'll wager dollars to donuts that it is a ballistic match for his backup piece. Which, by the way, I confiscated from him as I was leaving the ER. I can't help but wonder why he bothered to off that two-bit dealer though."

Wendi spoke up. "I think I have an answer to that. Eddie has been dealing powder for Mano Piñeda for several months now. Knowing what a greedy little shit he was, I'll bet he tried to cheat Mano and Steve was asked to take care of the problem."

George's phone buzzed. "Melendez here... Yeah... you don't say? Now this is really strange. Okay. Thanks."

He shook his head and looked up at the girls. "The divers just finished checking everything on the bottom, for fifty feet in any direction." He shook his head again. "There's no body. Eddie isn't under the pier... And without a body, we're going to play holy hell getting Internal Affairs to indict. Dawn, you and Wendy need to lay low for a few days. Do you have a place to stay?"

DJ spoke up. "No problem, Judge. They can crash in the guest room next door. If you can get them some extra clothing from their place and drop it off tomorrow, we'll see to it they're fed, watered and kept safe and snug."

Body Switch

"Hey Tony! How goes it?"

Tony poured the cop a cup of coffee. "Goes good, George. Haven't seen much of ya lately. What have you been up to?"

"Well, to tell you the truth..." He glanced around to make sure nobody was in earshot. "I've been trying to hunt down one of our local scumbags. You might have seen him around. His name is Eddie Watkins."

Tony's face seemed to freeze for a moment. "Can you give me a few minutes? Stick around here and I just might have a lead for you."

"No problem. I'll hang around for a bit."

A few minutes later, his phone rang and he stepped aside to take the call.

"George, I've known you for a long time now and I've always seen you give someone a chance to explain their actions. I can help solve your Eddie problem if you will promise that the source of the information remains anonymous."

"Is your source wanted as well?"

"Yes, but not for anything they deserve to be in jail for... and they are volunteering to help you with this investigation if you ignore their other problems."

"I can't promise anything, but I will see what I can do to help."

Tony consulted with the person on the phone for a moment. "Fair enough." He hung up and turned his attention back to the Officer. "We need to head over to the Schoonerville Pub."

***

Don walked in. "Well, I'm here. What did you want to show me?"

"Detective George Melendez, I want you to meet Dr. Donald Samuelson and his wife, Marsha Samuelson."

They shook hands. "Pleased to meet you. Why do those names ring a bell?"

"You probably saw reports on us from the FBI. I'm one of the developers of OmniPhage and my wife was the first recipient."

"So you two are hooked on some exotic drug? But I thought the people the feds were looking for were middle aged..." He stopped... eyes narrowing and then it hit. "You're telling me that drug really is the fountain of youth?"

Donald gave a wry grin. "Pretty much, yeah. That is why we needed to talk with you though. When Tony told us who you were looking for and why, we had to let you know what happened here a few nights ago."

"Go on; I'm listening."

Marsha picked it up. "We were cleaning the kitchen, well after midnight, when there was a banging on the back door. That's the one that opens on the alley. When I opened it, Eddie Watkins was kneeling on the step, half-drowned, beat all to hell and back, and bleeding like a pig."

George interrupted. "Do you mind if I record this for my notes, Mrs. Samuelson?"

She shook her head. "Go ahead. You've already got us if you want the reward."

He gave her a dirty look. "I don't work that way, ma'am. Please continue."

"He was half dead and had lost a lot of blood. We were going to call the police when he pulled a knife and held it to my throat. Then he demanded OmniPhage. It seems that he had been following all the techno blog reports on the internet and, after seeing us arrive, he put two and two together. He was going to turn us in for the reward, when that cop tried to kill him. When those strippers distracted Steve, Eddie managed to untangle himself from the chain and hide under the dock. He had several broken ribs, bad lacerations of the neck from that chain, and a broken wrist. He was in a lot of pain, but still very dangerous. He said if we gave him a shot of OmniPhage, he would leave as soon as he recovered and nobody would be the wiser."

"Okay. That explains why he seems to have flat faded into the woodwork. He was a pretty young fellow already though, he wouldn't look that much different, right?"

"I told you he had been following the techno blogs on the internet. It seems that there are some things you can do with OmniPhage that we had never considered. And they are going to play hell with law enforcement in the near future."

"Explain, please. What sort of things?"

"Are you familiar with how OmniPhage is administered?"

"No."

"Well, it is a dry, crystalline powder in basic form. You put a half gram or so into a syringe, insert the needle into a vein and suck some of your blood into the syringe. The OmniPhage goes into solution instantly and it examines all the DNA samples in that blood, fixes any broken chains so they are perfect new ones, and then you inject it back into the vein. A few moments later, the OmniPhage that is now encoded with your perfect DNA pattern, spreads through your body and it repairs whatever injuries or diseases you may have. With me so far?"

"Yeah, so far."

"Well, some people have been experimenting and this is what Eddie had read about. If you pull some blood from a person and then withdraw the needle and inject the sample into another person, then the second person will slowly, over the next day or so, take on the appearance of the first person. They become their clone, except much healthier."

The detective leaned back and whistled. "Holy shit! You're right. This is going to play hell with us." He shook his head for a moment. "Well, who does the little shit look like now and where can I find him?"

Marsha giggled. "It won't be too hard to spot, officer. He looks just like me only about fifteen pounds lighter and really paranoid right now. Since we couldn't really call the cops, for obvious reasons, as soon as she woke up, we gave her something to wear and kicked her ass out."

George filled in the Chief and an internal affairs investigation was started on the brothers. Without Eddie, however, they wouldn't be able to indict for anything serious. Surveillance was increased on Mano Piñeda in order to confirm the drug connection.

Lazy Fair

That Saturday, the Lazy Fair was in full swing. The parking lot was full and people were parking on side streets for two blocks in either direction. The Schoonerville Pub stayed busy and every merchant from the truck farmers and honey vendors to the tattooed fellow selling knives, swords and martial arts equipment were smiling at the flow of money.

Detective George Melendez was slowly cruising the market, not really working as much as enjoying the sense of community that the neighborhood had been missing for a long time. He walked up to a rough wood picnic table with four men, playing dominoes.

"Howdy Mr. Webster." He sat down next to the elderly Jamaican.

A sidelong glance, a nod and a friendly smile barely distracted him from his game. "And a good day to you, Officer Melendez. What's the latest from your side of the dock?"

"The usual. Washington is screaming about that new drug and Homeland Security is tightening controls on certain equipment and chemicals used to make it. Personally, I don't see what all the fuss is about..."

"Money, my dear sir, money. The root of all evil. When that drug is finally available on every street corner, then all the doctors and pharmaceutical firms are going to be hurting something terrible. This is starting to look just like the prohibition on marijuana."

They finished the game and David Webster turned to his official friend as their fellow players excused themselves. "George. I've got a bit of a problem. Perhaps you can help me sort it out."

"I'm listening."

"Well, there's this really young hooker in the area. Her name is Beti and the young lady's had it really rough. I've been trying to get her off the street, but that's the only way she has of making a living at the moment. I'm pretty sure she's hooked on crack and it won't be long before she loses it completely. Now, I understand you've got a little personal thing going with Detective Turner." He waved a hand in dismissal. "No, never mind the official line. The reason I bring it up is because both Beti and her roommate, Tina can provide you with some testimony on that scumbag. The biggest problem is they are both scared shitless of him. If you can get Beti into a program and find a real job for Tina, then I'm sure they could be useful in your investigation."

"Hhhmmm... I will see what I can do. Where can I find them?"

"When you think you have something lined up for them, just come by my place before noon."

"Thanks. I just might do that."

"Oh, and George... You heard anything more about that new drug... OmniPhage? I know it appears to be a north east thing now, but I'm sure it will show up here, sooner or later."

He smiled. "Why? You lookin' to hook yourself up with a new

body?"

The old Jamaican just smiled softly. "I've got diabetes, high PSA, and a bad back... wouldn't you, in my shoes?"

After thinking it over a moment, he shrugged. "You know... I'd really have to think on that a bit."

Downstairs, at the Lazy Fair office, Don Samuelson was holding an official document and looking worried. "I'm not an attorney, Mr. Brandon. So why don't you tell me what this really boils down to..."

"It's actually very simple, Sir. This flea market is against the zoning codes for this area. The bottom line is that you are hereby ordered to shut down and evict your illegal tenants in a timely manner. Now the city authority isn't unreasonable. We realize it will take you at least the rest of the day to notify everyone and close up shop... but we expect you to be closed for business tomorrow and that all of the illegal additions you have done to this building will be removed within one week."

"But we have a valid business license that was granted by your office less than three months ago. What changed?"

The young attorney looked embarrassed. "Just between you and me, Sir... There are a lot of high-powered lawyers lined up by several mall merchant associations in the area and they don't like the competition. The city doesn't want to get involved in a long and costly legal battle."

"So, if we get the city council members behind us, then this will probably go away?"

"That's my guess sir, but keep in mind that several of them have significant investments in the larger businesses around town. They really don't believe in competition."

"What happens if we don't close tomorrow?"

"Well, I can't say for sure, but my best guess would be nothing tomorrow, but sometime in the next few weeks, there would probably be a police raid. You, your staff, and all of the merchants would be arrested, and all of the merchandise declared contraband and confiscated."

"Whew! That's rough. Well, thank you for your honesty and forthright answers. I will take this up with the rest of the team and decide if we're going to open in the morning or not."

They opened as usual on Sunday morning and Marshal Brandon Jr., Attorney at Law shook his head, expecting to get orders for a raid the following weekend. He was genuinely surprised on Thursday, when his office got word from the city council that a zoning variance had been granted and the Lazy Fair flea market was not to be hassled.

What was more shocking was that three of the five council members resigned via email the following day and rumor had it, they were retiring and leaving town. The following week, their homes were listed with local real estate agents and nobody could recall seeing them since they voted to allow a zoning variance for the Lazy Fair.

***

Tony and Annette were taking a well-deserved break and sharing a booth with Officer Roberts and David Webster. The elderly black man took a sip of his coffee before speaking. "Uhhm. This is good. I was worried that coffee would go the way of fresh bananas since all the ruckus."

"No problem there, my friend." Tony smiled and took a sip of his own. "A couple of freighters that weren't doing too well before the market collapsed, are now doing a brisk business in coffee beans and sometimes bananas from the tropics and machine tools and auto parts from the states. With any luck, we should be getting back to a fairly stable economy sometime soon."

Officer Roberts added. "I don't think most folks really understood what sort of financial house of cards the whole world had been working with the last few decades. It took a major collapse to bring us back almost to a barter economy and now, we're seeing some stability."

"Well, it would help if our government would give up on categorizing Omniphage as a dangerous drug and follow Sweden's lead." Old man Webster reminded them.

Annette tilted her head. "I'm sorry, but I must have missed that. What did Sweden do?"

"Just like the rest of the world, when the market collapsed and word got out that the 'Phage really worked, things went to hell fast. In order to limit the rebellions, Sweden, followed by France and within the last week or so, several other nations, had allowed limited use. They established government clinics, based on two simple criteria. The first was mandatory sterilization for anyone who used it in order to avoid overpopulating the planet. The second was that the person has to be over 70 years of age or terminally ill and beyond the help of conventional medical aid."

She nodded. "Let me guess. This means we should see it available here, in the very near future."

Officer Roberts shook his head. "I'm not sure about that. There are still too many ruffled political feathers up there in Disney by the Potomac. While the Swedish system appears logical and of course good for the gene pool, there is still a supply-and-demand problem. The stuff does take time to make and distribute. I've heard that access to private clinics means that politicians, corporate leaders, scientists, artists, movie stars and other political power-mongers are the only real winners. The average, lower or middle class working stiff will have to register at one of the very few public clinics and the waiting list for supplies is going to be very long, very quick."

"What do you think is going to happen?"

"I'm not sure, Tony. I expect international drug cartels are going to take up the slack. There is already a huge black-market with single treatments of OmniPhage going for a year's salary or more. Several Asiatic countries have handed out death sentences to anyone dealing in the black-market. To be honest, I don't think that will have much effect."

Money Times

The two young men in the crisp, black suits were out of place walking into the Schoonerville Pub. They ignored the lady at the register and headed into the back, where Donald and Marsha Samuelson were having lunch.

"Good afternoon, Dr. Samuelson."

"I'm afraid you have me confused..."

"There is no need to worry, sir. The bureau has been aware of you and Mrs. Samuelson's location and activities for several months now. We pose no threat. On the contrary, I have this for you." He handed an envelope to each of them.

As they opened them, he continued. "The bottom line is that those are full, presidential pardons for each of you. Furthermore, we have matching documents for everyone on your original team. As long as they haven't murdered anyone recently, they have a full pardon."

Don looked up. "Thank you. This is greatly appreciated; but why did it take two of you to deliver it?"

"Because that is only half of what I have for you, sir. My colleague is tasked with keeping our conversation private for a few minutes. I have a job offer for you and your wife."

"Job offer?"

"Yes. It seems that there is a new government project in the works and we would like you two to be part of it. We are putting together an ambitious project to get a better handle on OmniPhage as well as explore some alternate uses. The salaries are generous and you will have state-of-the-art facilities at your disposal. If we don't have the equipment you need, then your lab budget should more than suffice for any additional toys."

"What is the lab budget and how many people on the team?"

"Your team will only be part of the overall project. Currently, we have planned for sixty, but after you see the campus and assemble the rest of your team, if you need more, it shouldn't be too much of a problem. Your initial budget is two hundred million for the next five years. I trust that will suffice?"

Don's eyes widened in disbelief. "What are the other components of the project if our lab is only a part of it?"

"Sorry Sir, but I'm afraid that is classified until you accept the position and arrive at the campus."

"How long do we have to decide and what happens if we turn you down?"

"If you decline the offer, then you still have your presidential pardons and may continue as you are here in Tampa. We shall not bother you again. If you decide to accept, we have a jet that is being serviced now. It is going to leave at eight in the morning. Just be there prior to take off with whatever you can carry with you. After you get settled in, we can send a professional moving team to pick up any of the rest of your belongings."

Alexandria Council

The Grumman Gulfstream flew west and finally settled smoothly on a huge and well-maintained runway, nestled between high, dry mountains. As they stepped off, they were greeted by a white-haired gentleman in a military uniform.

"Good afternoon. I'm General Michael Hawthorne. Please call me 'Mike'. Welcome to Area 51."

Don had to ask. "Area 51, eh? Does this mean we finally get to see the aliens?"

Mike politely chuckled at the tired joke. "Actually, you are responsible for most of the aliens here. Some of your other team members have already arrived."

"Which ones?" Marsha asked.

Mike listed them. "John and Clare Witham, Kathi Long, and Robert Lorraine. The Withams have changed somewhat since you saw them last."

"Oh? Changed, how?"

A broad grin split his face. "I'm not going to spoil the surprise." Abruptly, he looked serious again. "I must remind you however, of the secrecy documents that you signed when you boarded your flight. We know that OmniPhage is no longer a secret, but there is a lot here that is classified and if you discuss it off this base, you will spend a very long time in a federal prison. Is this understood?"

They all nodded.

"What about Victoria Veski?"

"We've already spoken with her and she said she might join us later on. Right now, she is working on an associated project. She sends her greetings, by the way."

The relative chill of the auditorium was a welcome relief from the hot, dry desert air. They saw name tags on the entrance table for each of them. Glancing around, they saw seats for more than two hundred, but only a dozen or so people in the first couple of rows.

Marsha saw Kathi first and called to her.

"Hey there! It's good to see you guys made it too. Anyone come with you?"

"Nope. Just Don and me this flight. I understand the Witham's are here?"

A soft voice announced behind them... "Yes, we are. You're looking good, Marsha."

Don and Marsha spun around and their jaws dropped at the sight of the cat woman in tight jeans, heels and white blouse. She had long hair, prominent breasts, and obviously feline features. A muscular tail was curling about her thighs. Alongside her and holding hands was a petite female that could only be described as mousy.

Don recovered first when he recognized the mouse woman as a very young and sexy Clare Witham. "Clare? Is that you? What happened?"

The cat woman widened her grin, put her hands on her hips and struck a cheesecake pose. "I guess you don't remember your old friend John in this cute body, eh?"

"John? But what the hell...?"

She abandoned the pose and looked serious. "We screwed up, Don. A cat and a rat ran over the table where we were preparing our OmniPhage doses and we didn't think they had contaminated them. As you can see, they did. It has made for an interesting few months."

"I'll bet. Sounds like we've all got some good stories to share..."

General Hawthorne whistled loudly and spoke from the stage. "Attention everybody! Time to start the show folks. Please take your seats and we can begin." He waited while they joined the rest of the audience.

He introduced the dozen people seated in an arc behind him. Several of them represented major multi-national corporations. There were also representatives of the governments of China, Japan and Canada.

"Just for the record, I'm going to be representing United States Government interests in this project. In the event of voting disagreements, I will act as a tie-breaker."

One of the female audience members held up a hand. "Excuse me, but how about telling us what this project is supposed to be?"

He smiled. "Patience, please. That is the purpose of this meeting. But first, you all need some background information to understand how we have arrived at this point." He took a sip of water and continued. "As you have realized, OmniPhage is more than a fountain of youth drug, it is also the single most destabilizing invention ever made. Current government efforts to control it and the financial fallout are only stopgap measures. They will work just so long before our entire global society is going to dissolve in a series of wars. This prognosis has been agreed upon by many think-tanks and corporate research centers, worldwide."

There were deep frowns and nods of agreement from many of the audience.

"With this in mind, the organizations represented by the people on this panel with me, have been tasked with a very ambitious project. First, let me ask you... How many are familiar with the Media Lab at MIT?"

A few hands came up.

"Well, this team is structured in much the same way. Each of the organizations on this council have funded their seat to the tune of $200 million US dollars over the next five years. There are contingency plans to double this should the need arise. Furthermore, any and all technological advances we develop are going to be made available to all the council members."

"That still doesn't answer what we're supposed to be doing with all this money." The same person interrupted.

"I'm getting to that." He continued. "This council is to be referred to as Alexandria. In reference to the great library in Egypt that was destroyed prior to the birth of Christ. Hopefully this repository of knowledge will fare better. From now on, if anyone asks what you or your team members do; tell them you are working on gathering research data for government security efforts. Your real jobs are going to be much more difficult."

He paused for effect. "There are three real tasks for this project. Number one- gather, cross-reference, and archive the latest scientific findings so that if our society does collapse, we can act as a research library to jump-start the technological aspects of whatever takes its place."

"Number two- to determine what is really possible with variations of OmniPhage and improved methods for manufacture and delivery."

He paused and looked over the entire audience. "And finally, the most ambitious part of the project... Within the next ten years, we are going to establish a series of politically and sociologically stable, self-sufficient off-Earth colonies. The first one will be on the moon, then at the LaGrange points and eventually on Mars and the asteroid belt."

"Ridiculous! There's no way that is possible. NASA estimates it will be at least another fifteen years before we can put even a small research team on the moon. A colony is just so much science fiction."

"That is NASA's opinion madam, and they are entitled to it. Let me remind you however, they are a giant bureaucracy that is very much subject to the whims of Congress. If they had kept their original teams and followed the advice of real engineers and scientists back in the 1970s, we would already have a lunar colony. There is a lot of technology that the general public and even NASA is unaware even exists. The United States Space Command, for example, has no need of NASA shuttle services. We have our own systems which are much more reliable, faster, safer and cost efficient." He turned towards a large screen, over the heads of council members. "Allow me to introduce you to a small part of our contribution to the project." The screen cleared to show a video clip of a spacecraft that looked something like the shuttle, but was much smaller. "This started back in the nineties as Project Black Horse. It's a truly reusable spacecraft. It carries up to eight people and some small supplies and can achieve Low Earth Orbit, also referred to as LEO, on three hour's notice. At this time, we have a dozen of these beautiful ships on standby in two different locations. Six of them are here." He turned back to face the audience as a low murmur spread. "Don't worry. You'll all get a chance to ride in one as part of your cross-training."

He pretended not to notice the sheer terror on Kathi Long's face at this announcement.

John Witham held up his hand. "Excuse me, but much as I appreciate the pretty spaceships, you mentioned further research in OmniPhage? As you can see, my wife and I would be very interested in working on that part of the program." Don and Marsha Samuelson nodded in agreement.

"Don't worry, Sir, you're going to get a chance to work on the biological aspects. We do want people to cross-train however. There is going to be plenty of exciting work to go around."

Another woman in the crowd commented. "Well I'm still concerned about the idea of attempting to build a lunar colony when we have yet to build a stable sealed environment of any size, here on Earth."

General Hawthorne nodded at the woman. "You're correct there, Ms. Wate. That is why we have Project Mammoth and that is where I hope to utilize you and Mr. McDonald's particular skills."

He switched the projector to another series of images. "In the very near future, we're going to be using a rather barren piece of arctic wilderness as a testing ground. Using the same tools and procedures that we intend to use on the lunar surface, we're going to build a self-sufficient colony. This colony is going to have two purposes. Its prime directive is to act as a test ground and secondarily, to provide a safe retreat in case this base falls to civil war mobs."

"Do you honestly think it will come to that, General?"

"Yes."

Other hands and voices were raised. "What about out families?"

"Who's going to be in charge of this Project Mammoth?"

"I don't recall seeing this put to a discussion or vote anyplace. We're still a democracy, aren't we?"

At the last question, the General stood taller and held up his hands for silence. "Let me answer your question directly, Sir. The answer is no, this is no longer a democracy. You are in the middle of a multi-national project that just may preserve the entire human race. It will be run in a military manner. If you don't like this, then say so now and we'll kick your sorry ass outside the gate and you can fend for yourself in what is to come. I don't want anyone here that isn't willing to pull their fair share." He glared at everyone in the auditorium. "That goes for everyone else here, as well. This is too important a task to allow to fall to bickering and petty politics. If you don't like it, you get one chance to leave... but if you do, you will probably die in the anarchy that is coming."

Olde Phartes

Vicki was careful to keep the primered rat rod just a couple of miles over the speed limit. Cops tended to ignore you that way. Driving under the limit was just as bad as driving too fast if you wanted to avoid attention. Her luck held as she pulled into the parking lot of the assisted living facility.

"Hi. I'm here to visit Angela Veski."

"You must be her grandaughter, Vicki."

"That's right. Can I just go back? I know her room."

The nurse smiled. "Of course. If you need anything, just give a shout."

The old woman was wearing a threadbare bathrobe and sitting in a wheelchair with an oxygen bottle slung on one side.

"Gramma?"

It took a moment to sink in, but the woman slowly turned her head, chin quivering and hands shaking as she tried to lift them. "Victoria? Is that you? My goodness, but you have grown to be a lovely young lady. Come... sit and tell me what you have doing lately."

She took a seat and smiled, lovingly at the old lady. "You would not believe how exciting my life has been, the last few weeks."

Gramma chuckled softly, glanced over her shoulder at the open door. "Why don't you close that door, dear? I do feel a bit of a draft, don't you?"

Vicki closed it and turned back to see a smile on Gramma's face.

"You might call it exciting, but I would think my granddaughter would know better than get involved with a bunch of drug smugglers."

"That's just it, Gramma. We're not drug smugglers. That is a government lie because we discovered something even more dangerous than cocaine. That is why I'm here. You've been so very good to me over the years and now that I have the chance, I just have to return the favor."

"Whatever are you talking about, child?"

"What have you heard on the news about OmniPhage?"

"That its a new kind of killer drug that was created in an illegal lab at the university where you work. Isn't that right?"

"Well, I was one of the team that developed OmniPhage. But it isn't a killer. Quite the opposite, actually. It is a lifesaver. It is the ultimate fountain of youth drug. I have some pictures to show you, Gramma." She pulled a small package of images. "Do you recognize this couple?"

"Isn't that your boss and wife? She was at the picnic you took me on this past spring. Sam something, I think..."

"That's right. This is Donald and Marsha Samuelson. A couple of months ago, she was diagnosed with terminal cancer. They gave her less than a year to live."

"Oh my God. That poor woman."

She pulled up another picture of a young woman in an exercise leotard. "This is what she looks like, today."

The old woman stared at it for a long time. "I know that you would never pull such a cruel joke on an old woman. So what are you telling me? How does this work?"

Vicki explained not only the process, but why they were being hunted and the government was trying to keep a lid on it.

"So, did you bring me a shot of this stuff, granddaughter?"

"Well, I think that the more people are aware of the truth, the safer it will make everyone. And I couldn't just leave you here, when I'm on the run now, myself. So far, I've managed to stay ahead of them, but I know they'll catch up eventually. So, not only did I bring a shot for you, I've also brought enough for your friends, here. If you all take it after visiting hours, tonight... in a couple of days, you all should be up and around and ready to leave. Unfortunately, I can't stick around. As soon as I leave, I'm going to head up to Canada to see if I can slip over the border until things quiet down."

"But I don't know anything about giving shots..."

"You introduced me to Mr. Pateli, awhile back. He told me he was a medic in the Army. He should be able to give a shot to anyone that wants the treatment."

Lynn Hall was tired. She had been on shift for the last six hours and while they were short-handed, she had six more to go. It had been like this for months. She did notice however, that the young woman had invited old man Pateli into Veski's room. "I wonder what they're up to?" She muttered to herself, then turned on the hidden security cameras just as Vicki was showing the pictures and explaining it all again. Amazed and then intensely interested, she watched as they opened a sterile bag of white powder and prepared a couple of dozen blood sample syringes. What none of them noticed however, were the few odd hairs from the family of short-hair cats that provided companionship around the home. The hairs fell from the arm of Dennis Pateli's bathrobe and dumped a few strands of feline DNA into the batch.

It was almost dark when Vicki hugged and kissed her Gramma and left.

Lynn called her teenage daughter. "Honey. I'm going to be real late tonight. They have me working another double shift since Sally called off." Her daughter said it was too bad, but Lynn knew this would only be an excuse for her and her punk boyfriend to get stoned and use her bed. Somehow, that didn't seem to bother her as much as it usually did. Next, she called Sally and told her she could have the night off. The resident doctor told her he would be on call with his cell phone and waved as he left.

A quick check of the security cameras showed Angela Veski and Dennis Pateli had gathered three of their friends and were in deep discussion. She waited until it was time for lights out and left the newbie nurse in charge of the front desk while she made her rounds.

She walked in on the five conspirators looked at each of them and stated simply. "I want in on this."

Before they could work up too many denials, she told them she had been watching and listening on the security cameras. She should call the police, but if they will let her have one of the shots, she would help them all. Since Vicki had left more than enough, they agreed. Over the next hour, Dennis Pateli followed her around with a cloth-covered tray of syringes on his lap, while one, by one, she pulled a blood sample from each of the other residents of the home and then re-injected them with the OmniPhage solution. Finally, she helped Dennis into bed, treated him and when he dropped into the coma, she went back to the front desk.

"I'm going to grab a quick nap. Everyone is sleeping soundly for a change. Wake me in a couple of hours, okay?" The newbie nurse just smiled and went back to watching the late show.

Two hours later, she went back to the nurses lounge and tried to wake the older nurse. When she didn't respond, she turned on the light, saw a cat woman in a coma and screamed all the way to the front desk. The police arrived within minutes.

Dreamland Escape

General Michael Hawthorne could feel the hostility. He was standing in the middle of a recreation room. There were free weights and benches along one wall, treadmills on another, a beat-up pool table and bars on the windows.

He looked at one of the two dozen cat people surrounding him, stepped forward and held out his hand. "Dennis, isn't it? How's the leg?"

The suspicious fellow paused, then shook the General's hand. "It feels good, thank you, sir. It took almost a month to finally stop itching and growing, but now, it feels like new." His cat face split into a wide grin. "Hell, General, my whole damn body feels like new. But you didn't come down here to catch up on my health. What's this all about? When are we getting out of here?"

"That is just the reason I'm here. We now know what has happened to all of you and are prepared to release everyone. First however, I want to make you an offer."

He glanced around the room at his fellow cat people; then focused back on the General. "We're listening."

Over the next few minutes, he explained how OmniPhage works and why they all looked like refugees from a 1950s horror movie.

"Regardless of where you ask us to let you go when you leave here, you are going to run into a lot of fear and prejudice from the general public. This has already turned deadly in certain parts of the country. That is one of the reasons I'm here. I've been authorized to offer all of you federal jobs... positions as team members for a new project."

"What kind of project?"

"Well, most of the details are classified at this time, but what I can tell you is that you will be helping to design, defend, and build a new society. We know that many of you have excellent work ethics and I'm in a position to offer you a new home."

A voice from the back of the room questioned... "What about these cat suits we're trapped in?

"At this time, we're still testing variations of OmniPhage that might be used to restore you to fully human. It is still too early to tell if it will be successful. As part of our team, naturally, you will have first crack at a cure when it is available."

"Why us though? Why do you need a bunch of furry freaks?"

Mike Hawthorn turned back. "Dennis? I think you and Dave Kowolski can answer this one better than I can."

"What do you mean?"

"Well, it seems to me that it was just last week, that you two got bored here, managed to sneak by five guards, two layers of security, and spend a day and a night exploring the base and the jungle around us. Isn't that right?"

Dennis looked at Dave and they both broke into wide grins. "Yeah... so?"

"Well, your military training, coupled with the ability to see in very low light and move like shadows, combines the best of your new physical bodies and your years of experience. I for one, don't want to see that go to waste. All you need is some tutorials on some of our high-tech toys and I'd be happy to have either one or both of you under my command."

"And let's just say we agree... How long would this enlistment be for...?"

"Four years with an option to renew at four year intervals. Naturally, this won't affect your current retirement benefits. Besides, I think you will all love a chance to make new lives for yourselves and that is perhaps the biggest benefit I can offer."

"How long do we have to talk it over?"

"My transport aircraft is being serviced tonight. I'm planning on leaving before noon, tomorrow. If any of you want to be dropped off in Florida, we will do that and give you debit cards with a thousand bucks. That way, you can make it to anyplace in the USA with some cash to spare." He paused and his gaze wandered around all the faces before he continued. "If you decide to join our team, we'll be heading to a base out west."

"Nevada? You don't mean, Dreamland, do you?"

The General smiled. "Actually, it will just be an initial outfitting and jumping off point. Your final destination is classified and you're not part of the team... yet."

Planned Hope

For the first time in the several months they had been there, the auditorium was full. There were more than three hundred seats filled, another couple of dozen on the stage and perhaps twenty standing around the sides.

Mike Hawthorne stepped up to the podium. "Good morning everyone. The time has finally come when all of our separate projects are going to come together. You all know our general goals but now we are going to take the first major step in realizing them."

The house lights dimmed and a video showing ocean waves filled the large screen.

"During one of our first briefing sessions, someone asked how we were going test our system to ensure they really would be able to keep us alive and comfortable on the moon. That has been a valid concern and here is the answer."

The video was showing an extremely rugged rock-strewn beach taken from a helicopter. As the view widened, it revealed a rocky cliff with a plateau behind it. The rugged terrain seemed to fade into the distance.

"What you are seeing is Little Lyakhovsky Island. This is the second largest of the Lyakhovsky Islands belonging to the New Siberian Islands archipelago in Laptev Sea in northern Russia. It has an area of a slightly more than thirteen hundred square kilometers. It should be no surprise to anyone here that our project is a multinational effort. Some extremely wealthy and influential people in Russia have thrown their support our way and this is where we are going to establish our first colony."

There was some unhappy muttering from around the room and the General replaced the aerial view with a satellite map image.

"Now from a terrestrial standpoint, this is a barren wasteland, totally unsuited for human habitation. It is actually quite hospitable when compared with the lunar surface. So with the permission and full cooperation of the Russian government, we are going to use it as a test bed for our lunar colony. Starting in a couple of months, we are going to be air-dropping the exact same payloads we would use to establish an off-Earth colony. Then, our assembly teams will don our next generation spacesuits and we will land them next to the supply drops. It will be up to them to live in these suits and build a warm, sealed, comfortable base. I say 'sealed' because we are going to treat this as if it were the real thing. We will not use arctic air, we will use air we ship there. Same goes for water, foodstuffs, etc. Questions?"

A hand was raised a few rows back. "What about environmental impact?"

"As I mentioned, the island is a bit more than thirteen hundred square kilometers. The current human population is less than four hundred hardy souls. At our peak of operations, we are going to be using less than twenty square kilometers in the center and expect to have minimal impact. Considering the overall importance of our project, we're not concerned with displacing a few penguins."

Someone interrupted. "There are no penguins in the arctic. Only some species of puffins. This would indicate there has been no environmental impact study."

General Hawthorn stared in disbelief for a moment before responding. "We are talking about the entire human race here. Puffins, penguins, or god damn arctic aardvarks are totally irrelevant."

A tentative voice from the front row. "What about food, water, power, sewage... all the other things we take for granted? How many people are going to use this?"

"Good questions! Since this is a testing and training ground, we're going to emulate the lunar expedition as closely as possible. That means the initial construction teams will be small and we will take advantage of all the technological tools at our disposal. One of the first projects will be to setup both solar and portable nuclear power plants. We are going to make no allowances for terrestrial power sources, such as wind and geothermal since they will not be available on the moon. A secondary project will be to build multiple sealed greenhouse facilities that will provide food and clean air for the colony. As production increases, we will send more people and they will bootstrap the systems to build larger facilities. In this way, we hope to mirror our lunar project and safely work out any bugs."

Another hand was raised. "What sort of time frame and how many of us are going to be stationed there?"

"Our Russian counterparts have already taken care of all the paperwork on their end. A couple of hardware assembly teams have already started assembling the first loads. I would expect the first supply deliveries to take place in a month and the initial construction team to deploy a month later. After that, we will probably send additional teams on an as-needed basis. As designed, if all goes well, the project will be finished in two years and at that point we will be ready for our first lunar expedition."

"What did you say the name of this island is?"

"It is called Little Lyakhovsky Island, but in keeping with the rest of these projects, we are going to call it Alice Island. That way, if anyone of us is off base for any reason and a civilian hears us talking, they won't know where we are talking about."

His confident smile faded. "I know it has been rough these last few months, watching the unemployment riots in major cities and listening to the President declare martial law. I know that many of us here have lost touch with friends and family members. We just have to remember that we are doing this so that the ones that remain will have a chance." He paused for a moment. "Just for the record, Alice Island won't be the only testing and training facility. We have agreements with the Chinese and Australians as well. When we are through building Alice Island and these other Terran colonies, they are going to be used as protected enclaves of education, reason and culture until this old world stabilizes once more."

Holiday Blues

Midwest winters were seldom pretty. A whispering wind scattered flurries of snow that only served to accentuate the empty cornrows and skeletal trees. Even the dark green of the row of evergreens that sheltered the north side of the house looked cold.

Out of habit born of several months necessity, she backed into a space in the machinery shed. Even with the presidential pardon in her pocket and photocopies scattered with friends, she was still more than a little paranoid.

She couldn't help but break into a grin as she saw her Dad and Mom shrugging into hooded coats and coming to meet her. They group-hugged for a moment, traded kisses and headed back to the house as the late afternoon wind started to bite at tear-stained cheeks.

"Welcome home, Vicki."

"Thanks, Mom. You don't know how much I've missed you and Dad."

"Well, we're all here now and everything is going to be alright."

"I sure hope so, Dad. But what I've seen in the last couple of months doesn't make me feel any better. Have there been any incidents around here?"

"Later, honey. We can talk about it later."

Once inside the kitchen door, things seemed to brighten in the dry warmth. Gaudy strings of Christmas lights blinked cheerfully as they sat at the round oaken table and sipped at steaming mugs.

"I'm sorry about the El Camino, Dad. I had to leave it back at the cabin when all this started."

"Oh don't worry about it. I got the dang thing back."

"What? But the last I heard, it had some bullet holes and the feds had confiscated it."

"Yep. That's what happened at first, but when those fellows showed up with a pardon for you and requesting us to contact you, I made that part of the deal. They had to return it since they no longer needed it as evidence. I have it out in the barn now and there were only a few small dings from the double ought buckshot those fools were throwing around." His smile faded as he grew serious. "I guess I don't have to tell you how extremely lucky you were. One of the pellets must have ricocheted off your cargo and left a small chip in the back window glass right by where your head would have been."

"Well, they missed and I'm here and I'm looking forward to spending Christmas. Unfortunately, I didn't bring any presents. Being on the run for a few months has eaten up all my spare cash and..."

"Oh hush there!" Her mother chided her. "Things are tight all over and we're very lucky to have food and warmth right now. The lights were off for almost two weeks awhile back and the oil man told us to be stingy with the heater since there was a good chance we might not get another delivery this winter."

"Yeah, those riots down south took out that one refinery and things have been really tense all over. What other effects have you seen here? What sort of preparations have you made?"

"Now don't worry about our preparations. We have a full cellar of sealed, dry goods and when this started, I got busy trading with the neighbors and doing a lot of canning. If push comes to shove, we have enough food and water stashed away for all eight of us for the rest of the winter."

"Eight of you?"

Her Dad looked grim. "Yeah. Your uncle, his wife and their three kids are living in the trailer down on the corner lot and have been working on our place and other farms in the area for the last two months. The insurance agency he was working at, the car dealership she was working at, and their home were all torched in the riots. They were lucky to get out with their skins intact. A good quarter of the town is still a burnt wasteland. FEMA sent some people, but checks have been slow coming and when they do, the banks want to hold them until the feds actually send them the money. It seems that Uncle Sam's checks have been bouncing recently."

Elizabeth continued. "Just last week, your Dad had to chase some fools off at gunpoint. They showed up at the Miller's place a few day's later, when only the women folk were home. Old man Miller and his two sons were working on the other side of the farm. When they got home, they found all three women dead on the back porch and the place had been set on fire. It started to rain hard and that put out the fire before it spread too far. It didn't matter though. The place had been gutted of any useful food, medicines, or weapons." She took a long drink from the mug before going on. "They followed the tracks down the road and found a car in the ditch with four drunks in it. It was full of stuff from their place."

"What happened then, Mom?"

"They got them out of the car and held them at gunpoint while Mr. Miller tried to get 911 on his cell phone. When he said he couldn't get through, his youngest boy, Tom just said "Gee, that's too bad." And shot all four of the bastards."

They were all quiet for a moment before old man Veski picked up the events. "They came by afterwards and told us what happened. Me and your uncle followed them with our backhoe and dug graves in the edge of the woodlot. We let them get cleaned up and fed and they spent the night. The next morning, a couple of officers came by. It seems like someone had reported the car in the ditch and the four bodies. We told them what had happened and they said they were sorry, but they couldn't have vigilante justice like that and would have to arrest the Miller boys. About that point, we all pulled weapons and told them that if they were stupid enough to try, a lot more people would die. And that since they had proven they were tits-on-a-boar-hog useless for protection out here, they better mind things a little closer to their own homes. They weren't really that dumb, thanked your mother for the coffee and left. We passed the word to the rest of the farms and nobody has seen a town cop since. We've actually setup our own citizen watch patrol using our old CB radios and there are at least two people on a random patrol between the five farms between US 30, our place, and the firehouse a couple of miles over. So far, it appears to be working. None of us goes unarmed now."

"That is about the same story I've seen in most rural areas, Dad. There have been some attempts in the big cities, but they don't seem to work until after a third of the neighborhood burns down. The fire departments and EMTs seem to hang in there, but they only respond to calls in their immediate area. Any calls for mass help outside their neighborhood are ignored. We're seeing a lot of midwives, lifeguards, and ex-military medics doing volunteer work with neighborhood watch programs."

After dinner, they cut back the thermostat to save oil and built a roaring log fire in the fireplace. A forlorn wind was prying at the eaves as Uncle Roy and Aunt Martha joined them for the night. Wrapped in comforters, they traded horror stories they had witnessed over the last couple of months.

"So tell us, Vicki..." Roy took advantage of a few moments of silence. "What are you going to do now? I head the government was going to give you a cushy research job."

"I looked over their offer pretty carefully, but decided it wasn't for me. I'm thinking there is a bit more I can do out here, instead of being locked up on some military base. I still hope that we're past the worst of it, but I'm scared that this is only the beginning."

Roy nodded, started to speak, paused as if steeling himself for something unpleasant and continued. "What about this fountain of youth you guys found? Is it really... I mean you can't really turn into some sort of cat-freak, can you?"

Once more, she explained the basic theory of OmniPhage and why there were cat and mouse people running around and why it was safe as long as you kept it sterile.

"Do you have any of it?" He asked hopefully.

"Yes and no, Uncle Roy." She looked him right in the eye. "Are you on the verge of death right now?"

"No, but..."

"No 'buts' about it. I've got a very small supply stashed in a safe place. I will get it out only for life-threatening injuries, or if somebody is dying of disease. Right now, I have no way to make any more and there are still a lot of things we don't know about it."

"What does it take to make more and how much does it cost?"

"I need some lab equipment and a sterile room. It's not that expensive to make, but you do need some fancy equipment, and the last I heard, the government is clamping down on anybody purchasing it without being part of a recognized research facility." She grinned at him. "I've seen that look on your face before. What are you thinking?"

"I'm thinking that this stuff is worth a lot of money and it's going to be a long, cold winter. If we had a supply of that stuff, we could trade it for extra gas, fuel oil, ammo, and spare parts. It might mean the difference before spring."

She was thoughtful. "You may be right there and that has occurred to me, but where are you thinking of getting the equipment?"

"Well I'll tell you what Vicki, how about you leave that to your ol' Uncle Roy. Just give me a list of what you need. I'll let you figure out where you're going to set it up." He turned to his brother. "Hershel, you still have that old shake-n-bake flatbed car hauler, don't you?"

"Yeah, why?"

"I'm going to see if the Miller boys want to give me a hand in a couple of days. We'll need to borrow the flatbed and that old VW dune buggy for an escort. Can we put things together in your barn, Hershel?"

Trading Network

"You wanted to see me, General?"

"Yes, Mr. Kowolski." He returned the salute and motioned towards a chair. "Sit, please. This is going to take a few minutes. Care for coffee?"

"No thank you, Sir."

"Hell man, you're an old war dog, just like me. Here, in private, please call me 'Mike'. I was within a year of retirement when the shit hit the fan."

Mike looked very tired as he paused before handing over an envelope marked TOP SECRET. "You are welcome to read that, but not pass on any of the info just yet. The bottom line is things are starting to get even further out of hand than the media is letting on. The President and Joint Chiefs are trying to keep a lid on things, but it's not going to last too much longer."

"I believe similar rumors are popping up from those that have been able to contact their families. In my team alone, I've had at least a dozen requests to bring in family members. I keep telling them that we have finite resources here at the base and unless they can provide a critical service, nobody else is coming on board."

"That's right, Dave. And that is also why you're here right now. I have a job for your team that is a dual mission." He pointed to a US map on the wall. "See the bright yellow pins? We're going to insert you at the top point and your first task is to establish contact with certain people. Once you are sure of their relative stability, you will deliver a series of communication devices. This is in order to develop a new intelligence net that is not dependent on existing comm channels. You secondary mission is to gather detailed first-hand intelligence on the immediate areas."

"How are we to be deployed, Mike?"

"Six man teams that will be flown into local airports."

"What if these people don't want to be part of our little spy network?"

"You will be authorized to offer trade goods for info. No money will change hands, but survival rations, emergency kits, the aforementioned communication devices..."

"What about OmniPhage?"

"No! We're still under orders to keep the wraps on that and limit it to research for now."

He shook his head. "You mean they are still trying to pretend it's a dangerous drug?"

Mike ignored him. "You will also be able to order a supply of weapons and munitions. In some cases, this may be the most valuable item you can trade them."

Two days later, two cat men, one cat woman, two humans and a wolfman look-alike, rode four motorcycles and drove a large SUV with tinted windows out the airport gate. Each bike had hard cases and large duffel bags strapped on and each rider carried a full backpack. An hour and a half later, they were slowly pulling up the gravel drive with the Veski mailbox.

When they had all dismounted, a voice hollered from the barn. "Hold it! We have you in our sights. Who are you and what do you want?"

David slowly turned around and kept his hands out from his sides. "My name is David Kowolski, this fellow is Dennis Pateli and that lady..." He pointed at the cat woman next to her bike. "...is Angela Veski. We want to speak with any of the Veski family if they are still here."

The back porch door opened and Vicki was already running out. "Gramma! I just knew you were going to make it!"

After tearful reunions and introducing everyone, Hershel Veski pointed towards the barn. "Park your bikes under the barn in that shop area and be sure to close the door. Then join us inside, where it's warm."

Hershel closed the door behind them and peeled off his jacket. "I think you all look like you could use some hot coffee."

They shrugged out of their backpacks in the living room, hung their coats and lined up the helmets by the door. Dennis opened his pack and removed a laptop computer.

"That's not going to do you much good here, Dennis." Vicki said softly. "There hasn't been a working cellular tower in months and the land line is so noisy we try not to use it."

Dennis smiled and turned it around so she could see the Yahoo homepage.

"What the... oh! I get it. You have a bunch of sample pages cached..."

He shook his head. "Nope. We just have a new comm system that makes the old network look like twisted-pair copper wire. Much of the old Internet backbone is still there. It's usually only local access that is suffering from neglect and broken down equipment."

Suddenly hopeful, she sat next to him. "What sort of comm system? Is it satellite linked or what?"

"Do you recall reading about some quantum entanglement research a while back? Well, this is the latest. We only have a few of these systems and if you folks like our offer, we're leaving this one here. It can be charged off of the regular household current, or you can use the photocell in the side pouch of the pack to charge it with sunlight. That is very slow, however, but it will work. With this system, you can chat, file reports, send email, or surf the net on a very high speed connection and..." He was grinning widely. "it will work anywhere."

"Wait a minute! Reports? What reports?"

Dave spoke first. "That is what we're here for... to trade you some equipment, supplies, and information, in exchange for some regular reports of the situation as it will evolve around here over the next few months."

"Dad? What do you think?"

"Sounds like a fair trade to me, Vicki. We can sure use some supplies and it would be nice to know what else is going on around us."

"Mr. Veski?"

"Just Hershel, please. David is it?"

"Yes, Hershel . How are you folks fixed for weapons and ammo? I'm asking because we thought you might be low."

"Well, we have been hoarding it, just in case, but could sure use some more. We've several 12 gauge shotguns, a 308, a 30-06, a couple of Colt 1911s, and a pair of Beretta 9s. You have any of that?"

Dave smiled. "Yep. I can give you a case for each."

"Hershel? I must admit, I'm rather curious. Although we saw some burnt-out areas in town and a couple of obviously empty farmhouses on the way over, it did seem rather quiet. What have you used all your ammo for in the last few months? Have there been some riots that we weren't aware of, Sir?"

Hershel looked at Vicki and she appeared to change the subject. "How is the OmniPhage research going? Have you been able to mass-produce it with the original formula?"

"There are some emergency supplies being created now, yes. But we don't carry any supplies with us. Is someone here in desperate need of being rejuvenated?"

Vicki looked embarrassed. "No. Actually we are in pretty good shape there. You see, about six weeks back, when the riots broke out in town, we lost more than half of the local police force and a few national guard people as well. About a quarter of the town burnt. If it hadn't been for all the rain, we might have lost the whole damn town." She shook herself and continued. "One of the places that got hit hard was the local zoo. Almost all the animals were killed and half the buildings were burnt."

"That's too bad, Vicki. But what does that have to do with OmniPhage?"

"Well, my Uncle Roy used to work at the zoo and remembered that they had a pretty extensive laboratory. It was hidden in an artificial hill that was part of the African exhibit. A bit more than a week ago, he took some friends and went exploring in the ruins and found the lab still intact. They loaded up all the equipment and supplies, hauled them back, and I setup a laboratory in one of the old milk rooms in the basement of the barn."

David started to smile. "I get it. You've setup an OmniPhage lab so you will have some valuable trading material later in the winter."

She smiled back and nodded. "Yep. Right now, we have more than a hundred new doses and I expect to have three times that many by Christmas."

"Who are you planning on selling it to and what are you going to charge?"

"We're not into that whole cash economy thing nowadays. We have an agreement with the local fire department and EMTs. They let people think they have some leftover OmniPhage supplies from a police bust awhile back... and we trade them for things we need around the farm. The question I have is, do you guys need any for trading?"

Dave looked at Dennis and the other members of his team before answering. "As a matter of fact, that does sound like a good idea. How are you packaging it?"

"I've been putting a single dose in a syringe, slipping that inside a piece of closed cell foam tubing insulation and then vacuum sealing the whole thing. You can toss it around and it is safe. We figured that would make for a good sterile environment and the right size for trading. One more thing though... how many other cat people are there?"

"Well Vicki, there are a couple of dozen of us from that nursing hell hole, a cat and mouse couple down in southern West Virginia and rumors of perhaps a dozen more. Why?"

She smiled. "Yeah. I've heard from a couple of furrys in West Virginia. They managed to get a message to me a few weeks back. You know who they are, don't you?"

"No. Should we?"

"It's the Withams!" She was grinning broadly. "They had an unfortunate accident with their OmniPhage dose and were lucky to find some open-minded and charitable friends to help out. So far, things are going well for them."

Dave looked at the rest of the team. "Well, it looks like our next stop has been changed. Do you have an address so we can drop off one of these comm units?"

"No problem. I'm sure they could use some extra supplies as well. Can we send some of our OmniPhage with you?"

"I think we'll have plenty of room for some samples. Oh... one more thing. Don't mention this in any of your emails or chats. That network is closely monitored and the government is still trying to keep a lid on it. Although, yours isn't the only lab that has sprung up. We've heard rumors of several others. There have also been some horror stories of impure batches. They are being played up as how very dangerous it is... and why it needs to remain a tightly controlled substance."

"Don't worry. Like I said, only a handful of EMTs know we have a source. And they don't know that we are making it or where."

"So tell us about the Withams. We had heard the pair in West Virginia was a lesbian couple. Is that part of their disguise?"

Vicki laughed again. "Oh don't worry... you can't miss them. They are well-known in town."

Alice Island

"Five, four, three, two,.." The glaring flash of orange flame was quickly hidden by billowing white smoke that obscured the base of the brilliant white tube. "One... Liftoff!!!" The base clamps flew back and the rocket seemed to hurl itself into the clear, California sky.

Over the next few minutes the monitors showed it arcing high over the Pacific, heading northwest.

"Sir! Both the Chinese and the Russians have confirmed trajectory. It will come into visual range in about three minutes."

There were three sixty inch wide monitors high on the wall. Two of them showed nothing but a deep blue sky, while the third was slowly panning over a rocky, barren landscape. Only a few wisps of pale green were visible in the distance.

"There! There it is! Monitor Two!" A small speck of white had appeared on the display and within seconds, the camera had zoomed to reveal the top stage of the rocket on a downward arc.

"Standby for ignition in three, two, one.." A bright tail of flame sprouted and the camera zoomed back a little. "Main engine stable at forty percent, initiating roll now..." The craft started to turn its nose up and the engine flamed higher. Moments later, it was falling tail first and slowing.

"On course and coming to hover now..." Vertical and balancing on a plume of shock-diamond fire, the craft seemed to drift for a moment and then slowly lowered itself the last few hundred feet to the rocky valley floor. Three legs extended to provide a wide base and barely bounced as it settled to rest. "Main engine shutdown. We're on the island!" Spontaneously, a ragged cheer grew louder as team members jumped around and hugged each other.

Over the next week, two more rockets also delivered their loads with the same precision. Standing tall and proud within a few hundred meters of each other.

Tampa Burned

The Police Chief was scared. They all were. "Okay everybody, listen up!" Officers in uniform and a few detectives stopped talking when he spoke. "It's been two days since we've seen any fresh produce trucks. Most of the grocery stores are out of eggs, milk, and vegetables. The Mayor has been asked to call in FEMA. The bad news is that he already tried and was told that they are stretched too thin with all the north east troubles and we'll just have to wait our turn."

He lowered his head and took a tired breath before continuing. "I am authorizing overtime and canceling leaves as of today. People are hungry out there and I know it's going to affect us as well. All units are to carry full riot gear. We're going to try to just keep a lid on it, but the next food supply truck that opens its doors is going to be mobbed. We need to make sure it doesn't get nasty. Any questions?"

A hand went up. "Chief... what about the Lazy Fair? They are not supplied by the grocery chain trucks. All their stuff has been coming in from the surrounding farms. It was really busy last week and with the normal shelves empty, I think it has a chance of turning nasty."

"You're right, Bob. It seems to me that the other green markets in town will also be mobbed in the next couple of days. I want two officers to cover the Lazy Fair. One can circulate the sales area while the other will patrol the parking area and entrance. That should show the colors and hopefully keep things peaceful."

***

It was already hot and the eastern sky was just getting the pink tinge of false dawn. Tony Grenelli smiled at the small group of vendors and customers that were already waiting at the elevator. "Good morning."

"Hi Tony. Looks like we're going to have a busy day. I was talking to Charlie yesterday and he said he's bringing in a small load of corn, tomatoes, and eggs."

"Yeah. After how sales have been climbing the last few weekends,

I think all our regular farmers will be bringing stuff. Prices are going to be high though. I'm worried about that. With half the city out of work and the grocery stores empty, things might turn ugly."

He unlocked the elevator and headed up with the first few vendors then went back down to unlock the vehicle security gate . Two trips later, the sun was peeking between the buildings and the Lazy Fair was in full swing. That's when the two cops approached him.

"Good morning, Officer Roberts, Officer Gambol. How are things going?"

"Okay for now, Tony. Just wanted to let you know that we're not going to be patrolling just a few blocks; the Chief assigned us to cover the Fair today."

"That's some good news. This is three times the normal crowd already and I only recognize a few regulars..."

A shrill voice interrupted him. "You son of a bitch! That's highway robbery!"

They turned and saw a middle-aged couple in worn clothing confronting a fellow with a pickup full of corn and tomatoes.

"I'm sorry, lady. But the money just isn't buying anything I need now. Gas is over five a gallon and..."

"Don't give me that shit! I know my rights and you're going to sell me this for the same price you did last week."

His face hardened. "I'm sorry you feel that way, but I have customers that will pay that price. Take it or leave it." Two other people were handing him cash and pointing at the bags of corn. He turned away to pick one up as the man was trying to pull his wife away.

"You bastard!" She pulled away from her husband, shoved the man against his tailgate, grabbed a bag and turned to run... right into the arms of Mark Gambol.

"That's far enough, lady. Now just pay the man what he asks and we can forget this whole thing."

She stared at him for a moment... then broke down in tears. "I... I can't. We don't have it."

Her husband looked took the bag and handed it back to the farmer. "I'm sorry. My wife... We've been out of work for more than a year now and..."

An understanding look passed over the farmer's face. Then he suggested. "Look. Do you have anything to trade? I can use gasoline, oil, medical supplies, tarps, rope, clothing, ammo..."

"I have a couple of those blue tarps that we used for a couple of months while waiting for our FEMA check to come in awhile back. What will those get us?"

"Tell you what. I'll put a bag of corn and a few tomatoes on the front seat. If you bring me the two tarps by ten this morning, I'll trade ya. If not, I'll have to sell them and go home. Fair enough?" He held out his hand.

The older gentleman shook it and smiled. "Fair enough. Thank you!"

There was some grumbling from the crowd as one of the people in line spoke up. "I don't think it's fair enough. I've been out of work too and have been waiting in line. I have a large family and need four bags of corn and..."

"Yeah! And I need four too."

"Wait a minute. How about the rest of us?" A skinny guy in the back hollered.

Officer Roberts held up his hands. "Take it easy folks... they were here first and it's first come, first serve. There looks like there's a lot on the truck and there are other trucks here..."

"Yeah and they all have lines and not enough. I think it should be rationed so we all get some. Not just the rich pricks."

Tony stepped aside to let the officers handle it and saw the crowd had grown. He knew it was no use trying to get supplies for the restaurant this weekend. They'd have to close or just serve beer, tea and coffee... at least until those supplies ran out.

He looked around the rooftop sales area and realized it was much more crowded than usual and the customers were not happy. Looking over the side, he saw a traffic jam for a block leading up to the entrance and people were parking on the curb and running into the building, worried they were too late to get any foodstuffs. They probably were.

He heard popping sounds in the distance and they were quickly followed by others. "Gun shots?"

The radio cackled some police gibberish as the two officers tried to keep control. Tony realized things were getting bad.

"Oye, mano..." The soft Latino voice behind him was Mike "Rabbit" Garcia.

"Hey Rabbit. What's up?"

"It looks like things are getting spooky, Tony. I have a suggestion though."

"What's that?"

"Well, I know you don't care much for my compadres in Poison, but there are a few of us that can be trusted to keep a deal. Comprende?"

"Si, comprendo. But what's that got to do with these problems?"

"Well, them cops are good men. Trying hard, but you and I both know they're gonna get run over if it gets worse. How about if I bring up some of my pals. We've done the crowd control thing at concerts before, you know that. I'm thinking two guys on each floor and four in the parking area to help control the flow of people so we don't have so many at once. Make sense?"

"Yeah, Rabbit. But just what is this gonna cost me?"

"No money and no foodstuffs if that's what yer thinkin'. I'll let mi familia work that out on their own. We're used to not having a lot. But what I want is a safe place for us. You've got a good thing going here, bro. We'll help you protect it if you will let us live in peace here. Let's just call it a 'free trade' zone and I'll agree to treat this place like home. No stealing, no jacking, and we'll all live nice and peaceful-like. That work for you?"

"How far does this zone you are talking about extend?"

"The Lazy Fair, your other two buildings and the facing block. That's all I can promise manpower for at this time. We can work out the details later if you'll trust me."

Tony looked at the young man. He'd been a fairly rowdy kid and there were rumors of gang banging... but he had always behaved around the neighborhood. The voices around them were getting louder and the cops were starting to look scared. One vendor had left their van closed and was sitting inside, too scared to come out and sell.

"Okay. You got a deal." They shook hands. "How long?"

"I'll start now, bro." Rabbit turned to his fifteen year old brother. "You heard us, Chukkers. No stealin' here from now on. Comprendes?"

"Si hermano." He didn't look happy, but he nodded.

"I saw Vieto and Marco with their ladies downstairs. Go tell them what's going on and then head back home and round up whoever you can. Explain the rules and tell them I'm running this gig. If they have any questions, let me know. Now, corale! Get going!"

There had already been a few scuffles on the second floor, but the crowd seemed more subdued since most of the vendors were housewares, electronics, furniture and antiques. A camping supply store had some problems when he said he was all out of MREs and somebody saw a box under the counter. The merchant said it was for him and his wife and several other costumers and merchants had to step in and stop the fight. The owner of the camping shop thanked them and, nursing a bloody lip and swelling eye, he stuffed a couple of backpacks full of gear, locked the door and left.

A tall blonde in a police uniform waded through the top floor crowd. "Officer Roberts!" She called as she put her hand on her weapon.

The main group of about two dozen were crowding Bob as he was protecting a stake-side pickup only a third full of baskets of tomatoes, green beans and squash. The van next to it had finally opened and the nervous farmer and his son were selling eggs and fresh chickens from several coolers. Officer Gambol was standing on the back bumper with his hand on his weapon and trying to look intimidating.

"Officer Behr! It's good to see you."

The crowd realized there was another cop behind them and with some angry muttering, seemed to calm for a moment, then get uglier.

"Hurry up, man. Gimme my damn bag and let me outta here."

The harried farmer handed him the bag and as he turned to put the money in the cash box on the tailgate, three people at once, grabbed a basket of produce, turned and shoved between the crowd. Several of the squash on the top of each basket were stolen as they passed other hungry people but they didn't slow down. The mob lost all control, knocked the farmer to the ground and he crawled under his truck for protection.

The cops drew their guns and were shouting for everyone to stop and step back, but were being ignored.

Suddenly there were two shots from behind them and every one froze. Rabbit was standing on the roof of a car and was now pointing his handgun at the crowd.

"Everyone just shut up and pay attention to the cops. We are going to be peaceful and friendly here today. The next person that breaks the peace and quiet will get shot."

"You can't do that. It's not legal."

"Stealing from your friends and neighbors isn't legal either and you people need to show some respect. Them cops have a lot of paperwork to fill out if they shoot one of you. Me and mi compadres in Poison don't worry about fucking paperwork. You will behave yourselves or I'll shoot your sorry ass and toss ya in the bay."

Several gang bangers had also drawn guns and were holding the vegetable thieves. They led them back to the pickup as the farmer was crawling out.

"Put the baskets down." One of the gang told the terrified thief.

When he did, the gang member looked to Rabbit. "What now, jefe?"

"Let them go. They are through shopping for the day."

As they hurried off, Rabbit signaled his men and they holstered their weapons. Some of the crowd went back to quietly purchasing what remained on the truck.

"Hey Rabbit. May I speak with you a moment?"

"Sure Officer Roberts. What can I do for you?"

"I just wanted to thank you..."

"Wait a minute." Mark spoke up. "You're not going to let this gang banger get away with that are you?"

Bob Roberts shook his head. "Junior. You need to realize that this man and his friends just saved our skins and even though I may not approve of his lifestyle, we needed the backup."

"But... this is... he..."

"You're stuttering, Son. Close your mouth and let's get back to work."

Rabbit winked and grinned as he turned away. "You're very welcome, Bob. I'll try not to leave too many bodies floating in the bay."

Regional Aid

The next morning, things were still a bit tense, but the presence of obviously armed men with Lazy Fair staff t-shirts as well as the two cops kept anyone from outright violence.

As the business day was winding down and merchants were packing, Officer Roberts smiled at the gang leader. "Hey Rabbit. Any problems?"

"Nada, jefe." He stopped and stood alongside the officer. "Did Tony tell you about our agreement?"

"Nope. He's been real busy today. What agreement?"

"Well, just so you know and you can pass the word uptown. Poison has this community involvement thing going from now on. We've formed a kind of neighborhood watch program. The Lazy Fair and the two blocks immediately around us are a new kinda Free Trade Zone.

You have my word that there will be no stealing, break ins, car jacking, or any kinda violence allowed. If one of my people breaks the rules, I'll take care of it. If we catch somebody else doin' it, we'll give you a call."

"Okay. But what's in it for you?"

"Same thing you want, bro. Peace and safety for our families. Things are really starting to get ugly out there and I want to be able to sleep at night. You cops are spread way too thin and when the shit hits the fan, it's gonna be anarchy. This little four blocks ain't much, but it's my home and this damn flea market is the best thing to happen in a long time. It gives us all a sense of community and a sense of hope. You have problems down here, gimme a call."

"I'm not sure the Chief, City Attorney, City Council or Mayor will take kindly to having a gang run even a few parts of town."

"Well then, there are two ways to handle it." He held up a finger. "One, we tell them to fuckin' grow up and get over it..." Another finger raised. "Or, this can be between you, me and your partners that work this shift. We all have a vested interest in keeping things cool and my folks seldom attend city council meetings."

They were interrupted by a beep from a GMRS radio on the gang leader's vest.

"Si? No me digas... Cuantos? Gracias." He looked towards the ramp. "Heads up, Bob. We have company coming and I'm not sure what it is."

"What kind of company?"

"That kind..." He nodded at the group slowly walking up the ramp.
***

Given the recent food riots, Dave had decided a show of force might be better than stealth since four members of the team were furrys. He saw the cop and the fellow with the staff t-shirt, waved and smiled. "Hey there! Can you tell me where I can find Tony Grenelli?"

The cop recognized military fatigues and weapons, but couldn't place the insignia. But, he smiled and pointed towards the office that was on one side of the elevators. "What unit you with, Sergeant?"

"Army Intelligence, special SITREP team from DC. If you're willing to stick around for a little while, we'll catch up with you." He knocked on the office door and walked in at a muffled greeting while two members stood guard outside.

Bob watched them for a moment, then turned to look out. "You know, Rabbit... I have a funny feeling things are going to get even more interesting."

"De veras, hombre, de veras." He agreed.

A few minutes later, Tony stuck his head out. "Hey Officer Roberts... yeah and you too, Rabbit. Can you join us for a minute?"

Tony was smiling. "I've some good news for you guys. This is Sergeant David Kowolski."

"Tony has just filled me in on what you guys have got going here. You'll be glad to know you're not alone. There are very similar neighborhood protection groups popping up in many urban areas. Now my group has no 'legal' authorization to support you in any way... But if an unmarked truck full of supplies shows up in a few days, I'm sure you won't look a gift horse in the mouth. Of course, we're depending on you to make sure they are distributed fairly."

"No problemo, compadre. We will work with the cops and FEMA or whoever is willing to help out."

"Well now... that is where there might be a wee bit of a problem. You see, we don't want you guys broadcasting it and that means no paperwork of any kind." He looked at Bob. "I'm sorry to say that means you don't put it in your shift report, Officer, and nobody downtown needs to know about it. We have very limited resources and we're only going to be helping out a few extremely small areas. Understood?"

Bob looked worried. "Well, you'll have to excuse an old cop for being paranoid, but just what did we do to rate such special treatment?"

"Fair enough question and I'll give you a straight answer. You are in the right place, with a working system already to go, and most importantly, some of your neighbors have friends in high places. Most of what we are going to do is aimed at long-term survival and that means we have to focus efforts where they will do the most good. This means we'll probably be breaking a whole shitload of rules and regulations along the way. If that bothers you, say so now."

He just smiled. "No bother at all, now that I know where we stand. What kind of supplies can we expect?"

"In your case, mostly food, portable water distillers, and ammo. I understand your police issue weapon is a Glock 40. What other rounds do you need?"

Rabbit was suspicious. "What about us? Do the cops get it all?"

Tony interrupted. "Don't worry, Rabbit. You're standing here right now, because you and your friends are part of this show. We're all familia, eh?"

Dave was more to the point. "So what kind of supplies do your people need, Rabbit?"

"Well, besides the food, we can use medical supplies and batteries. These radios eat double A cells like mad."

"That is an easy fix. We'll hook you up with some military grade comm gear that recharges with solar panels. What about ammo?"

"Most of the folk I know are partial to 9mm but a few Glock 40s and some of those Chinese assault rifles that were popular a few years ago."

"You mean the STS rifles... they look something like an AK47 but fire 7.62mm rounds?"

Rabbit nodded.

"Yeah. I can get you a couple of cases of ammo for all of them." He was enjoying the disbelief on their faces as he continued. "We're going to leave some communications gear and about once a month, we'll let you know when to expect an aircraft. It will be up to you to supply a team to guard the drop, unload it, and transport back here. Can you handle that, Officer?"

"No problem there. Looks like things aren't going to be as bad as we thought."

Dave shook his head sadly. "Don't count on it, Sir. Don't count on it."

General's Pride

"I still say it's discrimination." Angela Veski was ticked at the commander.

"Yes. But it makes sense. The current batch of spacesuits are enough of a problem to fit without making allowances for your fur. We can't have you shaving your whole body every day, so until we have tested a safe way of restoring your DNA to full human, all of the furs under my command are restricted to Earth airspace." He smiled at her expression in the dim light, reached out and caressed her cheek. "Besides, I have grown very fond of my kittygirl."

She understood, but didn't have to like it. But she had found a kindred soul in General Michael Hawthorne these last few weeks. He was the first man she had let into her bed in many years and was amazed that he wasn't put off by her furry appearance. On the contrary, it seemed to have re-energized his flagging libido.

"I'm still wondering why we've not heard from any furs who have tried to use OmniPhage to restore themselves? It would seem to be the simplest answer."

"We have. I have several reports on my desk. The problem is that we are still not authorized to use it on humans here. The powers that be are still running scared."

"What? You never told me?"

He smiled. "I just got the reports in the last couple of days and I have been working with some others to get the ruling changed... At least for the furs who want to return to basic human form. I expect that we'll be able to take care of this in the next few days."

"What are they so scared about?"

"Do you think there are any pure blood or tissue samples of yourself, prior to your rejuvenation?"

"I doubt it. Why?"

"Well, the way I understand it, if you want to go back to being one hundred percent human, then you have two choices. One, is to wait until we can find a way to remove just the feline DNA strands... Or two, we let OmniPhage work on a blood sample from someone else to initialize it and then inject that into you. If we do that, in a few days, you will become a physical clone of that person. You will lose any of your previous physical characteristics. Is that what you want?"

She thought about it for a moment. "I see what you mean. I guess I can wait a little while longer. As long as you are having fun with the kitty."

As he leaned over to kiss her, she held a finger to his lips. "If it does get to that point, though... I want you to pick out my new body. I don't care who, as long as she turns you on. Agreed?"

Project Mammoth

Balancing on a column of flame, the spacecraft slowly settled to the rocky surface.

"Touchdown and main engine is off! Dreamland, we have arrived and all systems are stable."

"Congratulations, HatterOne. You have one hour for cooling, then deploy your team as planned."

"That went smoothly, General."

"We've way too much invested to take chances. The way I see it, if we can build a totally self-sufficient colony strictly by supplying it with rockets from here, the only difference on the moon will be bigger

rockets and a longer ride."
*   *   *

Steve Saunders loved his spacesuit. His engineering degree, respected architectural firm, and family money had given him a great lifestyle and let him invest in Bigelow Aerospace. Their inflatable habitat designs had already flown to space aboard NASA rockets. When the OmniPhage formulas hit the net, he was one of the first to download and quickly put together a lab. Inside of a week, his arthritic sixty five year old body had been rejuvenated and he had a few hundred doses for trading material. A couple of calls to influential friends and he found himself on a plane to Groom Lake and a new career.

He smiled at his good fortune to be in the right place at the right time, with the skills that were needed. "HatterOne, Saunders... I've just completed a walk around of the T-ArcOne and she appears intact and undamaged. I'm going to trigger deployment sequence."

"Roger that, Saunders. We have you on camera."

He opened a panel on one of the landing struts and entered a code into the exposed keypad. A moment later, the craft seemed to split into three panels that slowly deployed like a flower opening. Each panel had sealed equipment bolted to it. When the petals were all laying flat, he signaled the rest of the team and they went to work. One of the first items was an electric tractor that looked like a 'Bobcat' except it had four huge, wire donuts for tires. This design was sturdy, lightweight and didn't require air. Once it was free, the driver used it to move the rest of the equipment and supplies to a nearby staging area.

The spacecraft had brought a team of six and with one driver in each tractor and a helper to direct and manage the operation, it only took a couple of hours to unload the cargo ships and remove their cargo-carrying side panels.

The side panels were shaped like feathers with flat bases and, when assembled using other bracing and strips with clear window panels, they made a single, metallic teepee about thirty feet high and slightly more than twice that diameter at the base. At six points around the base, there were sealed doors.

It was getting dark and the teams had been working steadily for almost five hours, so they all retired to their landing ship to eat, catch up on news and get some sleep.

"Man oh man... Steve! Did you see it when I almost lost that panel? The wind grabbed it so hard that it was pulling the tractor for minute. I'm glad it didn't kick up when we had the first few panels up, but not nailed down yet."

He shook his head at how close it had been. "Yeah Mark, It's good to know we won't have the wind to deal with on the lunar surface. But it is something to be aware of here and we don't dare make a mistake."

Military 'Phage

His Secure BlackBerry was vibrating insistently. "Hello?" He resisted the urge to come to attention when he realized who was on the other end. "Yes, Sir... I understand... I'll notify the teams of your decision. Thank you, Sir."

He took a deep breath and smiled before answering the unspoken questions. "That was the President. He just signed an executive order allowing the production and use of OmniPhage as a life-saving measure for all active duty military personnel. Not only that, but the order also covers civilians on our teams. There is one caveat though. In order to avoid a super population surge, any recipients are to be 'fixed' in one way or another."

"So, it's going to be part of our first-aid kits?"

"Eventually, yes. What worries me now, is how many of our teams are going to ask for it the first time they get a hangnail." A wry grin spread over his face. "How many doses do we have and how long to ramp up production?"

"When you told us to expect something like this a while back, we've been slowly ramping up based on Vicki's formula. It seems the most stable and easily transportable. I think that right now, we should be able to treat a couple of hundred."

"Well, get them to the infirmary this afternoon. I'll email the staff authorizing immediate treatment for any life-threatening patients and as they clear them out, any quadriplegics or chronically ill will be treated next. Over the course of the following month, I want our infirmary to deal with head colds and emergencies only."

***

In Washington, a very, very tired man stared at the phone. "I hope that will help maintain some stability in the armed forces and near bases."

"It can't help but give them some hope, Mr. President."

"I hope so. That may be all they have shortly. Where is your family, Charlie?"

"I took your advice, Sir and sent them to volunteer down in Quantico. They are in temp housing. Why?"

"Tell them to stay there. Did you see the fires last night? Three more blocks are smoldering right now and another fireman is dead. He was shot while working an apartment fire. I've been told that there are several large areas of the city that emergency personnel refuse to enter. I can't say I blame them."

"If I may ask; why haven't you called in the National Guard, Sir?"

"The ones that have been called up are going to remain on duty for a long time to come. I'm not going to call up the rest, unless it is for a cleanup operation. Every time I call a group, within 48 hours, their homes and families are attacked. The fact is that this whole house of cards has started to collapse and it is going to get a lot worse before it gets better. I fully expect to have protective troops quartered on the mall soon. I've been looking at setting up a perimeter for the downtown area. Perhaps we can save the museums and monuments."

"What about the rest of the city, Sir?"

"There are a lot of hungry people out there... and many of them are violent. I think we're past the point where we can save them all. If the mobs want to burn it down, then we'll just have to do what the rest of the world is doing and watch it on CNN."

Southern Jam

The pink neon strips edging the ceiling of the Schoonerville Cafe was fighting with the brilliant orange and red of the sunset as John McDonald and Helen Wate enjoyed desert. "You sure do make a great key lime pie, Annette."

"Thanks, John. What are you all gussied up for, Helen?"

"Well, even with all the craziness that has been going on lately, they are still trying to hold conventions downtown. LatexCon is starting tomorrow and since so many of the regulars called off, they came around all the clubs, asking for volunteers." She shrugged and took another bite. "The pay isn't bad since the adult industry appears to be one that isn't losing money as fast as the rest of the world."

"Well that explains your makeup then. You need to overdo it a bit so it looks good for the cameras."

"That's right. And in order to keep the models safe, they're even sending a ride. It's going to circulate between the hotel downtown and Ybor City."

"What's this about Ybor?" Rabbit grabbed a chair from a facing table and pulled it to the end of their booth. "Hey there, John, Helen... What are you doing heading over to Ybor?"

She explained the convention and why they were getting a ride.

"Well, just remember that right now, Poison has been taking care of security only within a two block radius of this place."

"I know and you've been doing a great job."

"Thanks. But I will tell you that you may see one or more of the gang cruising your convention. Call it surveillance, eh?"

They were laughing when the Hummer arrived for them.

***

"How are you feeling, Helen?"

"You know I love high heels and strutting my stuff... but after 12 hours in these FMPs, I'm ready to grab a bath and relax. This has been one long damn day!"

"Understood, hon. I'm wondering what the holdup is on our ride though." He was looking around the crowded lobby, hotel bar and lounge area. Then, he noticed the police officers escorting one of the convention organizers. She went up a half dozen step of the sweeping grand staircase and turned to face the crowd.

"Listen up! Hey! Everybody! Listen up, please. I have an announcement."

The crowd quieted somewhat.

"I've just been told that all our vans, limos and cars are going to be grounded for a little while longer."

There was some angry muttering.

"Please, bear with us. The police have asked us to keep everyone here for a little while because there is a large riot going on over in Ybor City right now. One of the clubs, not the Castle thank goodness, is burning now. There have also been reports of roving gang bangers shooting out car and shop windows and that at least here, in the hotel, we can remain safe."

"How long is this going to go on, Stacy?"

"I really don't know. The hotel tells me they have enough food for the rest of the con, so we should be fine."

"What about those of us that don't have rooms at the hotel, Stacy? I mean, I live around here... and I need to get back, eat my own food, get a shower and sleep in my own bed."

"We're working with these officers to arrange for escorts for local people. But there are only a few of them and this will take a little while..."

Suddenly, there were shots from the street and several windows developed star burst patterns. One window shattered, covering dozens with shards of glass and one of the chandeliers spun around in a hail of full-auto rounds. Instantly, screams of pain, fear and anger spread through the lobby as the first of several cars drove by, spraying the lobby with an almost continuous stream of bullets.

John threw Helen to the carpet and covered her with his body. She had a glimpse as one officer and another man grabbed Stacy and pulled her behind the bar. The other officer was laying on the steps with a pool of blood forming under him.

"Fuck this noise! Let's get out of here." As soon as the initial fusillade stopped, John grabbed her and hauled her towards the side of the front door. "Stay behind this pillar. It's concrete and steel. "He peeked around the side and saw their Hummer, parked by the curb with a dozen other vehicles. Most of them were bullet-ridden and there were at least three drivers, including theirs, sprawled dead on the sidewalk. "Wait until I call you."

"Wait a minute. There's Old man Webster, Beti, and Tina. We can't leave them here."

"Get them lined up by the door. I'm going to get our ride and when I stop, all of you pile in before those assholes come back for a second round."

He ran out, confirmed their driver was dead and went through his pockets for the keys. A moment later, he drove the Hummer over the curb and within a few feet of the door. "Get in!" He hollered. There were several cars turning the corner a block back and none had blinking blues.

"Stay down!" He punched the gas, drove over the curb and turned the next corner just as more shots filled the night. Their back window blew in and scattered little crystalline shards through the interior of the limo.

"Everybody okay?" The women reported fine, but David Webster was clutching his chest. "I think I'm having a heart attack", he whispered.

John looked in the rear view mirror and saw at least two older cars chasing them. "I'll get you to a hospital..."

"No! Get me home! They can't do shit in the hospital with all this shooting that's going on. Get me home, now... Uhhh...Uhh." He gripped his chest and closed his eyes.

Beti grabbed John's shoulder. "Get us back to the Schoonerville Cafe. They have a doc there that can help him. I know it for sure. I've overheard them talking."

Another shot dinged off the back bumper of the Hummer.

They turned down their street and could see the lights of the Pub and the security lights on the Lazy Fair. There were a couple of cars parked sideways, partially blocking the street. John skidded to a stop and rolled down the window.

"Don't shoot! We live here!"

He recognized several members of the gang Poison and they smiled and waved him on just as the other two cars came skidding around the corner, guns pointing out the window.

John punched it again and wove between the barricade just as the defenders opened up on their pursuers. He parked in the alley alongside the Cafe and they carried David inside.

What the hell?" Tony didn't like people bursting into his kitchen. "What's... Oh shit!" He cleared one of the stainless counters when he saw them carrying the old man. "Put him up there. Use those towels for a pillow. "Annette! Lock up! We're closing early." He turned back. "David? Can you hear me?"

The old man blinked a couple of times, groaned and whispered something... then seemed to pull back, into himself.

John spoke up. "He said he thought he was having a heart attack. We wanted to take him to the ER, but he said he'd be better off here. And with the war that's going on tonight, I thought he was right."

Suddenly they were shaken by the sound of a large explosion. John cracked the alley door for a peek and then pulled it wide... Just in time for Chuckers and another member of Poison to stumble through the door. They were covered in blood and clinging to each other. The older man was clutching his stomach where he'd been shot and almost fell into the kitchen.

Chuckers cradled the man's head. "It's okay, compadre. We're safe here. You're going to be fine." He looked up at Tony and Annette. "Get me the 'Phage! He needs a shot now!"

Tony nodded at Annette and she ran into the back and up the stairs. She returned in less than a minute with a child's school backpack.

"Just hold him still, Chuckers." She broke the vacuum seal and held the syringe up to the light to make sure it had the crystal within. Tony had a piece of surgical tubing wrapped around the gang member's upper arm and was checking for a vein.

"Move over, honey. Just hold him still for me." She deftly slipped the needle into his arm, pulled back on the plunger and watched the deep red blood partially fill the syringe. As she had been taught, she held it for a slow thirty second count and watched the slight color shift. Then, she pressed the plunger back home and withdrew the needle. "Chuckers! Look at me." He did. "Keep him as still as possible and if he asks for anything to drink, ONLY give him water. NO alcohol of any kind for the next three days. Understand?"

"Yes. I know how it works. We've done it before."

She started to say something. Then, just nodded with a wry grin, and turned to old man Webster.

He had been watching the whole thing and seemed to be alert, although still that ugly grey color and his hands were ice cold. "Is that the new fountain of youth stuff I've been hearin' 'bout, lady?"

She nodded. "Since you're awake, I'll ask. Can I give you a shot?"

He looked at her for a moment... grimaced at a wave of pain and nodded rapidly.

Situational Awareness

Just after dawn, John met Rabbit on the roof of the Lazy Fair.

"Hey there." He turned to shake John's hand. "Thanks for helping my guys last night. I know you don't have much of the 'Phage left, so it's appreciated."

John shook his head. "No thanks needed. Your men saved our asses last night. How many more injured?"

"There's a bunch of minor shit and two deaths. I think we got off lucky though. Look around, man. This sucks big ones." He handed him a pair of binoculars and pointed at the clouds of smoke billowing from a dozen large fires. It looked like half the city was in flames and there were still random gunshots and burst of automatic weapons.

"I've been listening to the radio stations. Only a couple of the out of town ones are still on the air. All of the stations with studios in the city have been shut down. They called the national guard, but only a handful showed up and they're all guarding the hospitals. It looks like folks just went crazy and it has been winding out of control all night."

He handed the binoculars back. "Tony wants to hold a meeting down on the 2nd floor stage around noon. Can you be there?"

"Wouldn't miss it for the world, bro."

"Yeah... he was hinting that he'd called in a favor or two. We'll see what that means."

Rabbit just nodded.

***

Tony stepped up on the small stage. "Hey everybody! Listen up, please. I know we all have lots of work to do, but I wanted to make sure everyone knew what was going on."

"Yeah, man. Whazzup? When you gonna start giving out all that food yer hoardin', eh?" The latino voice was beligerent.

Rabbit stood up. "Cayate, whey! These people are trying to help and we're all in this together. I've seen their back rooms, they ain't got much more shit than we have stashed away." He turned back. "Sorry, Tony, but some of the troops are a bit nervous."

"Nervous, you call it? Heh. I hate to say it, but I'm scared shitless, man." That got some grins of agreement. "Anyway... here's the scoop. We've been running a solar still on the roof for the last couple of weeks and storing water. When those furry military people were here, last month, they left us with a stash of MREs and ammo. I've already shown it to Rabbit and I'll let him decide how to ration it to Poison. If that was our only concern, I'd say we would be in good shape. The problem is, that we're already starting to see refugees from other neighborhoods. We can let them camp in some of the old offices, but food, water, and sanitation are already starting to be a problem. In case you haven't noticed, the city water went offline about the same time as the power, last night. Until things get peaceful and the burning and looting stop, they're not going to attempt to bring it back online. That means at least forty-eight hours. Now, the stoves at the Cafe run on gas and I just had the tank filled a while back. I'm willing to setup a soup kitchen to get basic survival food out twice a day. I'm not going to put a price on it, but pregnant women, children, people that have been defending our gates, or anybody that can bring in food to help out, get served first. Any questions?"

Catboat Refugees

The insurance offices over the restaurant had been cleaned up and now housed the operations center.

Chukkers stuck his head in the door. "Hey Tony! Captain

Culligan's here to see you."

The two men shook hands and sat down.

"I know you're really busy holding all this together Tony, so I'll get right to the point. We're all running low on food. The few farmers inland are too scared to drive into the city and the government supplies are just not enough. You have a solid, safe beach head here, but it is way too small for all the folks that are leaning on you."

"You have any answers, Captain?"

"My barge is docked next to my warehouse. There are two other warehouses inside that marina along with one dry dock and a large dirt parking area. The entire marina is surrounded with a heavy chain-link security fence with concertina wire on top. We've had no problem keeping it safe."

"Good for you. What are you suggesting, to help our situation though?"

"The marina is four blocks wide and about six blocks away from here. In between, there are a few offices, a four-store strip mall and a half-dozen apartment buildings. More than half of them have been burnt and abandoned. Right now, my barge and warehouse are full of friends and friends of friends. All good people, just trying to stay alive. At least half of them are armed and willing to defend our turf. Let's setup a series of road blocks on all the side streets and expand both our safe zones to include the area between us. That will give us enough shelter for everyone and we can start the green thumb types growing gardens in the vacant lots."

"Gardens will take too long right now. Even the green thumb types won't get food out of a garden for at least four or five months."

"Well, the marina has a series of small, fast boats and a fuel storage tank that is untouched. There are some drug-smuggler friends of mine that say we can easily arrange for some food drop points up and down the coast. If we send small teams to the surrounding farms with fuel for their tractors and other things they are running low on, we can have them drop shipments on the beach. Our boats can pick them up and store them safely in the warehouse."

Chukkers spoke up. "What about fishing?"

"Everyone has had the same thought in the last few weeks. Hook and line is fine for sportsman, but useless if you want to get any real food supplies. We're trying to dig up and repair some long nets now. But that will take people with boat-handling experience. I've only got a couple right now."

Rabbit added, "You will need to have armed guards watching the nets too. Otherwise, they will be gone before you get back to harvest them."

For the next hour, they knocked around the idea and finally, Tony held up his hands. "Enough! We can discuss this for days, but we don't have the time." He stood up. "Rabbit, right now, Poison is the only real defense force we have. Can your people handle the increased area?"

He shook his head. "Not without reinforcements, man. We're stretched pretty thin right now."

The captain interrupted. "What if I can give you two dozen new recruits? There are plenty of folks in my warehouse just itchin' for somethin' to do to help out."

"If they're willing to follow orders and fly our colors so they don't get confused and shot, I'll take 'em."

"What about the cops?" Everyone knew Chukkers still didn't trust the police. "There are a few that are willing to work with us and they are welcome. But there are some that just want to enforce all the bullshit laws from City Hall."

"Well, since City Hall is mostly empty for the time being and they are just trying to cover their own asses, I think we can just ignore them. This is our neighborhood now, and we will do what we can to protect our selves."

Rabbit laughed. "You know we can't just keep on calling this our neighborhood. It's part of Ybor City and part of the docks and the Lazy Fair is going to be the center of it all. And what is more important, is who is in charge." He pointed at Tony. "Since you've been running things, we've all survived and have a semblance of civilized society. I hereby nominate Anthony Grenelli for Mayor of the new community of Ybor Commons."

Tony waved his hand in dismissal. "Ybor City and Tampa already have a Mayor and City Council, elected by the people."

"And where the hell have they been while all this shit was going down? Fuck 'em, bro. Half are dead and the other half are hiding. This neighborhood is our turf and Poison protects what is ours. I'll let you in on a little secret, Tony." He paused with an evil glint in his eye. "I'm a bit of a history buff. And this looks to me like it is time for a bit of feudalism. You're the Lord of this manor, we're all depending on you to get our asses through this rough time without a lot of bullshit bureaucracy. You make the decisions and we'll help you implement them. After things are stable, you can call for new elections, but for now, I just want my familia to survive, comprede?"

Tony looked around the table and everyone was nodding agreement.

Lord of Ybor Commons

When Tony informed their government benefactors of his new title, they weren't surprised. Similar things had sprung up all over and they weren't the only one in the Tampa area, either. A farming community near Bartow had formed around the local CoOp and had declared their independence as well. They had armed guards on their farmer's market. Convoys of foodstuffs were already trickling into larger supermarkets in the city.

Another shipment of ammunition, corn, wheat, and rice arrived in several containers on railroad cars. The ammo was divided up to replace what was lost earlier in the week and the rest warehoused. Officer Barbi Behr and her partner, Officer Mark Gambol volunteered to escort a small convoy of trucks to the Bartow Farmer's Market. They traded ammo and fuel for a small herd of goats, a flock of chickens and a couple of cows. These formed the basis of the little farm area that had sprung up between the docks and the Lazy Fair.

***

Two weeks after the riots had died down, one of the Tampa City Council members showed up with Officers Steve and Pete Palmer in tow. He told them they were breaking all kinds of zoning laws and had to turn in their illegal farm animals and weapons.

Tony wasn't pleased. "And just who are we supposed to be turning them over to, eh?"

The councilman had no real idea what he was saying. "Officer Palmer here, can arrange for transportation out of the city."

"And what are you going to give us for them?"

"They are contraband. Illegal to own in the city limits. There are a dozen ordinances..."

"And while you're at it, you can turn over some of the criminals I saw walking around outside this office." Steve Palmer was enjoying his uniformed position.

Tony's eyebrows raised and he sat straighter in his chair. He glanced around the office. "And just who might these hardened criminals be?"

"I saw Dawn Smith and DeeDee Miller. They are wanted for assault on a police officer. Captain Culligan and Jim White, you know him as Cardinal, are wanted for harboring the fugitives. They also are suspected of having a great deal of contraband in their warehouse."

The door opened and George Melendez walked in. "I think I've heard enough. Thanks for inviting me to listen in, Tony."

Steve Palmer was pissed. "Where the hell have you been all this time? The chief wanted all hands to help guard City Hall."

"Fuck City Hall, I was busy helping these folks stay alive while you were all hiding in the basements, downtown. I'm surprised you had the balls to drag this windbag up here."

"Now you just hold on there." The councilman was almost apoplectic. "We are trying to enforce the law here and you are supposed to be a police officer. I'll have your badge for this."

Tony shook his head. "You are going to do nothing. I happen to know that you've been under investigation for months for misappropriation of city funds and now that you're here, trying to steal our hard-earned supplies, I see nothing has changed."

"Those are unsubstantiated lies and innuendo. I have the full backing of the police department and will demand respect and adherence to the law!"

George looked at Tony. "You want me to throw them out, boss?"

Pete Palmer pulled his weapon and his brother was a half-second behind him. Steve looked right at the older cop. "You are under arrest for dereliction of duty, harboring a known felon, and trading in illegal ammunition and weapons."

The door opened and DeeDee Miller ignored the drawn weapons and walked in. She was holding a covered tray. "Where do you want your lunch, boss?"

Tony looked at her in disbelief. "What?"

Steve looked disgusted. "You fucking whores never learn, do you?" He pointed his gun at her.

She smiled. "Actually yes, we do learn." The Glock 40 she was holding under the tray spat two rounds and Steve folded in half. His brother managed to fire a round at the girl and she stumbled backward. Before he could get a second round off, he dropped to the floor with the back half of his head blown away from Rabbit's Glock.

The councilman was back against the wall, eyes wide and making a pitiful whining sound. "You murderers! You're all going to burn for this..." He fumbled his own weapon free of a jacket pocket, but Rabbit shot him before he could aim it.

George dropped to one knee to check DeeDee. "You're going to be okay. The bullet went clean through that shoulder muscle. It will be sore for a few days, that's all."

Rabbit looked at Tony. "I never voted for him anyway. He's always been a thievin' asshole."

Tony gave a wry grin. "You never voted anyway. But you're right. What bothers me is that I think we just declared war on Tampa."

Rabbit shrugged. "No problem. We'll win."

Not Alone

The Summer of Fire as it came to be known, was not limited to Tampa. Every city in the world had a similar tale. As a desperate measure, bulk shipments of corn, rice, and wheat, along with instructions on basic survival foods, were released from government warehouses. Under martial law, the military guarded trains that delivered the basic supplies. The food trains were too little, too late for more than half of the population.

Those that remained were strong, resourceful, and very distrustful of big government.

Sergeant David Kowolski waved to Rabbit from the back of the railroad passenger car. "Come on up." He hollered. "I've got something to discuss."

The sat on the bench seats, facing each other and when they were each sipping on a rare, cold beer, Dave started the discussion. "Your guys have done a great job. Ybor Commons is one of only a half-dozen stable and relatively crime-free areas in this county. Most of the rest is still pretty rough."

Rabbit nodded. "Thanks. We're just taking care of our homes, that's all."

"Well, besides the two containers of ammo and tanker of fuel, I've also come asking a favor."

"What can we do for you?"

"There is a big project going down that needs some volunteers. I can't give you any details except to say it will be dangerous, but nobody will lack for food or medical care. We're looking for individuals and couples without children for now. And they must be able to speak, read, and write English."

"How does it pay and for how long?"

"It will be a military enlistment and I'm prepared to pick people up on the way back. They will be gone at least four years, maybe more. They can remain in contact with their friends and families until after boot camp. As soon as they are assigned to their duty, they will be out of communication for at least six months, maybe more."

"You still haven't mentioned pay."

"They will get basic enlisted pay through boot camp. After that, it depends on their job skills and training. All I can say is they will be well-fed and housed and will have an adventure like no other in history."

Rabbit's eyebrows raised. "An adventure? I think just surviving the last six months has been more than enough adventure for most of us."

"I wish I could say more. This train is going to continue down to Port Charlotte and we'll be back here in four days. At that time, we'll stop for long enough to sign up anyone who wants to join the team."

***

Four days later, DeeDee Smith, Dawn Miller, Judge Robert Smith, Sarah Culligan, a now-young David Webster, and the two young hookers that had been crashing in his basement joined up.

Dr. John Witham and his wife Clare had received another request to join their old team members and decided to take the train instead of flying. Cryptically, they said they wanted to see a bit more of the country before joining the team.

In a real surprise, Chukkers decided he needed to see more of the world too.

***

"Are you sure you want to get involved again, Vicky?" Her mom was worried.

"Yes. This is what I've trained for all my life and although I'm glad I was able to help you guys setup the lab here, it is now old technology, and any of the people that have helped out over the last six months can run things without me. The whole team is going to be back together and Dr. Samuelson has promised me that our new facilities are awesome."

Hershel Veski looked torn between pride and the thought of losing his daughter once more. "What about you car? You gonna drive it out... wherever you're going?"

She shook her head. "I'm afraid I can't this time. It's going to be on a top-secret military base. I still don't even know where it is. You'll just have to keep it running for me, Dad."

    ***

Six weeks later, the boot camp graduates are staring at their orders.

"Where in the hell is Project Mammoth?"

Vicky grinned. "Chukkers, I have been trying to get my grandmother to tell me that ever since I told her I was going to join up. She says I will both love and hate it."

"Yer gramma is there? The same one you told me was a furry?"

"The very same. She's there along with some of my old friends from the lab. None of them will talk about it."

"Well, they are flying us out really late, tonight. Looks like we'll know by tomorrow."

Dawn, DeeDee, and David Webster had similar orders and they all rode in a military bus with blacked-out windows. When it stopped, an officer in a pressure suit climbed aboard. "I will remind you all that you signed security documents. What you will see from now on is top secret. You will discuss it with no one outside of the base, nor will you even admit the existence of this program." He paused for effect, then turned with a, "Follow me."

They each took a second to stare when they got off the bus.

"That looks like a space shuttle." Chukkers voice was almost a whisper.

David shook his head. "Nope. Nowhere near big enough."

"The design is the same and it looks like it has seen some rough use. Look at the scorch marks on the bottom."

Their pilot gave them a minute to stare, then grinned and ordered them aboard. "No time for chatter. Pick a seat and strap in. We're in for a bumpy ride."

The craft was a lot noisier than a commercial airliner. Each seat had a small, round porthole window and they all watched as they took off.

David was watching over the pilot's shoulder and saw the lights of a large aircraft ahead of them. "Is that a tanker?"

"Yes sir, it is. We just burnt off about a third of our fuel just getting up to altitude. That is going to top us off with both fuel and lox."

"So this has a rocket engine as well as the jets I heard?"

"Yep. As soon as we're topped off, the real fun ride begins. Oh! And be sure to tell the rest of the passengers there are airsick bags in

the seat pockets. Get them out now. You will need them."
***

The pilot wasn't joking. When their rocket plane hit apogee, they were weightless for more than five minutes. Dawn and DeeDee were the only ones that didn't lose their cookies.

They set down in the middle of a desolate area with patches of snow and some simple mosses the only decorations.

"Welcome to Project Mammoth and beautiful, downtown Little Lyakhovsky island. Watch your step when deplaning."

They had to wait while the plane was towed into a hangar. This allowed it to cool down and also gave them some protection from the elements when they got out.

"Vicki!"

"Marsha! It is so good to see you again. So this is where you've been hiding." The two women traded hugs and air-kisses.

"And you are the last of the team to join us. We've got a lot to catch up on."

Don Samuelson hugged his protégé'. "Welcome to Project Mammoth."

"Thank you, Doctor. But, just where the hell are we anyhow?"

"This is an island on the northeast coast of Russia. It is way above the arctic circle and perfect for the experiments we've been running. Hold your questions for a moment, though." He shook hands with their pilot. "You said on the radio you wanted to ask a favor?"

"Yessir. Those two girls, DeeDee and Dawn... I want them assigned to my crew."

"Let me guess. They were the only ones that didn't puke on their first rocket ride."

The pilot just smiled and nodded.

"Okay. I'll take care of the paperwork. Better grab them before they get lost."

Baby Steps

Vicki scanned the faces of her friends, shook her head and spoke at John Witham. "I just cannot believe they want us to establish a colony on the moon. Don't we have enough problems trying to fix all the broken things here?"

Clare Witham covered her friend's hand with her own. "I don't think that is your real argument is it?"

"What do you mean?"

"You're a damn good scientist and I recall discussions back at the lab, when you agreed that we needed a backup plan so all of humanity wasn't in one basket, so to speak."

"Yeah, but..."

"And now that we're actually going to be a part of it, I get the feeling you're nervous about something else."

Vicki's brow creased. "Okay. I hadn't planned on being locked up in a giant tin can. I'm not really claustrophobic, but I do like open spaces. This habitat is comfy, but it is still way too many people in way too small a space for me."

John was watching the emotions flickering over her face. "General Hawthorne is aware of this problem and that is one of the reasons for building this facility. Besides testing the actual hardware and construction techniques that we'll use on the lunar surface, this place helps to thin out those of us who aren't suited for living in enclosed spaces. We've already shipped back a dozen of the construction team that got cabin fever in the first month." He smiled. "Don't worry, Vicki. We're not sending anyone to the moon unless they not only want to go, but are perfectly suited for the mission. It's way too important."

Potomac State

Jonathon Tellermann was one of the first to realize things were going to change. As a network engineer for the primary Internet Service Provider in the Keyser, West Virgina area, he had more than a dozen major news organizations on-tap at all times. When CNN, the Washington Post, Slashdot, and several others all started spitting out obviously-rushed reports of the genetics research drug bust, something didn't seem right.

That evening, he had a date with Leslie Symones to attend a Catamount soccer game with his old friend, Mition.

They cheered with the rest of enthusiastic crowd as Mition's high school sweetheart, Regina Castleri, made a goal and afterwards, the four of them were chatting over pizza.

"So what has you all worked up over a drug bust and a media frenzy two states away?" Regina's question got a nod from the other two.

"Something about how the media was spinning this and that lunatic preacher just didn't sound right to me. So I did some research. Every one of the people they said were involved with this are involved in cutting-edge research. They have spotless records and are working with some serious grant money. Turning all that into some new recreational pharmaceutical just doesn't jibe with the personalities."

Mition finished his bite and between chews, "So you think this is some sort of cover up?"

"Too early to tell, but I'll be keeping an eye on it for the next few days. There's bound to be more to the story."

Leslie interjected, "What about that bit about a fountain of youth drug? That sounded kinda odd, no?"

Gina chuckled. "If they have found it, then the first thing I'm doing is dumping my medical insurance."

    ***

The next morning, Jon was on the phone to Mition. "Listen Mits. I don't care what classes you have today, empty your truck, and get your ass over here. This is an emergency and I'm not going to talk about it on the phone."

A half hour later, Jon met his old friend in the parking lot of the ISP. "Come on, I want you to read something where we can talk in private." He dragged him down to the sandwich shop.

Mition read the handful of pages and his eyes got wider. "Is this some sort of joke?"

Jon shook his head. "That is the read-me from a two gigabyte arc file that hit the net this morning. It has been spreading like mad since it was released and explains all the panic and crazy media reports."

"You want me to believe these guys have really found a fountain of youth drug?"

"I'm not a physical chemist nor a genetics researcher, but from the buzz I've been reading over the last three hours, it looks like this might be the real thing."

Mition put the papers down, sat back and took a long swig off his soda. "Okay. This is some earth-shaking news, but why did you drag me out of class?"

"I want you to go shopping with me, right now."

"Shopping?"

"Yeah. I want to fill both our trucks with dried foodstuffs, ammo, and some new weapons. Whatever our credit cards and bank accounts can handle."

Mition stared and his eyes narrowed. He kept his voice low. "You can't be serious. Why?"

"I'm convinced that this is real. I'm also convinced that there is no way the government or big industry is going to keep a lid on it. They will try, but within the next week, you're going to see all of the pharmaceutical stocks crumble, medical insurance will follow, and that will trigger a massive sell-off of the entire market. Even these rumors are starting to have an effect on the market. Inside of a month, this will make the housing industry crash look like a fart in a hurricane.

"But food and ammo? That sounds like you're preparing for a revolution."

"The way I see it, before the year is out, that stuff will not only be worth more than gold, it might mean survival for us and our families."

"You're scaring me, Jon."

"Good. Here's a list I've made. I'm going shopping and I'll leave it up to you if you want to join me."

"Why the rush? Who else is doing this?"

His skinny geek friend shrugged. "From the chatter on my mailing lists over the last hour, I'm thinking there are thousands of people heading to stores right now. I want us to be among the first, before a full-scale panic sets in. There are two others in my office out shopping right now. I expect they have told their families."

    ***

Two weeks later, the four friends were sitting in the living room of Mition's rental house.

Gina shook her head. "I know we've been expecting it, but I really can't believe they've closed the college for the rest of the semester. What are we going to do now?"

"We're lucky in that with a small town, we have farms all around. But this is harvest time. It won't be long before nature's bounty wears off around here. With the major supply lines breaking down due to the layoffs and big-city riots, things are going to be bad in this area as well."

"That doesn't answer my question, Mits. What next?"

Mition shrugged. "Not much choice, I would say. Let's just pack our stuff and head back home. We can hunker down on the farm until this blows over. What do you think, Jon?"

"Yeah. My job here is okay for the time being, but the boss has already made some noises about taking his wife to the Virgin Islands for a vacation. I'm thinking he's going to grab all our cash reserves and let it collapse. The network will run fine by itself for awhile. But sooner or later, something is going to break and a lot of folks will lose connectivity. I don't want to be around when that happens. What about you, Les?"

She looked scared. "I really don't know. The hardware store laid off Dad, earlier this week. We have almost no groceries in the house, so naturally he and that scrawny bitch are down at the bar, getting drunk."

Jon put an arm around her shoulders and pulled her close. "Hey. I have an idea."

The girl looked up at him. "You have a cure for alcoholism and irresponsibility?"

"Nope. But I do have a nice room in a double-wide back near Capon Springs. If you don't mind folks joking about trailer trash, I'd love to share."

She thought about if for a few seconds while staring at his face, then a tear leaked and she kissed him.

Gina took Mition's hand and they both grinned at the other couple. "I was hoping you'd come along, girl. There's really nothing keeping the four of us in this Podunk town now. Let's saddle up and head for the hills."

Home Sweet Home

Jonathon and Leslie left their friends at the driveway and Leslie was envious. "That place is pretty as a painting. How big is it?"

"Yeah, they have a really nice spread. Mit's great-grandfather was a Union officer during the civil war and when he was discharged, he invested all he had in that property. He married a local girl and the farm has been in the Devon family ever since."

"Must be nice to have those kind of roots."

"Well, my place isn't as big or fancy, but it is paid for and with the supplies in the back, we should be in pretty good shape this winter."

"And after that?"

***

The twenty year old Chevy Blazer bumped up the dirt drive and turned into the level parking area. It looked downhill to the blacktop county road and behind them was a four-bedroom, two bath manufactured home. Two other buildings were on the property. One was a slope-roofed, four-bay machinery shed they used for a shelter for Nicholas' truck, backhoe, and other tools. The other was a closed work shop.

The two half-breed wolves met them with vicious-sounding growls until Jon got out and hollered. As soon as they recognized him, their tails started to wag and they sat down, tongues lolling.

Leslie got out and smiled as Catherine Tellermann came to meet them. "My goodness, it's good to see you two. I was starting to get worried. When you told me you were leaving, I expected you hours ago."

"We ran into several roadblocks around wrecks. Things are getting rough out there and the police are way overworked."

Her smile faded. "Nicholas has been having a lot of the same problems. After that riot over in Winchester last week, the Guard closed the enlistment office and sent him home. They told him to make sure all his gear was ready, because they expect to call him up in the next round."

"How are you fixed for food?"

"I've been canning all the vegetables that we can find around here. Same with most of the neighbors. We're trading some stuff to balance our diets. Your dad managed to get us a few cases of military rations that we can hit if things get too tight."

"Well, I've got four large bags of rice, a couple of cases of canned pork-n-beans, and a bunch of freeze-dried noodles."

Leslie added, "I've brought a case of sea salt and a bunch of spices that are not native to this area. I also talked Jonathan into some big bags of sugar, cinnamon, and other baking supplies. We can at least have desert once in a while."

Catherine grinned at that. "I have several bushels of apples that would make great pies. Come on. Let's get your stuff unloaded."

    ***

"Hi there, Nick!" Jon found his stepfather out behind the machinery shed. "What are you up to?"

The muscular Latino was loading some large, plastic tubs on a four-wheeler. "Just taking out some insurance. I'm glad you're here and can help."

"Insurance?"

"Well, since you gave me a heads up, I have been watching things get worse and worse. I've come up with a backup plan." He slapped one of the tubs. "These are sealed and contain MREs, ammo, clothing for all of us, and some basic hand tools. First thing in the morning, you and

I are going up to our old hunting camp in the National Forest."

"You mean the wide-spot clearing on that ancient railroad grade?"

"That's right. I know that only a half-dozen of us have been up there in the last ten years. It's a pretty secluded campsite with a good view of the approach. You, me, your mom, and your girlfriend are going to drive the pair of two-wheelers and the backhoe up the old logging trail until we get to the railroad grade. We'll follow that to the campsite."

"Why the heavy equipment?"

"We'll use the backhoe to help dig out a small area I scoped out near the campsite. We're going to bury these tubs there and then replace the brush and loose stuff to hide it. I also want to prepare a sheltered campsite and start work on a log cabin."

"But that's National Park land, you can't just build on it."

"You really think Uncle Sam is paying any attention to that sort of stuff right now? The way things are going, all the park rangers are going to have their hands full, just keeping the main campsites from being over run."

Jon shook his head. "I really hope it won't get that bad, but I think you may be right."

Nick put his hand on Jon's shoulder. "Son, I know that sometime soon, I'm going to get my marching orders. It might be to keep order in Winchester, but rumor has it that the President is going to focus all nearby Guards to DC. If so, you're going to have to take care of this place and our women."

Jon just nodded.

Fire Downtown

Almost all of northern DC was on fire and a dense pall of smoke covered most of Prince George's County. The stores that weren't on fire were being looted.

National Guard heavy weapons formed roadblocks all along K Street NW, Massachusetts Avenue to Capital Hill, and down to Interstate 395. The troops and their support staff were garrisoned on the Mall and tasked with protecting the government buildings and museums. Anything outside that zone could not be helped.

Heavy equipment had brought in Jersey barriers that blocked anything other than military traffic. Only those support staff that volunteered were allowed in to maintain the government buildings and museums. Roving bands of rioters moved in waves through the surrounding communities. Smoldering destruction was their legacy. In some areas, local community watch groups had evolved into vigilante militia and when they found groups looting and setting fires, they shot the rioters and left their bodies on barricades as a warning. After a few days, the smell of unclean death was mixed with the smoke.

A small group of people had formed a caravan of motorcycles, cars, trucks and SUVs. They were looking for food and medicine. A few of them had been wounded in the rioting around Bailey's Crossroads and they had fought their way out Route Fifty to Interstate 66. At the exits for Manassas, Front Royal, and Strasburg, they had been met with barricades and armed groups, waving them on. They found a gas station with supplies and paid exorbitant prices for a fillup and some stale snacks.

With their homes burned, no food, and nothing else left behind them, the weary travelers followed their leader into the mountains. The man in the front car had attended an executive retreat in better times, up in a little hole-in-the-wall village called Capon Springs. He figured that with all their guns and desperation, they could find a place to steal food and hole up until things quieted down.

They followed the winding dirt back road up to the resort until they came to a chain between two trees and a couple of men holding hunting rifles and standing beside a Jeep.

"That's far enough!" The younger man shouted. "This road is closed."

The leader killed his engine and slowly stepped out of the car, holding his hands out to the side. "We just need shelter, brother. We're refugees from the fighting and have women and children in the cars. All we want is..."

"It doesn't matter what you're running from. We have barely enough for ourselves and no room for any more refugees. You're just going to have to back track to the main road and continue on to Wardensville."

"But all we need is some food and water."

"Sorry mister, but that is in short supply everywhere. You need to turn around in the wide spot there and head back where you came from. There's no supplies to be had up here."

The leader lowered his hands and shook his head. "I'm really sorry you feel that way, brother." He turned and walked back to his car and when the door was opened, he pulled a handgun from the seat and cranked two rounds at the guards. Both rounds missed, but it had the desired effect of making them duck. Before they could return fire, several of the men behind him opened fire. They shot for effect, aiming at the legs and feet of the men trying to take cover behind their Jeep door. When the men fell, additional rounds ended their lives before they had a chance.

People at the Resort heard the shooting and grabbed their own weapons. When the rioters rolled into town a few minutes later, they were met with a hail of gunfire.

With cars and SUVs scrambling madly about the narrow road, several of them managed to get past the defenders. They ran the gauntlet and found themselves on a blacktop road heading downhill, towards Wardensville.

In the middle of a short, straight section, the leader stopped to check on who made it through. He was left with only three cars with four men in each. Two were dead already and three more had serious wounds. They needed to find shelter and medical supplies quickly.

"Hey boss! Take a look." One of his men pointed up the road and to the left. "See that redneck trailer up in the woods? I think I see a couple of goats and some chickens. I'll bet they could feed us and hide these cars if we ask real nice."

The leader nodded. "Let's do it then."

Leslie and Catherine had heard the gunfire. Nick had been called up to defend DC the week before. Jonathon was on a four-wheeler, back in the forest, collecting firewood for winter.

The dogs started growling and howling. The two women had been briefed on what to do if they saw strangers coming up the drive. Leslie grabbed her pistol belt and rifle and went out the back door. Cathy grabbed her weapons and hit the autodial on the phone.

"Hello?"

"Hey Gina. This is Cathy, we've got three strange cars in the drive that are full of men and look like they were just in a shooting back up the Springs."

The dogs were still raising hell in the background. The leader saw they were chained, so he told the others to ignore them. They might prove handy later. "Hello inside! Anybody home? We just need some food and medicine and we'll leave quietly."

Cathy left the phone on so Gina could hear what was going on. She cracked the door and let the rifle barrel show. "We don't have any spare food or medicine. You need to head down the road to Wardensville and check at the fire station. They have some emergency supplies there."

"If I remember, that is a long way and I have some wounded men here. A bunch of crazies shot at us back up the road. Let's not be unreasonable, lady. Just let us come in and put some band aids on my friends and we'll take a drink from your well. That can't hurt, can it?" He started moving towards the steps.

"Stop! Get back in your car and drive off. We have nothing here for you. Now go away."

The leader stopped and the fake smile dropped away. He scowled at the middle-aged woman. "I don't see anybody else around, lady. We outnumber and out gun you. If you don't open that door and be polite, we'll just have to do it the hard way."

Cathy closed and locked the door. Then, she ran over behind the overstuffed couch. She could lean over the top of it and had a clear view of the porch and two of the cars in the drive. She hollered once more. "Go away right now! I've already called the cops!"

The man backed up to his car, opened the door, and like before, pulled his gun and fired two wild shots at the house. Two windows lost their glass and made Cathy duck. They were followed by another dozen shots from the other cars, that tore into the thin siding.

From the low wall on one side of the machinery shed, Leslie took careful aim through the rifle scope. She hadn't had too much practice, but Jon had insisted that she learn how to handle it. Her first shot was perfect and the leader's head snapped to the side in a shower of red. She managed to get two more rounds off, killing another of the men with a chest shot and wounding another in the leg.

When the remaining men turned to shoot at Leslie, Cathy leaned over the top of the couch and cranked two rounds in rapid succession. The first round missed, but the second hit her target in the shoulder, spinning him around. She was aiming for another man, when the one she hit emptied his clip towards the house.

Jon had heard the first set of shots and was on his way back when he saw the dust from the cars rolling up their driveway. He shut down the four-wheeler, slung his rifle and ran down the trail, behind the house. Just before he got to the house, it hit him and he had to take shelter behind a tree and suck on his inhaler for a minute. Not for the first time, he cussed his asthmatic body. It only took a few moments for the drugs to take effect and help clear his airway, but he knew he didn't have much time.

He had just made it to the tree line behind the machinery shed when the firefight started. A fallen tree gave excellent cover and he found himself slightly above Leslie's position. He saw two guys running down the drive, trying to outflank her while she was shooting at the others.

Jon compressed his lips, took careful aim and put a shot dead center in the chest of the first man. The second one dropped behind a tree and tried to figure out where the shot had come from. An almost feral grin spread over Jon's face as he saw the man first peek out and then lean farther out from around the tree. The cyber geek let half his breath out and squeezed the trigger. The other man's head snapped back and it was over.

There was only one survivor. The man who had been shot in the leg was whimpering and clutching his leg. Jon kept him covered until he got close enough to kick the man's handgun out of reach. When he realized someone was standing over him, he stopped crying and looked at the young man. He let his gaze slip around to see all his dead companions, then looked back at Jon. "My leg. She shot me in the leg. Damnit! Don't just stand there. I need a doctor."

Jon's face was blank and his voice was almost a whisper. "No you don't." Even after all the gunshots, that one seemed louder than the rest.

***

"You Nicholas Martinez?"

Nick opened one eye. "Yeah. I just got off watch. This had better be important."

The private shrugged. "The lieutenant wants you ASAP."

Two minutes later, he stood at attention.

"At ease, soldier." The lieutenant pointed at the fancy leather government couch. "Sit down."

Nick sat while the officer opened a bottle and poured two shots. He handed one to Nick.

"What's the occasion, Sir?"

He held the up the shot glass and toasted. "To absent companions."

Nick echoed the sentiment, tossed off his shot and sat forward in his seat. "Thank you, Sir. Now... what is the bad news?"

"I just got word of a group of rioters that made it all the way out to your home town. There have been casualties and I'm afraid your wife is among them." He handed Nick an envelope. "Those are a set of temporary leave orders. You've been here for two weeks and things seem to be quiet right now. I'm giving you three days to see your family and take care of business. I've also authorized a full tank of gas for your personal vehicle."

Nick let his words soak in for a minute, then stood up. "Thank you, Sir. I'll be leaving in a few minutes."

"Just hurry back, soldier. You're not the only one."

***

It was bitter cold and an early-morning snow flurry dusted the leaves for Cathy's funeral.

Back at the house, Nick took his stepson aside. "I have to leave for DC again tomorrow."

"I know. Les and I will take care of things here."

I know, son. I know." He paused. "How are you fixed for your inhalers?"

"I've only got a couple left. I don't know what I'm going to do when they are gone. None of the local drug stores have any left."

Nick opened the back door of his Suburban and handed Jon a small, black nylon backpack.

"What's this?"

"You know that drug that started all this shit?"

"OmniPhage, yeah. Why?"

"Well, it turns out it really wasn't all that evil stuff the government said it was. They have released limited supplies of it to military personnel and their families. There are a dozen doses in there, along with instructions. Don't tell anyone you have it."

Jon nodded. "I was wondering when we would see some of it. I'm not sure it will do me much good though."

"Why's that?"

"It works on your original DNA. My asthma is probably genetic, so it might not cure it."

The man's voice sounded a bit rough. "Well either way, it might just keep you or one of the others alive this winter. I only wish I had been here in time for your mother."

Jon hugged him. "It wouldn't have mattered. She caught at least three bullets and one was to the head. She never felt a thing."

Somehow, Nick seemed like he was much older as he turned away, crying silently.

War Wolves

Two weeks later, the first real snow of the season left three inches of holiday card white in the mountains. Jon and Leslie pulled up the Devon driveway. Gina met them on the front porch.

"I'm so glad you could make it, I've been really worried."

Leslie hugged her. "We're only a couple of miles away. How could we turn down a Thanksgiving dinner invite?"

"Oh, it's not dinner, it's Mits. He's not doing too good."

Jon nodded. "He told me on the phone that he wasn't feeling so hot. What's up?"

"Well, that bullet he took back during the battle of Capon Springs did more than a little damage. At first, the docs thought it would heal, but he's getting worse."

"What sort of damage?"

"There's some nerve damage to his leg and now it looks like the infection is spreading. After that first batch of antibiotic, we've not been able to get any more."

***

Mition had lost weight and was in a foul mood. "Hey there, Jon. You stop by to tell me every thing's going to be alright like the rest of those liars?"

His friend held up his hands in mock surrender. "Whoa there, pal. You know I wouldn't bullshit you like that. We were coming up for dinner and I just heard you had taken a turn for the worse." He grew serious. "How bad is it, Mits?"

"The doc was here early this morning. He said if it isn't better in two days, then he will have to amputate to save my life. This is just like those civil war stories we used to hear. No antibiotics, no anesthesia. The best he could offer was to send me to the hospital over in Winchester and they had a supply of anesthesia for the operation. I'd be on my own for recovery, though."

"I think I have an answer for both our problems."

"Oh?"

"I have some OmniPhage."

Mition's eyes grew wide. "That's the shit that started all this? Does it really work?"

"Yeah. It works okay. Nick brought me some that the military is handing out to the troops in the field. I wanted to talk to you about something though."

"What's up now?"

"I'm on my last inhaler and if we come under attack again, I'm going to be damn near useless. Hell, I could even die if I get stressed really bad." He waved Mition to stop his interruption. "I think I have a solution, however. But I wanted to run it by you as well."

"Okay. I'm listening."

"You know those reports of cat people and dog people that have screwed up OmniPhage?" Mition nodded. "Well, I've been following them, including interviews with those that were actually affected. In every case, some hair or other tissue from a cat or dog got into the Phage before it was used. The only way to return a person to their original body is to have some of their original genetic material. So, with that in mind, I got a blood sample from Nick before he left and stuck it in the freezer."

"So, you're going to use his DNA so that it will cure your asthma?"

"I could, but then I would look just like him. Not that I mind, but it might get confusing. I had a better idea. It looks like these riots and troubles we've been seeing are going to continue for awhile. We're essentially on our own to defend what little we have."

Mition agreed. "Yeah. I'm worried that I won't be able to help around here, this winter."

"I want you to talk it over with Gina, but I want to improve both of us for the duration of these troubles. After things cool down, we can go back to normal."

"What do you mean, improve?"

***

Later that evening, after a turkey feast, Jon and Leslie were in bed. "I had that discussion with Mits and he agreed on one condition."

"What's that, love?"

"That if it all works out for me, then he wants the same treatment before they chop off his leg."

"That makes sense. Has he talked with Gina about it?"

He gave a wry grin. "He's going to wait and see how I come out."

"I don't care what you do, Jon. I'll be here for you."

They kissed for a few minutes and then Jon opened one of the syringes. "Mits let me take a blood sample earlier. This is it. Only one more thing to add." He carefully pulled back on the plunger until it came loose. From an envelope, Leslie picked out a single hair with tweezers and dropped it into the half-filled syringe of blood. Jon replaced the plunger, inverted it and slowly worked all the air out.

"This is it, Les."

"Don't worry, love. I'll be by your side until you wake up."

He winced as he found the vein, then forced the concoction into his arm.

***

Two days later, there was a knock on Mition's bedroom door. "Oh for Pete's sake, who the hell is there now?"

The wolf man that entered was the same height and build as Mition, but was covered in a silver-gray pelt and had a muzzle full of nasty-looking teeth. Even so, his lips pulled back in a grin and yellow eyes held a gleeful sparkle.

"Who the hell... Jon? Is that you?"

The voice was a bit deeper but still recognizable. "You expected maybe little red riding hood? Yeah. It's me, bro. I just got cleaned up and decided to let you see what your genes looked like with a dash of timber wolf added."

"Well, you certainly look intimidating. Is this really what you expected?"

"Yeah. I froze some of my own blood samples just in case this didn't work out, but damn Mits, I feel great. I actually ran all the way over here, through the woods."

His friend stood up, grabbed a crutch and limped around, looked him over carefully - like he was trying to memorize the new version of Jon. "What does Leslie think of this?"

"That's the best part. You know she's been into cosplay and live-action-roleplaying for years, right?"

"Yeah, she's tried to talk all of us into joining her LARP group back at school."

"She just looks at this as another, rather kinky costume. She is trying to convince me to let her try something similar."

"You going to let her?"

"I'll give it a month to see what sort of long-term effects there might be, but if I still feel this good, then yeah. I'm kinda curious to see what she chooses for herself." Jon lowered his voice. "How's the leg?"

Mition winced. "It hurts like mad in places and it is totally numb in others. It also stinks when the bandages come off. The doc said they will have to operate in the morning."

Jon went back to the door and checked to make sure no one was standing behind it. "I brought the 'Phage. You ready to get fixed up?"

"Yes, but one condition."

"What's that?"

"I don't want to just be repaired. I want the same treatment you gave yourself."

"What about Gina?"

"I've already got several blood and tissue samples stashed away in case she freaks too bad. I can switch back after things die down and we can feel safe in our homes again."

Jon nodded and pulled a padded syringe pack from inside his jacket. He drew some of his own blood and they watched the tiny sparkles and color shift as the OmniPhage worked. Moments later, his friend was in a coma. "Good luck, bro. I'll go tell the others."

New Guard

Nick Martinez was an old hand at driving just about anything the National Guard used. This time, he was behind the wheel of a humvee full of medical supplies and a few cases of OmniPhage. As the middle truck in a five vehicle convoy, he didn't expect too much trouble. Local vigilante groups had cleaned up most of the real troublemakers and as long as you approached an area by the main street and stopped at the roadblocks, there were no problems.

Nobody had planned on a greedy junior officer who had seen his rather cushy peace-time military career turn nasty. He wanted to desert but needed some security, so he put together a small team of like-minded traitors and set a trap.

Each of his team were military and had an assigned task. They wore used civilian clothing and covered their faces with do-rags. When the convoy slowed to work its way between a Jersey barrier bottleneck, they opened fire from both sides and killed everyone in the front and back vehicles. Only the center hummer and its valuable cargo were spared from the heavy weapons.

When Nick reached for the radio microphone, shots from two snipers shattered the side windows. His passenger died instantly from the head shot, but Nick only got a round in the shoulder. Flying glass cut his face and he knew his only chance was to play dead. He held his weapon under him so that if someone tried to pull him out, he could take at least one with him.

They didn't bother. He heard the back doors open and the cases of

'Phage were removed to a waiting civilian Suburban. As they drove off, he heard a pop, smelled smoke and realized they had set everything on fire to destroy evidence of their treachery.

Nick flung open the door and ran through the spreading pool of flame. His pants and jacket caught fire, but he made sure he was away from the burn zone and dove into a muddy ditch to douse the flames.

"Damn! That smarts." He muttered to himself as he stripped the smoldering uniform. His left arm was all but useless with the bullet still lodged in his shoulder. He knew that when the convoy didn't report or show up in the next hour, they would send out a search party. The smoke from the burning hummers would show for miles. Nick only had to hide and be patient for a couple of hours at most.

Gritting his teeth against the pain from his burns and the bullet wound, he stumbled past the barricades to a bridge overpass. The washed-out area behind the bridge abutment would provide some cover and give him a clear field of fire until help arrived.

Less than an hour later, he was shaking, could barely lift his hand gun and realized that lose of blood and shock were probably going to kill him if he didn't do something fast. When the cavalry arrived, they would search the area looking for evidence and would be sure to find him. Reluctantly, he pulled the foam covered tube from inside his flack jacket. At this point, the 'Phage would either kill him or cure him.

When he opened the tube, shards of shattered glass and a few wisps of crystal powder slipped out. It looked like the near-passage of the bullet had destroyed his last chance.

"Now that sucks." He muttered to himself as he laid back against the cold concrete. He had to close his eyes for just a second to gather his strength.

The Crew

Somewhere, deep inside, Chukkers always knew playing all those video games would pay off. His breath was low and slow as he delicately adjusted the controls. Apparently unblinking, he was totally immersed in the moment as the spacecraft balanced on a column of hot gases. Slowly, inexorably, he let it slide down until all three landing gear indicators turned green. A tiny smile slid over his face as he realized there hadn't even been a jerk when the gear had touched.

"Congratulations Mr. Garcia. That is the third time in a row that you've had a perfect score in the simulator."

"Thank you, Dr. Anderson." Antonio Garcia still wore the gang tattoos, but when the induction team realized how the public school system had failed to reward his one hundred and forty plus IQ, they had turned him over to Dr. Steven Anderson's team. The electronic engineer and computer scientist immediately assigned him a full schedule of interesting work. Much of the work was just beyond his knowledge and skill set so that the boy had no choice but to learn on the job. When he couldn't figure something out, his mentor assigned some reading and showed him how it was done. Both Stanford and MIT had instructors in the Alice Island project and it hadn't taken long to establish a high-tech school for anyone willing to study.

Although the voice had the authority born of experience, Dr. Anderson had already had an Omniphage treatment due to his age and heart condition. These days, he looked like he was in his late twenties and kept himself fit with regular exercise. "That's it for today, Mr. Garcia. I've got to get back to some mission planning meeting and I believe you have some physics homework to attend."

Chukkers nodded. He had given up on getting the doc to use his gang name or even his first name. He had to admit the man had pushed him far beyond what he thought he would ever achieve. Another few weeks and he would graduate with an engineering degree. "Thanks again, Doc. I'll see you on Wednesday."

The lab, just like every other part of the Alice Island base, was inside a tube about twenty four feet in diameter and twice as long. Each of these tubes had a door at either end. Detailed, three dimensional drawings of the base looked like rows of connected sausage links, laid out in a circular pattern. More links formed the spokes of a complex wheel.

The young Latino felt at home in the maze of tunnels that comprised the Alice Island base. A city boy at heart, he didn't mind the hustle of people packed into close quarters. Every other ring of segments had large openings where the doors were kept open except during emergency drills. This allowed a continuous flow of two-way traffic. He looked both ways, then joined the rest of the joggers in the fast lane. In order to keep things flowing and allow everyone to stay in shape, the main rings had roadways with six, three-foot wide lanes. The outer lanes were only used for loading, to park electric carts or to chat with friends. The next lane in was for those walking while the innermost lanes were reserved for joggers or electric vehicles.

Over the last two years, since the first landing, the base had grown from a dozen segments and two dozen inhabitants to more than three hundred segments and more than a thousand full-time residents. Eventual plans called for the facility to grow to more than three times this size and act not only as a learning center, but a staging area for the colonial efforts.

Chukkers stepped into the Cantina and took a quick look around. His eyes landed on the gorgeous redhead at the same moment she saw him. She broke into a huge smile and waved.

"Hey there, Garcia! Nice of you to take time for us poor mortals." She followed the chide with a hug.

Deedee's grin was infectious and he had to answer. "Somebody has to know how to fly if they ever decide to let us go."

"I guess you haven't heard, then." The soft voice belonged to Kevin O'Conner.

"Heard what?"

The ace cameraman took a slow swig of his beer before answering. "I just got word that the last two supply missions just launched and they are going to announce the first teams tonight."

Chukkers felt a sudden nervousness. "When?"

Kevin just shrugged. "Dunno. Just what I heard, that's all."

Just then, the bartender raised the volume on the large monitor, over the bar. Samantha Wilson had been the project media spokesperson ever since the Ybor City riots.

"... and now, we have our Director of Operations, General Michael Hawthorne. Mike, I understand you have an important announcement for us, this evening."

"That's right, Sam. It's something the majority of us have been working hard to achieve and the time has finally arrived." He turned to face the camera and glanced down at a data tablet. "I was just informed that the last two unmanned supply ships have landed safely on the lunar surface. All the initial materials for our base are now in place. I'm now going to share the launch and crew schedules." He paused.

Chukkers felt Wendy "Deedee" Miller take his hand and squeeze it. She knew just how much this meant to both of them.

The Director continued. "The first mission will be three ships. The crew breakdown is as follows... Lunar Ship One, Pilot and mission commander Steven Saunders. Co-pilot and Engineer, Scott Chambers. Equipment Operator, Wendy Miller."

A rash of whispers around them. "You got it, Deedee! Congratulations!"

"Shhhh... there's more."

"... and the payload specialist will be Anthony McGregor."

The General looked back at the camera. "Congratulations to the first crew!" A round of applause followed. "And now for the crew of Lunar Ship Two, we have as Pilot and Mission Commander, Charlie White. Co-pilot and Engineer will be Antonio Garcia..."

The rest of the announcement was lost as Deedee threw her arms around the young Latino and hollered in his ear. "You got it! You got it! We're on our way!" Then, she pulled back just enough to meet him for a kiss.

***

Dennis Pateli walked into the Director's office and came to attention with his eyes focused six inches over the General's head.

"At ease Major. What's with the formality?"

Despite the military uniform, the Marine and nursing home escapee looked like an extra in a Hollywood urban fantasy. The Omniphage that had renewed his life along with several others, had been contaminated with cat hair.

"The rest of my squadron and I have been talking and we'd like to run an idea by you, Sir."

"Go ahead. I'm listening."

"Things have been going very smoothly around the base and our skills are getting rusty. We feel as if we're not being very productive. We want to be included in the colony efforts."

"I would love to, but we've already discussed the fact that your fur prevents you from wearing a space suit for more than a few minutes."

"I think we've found an answer to that, Sir. We've been talking to the gang in the R & D lab and they have told us that there is no way in the near future, for them to remove just the feline DNA. So, rather than wait, we want to reform our squadron using volunteer DNA."

"That means you will look exactly like someone else and you will not be able to look like yourselves before you acquired the feline 'phage. You understand this, don't you?"

The catman nodded. "Yes, Sir. We've discussed it and each of us had chosen someone and they have volunteered their DNA. As for the identity problems this might generate, we've a solution to that, as well. After we heal and stabilize in our new bodies, each of us is going to get some distinguishing tattoos. These tats will be added to our service jackets for future identification."

"Let me talk it over with the lab guys and if there are no qualms, I'll go ahead and authorize it. As for the colony teams, your names will be added to the lists as soon as we find replacements for your current security details."

The catman snapped to attention, a smile on his muzzle. "Yes, Sir! Thank you, Sir!"

Touchdown!

Chukkers was running his third lap of the B ring when his earpiece dinged. He tapped it. "Garcia." He answered.

"Mr. Garcia. This is Steve Saunders. I thought you should know that Charlie White was just checked into the med lab with a nasty head cold. He picked it up while visiting some relatives back at Dreamland."

"What? But we're taking off in three days. I'm supposed to check into quarantine for final lab tests, tomorrow morning. Can't they just hit him with some 'Phage and get over it?"

"Well, I'm afraid Mr. White won't be going with us. The medical corp has been working with some researchers at the CDC and they have prohibited the usage of Omniphage for non-fatal, common diseases. They are worried that if people start using it like an aspirin, then we will eventually lose all our natural resistance to cold and flu bugs."

Chukkers felt cold but he had to ask. "Does this mean our flight is delayed?"

Steven chuckled. "I suppose you might consider this the upside to it. I spoke with your mentor and with General Hawthorne. You've just been promoted to Pilot. Congratulations!"

He had to take a couple of deep breaths. "Thanks! Who's taking my seat, then?"

"Someone you've worked with in the simulator on several occasions. Dr. Anderson."

"But... But he's head of the training team!"

"He put in for the colony last year and had to pull strings with some old friends, but Mike Hawthorne just approved it. After all, he's one of the ones that pioneered this whole thing. He's also a damn good spacecraft pilot."

"Yeah. I know. He taught me everything I know. It just never occurred to me that he'd want to get out of his lab."

***

The ride to LEO or Low Earth Orbit was the adrenaline rush that let Chukkers know he was finally on his way. All the hard work, training and late nights, hitting the books was finally going to pay off.

He took a deep breath and closed his eyes for a moment as the rocket engines cut off and only the straps held his body in place. An hour or so later, gentle tugs first one way, then the other, aligned them with their spacecraft.

"Welcome to LEO terminal. Lunar Ship One is departing shortly, so please gather your gear and watch your step when deplaning. Thank you for flying Black Horse Airlines." The pilot was known for his banter, but Chukkers wasn't paying much attention.

None of the virtual reality simulators and models had prepared them for the view, when the hatch opened. A brilliant white ship with the proportions of a huge ice-cream cone, hovered a short distance away. Half of their field of view was taken with the Earth and the rest a deeper-than-black star field.

An astronaut with a maneuvering pack had just attached a cable to a ring inside their hatch. Chukkers heard his voice on the radio. "Welcome to LS One. Be sure to hook yourselves to the cable and just head on over. Both inner and outer lock doors are open so you can all enter at once. As soon as you're settled in, we'll seal and pressurize from the tug." He pointed toward another, much smaller craft, covered in pressure tanks and clearly designed never to enter an atmosphere.

***

Even though their ship was pressurized, all four crew members were still in their suits and kept their helmets closed.

"Five... four... three... two... one... ignition!" After several hours of weightlessness, the sudden push of the rockets felt different. His eyes never stopped scanning all the data screens, but everything was working perfectly. At this point, he was just along for the ride.

"LS2, this is LS1."

"Go ahead, LS1."

"LS2, at the last moment, we have an abort situation here."

"What is your situation?"

"The launch computer shut us down due to an overheating in one of the feed pumps."

"But you haven't even been running yet."

"We'll let you know."

Several hours later, they got word that it was a faulty reading. The appropriate sensor had been re-calibrated and they were on the way, but well behind LS2.

That is when it dawned on Antonio Garcia that he would be the first person to land on the moon since the original NASA trips, back in the nineteen seventies.

***

Although the two craft arrived in lunar orbit a few hours apart, the decision was made to follow the original landing order. Tony's ship landed first.

He noticed that his hand shook when he reached for the hatch release. He took a few deep breaths, closed his eyes, and moved the release. As soon as the hatch swung wide, he climbed down. Antonio Garcia, the kid from Ybor City that had been on the verge of being just another Latino gang-banger, was the first person in more than forty years to set foot on the moon.

He gazed at the the sharply-defined crater walls and deep shadows before speaking. "And so it begins."

One of his crew answered. "What ever happened to one small step?"

"It's been done and now it's time to grow up."

As they busied themselves with the unloading and establishing their new base, Tony couldn't help but wonder what it would look like in a few years.

Book Two: Selenaphiles

Desert View

He stared at the bleak landscape and muttered to himself. "Dust. Nothing but dust. I hate dust."

"What's that, hon?" His wife's voice was gentle over his shoulder. She put a plate of eggs and toast on the table and leaned over to see what had his attention outside their trailer.

He gave her a wan smile and a quick kiss. "Ah, nuthin'. I'm just bitchin' about this damn desert."

As Cheryl got her own plate, he asked about the kids.

"Charlie has been doing really good on his geometry and general science lessons, but I'm having a hard time getting him to focus on history. Wendy is going to be a pretty good writer, but I'm worried about her math skills. They're both well above normal on reading speed and comprehension." She took a bite of her breakfast, then asked, "What about you, Buster? How's the project?"

He finished chewing a mouthful to delay. "It's almost done. I've had to let most of the crew go and we're getting final sign off on the entire site sometime in the next week or so. After that..." He shrugged.

"Still no other job offers?"

"Nope." He waved out the window. "You've noticed that even though only a few of us are still employed, nobody has left the camp yet? There's no place to go. There are no more large construction projects scheduled since the riots and any rebuilding jobs are going to cheap, local labor."

She took his hand and tried to be positive. "Well, I'm not going to worry too much right now. We've been pretty careful and there's some cash in the bank. Where do you want to go when we're done, here?"

"No place. This trailer is paid for and I've managed to talk the company into lettin' anyone on the team remain on this land, rent-free for the next year. That's all they will allow us to find new positions. The problem is that nobody is hirin' and since all the riots, the big cities are just shells. Everyone that could has settled where they can farm and grow their own food. The few city folk that don't know any better or can't afford to move, are dependent on rapidly-dwindling emergency food supplies. We're safer out here in this damn desert and we are close to the power from the hydro plant we just finished, but we can't grow anythin' in this damn dust."

***

He parked next to the project trailer and paid no attention to the black Suburban in front.

"There you are!" It was the government project manager. "Come here, Buster. There's somebody you want to meet."

"Mr. Simmons, this is Charles Mathias. Buster, I invited this fellow to meet you. He has a proposition."

They shook hands and the PM told them to go ahead and use the conference room. Then, he escaped to some other meeting.

"So, Mr. Simmons, what can I do for you?"

"Call me John."

"Okay John and please call me Buster. Most everyone around here does." He leaned back in the chair, glanced at his watch and decided to get this over with. "What is it that you're selling?"

"A fresh chance for you, your family and some of your team." Before Buster could ask, he continued. "I know that this project is almost over and you're going to be available. I represent a group that has a very large, long-term project already started and we're in need of people like you and many of the folks on your present team. We're prepared to offer you a chance at a new life."

"I'm not sure I follow. How about some details, like what kind of project, where and what sort of timeframe?"

"You've heard that we have a base on the moon, right?"

Buster nodded.

"Well, it has finally grown past the research station stage and we're engaged in a series of massive construction projects."

Buster held up his hand. "Whoa there, mister. I'm way too old to be spending months at a time ramrodding some rocket base on the moon. And I'm also not going to leave my wife to finish raising our kids while I'm away for months or years at a time. Forget it!" He started to get up.

"Wait a minute. I think you misunderstand. We don't just have some small base up there. We're now at the stage where we are going to start colonization with entire families. If you take this job, your wife and kids are going along too. And there are some great fringe benefits..."

"Take my family? To the moon? Now I know you're nuts. Things are cramped enough in our trailer, but at least they can go outside to play soccer or go hiking. I've been in a submarine before and if I told them we were going to be living in a pressurized tube, sleeping in bunks and no soccer field, I'd have a riot on my hands."

John smiled and continued. "I think you have the wrong idea of what stage the colony is at. We let the media think it's just a bunch of inflatable tubes on the lunar surface, but right now, I can offer your family a three bedroom, two bath apartment that is easily twice the size of your current trailer. Not only that, but we have an amphitheater, park, and playground area that is more than ten acres of open space."

Buster's eyes narrowed. "That doesn't sound like any of the news reports I've seen. How many people do you have up there and just how big is it?"

"All the information we give to the media is at least a couple of years old. We aren't quite ready for the land rush, just yet. That's where you come in."

"That's all very interesting, but I still don't think I'm ready to go blasting into space with my whole family. Hell! I'm forty seven years old and doubt I could even pass the physical."

Buster tapped on his tablet computer and turned it around to show Buster a slide show. "Take a look at these images that were taken in the past month or so. I mentioned fringe benefits, how old would you say I am?"

Buster watched images of a tropical garden with overhanging tomato vines and other vegetables slide by. His eyes skipped for a second to give a quick evaluation of John. "You look like you're about twenty five or twenty six, why?"

"Actually, I celebrated my eighty fourth birthday a couple of months ago. One of the benefits is totally free health care for the entire family. Once you're part of the team, every member of the family gets a full physical. If there are any major problems or if you're feeling the effects of age, we offer free Omniphage treatments. The same applies in case of any injury. If you're hurt and we can keep you alive long enough for a shot of the 'Phage, then you'll be up and at 'em inside a few days."

The slide show had switched to images of tall, wide tunnels with people walking and standing in them. Then, the photos showed what looked like a modern, luxury apartment.

"Why do you want me? I'm no rocket scientist. My degree is in mechanical engineering and it's about twenty five years old."

John waved his hand dismissively. "That's why we want you. We have rocket scientists, astronomers, physicists, chemists, and space pilots out the ass. The colony has reached the point where we need people with construction and heavy equipment experience. Riggers for long-line work and bridge builders. The next stage is going to be massive and you and your team's experience is going to be critical."

"I'm almost afraid to ask... What is this next stage?"

John leaned forward, picked up the tablet and selected another image. "This is a photo of a crater and some mountains on the south pole of the moon. See that large crater?" He pointed it out.

"That crater is more than one hundred and sixty five miles wide." He zoomed in to a smaller crater near the edge. "This crater is about fifteen miles wide. Our current colony is working its way around the edge of the smaller crater right now. We've got about a mile of tunnels so far and more than a hundred apartments ready to move in."

"That sounds more like a job for miners than riggers and bridge builders."

"That is only part of the project and our existing teams have the tunneling operations well in hand. What we want you for is a wee bit larger." He selected another image that showed a spider-web of lines criss-crossing the crater. "We're going to build an airtight dome over the entire crater."

Buster stared at the next few artist sketches, showing the frame work growing and getting covered. "Excuse me, but I think I heard you say that crater is about fifteen miles wide?"

"That right."

"Impossible."

"Nope. We have plenty of reason to think it is not only possible, but a requirement. Keep in mind the moon only has one sixth the gravity of the Earth."

"But even so, how thick would steel cables have to be to support a roof? And what would the roof be made of?"

"We're making all the materials on-site. The cables are a type of braided carbon fiber that is much stronger than steel and less than a third the mass. Also remember the moon has no appreciable atmosphere. Once the crater is sealed, we're going to pressurize it to about one Earth atmosphere. Spread that under a dome that size and there is a lot of additional support"

"But fifteen miles. That is mind-boggling."

"Don't worry, Buster. We're going to do it." He stood up. "Keep that tablet for show-and-tell. I'm going to be here for the next couple of days. Then, you'll be able to reach me at this email address." He handed him a card. "Don't take too long to make up your mind. If you don't take it, I'll find somebody else. We need a team in place in the next six months."

Diaspora

"The moon? You did say the moon, didn't you?" Cheryl repeated slowly while shaking her head.

He nodded while she stared at her husband in disbelief.

"As if things aren't bad enough here, you want to send us to live in some underground tunnel on the moon?"

"At least give me a chance to show you why I'm considering it."

Her voice reflected her sense of trepidation. "Okay."

He showed her the images and gave her the same spiel Mr.

Simmons had given him. Then, he went further. "Right now, there is no way to produce any serious food in this damn desert. The only places that are hiring folks like us are some of the inner cities that are trying to rebuild after the riots. They are paying pennies on the dollar. As you well know, they are also a very dangerous place to bring up kids. Not one of the governments have any money to spend on major projects like this hydroelectric plant we just finished. One of the reasons they want people like us, is that families tend to give you stability. They already have a small school and a group of kids up there. It's not in the news yet, but the first baby has already been born on the moon. They are building a new society and we can not only be a part of that, but we can help to shape it."

"You sound as if you're already sold on the idea. But what about the kids? Do you think they will want to leave their friends and their school?"

He shrugged. "We've been living in this damn dust bowl of a desert for the last five years and I've heard both of them griping about it almost as much as I have. Not only that, but the contract is not just for us, but for any other families I want to bring in as part of the team. They have places for two dozen of us right now and as soon as the new batch of apartments are ready, they will have room for another couple of dozen. They fully expect to hire more than two hundred construction people within the next couple of years."

"What happens when that crater job is finished?"

He got a wistful expression. "I asked that too. You know what he said?"

She looked suspicious.

"They expect all the heavy rigging and construction work on this job to last for at least another six to seven years. After that, they plan another, almost identical job in a nearby crater. He says we should have work as long as we wish. And, we'll be able to take regular vacations to freshen up."

"Vacations? Where, for Pete's sake? This is the moon we're talking about."

He showed me some of the recreation areas we're going to be working on. She was reminded of luxury resorts in some of those old travel magazines.

Her arms were folded under her breasts. He reached out and put his arms over her shoulders and pulled her close. "I really think this will be a good move for us."

She just stood there for a moment, then put her arms around him and whispered in his ear. "You know you're a damn lunatic, don't you?"
***

They didn't tell the kids right away. Instead, he spoke with the rest of his team. Five others decided they had had enough of the desert and no job prospects and signed on. They organized a group meeting with a big-screen projector and all the kids. There were some panic moments, but when they youngsters, ranging in age from six to seventeen, realized they wouldn't be alone, but all their friends were going with them, the complaints dropped to a muttered rumble. They did stare at the rugged plastic box with the multiple snaps around the lid.

"What's that for?" Asked a fourteen year old Charlie Mathias.

John Simmons released the snaps and opened the lid. "This is what you can take with you. It holds approximately one cubic meter and is rated to hold up to one hundred kilos. That is your personal weight and space limit. There are only a few restrictions. Nothing living can ship in it and that includes plants. Also no aerosol or other pressurized containers. Nothing in the form of explosives. This includes firearms. We have many folks in the colony that can teach various self-defense arts if you wish to learn. I have a list for each of you that recommends things that are in very short supply. It is highly recommended that you pay attention to it.

One of the teenagers held up his hand. "What sort of things are the rarest?"

"Fine wines, good coffee, and good tea. We grow lots of wonderful vegetables and fruits, but so far, we don't have the room for tea and coffee plants. That will have to wait until the larger dome is finished. Also, fine wood products are very rare because wood is so heavy and bulky. We are going to start our own lumber industry when the larger domes are ready, but it will probably be thirty to fifty years before we see any lunar wood products at all."

Wendy couldn't believe she had to cut back on her wardrobe. At sixteen, clothing and her own gothic lolita style meant everything. She held up her hand. "What about clothing? What's it like up there?"

He folded his arms and held one finger up to the side of his face, as if trying to recall something. "You're Wendy Mathias, right?"

She nodded.

"I think your mom told me that you do a bit of sewing and are into costume design."

She nodded again.

"Well, we're putting together a theater group and there is a budget for raw fabric, thread, and sewing machine needles. I would highly recommend you have your sewing machines serviced, order some spare parts that might wear out and pack it along with some of your favorite garb. The one thing we don't have a lot of is shoe stores. So, a few different styles might be a good idea. You can leave the old sneakers or running shoes home though. We provide more than a dozen styles of basic work shoes as part of your housing allowance."

Charlie Mathias held up his hand. "What about my table top gaming figures, books and video game console?" Several other kids nodded in agreement and started muttering.

John held up his hand. "Please keep it down and I'll answer your question." He continued. "First off, let me say I like to build models, too. And my apartment has a bunch of them. I would not recommend taking any of your models or books with you, though."

A bunch of the kids and a couple of the adults looked shocked at this.

"There are two reasons for this. Number one, all the gaming books, magazines, and support manuals are available in electronic format and if we don't have one of them on our servers, we can get it within a day or so. The second thing is that we have dozens of small-scale fabricators that can build just about any design you can think of using local materials. That saves us from shipping all that weight up from Earth. Just for example, I like to build model airplanes. There are more than a dozen in my apartment. They are all made from plastic kits that I ordered from one of our fabricators. I assembled and painted them myself as my idea of relaxation. I have friends that are table top gamers and they have made entire armies of small figures that they assemble, paint and then use in their games. There's no need to waste your valuable cargo space. Just be sure to check the recommended packing list."

Another hand went up in the back "I haven't been able to afford a new computer. How am I supposed to see this list you keep talking about?"

John pulled a tablet from his vest pocket and held it up. "Part of your hiring bonus is that everybody will get one of these slates. They are a brand new design and employ an extremely broad-band quantum connection that will let you access both the public web here on Earth and the lunar net. It has a great deal of information as well as the recommended packing list." He paused and smiled conspiratorially. "And it is also a full video phone with unlimited minutes."

That announcement was greeted with a great many nods and smiles.

Starlight Dream

The moon! Wow! Charlie thought to himself. Talk about living a science fiction dream. His mom and dad had just broken the news to some of their grandparents and cautioned them not to spread the word to their friends just yet. But wow!

The fourteen-year-old stood out behind their trailer, staring at the full moon, just clearing the horizon in the distance while the brilliant colors of a desert sunset lit more than half the sky.

"Hey Charlie!" The voice belonged to Jimmy Tsu. "Have you heard?" Jimmy skidded his mountain bike to a stop.

Charlie only glanced at his friend, then went back to staring at the moon. "Yeah. I heard all right. Let me guess, your family took the job offer, too."

"Yeah. Man, can you believe it? We're going to the moon." He leaned forward, arms folded on the handlebars and stared at the moon with his friend for a moment. Then, in a conspiratorial whisper, "Wonder how many cute moon chicks we're gonna meet?"

Charlie shook his head. "You've been watching way too many of them old movies." He paused for a second. "But then again, with Omniphage, who knows? Maybe we will meet some really hot moon chicks."

His sister heard their conversation while looking out of the trailer window. She shook her head. "Boys." She muttered to herself.

"What's that, dear?" Her mom asked from the other side of the kitchen.

"Charlie and Jimmy seem really excited about this move. I'm glad somebody is."

"Oh, you're going to love it. Think of all the fantastic things we're going to see and experience that most people only dream about."

"Yeah. And one of those experiences might be getting blown up with some rocket failure, or freezing to death when the power fails, or feeling all the air get sucked out of our lungs..."

"Oh stop it!" Her mom was exasperated. "Why are you trying to be so bleak about it? There are hundreds of people already up there and we're going to be fine. You might just take a tip from the boys you were grousing about."

With an incredulous look, she stared at her mother. "A tip from them? What are you talking about?"

Her mother grinned conspiratorially. "You are probably going to meet some really handsome, intelligent and oh-so-sexy young man up there."

Wendy just rolled her eyes and banged her forehead on the table.

Riding Up

You never quite get used to the sudden absence of acceleration. The first few seconds of micro-gravity always feels like you are falling. This was only his fourth trip to Low Earth Orbit, or LEO as it is called, so he was still excited as the Appaloosa4 coasted up the rendezvous trajectory. The brilliant blue curve of his home world filled most of the small portal.

A few minutes later, he felt a few, brief bursts from the attitude jets and their destination eased into view.

"Beautiful, isn't it?" Terri was just as excited as he was.

"Yes. I don't think I'll ever get bored with it." He glanced over to see her face behind her helmet shield. "You ready?" He half-joked.

"I was born ready, Steve. You know that."

A few more minutes and there was a slight jerk as they docked. "Docked and locked, ladies and gentlemen. You may release your seat belts, grab your personals, and leave when the hatch opens. Thank you for flying Hot Stallion Aerospace."

His seven passengers all chuckled at the cliché. The 'Hot Stallion' referred to the Air Force black box project that had kept this LEO shuttle and five sister ships flying in secret for more than ten years. Only the final cancellation of NASA's ill-conceived 'flying pickup truck' and the global market collapse had forced the military to reveal they already had a much-superior system in place.

Once through the hatch, they found themselves in a long, narrow cylinder, lined with small portals. Each portal showed a flat panel with a label describing the contents.

One end of the cylinder ended in a series of cable storage reels, instrument panels and emergency parts lockers.

They pulled themselves along the cylinder to the other end, where there was a larger, circular room with galley, toilet, food, and table.

Following the ladder up another level and they were on the flight deck where three acceleration couches were on each side. Alongside each couch was a series of monitor screens and storage for their 'personals'.

Four of the couches were already occupied. They smiled, nodded and shook hands, then strapped themselves into the remaining seats.

The shuttle disengaged with another soft jerk and moved away from the larger craft. When it was a safe distance away, their main engines fired and they rapidly pulled away from LEO and started their three day journey.

"There is one thing I've been looking forward to, Terri."

"What's that, Steve?"

"I've heard a lot about it for years. You might laugh, but I'm really looking forward to seeing and feeling that famous lunar dust."

First Digs

"Damn! I hate dust." Steve Saunders muttered as he shook himself and waited for the vacuum to suck the fine lunar dust from his work suit. A far cry from the incredibly bulky spacesuits of the early days, this was essentially a sophisticated version of a diver's wet suit. Made from a very tough material that was all but puncture-proof and did not stretch, it had a built-in air conditioning system that help wick off sweat and either heat or cool different parts of the body as needed. Extremely thin metallic layers provided some radiation shielding.

"What's that, Steve?" Questioned his best friend, Mike Gates.

"Oh, just the usual bitching about all this dust."

"I'd rather have it cleaned off here, than track it through our living spaces. Speaking of which, have you gotten used to your new digs, yet?"

Steve gave him a wide grin. "Damn straight! Anything is worth getting out of that hamster run."

He was referring to the original moon base that was almost a duplicate of the Alice Island project. During the first three years, a trio of cargo ships had brought tightly-wrapped packages that when inflated, formed sturdy living quarters and work spaces. Connected like sausages with two and four port hubs, once in place on the surface, they had been buried by small robot tractors. This base had grown to include more than a hundred segments.

The mandatory cleansing process over, the two friends, dressed in simple coveralls and pull-on booties, walked out, into a large, well-lit tunnel. It was about ten meters square with slightly rounded corners. Every thirty meters or so, there was a door on each side with an address plate above it. Every hundred meters, a cross-corridor led to another, parallel tunnel. Since it was the official end of a work shift, there were quite a few other people in the tunnel and they joined the rush hour, by taking off in the long, smooth strides that most humans adapted in the low lunar gravity.

They passed through two large gates that could be sealed in case of an emergency, then Steve held his palm up to a panel set beside a door. It only took a moment for the system to recognize him and open.

They walked into a roomy apartment with a four meter high ceiling and an open concept kitchen on the left. Shelves all around the room held various types of plants. Some had flowers while others appeared to be vegetables such as carrots and tomatoes. The far wall had a shelf full of small plants up to about waist height and above that, a picture window about a meter high by two meters wide.

"I'm going to grab a shower, Mike. Feel free to pour a drink."

His friend nodded as Steve headed for the master bedroom and the chance to get the last speck of dust.

***

Steve found Mike savoring a beer while staring out the window. He poured a brew for himself and joined him.

"You know, sometimes I have to just take a few minutes to stop and remind myself that this is not some sort of fantasy. We really are doing it." He nodded at the deeply-shadowed crater. If he leaned close to the thick glass, he could see the lights reflecting from similar windows on both sides.

"Welcome to Port Heinlein, Mike." They clinked their mugs. "Now that you're finally here, are you ready for some real work?"

"Hah! You don't think all those dog-and-pony shows back on Earth weren't work? I'm looking forward to a little rest."

"Well, you can rest until the first batch of newbies arrive. They will all be your cats to herd."

"Steve, that is at least a month away. In the meantime, how about bringing me up to date and please promise me we'll have room for all of them."

They sat down and Steve fiddled with his slate for a moment. A section of wall became a high-resolution display and he started. "I've put together this series of stills and video clips as a presentation you can use for the newbies. The first few minutes shows the tubes of Moonbase One which we are going to use as a cleanup, reception, and sorting area. They won't be there more than a few hours as each family or small group will get one of us old-timers as a sponsor."

The image changed to a tunnel scene and he continued. "During reception, we'll show them maps of both Moonbase One and the Port Heinlein tunnels." A map of the crater was next and a series of lines appeared to circle it. Only a short section of line, near the moonbase was solid. The rest were dotted, future paths. "I know that you've done a lot of orientation work back on Alice Island, but I don't want to take any chances. We're going to remind them every chance we get of the safety rules."

"Oh, you'll get no argument from me on that one. The last thing we need is for one of them to try and see what one of the new tunnel sections is like before we've cooled it. The laser tunnel-builders leave it hot for weeks." He took a swig of his beer. "Which reminds me. I know it was slow going at first. What are the tunnel machines up to now?"

"They are doing better than expected, Mike. Once we got them properly tuned, they are moving at between three and five meters per day. We now have six of them and we rotate them for servicing every week. Two are digging the primary and secondary tunnels one week, the following week, they are set to digging the side tunnels that comprise the apartments, garden and working areas. A week of that and they spend a week cooling down and getting cleaned and adjusted for their next shift. I see no reason why this schedule won't continue for at least the next few years."

"Now that is good news, Steve. I notice the streets are still pretty bare. Nothing but lights, marked walkways, empty shelves and address plaques."

"Blame the guys in hydroponics for that." He nodded at the plants on his shelves. "They can only grow so many extra seedlings at a time. The psych team told us the first priority would be to put as many as possible into personal living spaces. The public spaces are going to get several species of vines, flowering plants and small trees only after we take care of the apartments. Oh, and to answer your earlier question, all of the newbie families will have their own apartments, as promised."

He tapped off the display and turned back to face Mike. "Okay now, Mr. Gates. That's my update, now it's your turn. What's the latest from our home world?"

"Still pretty bad, I'm afraid. There are at least a dozen small fiefs established in northern Mexico and the southwest United States. A few of the cities have stabilized with neighborhood watch associations either joining forces or taking the place of formal police departments. The military is stretched way too thin to handle anything except major riots. And it appears to be much the same throughout the world. There are still some high-tech small industries and engineering around a few universities. One good outcome of the Alice Island genetics lab has been that they've come out with two new versions of Omniphage. Both of the formulas have been placed in the public domain and are in general use."

"What's so different and why two?"

"Remember all the furry anthromorphs that showed up the first few years it was out? The cat, wolf, dog, rat and all?"

"Of course. I had the pleasure of meeting and partying with a whole military special ops team that called themselves the Werewolves. They were at an Alice Island celebration right before I came up here."

Mike nodded. "The latest versions have been adjusted to reject any DNA structure that doesn't fit the human genome. Not only does it prevent the anthro hybrids, but if they use it on and existing cat, wolf or rat person, it will restore their human appearance."

"Well, that's good news for many of them I would imagine. What's the other 'Phage variation?"

"One version has a simple modification that makes the subject completely sterile. The best birth control there is. If and when a couple decide to start a family, they ask their physician for the version that restores their ability to procreate. Most of the hospitals have been instructed to give a woman the sterile version the day after birth. It restores her to full health and vigor a day later and she won't be able to have another child unless she and her spouse ask the doc. That way, they hope to keep the population under control."

"When do we get those versions?"

"You already have them. I brought the formulas up with me and they were handed over to your Emergency Medical Team earlier today. By the way, did you happen to check who else I brought with me?"

"Actually, no. I saw a few more get off the ship with you, but figured they were some of the replacement military team."

Mike laughed. "You might say that. Actually, they have recently retired and requested this as their discharge point. They used to be one of those werewolf special ops teams you probably met at that party. As part of their retirement, they got the new 'Phage to return to fully human and are now going to be part of the labor force, helping you to build Port Heinlein. Oh! And here's another little surprise. Do you remember General Michael Hawthorne?"

"Oh yes. How could I forget. He was in charge of Area 51 when I first joined this project. The last I heard, he had moved to training at Alice Island." He paused for a moment, thinking. "Wasn't he living with a cat-girl anthromorph?"

"You got it, first try. They actually got married last year and when the new 'Phage came out, she became this absolutely stunning redhead. Imagine Jessica Rabbit, come to life. Anyway, they were on the flight with me. They are going to be part of your new agricultural team."

Steve looked askance at him. "Farmers? But he's a general with years of military experience."

"Consider this, my friend. Now that Omniphage means that people can rebuild their bodies and live indefinitely, the idea of someone doing the exact same thing over and over for decades on end is going away. General Hawthorne, has already tried to retire from the military a couple of times. He's been serving for more than fifty years now. He told me he wants to spend another few decades as a farmer. After that, who knows?"

Steve thought about it for a moment, then offered. "I suppose this gives a whole new meaning to buying the farm, doesn't it?"

Homecoming

Wendy was pissed and muttering under her breath. "Damn it all to hell and back." Why in the world did she let her folks talk her into this insanity.

"What's that, dear?" He mother inquired.

"I was just thinking I could be dancing and playing in the band at Aunt Ethel's commune in northern California, right now. Instead, I'm breathing canned air and looking forward to living in this oversize rabbit warren."

"Perhaps you're forgetting the last time you went to spend a month at Aunt Ethel's, you were on the phone, begging to come back in less than a week because she had you out in a field, helping with the harvest. Look at the bright side, you're not going to get a sunburn here."

"Hhmph! Not unless I open the wrong door. And then, all the air will get sucked out of my lungs long before I notice the sun."

"Maybe you're forgetting that these tube shelters are part of the original moonbase and are only used as a mid-point and reception center for the rockets. After we are finished with the check-in process, our sponsor is going to show us to our apartment. You've seen the photos. They look lovely and you'll have your own room."

The family shuffled ahead in line and it only took a few minutes to register their hand prints. The woman behind the counter advised them that their sponsor would be there in a moment.

Wendy's mood was getting blacker until she heard someone call her name.

"Wendy? Wendy Mathias?"

She looked up and realized that her folks were standing and waiting for her. The voice calling her name belonged to a tall young fellow. Her eyes traveled slowly up until she met a pair of piercing blue eyes, a huge smile and a buzz-cut of light brown hair.

He held out his hand. "Hi. I'm Mark Chambers. Welcome to Port Heinlein."

She shook his hand.

"Well come on now. You guys are all cleared and I'll show you to your new home and help you find your way around." Although he was talking to the whole family, he didn't take his eyes off her until he turned to lead them down a long corridor. After they were well clear of the reception area, he turned and started to walk backwards, waving his hand about him. "The series of dome-shaped rooms you were just in is part of Moonbase One. It has been in constant use for the last six years. About five years ago, this tunnel was started. Once we got past the entrance airlock, it is the same size as most of our tunnels at ten meters by ten meters." He pointed up. "The LEDs are tuned to produce a very broad-spectrum of light, similar to Earth sunlight on a nice day. You might find it surprising to realize you can actually get a suntan here. The shelves and alcoves you see are empty now, but eventually, will be filled with plants and small trees."

Wendy tried to look as disinterested as possible, but when he turned to lead them further down the corridor, she couldn't help but watch his muscles shift under his white polo shirt and black jeans.

Perhaps there might be some fun to be had in this rabbit warren after all, she thought to herself.

***

Wendy sat on a queen-sized bed and looked around. She had to admit that it was huge compared to the dinky space she had in that old trailer. The closet looked big too, but that was only discouraging, since she had to leave well over half her clothing and didn't have enough left to make a dent in all that rackspace. The sealed transit case they had given her was sitting in the middle of the floor. She hadn't even broken the seal on it yet. They had given each of the family members a pair of extremely thin and lightweight jumpsuits in a bright white. They were to be used for travel and as working garb. She had been assured she could go back to her more comfortable gothic lolita garb after they got settled.

She had noticed that almost all the shirts worn by both male and females had a shoulder pocket with a flap. This was were everyone seemed to carry their slates.

Each slate was a bit larger than an Earth smart phone, but smaller than the tablets she had seen before. They were less than a centimeter thick and fit easily into the palm of her hand. She heard hers beep.

"What the heck?" She muttered while fishing it out of her jumpsuit pocket. "Hello?"

The screen cleared to show the same wide grin and piercing blue eyes she had admired earlier.

"Hi there, Wendy. It occurred to me that after that rocket ride, you're probably way too wired up to sleep."

"You're right there, Mark." She agreed.

"And I'll bet your folks are all about unpacking, putting up family heirloom junk, and going gaga over their view of the crater. Right?"

She nodded again and gave him a wry smile.

"You like music?"

This caught her by surprise. "Uh, yeah. Of course. I'm learning to play guitar and have a bunch of tunes stored on my slate. Why?"

"If I may make a suggestion, some of us get together once in a while to listen to tunes, dance a bit, and just hangout. Want to come along?"

She bit her lip and thought for a few seconds. "Okay. But give me an hour. I need to grab a shower and get into some real clothes."

***

"Wendy? Where are you going?" Her mom was still pulling things from her shipping crate. Then, she did a double-take. "And why are you dressed like that?"

Wendy glanced down at her black spandex minidress, fishnet tights and shiny black patent-leather clunky heels. She was wearing a deep red, long-sleeve fuzzy sweater on top. "I wanted something other than a brilliant white prison uniform."

"Why? We just got here."

"Maybe it's because I have a date." And with that, she walked out the door.

First Night

Mark was leaning against the opposite tunnel wall. "Wow! Look at you."

She blushed and asked, "You like it? I wasn't sure what to wear, since just about everyone I've seen so far has been kinda casual. Should I change?"

"No. Please don't. You look great and I know just the place. Come on." He turned and started a long lopping gait that quickly opened a gap between them.

Like most of the newcomers, Wendy had been taking it easy and walking slow to avoid jumping or bumping into things in the low gravity. The easy lope didn't look that hard, so she tried to keep up. "Hey! Wait for me."

He glanced over his shoulder, realized the problem and slowed down. "Sorry. It's something you'll get used to in a day or so.

She grimaced. "Any gravity is better than null-gee. The last three days have not been pleasant."

"Well, the trick here is to take it a bit slower until you learn the routes you want to take. It's easy to get going really fast, miss your turn and have to back up."

"Where are we going, anyway?"

Mark tilted his chin up to point down the corridor. "A couple of blocks that way, then to the right for another couple of blocks. I'm going to show you the Mall."

"The Mall? You've got to be kidding. Tell me there isn't a Mickie Dees there as well."

He laughed. "Don't worry. None of the giant franchises have made it out here, just yet. But we have our own stuff that's almost as bad for you."

A few minutes later, they stopped in front of a door that looked like every other one except it had a glowing sign over it that could be seen both ways. It proudly proclaimed "Lazy Fair".

Wendy nodded towards it. "What the heck is a Lazy Fair?"

"It was coined by a flea market down in Tampa that evolved into a whole community of entrepreneurs. A couple of the original landing team were involved with it and thought it was such a good idea, they reserved the first mall space for themselves. As the colony grows, we're going to use these malls as ways of defining neighborhoods."

"Neighborhoods? How many do you have now and how many are we going to have?"

"There are more than a hundred apartments like yours right now and it's just the first neighborhood. Eventually, Port Heinlein will have at least fifteen levels and run around the entire rim of the crater. Each ring will be a little more than fifty kilometers and there will be ten neighborhoods per ring. Allowing for some architectural variations, you can expect between two hundred and three hundred homes per neighborhood." He pressed his palm to the door plate and it slid open.

Inside, Wendy had to stop to take it all in. The space was the same sort of ten meter by ten meter tunnel as everything else, but she hadn't been prepared for the bustle of people, sounds and wonderful aromas. There were tables and chairs scattered in a seeming haphazard pattern. A two meter-wide path led down the center and was echoed by a balcony on each side. She saw some people leaning over an ornamental iron railing on either side. Mark led her a few meters into the room and she saw openings on walls. Glass storefronts with animated signs over each door, advertised their name and business. The first two were restaurants. The place on the right advertised Asian cuisine and the one on the left bragged on southern fried chicken.

"You didn't expect this, did you?"

She shrugged and tried to look blasé but it wasn't working. "My dad showed me some of the photos but I thought they were shot back on Earth, in some studio. I didn't think it would be this far along." She was glancing around, trying to take it all in and she noticed a double-doorway in front of them. The sign simply said "Showcase".

"Hey! Mark!" The voice came from behind them.

Wendy and her date turned to see another young couple. The voice belonged to a fellow wearing black dress slacks, black shoes and a black, long-sleeve teeshirt with a pocket on each sleeve. Wendy remembered that the sleeve pockets were for their tablets. The lady next to him was wearing what looked like a black wet suit with the tallest spike heels Wendy had ever seen.

"Wendy, this is Samantha and Kevin O'Conner. They own Showcase. Sam, Kevin, this is Wendy Mathias. She just got here, today."

Kevin stuck out his hand. "Welcome to Port Heinlein, Wendy." She shook and thanked him.

Sam held out her arms and gave her a hug. "Call me Sam. You have that deer-in-the-headlights look about you. Don't worry, we really aren't that strange and seldom bite."

"Thanks. I hope not. This has already been a heck of a day."

Inside Showcase, they were met with the sound of music, but before Wendy could ask, Sam pulled her aside. "Let's hit the ladies room first." A moment later, Sam asked, "Aren't you hot with that sweater?"

Wendy shrugged. "I wasn't sure what was proper around here and my dad still gets a bit twitchy if I show too much skin. I'd love to ditch it, but don't want to carry it on my arm."

"No problem. This place is still way too small of a community for anyone to get away with being a thief. Give it to me."

Wendy slipped it off and Sam hung it by the door. "I would suggest you use a permanent marker to put your name inside all your clothing. That way, even if it gets lost, it will show up back at your apartment within a day or so." She turned back, folded her arms and gave Wendy the once-over look. "Not too shabby. Did you bring any makeup?"

"A little bit, but it's still packed. They told me I would be able to get most anything I wanted up here."

"Yeah. But you know men. They have to develop the formula for a product, then load it into one of the replicators. They are so busy doing really important things, that they only stored a half-dozen shades of some generic brand of lipstick. Save your good stuff for now. When I get the chance, I'll get a small sample from you so we can add it to our replicator database."

"That's great. When I get everything out, I'll let you know. But I do have a couple of questions."

"Shoot."

"Just how in the hell do you walk in those heels?"

Sam laughed. "You forget. Here on the moon, we only weigh one sixth of what we weighed back on Earth. That means that we can get away with a lot of fetish garb that was reserved for bedrooms and photo shoots back there." She waved at Wendy's outfit. "What you have there is great, except for the clunky shoes. If you'll notice, everyone here is fairly good-looking. That means us girls have a lot of competition and we usually err on the side of sexy. It's a fact of life that most men like the way women look and walk in heels, so we oblige them when we're not working."

"I guess I'm out of luck then. I have a couple pair of sandals, a pair of hiking boots and three pair of dress shoes, like these."

"Don't worry. I'm one of several people that have access to a clothing replicator. Anything you have that isn't in our database already, I'll add. And once you have been here for a month or so, your body will adjust slightly. At that point, I'll get your measurements and anything in our database, we can make for you. We have regular parties and that gives folks a chance to dress up."

They rejoined the men and Wendy got a kick out of seeing Mark's stare when he saw the way she filled the spandex minidress. She had paid just enough attention to the one-sixth gravity to realize she didn't need to wear a bra and it was quite obvious.

Sam noticed it as well. She nudged her new friend and whispered, "We'll make a lunatic out of you, yet."

Bad Landing

Wearing a simple blue jumpsuit covered in pockets and slip-on sneakers, Buster figured he was ready to face the day. He found Cheryl in the kitchen and gave her a good-morning kiss.

"Don't go rushing off without breakfast. I know you still have time." She warned.

"I wouldn't think of it, hon. When did you have the time to shop though?"

"It looks like part of our house-warming present was a fully-stocked pantry and fridge. There are some things I don't recognize there, but we are set for some reasonable meals for at least the next few days."

"They told us we would have time to settle in. From what I understand, I'm getting nothing but tours and planning meetings for the next month or so. The project isn't supposed to start until the next three flights of colonists arrive."

"Well, it sounds like you're going to have it easy for now. I'm supposed to show up at nine for my tour of the garden section. Supposedly, they're going to turn me into a farmer until the place grows enough to need more teachers."

He nodded and sipped his coffee. "Uhmm. This is good."

"Savor it while you can. I'm going to ration us to one cup a day for now. Even then, we'll run out pretty quick."

"I thought we had both packed about fifty pounds?"

"That's right and I'm saving one package for celebrations in the future. We're only going to suck down the one and that will be used faster than you think.

Suddenly, they heard a loud and extremely annoying klaxon sound five short bursts, followed by a voice.

"Warning! Seal all doors and shelter in place. This is not a drill. This is not a drill. Seal all doors and remain in place until further notification. Personnel in exterior labs must don helmets. Warning! This is not a drill. Seal all doors and shelter in place."

Buster looked at his wife and saw the alarm in her eyes.

"Where're the kids?" His voice was low.

"The left for class about twenty minutes ago."

He nodded. "They're safe then."

"What's going on, Buster?"

"I don't know what would cause that sort of alarm..."

He was cut off by a sharp shudder that rattled the floor, under their feet.

"A moon quake?" His wife looked confused.

Buster shook his head. "The moon isn't seismically active. We do get some moon quakes, but from what I've heard they are very small and due to meteor impacts. It is very rare that one is strong enough to feel. I don't know what that was."

The same voice came over the public address system. "All systems have been cleared. All alarms are now clear. Resume your normal routine. Further information will be posted to the PHNews feed."

Buster grabbed the slate from his shoulder pocket and tapped the PHNews icon. A moment later, he saw a lovely blonde woman in front of a map of their crater and the surrounding area.

She was looking off to one side of the camera for a moment, then turned to face it. "Hello and welcome to a PHNews special report. I've just been informed of some very bad news. One of the incoming shuttles has suffered a major failure, overshot the landing area and crashed into Cabeus crater. That would account for the tremor we all felt a few minutes ago. At this time, I have no word on the crew or passengers. As we get more data, we will of course pass it on. This is Samantha O'Conner for Port Heinlein News." Her image was replaced on the tablet screen with a map of Cabeus crater and surrounding area. Port Heinlein and the landing area were small marks a short distance apart and on the lip of what looked like a tiny crater that formed part of the Cabeus crater wall. Before either one of them could say anything, a red dot appeared deep in the darkness of the larger crater wall. A couple of lines of text under it showed it as being almost forty kilometers away and about ten kilometers lower.

Buster shook his head, slowly. "I hope we didn't know anyone on that flight."

She nodded. "What's that term the old-time test pilots used?"

"They augured in. No way anyone could have survived that, even back on Earth. At least it was quick."

***

Steve Saunders shook his head. "Damn! I knew we should have pushed the landing zone farther away from the crater. I knew some of them."

This was the first general planning meeting that Buster had attended and the overall mood was grim.

One of the other managers added, "We've already suggested a different approach path for incoming shuttles. If something like this ever happens again, they will be pointed away from the craters."

"Something like what? I don't recall hearing what actually caused a shuttle that has made several dozen round trips over the past five years, to suddenly tumble out of control and augur into the lunar surface." Steve's corporate executive background became very obvious when he was stressed. He tended to bark commands and get things done.

There were no answers for almost thirty seconds, then one of the technicians tentatively held up his hand.

"Well?"

"I was monitoring their approach. They appeared to have all the proper landing profiles. The only thing I can think of would be a catastrophic system failure. I've reviewed all of the data files, both system data and audio transmissions and I don't think they had any warning at all. One second the shuttle was on a perfect approach. The next, she was tumbling and the main engines were firing erratically. I've ordered a complete systems check on the other two shuttles. They are still at low Earth orbit and will remain until we check all their systems as well."

Buster held up his hand.

Steve nodded towards him.

"Excuse me, Mr. Saunders. I know I'm the new guy on the block, but aren't we going to investigate the crash site for clues?"

"We have several robot crawlers gathering data within a few clicks. Two of them have been diverted and should arrive later today. At the speed they hit, I seriously doubt there will be anything larger than scraps of gum wrapper."

Holographic Game

Charlie Mathias had been really excited to go to the moon. Now, as he walked home from the first day at school, he wasn't so sure.

Jimmy Hsu was within a year or so of his own age and best friend since first grade. After landing, they had lost touch for a few weeks as their families settled into new routines. It was good to finally catch up with Jimmy, after classes. When Charlie had lamented having to leave all his gaming figures and books back on Earth, Jimmy told him he had the perfect replacement.

"Where are we going?" Charlie was trying to keep track of the turns.

Jimmy tilted his chin to show the way. "Just up the road to the library."

"Library?" I thought nobody brought books 'cause they're so heavy?"

"That's right. Library is just what its called, because it has a whole bunch of really large displays, comfy chairs and it's broken up into small rooms so a small group can gather to share lectures or brainstorm. But we've found a better use. You'll see. It'll be a surprise."

A few minutes later, they went into a room that was only about three meters by four meters. There were a dozen chairs scattered around and a single, large table in the center.

Jimmy grabbed a chair and tapped the table top. It lit up and the overhead lighting dimmed. "I think you said you missed Ork Wars, right? I've not played it in a while." The table top screen cleared to show a series of large, three dimensional icons for various business, research and gaming tools. Jimmy held his finger over the game symbol and the whole screen started to pulse slowly. He spoke slowly and clearly, "Enter Ork Wars Five, load player Jimmy Tsu." The table top icons faded away and were replaced with a fog that looked like cloud tops. As the fog cleared away, a highly detailed terrain showed, viewed as if from orbit. Jimmy spoke again. "Set next player Charlie Mathias." He turned to Charlie. "What are your character specs?"

Charlie told him what his last character had been while playing the game with figures and dice back on Earth. A moment later, he was looking at a ten-centimeter high holographic projection of the gaming piece he had been using.

"Wow! Except for the colors, that's the same figure. How does this work?"

"No problem, Charlie." Jimmy showed him how to change colors, weapons and other aspects of the figure. As soon as they were finished, Jimmy showed him how to control his character and suggested they drop into the game world to see who was there.

The table terrain map suddenly spread out and gave the impression they were dropping straight down at an enormous speed. They came down into a medieval city and just before hitting the ground, stopped at eye level. The two of them were looking over the shoulder of their game characters as they stood in front of a tavern.

"Follow me, Charlie. This is where we start most of the basic games. All the players gather inside to choose partners."

The first thing Charlie noticed was the holographic projection filled the entire room. The two of them seemed to be shadows, inside their characters. As the lights adjusted, only their characters were visible. He felt like he was still sitting down, but it looked like they were standing. The controller in his hand was out of sight, but lots of video game experience meant he could almost ignore it.

"Well, well... Looked what the cat dragged in. About time somebody showed up."

The looked to their right. Most of the figures in the bar were pretty basic game pieces. They were dull, and locked into a few basic movements. The voice however, came from a figure that had to have been custom designed. And what a figure it was. Charlie was glad she could only see his cool warrior character and not the open-mouthed geek that was staring at his dream girl. He had seen some well-built gaming figures before. Nordic Goddesses and their kind. But this one pushed sexy to the extreme. And she was only wearing a fur bikini with a sword belt and boots.

"I think this game is going to be fun." He whispered.

Jimmy cut him off with a shout to the warrior woman. "Hey there, Dahlia! Good to see you." He waved then motioned to his friend. "This is Charlie. He's new to the library so let's not try to get him killed right off, eh?"

Dahlia smiled and waved at him. "Good to meet you, Charlie. Let's go kill some orcs. I got a tip there's a group escorting a wizard on the coast road."

As they headed out for adventure, Charlie was now very sure he was going to like this version of the video game.

High Wire Work

Buster was not fond of space suits, but this was part of the job. At least they were a lot easier to put on, take off and work in than the early marshmallow man designs. He was standing next to a four-seat lunar rover that reminded him of a large, crew-cab pickup truck without body panels.

Steve Saunders had brought him and two more of his new team out to show what had been accomplished so far and what they were expected to do next.

"Gentlemen, notice this smooth road we're standing on. It sits a meter or so below the surface and is comprised, just like everything else around here, of molten and formed lunar dust and aggregate." He pointed further along. "Notice how the color changes a bit? Keep your eyes peeled when you're working around new sections of the road. The color shift means it hasn't cooled yet. If you were to take the rover back up on the surrounding surface and followed the road, you would find one of our tunnel machines moving slowly. It uses the same techniques as the ones that created our underground spaces. The ones working topside are programmed to follow the rim of the crater, staying about a hundred meters back from the edge. This is to avoid any hidden soft spots. The end goal will be when it completes the full circuit and we can reprogram it to work on other roads or tunnels. That won't be for another year or so."

"Excuse me, Steve." Scott Chambers interrupted. "I'm seeing a lot of heavy equipment work being done with variations on these robot tractors. What do you need a bunch of grunts like us for?"

"You under-estimate yourself, Scott. Even the most sophisticated unmanned construction machine we have is limited by its programming and speed. Now, it's true it can work twenty-four-seven, but they do break down. They need servicing and they are constantly getting into problem areas that we have to help them sort out. We already have a team of mechanics to handle all the repairs, but it will be your job to follow behind these road builders and build hard points to attach extremely large cables. The cables will be stretched in a spider-web every kilometer or so. Other hard points and cables will be overlapping. These cables will support walk ways and mounts for large racks of LED lights. It's going to be as automated as we can make it, but even so, we're looking at five years or so before we seal the dome over this crater."

Buster asked. "From the size of this project, I can't imagine getting that much in the way of raw supplies shipped up from Earth."

"Oh we don't get much from Earth these days besides colonists like you guys, and some new tools. One of the first things we did was ship up some nanotech fabricators. All they need is a lot of power and a source of raw ingredients. They can make just about anything we can code into them. When the first one arrived, we set it up in a sheltered area and used the first rover to feed it supplies of this ubiquitous dust. Then, we sent unmanned rovers down into some of the deeply-shadowed valleys to gather frozen water and a lot of other minerals. It was slow at first, but we managed to create more rovers, and enough parts for several more fabricators. These days, about ten percent of the output of each fabricator is devoted to parts for another fabricator. Another ten percent is devoted to creating solar panel arrays." He pointed towards a mountain that loomed off in the distance. "That is Mount Cabeus. One side of it is in direct sunlight except a couple of days each month. We have a solar farm that is providing most of our energy right now. Eventually, we will cover most of that side of the mountain and the surrounding plain with solar cells. We will not lack for power."

After touring the preliminary work and completed rim sections, they went back to the tunnels. Steve gave everyone a break to clean up and change, then asked the whole team to join him in the operations center. He stood next to a lectern with a semi-circle of comfortable chairs forming an amphitheater for several hundred people. The back of each seat had a flat shelf where the person behind them could make notes on their slates. Only about sixty seats were filled.

"Okay, everyone. Now that you've seen what we've accomplished so far, let's get to the meat of it." The house lights dimmed and the wall screen behind him lit up to show an orbital view of the crater. "The crater we've chosen for Port Heinlein is about thirty kilometers at its widest point. Much of the bottom of it has never been exposed to direct sunlight and mixed with the dust and scree, there is a great deal of frozen water along with thousands of tons of other elements. Some of it probably dates to the formation of the solar system, but much of the top layers are from slushy comet impacts. At this point, our little base is still dependent on weekly supply shuttles from Earth. We expect this will continue to be the case for the next year or so."

The wall image zoomed down to form a three dimensional cutaway display of the colony. He continued with a pen laser pointing out each item. "The first level of tunnels is at least one hundred meters below the crater rim. This is to provide radiation shielding and insulation. All of the outer cavities are for apartments. They all have one exterior wall with one hundred and fifty millimeter thick clear windows, facing into the crater. The back wall of each apartment has an entry with double doors that can, in an emergency, serve as an airlock. The tunnel directly behind the apartments is referred to in the working documents as Ring One. On the other side of each apartment, there are similarly-sized cavities which will be used for offices, shops, commercial centers and other small businesses. Behind them, there is the Ring Two tunnel. The cavities behind Ring Two are used for hydroponic farmsteads. Ring Three is merely a service and emergency tunnel."

A tall, slender woman held up her hand.

"Yes, Cheryl?"

"I've seen some computer-generated images of wide open spaces, with large trees. Although these tunnels are very impressive, the largest I've seen so far is the mall area and there are no trees. When and where are we planning to build the domes?"

Steve smiled. "I think you might have misunderstood. We're not going to build separate, small domes. We've going to put a domed cap over this entire crater. That is why you will notice we have wide ledges in front of each apartment. Eventually, those will be open patios with great views of the forest and lakes down in the crater. If all goes well, in about five years, we expect to close off the final peak of the dome.

Once the top center of the dome is about ten meters thick, we're going to start boiling off the frozen comet debris at the bottom. We're going to break it down, clean it up and use it to develop an atmosphere. Plans call for at least a year and probably several years before it is stable at something breathable by humans. The images you saw are what we hope to accomplish in seven to ten years. During the intervening period, we're going to continue constructing these tunnels until we finish a full circle of the crater. At that point, all the equipment will move down another hundred meters below our current level and start over."

The screen switched to a series of slides showing a lake with several islands, surrounded by gently-slopping hills covered in huge trees.

"This is our long-term goal. We expect, that it will take between twenty five to forty five years for us to totally stabilize the environment and turn the entire crater into a forest park. All of our living and working spaces will be in rings around the wall. Eventually, this crater will be a completely self-sufficient home to more than a million humans."

Mark Chambers spoke up. "And then what?"

"If you'll take a look at the orbital shots of the lunar south pole, you'll see this is a really tiny crater compared to some of them. This is only the first one and it's going to be a learning experience for all of us. Once we're satisfied that we've worked out the bugs in the construction techniques, there is Cabeus crater, next door. It's about one hundred and sixty five kilometers wide. That will be a really long-term project. Even with updated equipment and a hundred times the manufacturing capability, we expect that will take well over a hundred years to make habitable. Of course, by that point, it will be able to comfortably house twenty to thirty million people."

Mark's jaw dropped. "Wow! You guys don't think small, do you?"

Another Path

The odd five-four timing of Dave Brubeck's immortal Take Five resonated in the room. Jeff Perkins, eyes closed, moved his head with the music while his hands brushed the drums. His wife, Marlo filled in the counter-point with a twelve-string Chapman Stick.

As the last notes fade, they both took a deep breath and smiled at each other.

"Now that was perfect, Marlo."

She nodded and started to say something when the phone rang. "Hello?" She paused, then handed it to her husband.

"Who is it?"

"Says he's with the PetaByte Corporation and they want to set up a meeting to discuss your research."

He spoke for a few minutes and agreed to a meeting.

***

"Let me get this straight." Jeff paused to collect his thoughts before continuing. "You're interested in some of my theories on brain mapping because you have a new type of endless storage?"

"Maybe not endless, Dr. Perkins. But larger and almost instantaneously accessible. More than enough so we can finally combine several fields of research into a working prototype. We have a first-generation system that fits in a desktop cube less than forty centimeters on a side. It is based on a form of holographic storage in a crystalline matrix and is accessed with the same sort of quantum effects we have been using for secure networks the last few years. We'd like you to bring your insight into the team for further development."

"Exactly how much memory is actually in this device?"

The executive looked embarrassed for a moment before he answered. "To be totally honest, we don't know."

Jeff raised his eyebrows. "You've built this super memory device and you don't know how big it is?"

"There appears to be some quantum tunneling effect that changes with the slightest address variance in the holographic addressing. None of the preliminary numbers seemed to make sense, so we've tried just to run a memory test. A single cycle has yet to be completed and the numbers seem to have gone up exponentially. I expect it will be canceled shortly. "

"How long ago did you start it?"

"Three months."

"And how many petabytes are we talking about the last you looked?"

"As of a couple of days ago, it had gone past ten to the several hundred thousandth power of petabytes. There is some speculation among our team, that we have tapped some other dimension and it is, in effect, unlimited. We really don't know. That is just one of the reasons we want your assistance."

"But I'm not a hardware tech. My interest lies in wetware and human simulations."

"Give us six months, Jeff. Sign the non-disclosure agreement and let us pick up all the bills as well as give you a helluva bonus. I think that once you see what we're getting into, you'll want to stick around. Tell the university that you're taking a sabbatical and if you don't like it, you can come back to this modest lab."

Jeff gave him a dirty look, but realized it was only the truth. His school lab wasn't top of the line. "Okay. You have a deal."

Gran Prix

Charlie was bored. "Don't get me wrong, Jimmy. The gaming systems are friggin' awesome. But I'm tired of just school and really fancy video games. These tunnels need some action."

Fifteen-year-old Jimmy Tsu nodded. "I know it was a lot of fun to try and run in this light gravity, but once I got my lunar legs, it's just too easy. I kept wishing we could have brought our bikes, but then where would we go?"

"How about a game of handball? I saw one gym section where they had a court setup."

His friend didn't answer, but Charlie knew he was thinking hard on something. After a few minutes, he broke the silence. "Maybe we're looking at this the wrong way. We're thinking of Earth games and this is the moon. We need something different."

"Okay. I'll buy that, but what?"

"Dunno. Still thinkin' on it."

Charlie looked at the walls of the restaurant, then out, into the corridor. "Com'n. I got an idea. Let's look around."

Outside, in the second ring corridor, Charlie leaned against the wall and looked both ways. "You ever hear about the triathlon?"

"Thats' were you do three different sports, one right after another? Yeah, I've heard of it. Why" What're you thinkin' about?"

Well, most of the time the ring-two tunnel isn't too busy. I'll bet if we planned something carefully, we could arrange a race."

"You mean running? That might be fun, but I've seen folks jogging it a lot of times."

"Not just running. Let's add some stuff like they do in the Olympics. They have a winter game where you ski cross-country for distance, then shoot a rifle at a target, ski some more, than another target. The idea is that the hard exercise makes it very difficult to aim the rifle. We need to alternate between pure jock exercise, some mind stuff and some delicate control stuff."

"Well, it's a cinch they won't let us use guns. Because of the fear of an explosion, I seriously doubt there is a gun on the moon."

"They are planning on making this a huge community, a city colony for Pete's sake. They are bound to have cops sooner or later. They are going to have some sort of crowd-control ability. Maybe they have some phasers or stunners or some sort of scifi weapons."

"That makes sense. We can ask around. What else you think we need for this?"

"Some sort of vehicle. I know they have those small electric carts for moving tools and materials. I'm wondering if we can make some sort of electric cycle. In the meantime, let's see if we can come up with a new kind of game that will only work on the moon."

***

"Hey, Dad. You got a minute?"

"Sure Charlie. What's up?"

"You have a lot of hardware in the warehouse. Is there any chance Jimmy and I could get some spare parts and tools for a little project?"

"Well now, that depends. What kinda project are we talking about?"

"Since we don't have bicycles here, we were thinking about building something similar, but adapted for lunar gravity and use in these tunnels."

"In that case, I think we've already solved your problem, Charlie. In case you've not noticed it, this place is growing like mad. Up until recently, you could walk to any place in the habitable areas in ten minutes or less. But we've already reached the point where we're using the electric mules to shuttle stuff around. In the interests of physical health, they decided to limit their use for heavy materials and emergency crews. Now that the tunnels, office, commercial, and living areas have expanded, we were going to start making some personal transports." He paused to see their expressions. "I'll bet you guys would like to test the first few, wouldn't you?"

Charlie nodded, enthusiastically. "What do they look like and when can we get them?"

Buster tapped his slate and a moment later, showed the 3D CAD image to his son. "It's a variant on the off-road bicycles used back on

Earth. They can be setup for all sorts of different purposes. We can have a fabricator build one now. I will check the schedules to see where we can get one to build the first run. I think I have enough pull to make sure you and Jimmy get the first two." He paused. "There will be a cost involved, however."

Charlie's eyes narrowed in suspicion. "What kind of price?"

"The fabricator is going to spit out a bunch of parts from the CAD images. I'll assign a work area for you two, along with tools, but you're going to have to assemble and tune them, yourselves."

***

"You don't seem to be paying attention, Mr. Perkins. Do you find this dojo so very boring?"

Charlie had the sense to look abashed. "Sorry, Master Tsu. I've just been thinking of another project."

"Well, no sense in running laps, pushing weights, or handball if you're not paying attention. Any one of them can get you hurt. Tell me what seems to have you so distracted?"

Charlie liked Jimmy's dad and didn't see any harm in sharing the idea for a multi-sport lunar race.

"So, you're thinking of a bicycle race with extra sports to make it more interesting. But they need to be lunar games. Right?"

Charlie nodded.

"The bikes are going to turn into a pretty physically grueling race. Since you want something with fine motor skills for one segment, why not a variation on the medieval art of jousting? Hang some rings at various points along the way and each rider has a pouch with a small ball for each ring. If they miss the ring, they have to stop, grab the ball and retry until they get it."

"That's a great idea."

"Here's something to make it more of a lunar competition. Since you're going to be moving pretty fast, you'll want to wear helmets and other safety equipment. Make one of the rules that you have to stop at one point and put on a standard space suit. Then race the last part of the course with your suit and helmet sealed. That will add a real layer of complexity and endurance to it. That will also teach the competitors how to get into a suit in a hurry."

Another Room

Marlo was wondering what her husband had up his sleeve. He led her into a room in the basement of his office building with a half-dozen comfortable-looking recliners.

He pointed at one. "Sit here, hon." Then he picked up a cage-like affair with a bundle of cables attached. "Let me put this on and adjust it for you."

"Put it on? What th'..."

He set it down on her head and had her lean back so it formed a spring pillow. "There. Just relax for a moment and I think you're going to see what we've been so excited about the last week or so."

He sat in the chair next to her and fitted the same sort of helmet cage over his head. Then, he tapped on his slate for a few seconds. "Ready, Marlo?"

She nodded. "Go for it, Jeff."

Suddenly, everything went black and she felt a moment of dizziness. Then, the lights slowly started to come back up and she looked around. The chairs they were sitting in were now covered in some sort of butter-soft leather. There was old-fashioned shag carpeting on the floor and the room was a bit larger. The look of a modern office was completely gone. Instead, the walls were covered in a truly ugly red and gold wallpaper. Heavy red velvet drapes covered the window and the door looked like it was carved from an ancient oak. She was not wearing the cage helmet and there were no electrical outlets showing at all. The light appeared to originate in a flickering set of gas flames in two wall sconces and six chandelier globes.

"Jeff?" Her voice had a bit of a squeak to it. She was trying to remain calm. "How long were we unconscious and where the hell are we?"

Jeff had this huge grin on his face that was starting to tick her off. "Relax, hon. We haven't really been unconscious. We are now in a whole new room, generated by that new system I was trying to tell you about the other evening."

"Another room? But I didn't feel us move."

"We didn't move. Our bodies are still laying in a couple of lounge chairs back in the office. We are now in a totally computer-generated room." He stated proudly.

"But it feels so real." She brushed her hand on the back of the chair and felt the leather. Then, she walked over and touched the drapes, then pulled them aside. Outside the window, she saw a barnyard scene straight from a Midwestern farm.

Jeff stepped over, behind a bar and got two glasses from the shelf. "Would you like a drink, m'lady?"

She turned and looked at him in confusion. "Drink? In some sort of virtual reality game?"

"Sorry, but we don't have much of a selection right now. We've only had time to analyze a few drinks so far and no food items." He handed her a glass with a couple of ice cubes and a dark fluid. "Tell me what you think." He sipped his.

She sipped it. "Iced tea?" She paused and took another sip. "My goodness, but this is good."

She took another sip while thinking furiously. "Okay. I think I have this figured out, now."

"Oh?" His eyebrows raised.

"You knocked me out with some sort of brain stunner, then brought us into this room. Right?"

He shook his head. "You still don't believe it, do you? At this very moment, your body and my body are laying on lounge chairs. This actually is a special sort of reality."

"But the taste of the tea, the smell of the leather furniture, the slight breeze from that overhead fan. This is all in my mind?"

"Nope. Not really. It's all inside an impossibly fast computer with an unknown amount of free memory to work with. Our minds are merely linked into it right now. The only reason we're limited to this room is that this is a very small section that we have essentially programmed by hand. It started as a very simple CAD file for the shape and dimensions, then we added the rules of physics as we know them so far. That took more time then we thought it would. But after that, all we have to do is describe the chemical and physical structure of something, like tea leaves, water and a teapot for example, and we have all the makings for a great glass of ice tea." He pointed at the window. "That barnyard really exists someplace in southern Ohio. We setup a group of cameras to gather the basic visual information and that looks pretty good. Eventually though, we want to be able to walk out into that barnyard and the farm beyond."

She shook her head. A half-smile started to work its way over her face. "Well, it is breathtakingly real, but aside from a helluva video game, what good is it?"

"Our first thought was engineering and architectural uses, but as it grew and we realized how much territory we could store, we started looking beyond a simple farm or even an whole state full of farms and cities. The team is busy sampling every plant, animal, microbe, algae, rock, or insect that exists here on Earth. Once we have the structure of any one of them, we can provide the physical size limits and environmental requirements and let it join the party."

"That sounds terribly ambitious. This computer has that much memory?"

"From what we're able to determine, it's all but unlimited. We're seeing an exponential growth in the gathering of data since we've started it and I don't believe there is any reason why we can't have it create a duplicate of our own planet in the next few months."

Trial Run

Buster wasn't sure why the Port Heinlein Onsite Director ask to see him. Everything seemed to be going very smoothly and nobody on his team had suffered as much as a hangnail. The office door was open, so he stepped inside and looked around. Mike Hawthorne no longer wore a military uniform, but he still looked like he was carved from lunar basalt. He was pouring a cup of coffee and when he saw Buster, he offered, "Join me in a cup?"

Buster nodded. He could smell the lovely aroma of the dark brew all the way out in the hall.

"Go ahead a grab a seat." A moment later, Mike handed him the aromatic brew and sat down on a facing seat, rather than behind his desk. He took a sip and waited until Buster had enjoyed the first taste.

"Excellent! It's been ages since I've had java this good."

"Even though we're very limited on what we can have shipped up, I make it a point to see that anytime there's a spare kilo in a flight, it gets filled with some good java." He took another sip, then got right to the point. "I hear your son has a grand project worked up."

Buster stopped with the cup halfway to his mouth. "Project? I'm not sure I understand, sir."

"Cut the 'sir'. Just call me Mike. You've done good work on the dome rigging and we're actually a bit ahead of schedule. I was referring to Charlie's Gran Prix project."

"I hate to say it Mike, but I don't know what you're talking about."

The director laughed. "I see that scamp has been keeping it secret from more than a few of us. Don't worry. It's a good thing. Have you seen the bicycles he and some friends have been building?"

"The bikes? Sure. They are some pretty nice little rigs. He showed it to me a few weeks ago. I didn't think they were so secret."

"Well, he and some of his friends got the backing for a new sport from their marital arts trainer and he, in turn, pulled a couple of strings to get two full blocks of the latest section of Ring Two and Ring Three blocked off. They are using it for practice."

"I'm almost afraid to ask. What sort of game requires that much space?"

"That was my question, but those youngsters are thinking big. That is only their practice area and it can be moved ahead as we need the space. It's not critical right now, so I've approved it. They are actually working out the final rules, but it goes something like this."

He tapped his slate and the wall screen started playing some video from a corridor camera. "They have come up with a lunar Triathlon that uses a roughly oval course. First, they have to run for twenty kilometers, carrying a backpack containing a dozen high-density, silicon balls and their space suit and air supply. You know the ones we used to call superballs?"

Buster nodded.

The director continued. "At each corner along their running course, there are rings mounted on the upper side of the curved wall. They have to pull a ball from their pack and throw it through the ring. If they miss, they have to retrieve the ball and keep trying before they can continue."

Buster started to smile. "This is starting to sound interesting. Isn't that a variant on some old Mayan game?"

"That's right. I'm guessing they got the idea from one of their teachers. After the twenty kilometers, they mount their bikes and start lapping the course at bike speed. Each corner of the course has one of the rings and they have to toss four more balls through each ring and then finish two full laps. The final part of this little trilogy of terror is to stop, remove their space suit and helmet from the backpack, put it on and have a referee check the air supply and then back on the course for two more laps and the last four balls."

"That certainly sounds like a hell of a workout. Thanks for bringing me up to date on it. I guess he was going to surprise me with it."

"Don't be too hard on him. He's actually doing us hell of a favor. We've been trying to come up with some recreational activity that was purely lunar for some time now. The closest has been that insane handball game that uses a court about six times Earth-size. I did want to talk to you about it though, since he and his friends are likely to be stars soon."

Buster narrowed his eyes. "Stars? I don't thing this colony is big enough to have any of us hold that sort of title."

"The Powers-That-Be back on Earth are sending a talking head and a camera man that won some media lottery. They are going to work with our resident entertainment network to make a documentary on the current state of Port Heinlein. While they are here, I'm going to authorize the temp closing of much more than their little two block practice area so we can have the first Lunar Gran Prix."

"I hate to say it, Mike, but that's going to be a pretty big deal for a half-dozen kids and their bikes"

"Don't worry, Buster. I've talked to their sensei and suggested some variations to their rules. Just like in other sports, we're going to have different categories. Kids sixteen and under are in one class, seventeen and up are in another and there's a professional class for anyone that spends more than twenty hours a week in a space suit." He pointed at Buster. "That is where you come in. Your team does a lot of heavy work in suits. They are like a second skin to you and you're all hard as rocks from all the rigging. I want you to coach the professional team."

Buster grimaced, sat back and took the last swig of the now-cool coffee. "When are we going to hold this big event?"

"We just finalized the visit of the Celebrities from down the well for a month-long stay starting in about six months. You have that long to pick six people for your team and get them trained. I've put aside one whole warehouse complex as the Gran Prix Training facility. We'll leave the two blocks around it blocked off from regular traffic. Get with your son and his friends so they can move their bike shop to the new facility. Each of your team will have to borrow their bikes until yours are ready. Oh! And one final thing..."

"Yes?"

"Don't forget to have fun!"

Territorial Imperative

Kevin O'Conner wasn't smiling. "I'm not sure I really like the idea of being in front of the damn camera."

His wife was always camera-ready. "Oh come on, hon. It will be fun. Dawn Smith is well-known as the reporter that took my place back home, in Tampa. She's bringing a friend to run the camera. Our job is to give them a look at what really happens up here."

"I still think my place has always been behind the camera."

Sam hugged and kissed him, then whispered in his ear. "You're just not thinking of the fringe benefits."

"Like what?"

"You get to tour this place and share you wealth of knowledge with not one, but two beautiful women."

He pulled back and smiled down at her. "I don't need two. I just need one. And she's right here, in my arms, already."

***

On one hand, Charlie was happy to have a real Gran Prix Clubhouse and shop area, but what had started as some fun for him and a handful of friends was now getting complicated. He was excited about the big race though. That is where his mind was when he came through the shop door and heard the chanting and cheering.

"What the hell?" He slowly whispered when he saw the girls.

Four girls from his school were lined up while Samantha O'Conner showed them a dance move.

Each of them wore a bright blue spandex body suit that looked like it had been sprayed on.

Charlie stared for a moment until he felt a nudge from Jimmy Tsu. "You like 'em, bro? That was your sister's idea. Each of the teams will have their own cheering section complete with cheerleaders. That's our team, there."

"You know, Jimmy... I think all this complication is going to be worth it, after all."

Jimmy agreed with a grin, then added, "I've got more good news, too. We now have sponsors!"

"What? Sponsors? Who and why and... Oh, I dunno. Why do we need 'em?"

"The who is easy enough. A couple of restaurants, a photographer, a painter and the Port Heinlein Directorate. The restaurants are giving free meals for each of the team members during training and to the winners, after the race. The photographer is documenting the whole process for a Gran Prix Yearbook and the painter has designed some neat paint jobs and matching unitards for our team. This whole thing has gone viral, man."

"Wow! I guess it's pretty good then. But I can't see what the local businesses want to advertise. We all know where they are and there aren't too many of them right now."

"Oh, I wouldn't worry about that. It seems the biggest sponsor is the Directorate. They have some reporters coming up from Earth that will cover the race. They think it will draw a lot of new colonial volunteers. They are back-logged right now, but expect to double our living space in the next year and double that within another year. They want to keep us in the good graces of the folks back home."

    ***

Wendy did not want to be on the cheerleading team. She wanted to be the one they were cheering for! She had to qualify in the top three by the end of the week. That was when the trials would end and the team would start serious training.

She finished the running segment and fitted her backpack into the seat frame. With a glance over each shoulder to make sure it was clear, she pushed off and remembering her coach's advice. "Start slow and easy to build up speed. Reserve your energy for the sprint at the end."

Her tires and cable drive made a soft hum that belied the fact she was moving at more than forty kilometers per hour. She reached down to her waist where a fabric tube held a row of balls on the side of her backpack. As she barreled towards the high bank of the first corner, she pulled to the outside and started to lean into it. At the last possible second, she tossed the ball to the side and it hit the wall. A half-second later it shot through the hoop just as she passed below it, pinned to the banked wall while she kept on peddling. "Perfect!" She whispered between her teeth as she grabbed another ball and lined up for the next curve.

As she approached, her hand slipped for just a split-second and the front tire lost its grip. She spun to the side and was sliding down the track while the bike flipped end-for-end up to the wall and crashed back down to the infield.

She lay on her back, gasping for breath when she saw a familiar face loom over her.

"Wendy! Are you okay? Talk to me." The concerned expression on Mark's face was almost comical, but she realized it was serious.

"Whew!" She gasped, coughed a couple of times, then took a deep breath. "I'm okay, Mark. Just had the wind knocked out of me. Is the bike alright?"

"The bike is fine. They are built to take it." He waited while she got some color back, then helped her to her feet. She was actually feeling better by the second, but enjoyed the attention.

"You took a pretty good hit there. Let me help until we get you checked out." He scooped her up and carried her in his arms.

"Thanks. You're a doll." She leaned her head into his shoulder and smiled softly. Yep. She could get used to this.

Unexpected Development

"Well Matt, what do you think of our little creation?" Jeff Perkins waved vaguely at the world around them. His attention was focused on the tall, slender man leaning against the marble railing.

"Incredible. I had no idea you were this far along." The feel of a cool breeze brought deep forest scents and the sound of a waterfall and rapids to his senses. "I would almost bet we could climb down there and go trout fishing."

"If you want to, we can." Jeff smiled at his friend's startled look. "That is not just a matte backdrop painting for a video game. This world is almost completed. We're still working out some of the weather patterns, but the physical structure is ready to explore."

"I thought that you told me just a few weeks ago that you had to scan various animals, rocks, trees and things in order to fit them into this computer system. That takes time."

"We actually found some interesting shortcuts. It seems that we have a huge amount of genetic data from most species and that, coupled with existing photographs and video clips are all the host program needed to populate this new world." He waved expansively. "Once we started the process, we just let the system absorb the data at its own pace. This is truly the fastest system ever invented. And the AI systems that run it have been adjusting themselves to take advantage of what now appears to be an unlimited amount of quantum storage."

The artist shook his head. "Man, I'd hate to have a hard drive crash. What happens if lightening strikes your system?"

"That's just it. Everything that is actually a part of this doesn't really exist in our dimension. It's part of a holographic matrix stored in several adjoining quantum dimensions. That is as close as I can explain without dragging in some math that I'm not sure I really understand. The important point is, once the multiple dimensions were linked, they formed a real-time backup of each other." In the early days of this project, back when it was only a single room with a couch, bar and drinks, we actually tried to physically destroy it in multiple ways. We made three of the quantum bricks and made sure that each one had access to the same room. Then, we put one in a hydraulic press while it was turned on. We smashed it flat and the only thing that happened was we lost contact with it. Nothing untoward happened in the room. Later experiments with some animals and later, when I was in the room, showed the same thing. That portal just vanished as soon as it was destroyed."

"So, you started to develop a whole dang counter-Earth. But why so large? You only have six of those helmets, right?"

"At this time, we only have six, but as soon as our team is satisfied that this place is animal populated and stable, we're going to start licensing the helmet and interface design and mass-producing them."

The two men turned to see their wives come out, on to the balcony.

Matt stepped forward to meet and hug his lady. "What have you two beauties been up to?"

Brenda's mahogany complexion was darker than her husband's and proof of her Southwestern Hispanic heritage. Like Marlo, she was wearing tight, faded blue jeans, a button-down shirt and cowboy boots. "Marlo was showing me how to use the magic closet to pick out clothing. I think I'm going to like this place."

He looked confused. "Magic closet? Did I miss something, Jeff?"

Jeff looked at his friend's attire and then glanced down at his own. "I guess it's our turn. We'll meet you ladies down at the stables in a few minutes. Come on, Mark. It's time you met the Magic Closet."

He led Matt back through the same set of tall, French doors that the women had just come out of and into a large, luxurious bedroom. A side door led into a walk-in closet and further door led to the bath. Jeff stopped in front of a trio of mirrors, set back into an alcove.

"Look down. See the pentagram set into the tile?"

Matt saw the tiles forming a large pentagram with a floor-to-ceiling mirror on each of three sides. He nodded and looked at the scientist.

"Stand in the center of it and look straight at the center mirror. Then say 'Mirror, alter garb for riding.'" He continued. "Be sure to note how you appear in the other two mirrors as well."

Mark stood where he was directed and as soon as he said the word 'mirror', the two side mirrors changed. The one on his left showed himself as a direct view from the back and the one on his right showed a ninety-degree, right-angle view. It was disconcerting, and yet allowed a total view of what he was wearing. When he finished telling it riding garb, all three mirrors showed him in jeans, cowboy boots, colorful shirt, vest and black ten-gallon hat. "Impressive." He muttered.

"Now tell the mirror to change hat color to white."

He did so and the hat changed.

"Now tell it you want snakeskin boots."

Once again, the mirror followed his command and showed him wearing a very fancy pair of expensive snakeskin boots. "Very nice. Now what?"

"Tell the mirror you accept that garb."

Matt followed the instruction. There was a quick flash of light over his body and he found himself dressed in the same image as in the mirrors.

"My turn." Jeff stepped into the center and said, "Mirror. Set cowboy riding garb and accept."

Another flash of light and he was dressed in a similar manner.

"Come on, Matt. We don't want to keep the ladies waiting."

***

The horses followed a smooth stone paved street from the front gate, over a drawbridge and around the curve of the mountain. The were lost in a deep forest for a mile or so, until the road curved back to cross a bridge over a ravine. Clear waters rushed over a rocky stream bed below them. Back over their shoulders, they could see the fairy book castle they had just left.

"Jeff, I just can't believe this isn't some incredible dream. It actually seems more real than Earth."

"We're doing all we can. The only hangup now will be the delay in making some additional helmets."

Brenda spoke up. "Jeff, how far are we going to ride? Don't we have to get back before we wake up? It's been almost an hour already."

"That's it!" He snapped his fingers. "I knew I had something else to tell you."

The others looked questioningly at him.

"Sorry, but we found a way to speed up the system development and the AI systems implemented it just the other day. From now on, we are all working on a twenty-four to one time compression ratio. What that means is that every hour back on Earth counts for twenty-four hours here. So if we're asleep back home for three hours, three days have passed here."

"You mean the scheduled wake up call we agreed on is actually going to seem like three days, here?"

"That's right. And we also no longer have to worry about how healthy our bodies remain while in that fugue state."

"Why's that, Jeff?" Asked Marlo.

"We realized that a lot of people will probably get hooked on spending all the time they can here. And that would make for some terribly unhealthy bodies. The AI is now taking over our bodies while we are here. It has better control that you do and will tighten and relax every muscle in the body in a series of isometric exercises. It's a technique that would be incredibly boring to learn and apply for most of us, but the AI doesn't get bored. After a complete aerobic exercise regimen for an hour, it will then send the body into a very deep, relaxed state and assist in rebuilding tissue. Anyone that uses this system on a regular basis is going to be in great physical shape in a less than a year's time."

They rode silently for a few minutes until they came to an open meadow with a view of a lush valley below.

"Matt, Brenda, what do you think?" Jeff waved expansively at the scene before them.

"It's beautiful. I'd love to paint it sometime."

Her husband was smiling softly and nodding.

"Well, I've got good news for you, then. It's yours."

They both looked at him, but before they could ask, he explained. "In many ways, this world is like Earth. Unlike Earth, we can pick and choose who we let in here. If I gave you one of the brick controllers, helmets and power suppliers for it, you would be able to make another one, just like this. But it would not be this one. Our company and team have reserved these coordinates and nobody else can use this corner of the multiverse unless we let them in. So far, every member of our team has a very large parcel of land here. I happen to control everything within about a hundred mile radius of my castle. That means I can sub-let it if you will."

Ever the logical business woman, Brenda asked, "Just what does your offer entail?"

Jeff nodded back the way they had come. "My castle overlooks the next valley over. During the next few years, I plan on building a small city there. Down stream from my valley there's a wide, swamp with a few deep-water streams that lead to the ocean. This valley we're in now, is upstream. I want to leave the tops of the ridges on each side open for public parks, hiking and hunting. The area between those two arms and from that high cliff face behind us and then down to the river, is yours if you want it. I'll even show you how to create your own home. The reason I'm doing this is because I want you guys for neighbors." He looked at Brenda. "And you m'lady, will be able to sit on your balcony and paint this anytime you wish."

Undercurrents

The Port Heinlein Director needed an answer. "Well? Can we let them land, yet?"

"Not right now, sir." The technician hadn't slept in more than thirty hours. "I know they are running low on supplies, but they will have to wait another couple of hours." He paused and looked up at his boss. "I'm sorry to report that the crash was not a fluke accident. It was sabotage."

"What? How... And by who?"

"The first two are easy. I'm not sure on the who part. Here's what I've found out." He directed attention to the large screen in front of him. "This is a small part of the code that controls the attitude jets and main engines. I was part of the team that did the quality assurance testing."

"You're saying there was a bug after the testing?"

"I suspected something might be wrong when I looked at the preliminary radar data on their approach. I remembered that I still had copies of the original software we had tested, in backup files. I recovered it to my workstation, then I downloaded the same files from the two shuttles that remain in orbit. When I compared them to the original, they were much different. I GREPed the difference..."

"Grep? What the hell is that?"

"GREP is a Unix program that has been around for many years. That's not important. What is important is that it can do a byte-by-byte comparison of two files and tell you where the differences lie. When I looked at the additional lines of code, I discovered something horrible." He paused, obviously frightened.

The Director prodded gently. "Go on. What did you find?"

"The software would behave normally until a certain date, from then on, every time it got within ten miles of the landing area, it would kill the main engines, quickly rotate the craft until it was pointing straight down and then fire up the main engines at full power. The shuttle would immediately hit ten to twelve Gs of acceleration and power-dive into the surface. The pilots would have no time to respond and regain control."

"So what are we going to do? How do we get those two shuttles and their crews down safely?"

"I've double-checked my code and compared it to checksums from the same code base back on Earth. I have confidence that I have the proper software. With your permission sir, I'm going to shut down all computer systems on each shuttle for about ten minutes so I can give them a clean boot, delete the existing code and reinstall the proper software. After that, I'll restart the systems again and run the full checksum test against all the software to make sure none of the other core systems code has been altered. That should take another hour or so. If it all comes back clean, I'll let you know and you can schedule a landing sequence."

"How long until you know for sure?"

The technician shrugged. "I can't be sure, but I'm guessing two to three hours. After that, the next orbit should allow one of them down and the other can follow the next time around."

***

A collective deep breath flowed through the team when the second shuttle settled on its landing struts and the engines shut down.

Mike Hawthorne slapped the tech on the shoulder. "Good job!" He said in a normal tone, then elevated his voice to the military command level that got everyone's attention. "Ladies and Gentlemen, I think we all owe this man a round of applause."

Once the applause, whooping and ululating from the team quieted down, the director leaned down and looked the tech in the eye. "And now, it is time for you to go home, get drunk if you want and then take the next two day's off. We have a lot of work to do after you are rested."

"Uh, what's up next, sir?"

Mike's eyes hardened and his voice dropped another notch. "We're going to hunt down the bastard that killed all those people and might have destroyed this colony."

Earth Eyes

Kevin stood back a bit with a pair of gyro-stabilized HD minicams hanging from each shoulder. His vest held multiple batteries so the whole rig could record High Definition video and six-channel audio from four wireless microphones and the mics in each camera. His wife, in her role as the Port Heinlein News anchor was wearing her earpiece and microphone. She was holding two more ear and mic sets. Mike Hawthorne was wearing the fourth one. He glanced down at the production slate standing out from the front of the vest and made sure all the levels and each camera was working properly.

They were standing in the main entry to Port Heinlein from Base One. The airlock opened and the two shuttle pilots stepped aside to let their passengers pass.

The first one out was a beautiful young woman. The other was a slender black man wearing a vest similar to Kevin's. GNN patches on his flight suit and logos on the camera rig declared him part of the Global News Net.

Mike stepped forward and held out his hand to the unencumbered woman. "Welcome to Port Heinlein. I'm Michael Hawthorne, OnSite Director."

She smiled broadly and shook his hand. "Thank you, General Hawthorne. I'm Dawn Smith with GNN and," she indicated her companion. "This is my cameraman, David Webster."

"Please just call me Mike. I retired and gave up my military commission when I let them talk me into this job." He turned. "This is our news team. Samantha O'Conner of Port Heinlein News and her cameraman, Kevin O'Conner."

Before anything further could be said, the two women hugged and Dawn spoke. "I'm so glad we've got a chance to catch up. It's been ages."

"I know. And look at you. The big-city news anchorwoman. Wow!" Sam was genuinely pleased to see someone from Tampa.

Mike glanced at the cameramen. They both shrugged. "I take it you two already know each other, then?"

They both chuckled and composed themselves. Sam answered him. "Actually, yes we do, sir. We're all from Tampa and we've both been in the entertainment industry for some time now. I hadn't realized that Dawn and David were going to be joining us."

His smile held a wicked gleam. "Now that is wonderful news." He turned to Dawn. "I'm sure you want to get settled in from spending all that extra time in the shuttle. I'm hosting a dinner this evening and expect you will all join me. Naturally, I've got a pretty busy schedule during the day, but if you'll contact my office, I'm sure we can arrange a formal interview in the next week or so. In the meantime..." His smile widened. "I think it would be a good thing to leave you in the hands of our news team. Other than the areas of the colony that are under construction and very dangerous, you have free run of any of the public spaces."

    ***

Dawn and David were both impressed with the size of their quarters. "This is sure a change of pace from the cramped shuttle and those tubes where we spent the first few hours after landing."

On the way down, Sam had been describing the general size of the tunnels and interconnecting spaces. "And this is actually one of our regular apartments. The only difference is that each of the bedrooms has a private bath and door locks. This is as close as we come to a hotel or visitor center these days. There are seven private suites, a shared kitchen, dining area and a couple of meeting spaces."

"So, you're only setup for a very few tourists at this time?"

"That's right, Dawn. All of the colonists and the few military staff have their own places."

"I was under the impression this was a civilian venture. Why the military?"

"They handle all of the space transport, Moonbase One, and they are building a deep-space research center in a much smaller crater, a short distance away." Before another question came up, she held up her hand to stop. "I understand you're going to be here for at least a month. We will have plenty of time for in-depth interviews. I'm going to see you meet anyone that can give you details on various aspects of our little colony. But before that, I think you two need some rest and a chance to clean off the shuttle grime. There are some drinks and snacks in the kitchen. Kevin and I will be back in about six hours, so we can escort you to the Director's place for dinner."

    ***

The door opened to reveal a stunning redhead wearing a bright red spandex minidress, incredibly high heels and a warm smile. "Good evening and welcome to our home. You must be Dawn and David. I'm Angela Veski Hawthorne." She gave each of them a quick hug and air kisses. "Come on in. Dinner will be ready in a little while.

Before they stepped inside, she smiled directly into the cameras.

"Okay. Now that we have the formal greetings aside, I will ask you all to turn off your cameras and microphones before entering. My husband and I will be happy to give you a full interview sometime in the next few days, but this evening is going to be strictly for pleasure and we value our privacy." She waited while David and Kevin shut off their systems, disconnected the tiny cameras and stuffed them in the padded pockets of their vests.

Inside the entryway, Angela indicated the coat hooks where they could hang their vests, before entering their apartment. She then shook Kevin's hand. "Good to see you again, Kevin. Welcome to our home." Then, she shook David's. "Welcome to you too, David. And all of you, please call me Angela."

David stared at her hostess for a moment, then asked. "You seem really, really familiar. Have we met before?"

Angela chuckled. "Actually, yes. We've all met before. That was back when Mike was in charge of Dreamland. I was that catlady that used to shack up with the general and gave him a reputation for being a bit too kinky for the military."

Dawn slapped her head. "Now I remember. You had that calico pelt and were really short."

"Still am really short. Mike likes it that way and here with the light gravity, I can get away with wearing heels like these." She nodded, twisted sideways and held up one foot to show a platform with a stiletto heel at least eight inches long.

David mentioned. "I've already seen a lot of women wearing really high heels and now it makes sense.

A short time later, the six of them were sitting around the table and relaxing with after-dinner drinks.

Dawn held her glass up to the light. "Although I'm not much of a hard drinker. This is very good. And these glasses are beautiful. They must have cost a fortune to get up here intact."

Angela answered. "Actually, they are very common up here. Just about any sort of glass product is very quick and easy to fabricate. And what you are drinking is called Stardust. It's a form of corn liquor otherwise known as white lightening, that some of our scientists have cooked up."

"Isn't that illegal? How do you license and regulate it?"

Mike interjected. "One of the big things you'll notice up here is that we're not really big on fancy licenses and such. Everyone knows who makes it. If they make a bad batch, it will ruin their reputation and nobody will buy from them again."

David asked. "We were told that you guys are really big on privacy issues. They said we had to have specific permission not only to enter a private apartment, but also to record. How does that tie in with knowing who makes the booze? Wouldn't they want to keep it secret?"

"There has been a great deal of debate over how to balance privacy, business, and security in a closed environment such as we have here. Psychologists repeatedly have told us how important a certain amount of privacy is for long term happiness. That is why we have started working on a colony charter based on what we've learned back on Alice Island, in the running of Moon Base One, and here, as the colony has grown." He paused to take a sip, then continued. "When you were in processing, to come here, back on Earth, they took fingerprints, DNA, and a lot of other tests, didn't they?"

The two girls nodded.

"Everyone that ever leaves Earth has to undergo a similar battery of tests. Part of it is for health medical reasons, but the biggest part is to develop a solid, identifiable profile for you. If you will recall, you had to place your hands on a biomentric scanner just before takeoff from Earth. And then again, when you disembarked from the lunar shuttle."

Dawn nodded, then added. "That's right. I assumed it was just to confirm who we were for security purposes."

"Only part of it. Remember, they told you to leave all your money, credit cards and driver's licenses back in a lockbox at Earth Base? That is because once you were accepted into the program, you were issued a lunar bank account. We are very much part of a capitalist culture here in Port Heinlein. Everyone starts out with a base amount in their account. After that, you get paid for hours worked or for services rendered, and your account grows. We don't carry money around with us. It all flows through one of several banks and they all share our network. That is the reason we are so adamant about personal privacy space."

"Sorry, Mike. But I don't follow. Elaborate, please."

"Quite awhile back, a gentleman by the name of Scott McNealy was speaking at a large conference and said something to the effect, 'You already have no privacy. Get over it.' For many reasons, when it comes to money and movement, here on the moon, you really have no privacy. Every transaction, no matter how minor or major, is recorded in real-time. The same applies to your movements within the colony. Should there be an investigation by our security team, they can tell everywhere you have been since the moment you first walked through the airlock at Base One. The only places the video and tracking information stops is in a public bathroom stall and at the entrance door to any private apartment. That is why my lovely wife asked you to leave your cameras and recording equipment at the door. The only people allowed to record inside a private dwelling is the owner or owners of that dwelling. In order to protect hotel visitors or rental clients, as long as their bills are paid, they are considered the legal owners of that space. The only way anyone can record in a private space is with a court order or formal permission of the space owner."

Ever-practical, the business man in David had to know. "What happens to your financial data? Who has access to that?"

"Anyone who wishes to inquire. Keep in mind they leave a trail in asking, however. That way, nobody can get away with hiding their financial background. If you purchase some risque' underwear for example, there is a record of it. What you do with it once it is inside your home is totally private, however."

Five Years Earlier

"Finally! A decent score." Marvin Bently was excited, but didn't want to let it show. The Major was standing nearby, snooping around and looking down his rich-kid nose like he usually did. He saw Marvin glare at him, sniffed, shook his head and left the communications van. Marvin knew the major didn't approve of his less-than-perfect uniform and general give-a-shit attitude. But it wouldn't matter much longer. He was going to get even with all the holier-than-thou assholes who yanked him out of his cushy Beltway Bandit coding job and stuffed him into a stinkin' military trailer just outside of Manassas. What did he care if starving rioters were burning down the Capital?

"Private! What the hell do you think you're doing?" The Major's voice in his ear snapped at him.

"Sorry, Sir. Just checking my email." He quickly killed the browser and the field deployment map filled his screen."

"You can chat with your friends when things are quiet. In the meantime, pay attention to your job. If I catch you fuckin' off once more, I'll have you on report and you can explain it to a courts martial board."

"Yes, Sir." God! How he hated having to kiss this idiot's ass every five minutes.

An hour later, he handed his seat over to the next sucker on the shift. Marvin tried not to look nervous as he marched rapidly over to a waiting SUV. His three partners in crime were already to go.

"Well? Did they leave on schedule?" The driver asked.

"Yep! I checked just a few minutes ago and they had fueled up and were heading out sixty six. Did you guys plant the charges?"

They nodded.

A few minutes later, they had pulled off the main road, into a private drive. The house at the end had been foreclosed and abandoned months ago and the team had made it into a staging area. There were some woods out back that abutted the interstate and they had already made a trail and cut the fencing. The four of them dressed out in stolen weapons, ammo, and a pair of hunting rifles with scopes.

The SUV driver checked all their gear and made sure each man wore a do-rag like an old-fashioned outlaw. He was their leader. The whole thing had been his idea. They headed into the woods and spread out in the ditch on either side of the highway.

There were very few vehicles on the road since the gas shortages and riots. The military had just finished their first batches of Omniphage and it was in very limited supply. A local gang had arranged to pay them a small fortune for one case of the stuff. The convoy coming from DC had a humvee with six cases of MILSPEC Omniphage in field packs. They were going to sell two cases for hard cash, then each of them would take a remaining case and head for the hills. Let the damn city burn down. With a temp supply of cash and a case of 'phage, they could set themselves up like kings in some backwoods area.

As the convoy rolled past, they set off the charges just beyond the overpass. The humvees squealed to a halt and the two in front and the two in the rear were immediately and almost simultaneously hit with RPGs. The billowing flames and debris hid the sound of two hunting rifles. One shot hit the middle hummer passenger in the head and the other caught the driver in the shoulder, spinning him to the side. He dropped as if dead.

The bandits were in a hurry, so they ran to the back of the middle hummer, yanked the door and took turns grabbing a case of 'phage. A rusty old pickup flew up the bank from their hidden drive and they loaded their booty in the back. The whole operation took less than a minute with two in front and two in the bed of the pickup, they disappeared into the woods as fast as they had arrived.

***

Through a haze of blood and pain, Nick Martinez got a good look at two of them and recognized the traitors. All he had to do was crawl out of sight and tend his wounds until help arrived.

He found shelter from the blistering cold wind in the lee of the overpass. When help didn't show, he realized he was wounded worse than he thought. He reached inside his ballistic vest for the emergency Omniphage pack they had issued just a few days before. One of the rounds or some shrapnel had smashed the syringe.

He stared down at the torn envelope leaking crystal and shards of glass. "Now that sucks." He muttered to himself as he laid back against the cold concrete. He had to close his eyes for just a second to gather his strength.

The backup team found him almost dead, just a few minutes after he passed out. Twenty four hours and a dose of 'phage later, he asked to see the Major.

The officer returned Nick's salute when he entered the hospital room. "At ease and sit down. How are you feeling, soldier?"

"Better than new, Sir, thank you. I have some information for your eyes only, Sir."

"Oh?"

"I lied to the investigating officer and the medics."

"Why is that and why are you telling me now?"

"Because I recognized two of the men that attacked our convoy. They are part of this unit, Sir. When I realized they meant to kill all of us, I decided to play dead until I could get the word out. One of them is the officer that came in to interview me. I told him I had been staring at the hummer in front when it blew up and couldn't see anything from the glare, then when I was shot, I passed out from the pain and didn't wake up until everything was quiet."

The Major's eyes had narrowed and his face hardened when he heard this. "You said you saw two. Who was the other?"

"One of your 25B communications men, Sir. Goes by the name of Private Marvin Bently. I've seen him in your commo shack several times. That's probably who gathered the intel for them, so they knew who to hit and when."

A few moments passed while the Major thought it over. "The medics tell me you should remain on light duty for the next forty-eight hours. After that, you'll be as good as new. As soon as I get back to my office, I'm cutting orders for you to take ten days off and go see your family. That will keep you out of the line of fire while I have the MPs corral those two and get them to give up the other traitors."

The Major stopped at the door and looked over his shoulder. "Thank you, Mr. Martinez. Once again, you've proven your worth to this organization."

Marvin sat outside in his pickup and listened to the whole conversation with his earpiece. He was really glad the leader of their little band of outlaws had planted the bug under the hospital bed.

He thought about warning the others, but realized the Major would have the word out to arrest them within the next thirty minutes or so.

Fuck 'em. He muttered to himself and headed back to his place. With luck, he could score his case of 'phage, the go-bag of civvies and cash, and be out of the area within an hour.

***

Marvin parked a couple of blocks down from the club and took his time walking, bundled up in heavy jacket and gloves, he was just one more bum looking for a place to get warm. At the door, the bouncer recognized him.

"Yo, Marvin. Someone was lookin' fo' ya earlier."

"Oh yeah? I assume you told 'em you didn't know me, right?"

"Of course, mah good man. You're a payin' customer and gots rights, ya know?"

Marvin slipped him a twenty dollar bill and went inside. As planned, he got there right before last call and sat in the corner, drinking his beer. A very-well-stacked brunette was making love to the brass pole. She was good and when the music ended, garnered quite a few tips. His table was last on her route

"Hi there, Tanya." He greeted the cute brunette with just the proper padding to suit him.

"Oh! Hi there, Marv. I thought you were going to be busy doing Army things for the next few days?"

"That's not really important right now. We need to talk in private for a few minutes. Let me buy you breakfast." It was already past two in the morning and he knew they could hit one of the few Denny's that were still open.

She brightened. "That sounds great. Let me get changed and I'll meet you out back."

"Give me the keys and I'll warm up your car."

Ten minutes later, she hopped into the passenger side and he drove around the block.

"Where are we going, lover?"

"I left my truck back here and wanted to get something. Hold on." He pulled up behind the pickup, popped the trunk and quickly transferred the case of 'phage and his go-bag. He left the keys in the truck's ignition and drove off.

"What's this all about? Why aren't you taking your truck, too?"

"I need your help, Tanya. Remember I told you I had a big score going down? Well it's done and now I need to drop off the map for awhile."

"What did you do and who's looking for you?"

"I ripped off something very valuable from our beloved Uncle Sammy and they are not pleased about it."

She was instantly worried. "And now you've brought me into it? What am I supposed to do?"

"Relax. Remember you told me about those friends of yours that really hate the military-industrial complex and want to strike back?"

"Yes..." She said slowly. "What do they have to do with it?"

"I'm thinking I have a lot to offer them in their battle against the man. And in exchange, I'm just asking if they'll give me a place to lay low for awhile. At least until I can arrange an escape up to Canada."

Tanya thought about it for a few minutes. "In that case, let me get some stuff from my apartment. We need to hit the road."

"Whoa there... why? There are bound to be some military police patrols out looking for me."

"Look at this logically, Marvin. You've ripped them off and they are looking for you to leave town. The last place they will think to look for you is back into DC."

"Excuse me, lover. But isn't DC that place with all the rioting and where they are shooting white guys with short haircuts... like me!" His voice was raising with each syllable.

"Yep. But many of my friends are doing the rioting. They have safe houses and their own supply of weapons, which by the way, is what happened to the last couple of snatches you cued me into."

He thought about it for a minute. What th' hell. After the way the

Army had yanked him from his comfy reserve spot to bring him to this hell hole, he might as well join the other side. "Sounds good to me. Let's go."

      ***

Two weeks later, he sat in front of a large LCD screen with several windows of text and a command-line console all open at once.

A voice over his shoulder asked. "How are you able to get into all that military shit so easy, bro?"

"It wouldn't be easy except that I have been worried about this sort of stuff ever since high school. I took the Army National Guard gig for a six year reserve program just so they would pay for my college classes. It was pretty sweet at first. I only had to show up one weekend a month and do some grunt coding and system administrator stuff, and once a year, go make a bunch of noise on the rifle range."

"And now?"

"And then Omniphage hit, the stock market crashed, the whole damn world turned to shit, and the damn Army called me to active duty. They wanted a simple little computer geek to start shooting my own countrymen."

The tall, slender fellow behind him had been a student too, but the school was now closed and he struggled with the rest of the gang on the block to put food on the table and fuck up the cops and military whenever they could. He nodded agreement. "That sure enough sucks. But how do you still get in?"

"Every time I had access to a new server, I added at least one fake ID and password. Then, I installed some script files in unusual locations. Over time, I've got accounts scattered all over their systems and I can also piggyback some of their communication channels. Without getting too geeky, before I left, I installed a whole bunch of back doors."

Tanya strutted in, heels clacking on the cheap tile and obviously pissed. "I can't believe it! Do you know what those bastards have done now?"

The two men shook their heads. They knew better than to interrupt her when she was in this sort of mood.

"As if this country didn't have enough problems, we are now spending gazillions of dollars on a moon base! That's right! That's what I said. A fucking moon base." She slammed the bag of Chinese take-out on the table and paced back and forth, muttering and cursing.

"Thousands of people dying of starvation, no damn jobs, people like us forced to hide in the ruins of our own capital and those rich fucking bastards are still trying to escape to the moon. Somebody has to stop them! This is insane!"

Marvin got out some plates and silverware and dished out some of the house special fried rice. The other guy poured them some drinks.

After a couple of bites in silence, Marvin spoke up. "That would explain some of the files I saw on a classified server last week. I thought it was just research stuff, but now I see it was hardware controls of some sort."

She looked at him and asked. "What sort of hardware?"

"It was some prototype rocket controls. I've seen something similar for UAVs but this had a lot more safeguards and internal cross-checking. I can get back onto that server and snoop around some more, but I think it might be part of that moon project."

"Can you hack it?" Her eyes were bright with excitement and Marvin knew that the proper answer would mean a hot, sleepless night for him.

"Of course I can. What do you have in mind?"

"Something that would make it screw up really bad. Maybe if they see how stupid it all is, they will pay more attention to the poor people back home."

She placed her hands on top of his and he stared down her loose blouse. Yep. She was excited about this. Marvin nodded, licked his lips and looked up at her eyes. "I think I can fix things up just the way you want them, lover."

At that moment, the tall guy heard something outside. He pulled a drape aside and looked down from their second-story window. "Hot damn! Cops and Army, both!" He turned back, grabbed his coat from the back of the couch and opened the door. "Come on, you two. Time to get the hell outta heah!"

Marvin slammed the lid on the laptop, grabbed the power cord and stuffed them both into his backpack. Tanya put on her jacket and grabbed both of their go-bags. As soon as he zipped his backpack, she grabbed it so he could put on his jacket and they headed into the kitchen.

Marvin opened the window to the rusty iron fire escape, slipped on his backpack and then grabbed his go bag. "Come on." He urged her.

The fire escape stairway made a loud squeal and clang as it

dropped to the ground. They ran down the alley towards a snow-covered tarp. He tore loose some tie-downs, threw the tarp aside and stuck the key into the motorcycle. It took three tries, but started. Tanya climbed up behind him and he started moving forward, tires sliding in the fresh snow.

"Stop! Police! Stop or we'll shoot!"

Marvin punched it and the bike fishtailed, but with some strange burst of luck, he kept it under control. They flew out of the alley, past a group of military police running towards them. He recognized Nick Martinez trying to block his exit. The hacker gritted his teeth and accelerated right at him. Nick tried to jump out of the way, but slipped in the snow and fell. Marvin drove on and felt the bike first push and then clamber over the screaming body. He knew he's killed the bastard that had ratted him out. Cranking the throttle wide, he barely heard the shouts to stop.

The couple had barely made it a block away when he felt something shove the bike first one way, then another. Tanya gripped his chest with bruising strength, but he kept on going.

He detoured through several side streets, alley-hopping at breakneck speed in the lightly falling snow. His adrenalin was way too high to stop. Less than a twenty minutes later, he pulled into the half-fallen wood garage behind an abandoned WWII-era bungalow. It was one of dozens of similar ones that had been burnt out during the riots. The week before, he had reinforced the basement doors, installed new locks and stashed some supplies, including his case of 'phage and spare cash.

The silence was almost scary when he shut off the bike. "Okay, love. We're here. Let's go inside and get warm."

Her hands were still clinging to him and he realized she must be in shock from getting shot at. "It's okay, love. We're safe here. They won't find us." He gently pulled her hands away and stepped off the bike. When he turned to look at her, she was leaning forward, hands pressed down on the seat and trembling.

"Shhhh... It's okay, Tanya. You're safe now. Let's get off the bike and get inside. He cupped her chin and looked at her.

A trickle of blood was on the corner of her mouth. He realized her breathing was labored and there was a nasty burbling sound to it. It dawned on him that she was hurt. He dropped his backpack, helped her to shuck hers and saw that her back was covered in blood.

"Ohmygawd!" He muttered in horror. Then, put her arm over his shoulder and tried to help her off the bike. She stumbled and moaned loudly.

Marvin scooped her up and carried her to the basement door, fiddled with the keys, cursing under his breath until they got into the relative warmth.

Tanya laid back on the cheap leather couch, coughing, shivering and eyes darting back and forth. "Marv? Marvin?"

"I'm here, love." He took her hand and watched in horror as she coughed up blood of several shades.

"Promise me!" She whispered harshly. "Promise you won't let them do it."

"Anything, Tanya, love... Anything you want. I'll do it. Just don't die on me. Please. Just hang in there while I get a doctor."

She almost smiled at the idea. "Ain't no doctor comin' to the middle of this hell hole at night." She coughed more blood, gasped and moaned. Both hands clutched his and she gasped again. "Promise me. No fucking moon base. Just promise me that we're not going to let them piss it off like that."

"Yes! Yes, Tanya. I promise. I pro..." And with that he realized she had stopped moving. No more shivering. No more burbling sounds. No more breath at all. Her eyes were fixed, staring over his shoulder as he pulled back and moaned himself. Not in pain, but in sorrow.

He never really thought about how long he sat on the floor crying and staring at the only woman who had ever really given him love and respect. After he stopped crying. His mind was racing. He had to keep his promise, but how could he when every police force, military office and three-letter agency was hunting for him?

Then, he realized the answer was right at hand. He opened the shipping chest and got out a vial of Omniphage. The needle slipped into her arm and he had to pull on it a bit to fill it with half-warm blood. The crystal absorbed it and started to change color immediately. He put it back in the tube and set it aside. Then, he went through her pockets to gather her cash, identification and driver's license.

Tenderly, he carried her body through the pre-dawn snow, to a place several houses down. Also abandoned and only a shell. He laid her out, stared at the beautiful young woman's corpse for only a moment, then poured a gallon of gasoline all over her and around the room.

He never looked back as the house sizzled and crackled with the fire.

Back in his safe basement, he made sure the heater had enough fuel for a couple of days, bundled himself under some blankets and injected the now chilly solution into his own vein.

Race Day

Wendy was excited. In all the preparation for the big race, when they announced the date, she was amazed to realize it was actually a celebration of two holidays. All the lunatics were excited because it was their biggest annual cause for celebration, landing day. The anniversary of when the first shuttles set down to start construction of Moon Base One. The other reason was more personal. It was also her eighteenth birthday.

Buster Mathias was smiling. "I can't believe you're turning eighteen. This is going to be a great party. We have the Lunar Triathlon, celebrations in the mall and then all your friends can come over to help you celebrate here."

Wendy held up her hand. "Now wait a minute, Dad. I appreciate what you're trying to do, but I'm only coming home to get freshened up after cheer leading for the race and for some cake and ice cream."

"But I thought..."

"Sorry, Dad. But I have a date and I'm going out to dance and party with my friends."

He shook his head. "Were you aware of this, Cheryl?"

"No, dear. But she is an adult now. A big girl who can make her own decisions."

He shook his head, threw up his hands and left the room. Her mom watched him go, then turned to her daughter and grinned. "Lemme guess. Mark Chambers is going to get lucky, isn't he?"
   ***

Wendy had been watching the teams practice on their little two block long course. After only a few practice sessions, she realized she wasn't competitive enough and became a cheerleader instead. Nobody had been expecting the difference it made when they closed off and six blocks of the ground level of both Ring One and Ring Three and the two-block connector on either end. The six block run gave the bikes time to build up some speed and they were flying at almost sixty kilometers per hour by the end of block five. Then, they had to brake like mad to take aim, shoot the hoop and make the turn. The very first practice runs had four competitors misjudge and lose control while trying to corner and throw at the same time. One of the adults garnered a broken arm and leg the first day. Luckily, the course had been opened three days prior to the race, so he was able to compete although most bets had him playing it way too cautious with not enough practice time to be really competitive.

While the crowds were gathering on the elevated cross-walks, Wendy and the other cheerleaders toured the shop area. Strutting in spandex body suits that left exactly nothing to the imagination.

"Hey! Wendy! Over here!" The voice came from Mark Chambers. When he found out Wendy was going to cheer, he immediately joined the adult team.

She put on her best runway model strut as she walked over to him. "Hey there, Mark! Are you ready to go play?" The poor lad was all but drooling when she stood in front of him. "Oh! I almost forgot. You have a race today. Too bad. No time to play, I guess." She folded her arms under her breasts and smiled innocently up at him.

"After the race is over, I'll expect a reward for winning."

"That is assuming, of course, that you win. If so, I'm sure there will be some little thing we can do to make you happy." And with that challenge, she turned and strutted away. Let him stew on that for a little while, she thought to herself.

    ***

The PHNews announcer called the junior team to the starting line. Jimmy Tsu tightened his helmet strap, grinned at his friend and said, "Don't worry, Charlie. I'll keep the finish line warm for when you show up."

Charlie grinned back with the retort, "That's because I'll be taking my victory lap, bro."

They stepped up to the line and only then did Charlie realize the tough little game he and his teacher had dared to dream, was really going to happen in a big way. There were people lined up on all of the overhead walkways and every block or so, a couple of volunteers acted as safeties. The junior cheerleaders were wearing short, flouncing skirts and leotards in their team colors. The announcer let them finish a cheer amid applause from the crowd then handed the microphone to Dawn Smith, the TV star from Earth.

"On your marks... Get set... GO!" She shouted.

The four boys and two girls were between the ages of twelve and sixteen. They all had been working out daily for the past three months and were in perfect shape. One of the girls took the lead and was close-followed by one of the guys. Charlie knew better than to put all your energy into the first lap. He dropped into a sensibly-paced, long lopping run that kept him in the middle of the pack. After all, the run was only a few laps of the fourteen block course.

Everyone made their hoops at each corner. The lead traded places twice and Charlie dropped back to fourth. Jimmy kept pushing the leaders until, on the sixth turn, the guy missed his hoop shot and had to drop back, grab the ball and throw it again. By the time he made the hoop, he was in last place. With just two corners to go, Jimmy was in the lead, followed by the girl and Charlie. The other two were by now, more than a block behind.

On the seventh corner, Jimmy's ball hit the hoop frame and bounced back. He started to slow down. "Don't stop!" Shouted Charlie as he grabbed his buddy's ball on the bounce and threw it for a hoop. He followed up with his own ball, making it as well. The two of them made the eighth hoop and hit the finish line at the same time. A team mate took each empty ball bag and slung another over their shoulders. Another team mate held their bikes ready.

The two pulled away from the line almost wheel-to-wheel. The roar of the crowd was deafening.

The fifteen year old girl who had been languishing in fourth and fifth place during the running part of the race left the pits next and was hot on their trail. She had been conserving her energy for the bike part, which she knew was her strongest. None of the three leaders missed any more hoops, but on the final turn, Charlie pushed a tiny bit too hard and lost it. His bike careened off the wall, tossing him sprawling and by the time he got up, mounted and pedaling again, he rolled past the line in last place.

"Charlie! Are you okay!" The safety warden caught up to him as he rolled up to the pit area where his team held his spacesuit.

"Yeah! I'm fine. Just let me get my suit." He waved the warden off while ditching his helmet, handing the bike to a team mate and reaching for his suit. With skill borne of practice, he yanked it on, sealed it up and checked his air supply. While he slapped his helmet in place and straddled the bike, the safety warden double-checked his air, then swatted him twice on the helmet. That was his signal to go.

As he accelerated up the straightaway, he realized he was just a wheel ahead of the last place rider.

Although the latest generation of space suits was a far cry from the Michelin men suits of days past, they still were several layers thicker than the spandex bicycle suits of the first two events. They added an additional level of resistance to every movement and the helmets contributed to a small sense of claustrophobia. He found himself suddenly overheating and remembered he had forgotten to turn on the suit's environmental controls. A moment later and he felt a wash of nice, cool air on his face and the overall suit temperature dropped a couple of degrees.

He had no trouble passing the next two competitors but when he found himself chasing the back wheel of Jimmy's bike, it felt like he had hit 'the limit'.

"Having trouble... gasp... back there?" He was almost startled by the voice in his helmet. It belonged to the girl in the lead. They had spoken a little bit during the last few week's of practice, but he didn't expect to hear chatter during the race, itself. She had the nerve to tease them at this stage of the game?

Trying not to sound as out of breath as he felt, he replied. "Not at all... gasp... I still have... gasp... another couple of turns... gasp... and just enjoy... gasp... watching you two work so hard."

Jimmy's voice was next. "I can't... gasp... believe... gasp... you two... gasp... still have... enough... gasp... air to chat." And with that, he moved a bit to the outside and let Charlie pass.

Charlie waited a couple of more hard breaths and then decided that if she wanted to play mind games, he could do it too. "Hey, Linda. I'm right behind you. I now see why Jimmy was following so close. You do have a very nice ass."

"What?" She gasped, sputtered and her bike swerved just a little. That was all Charlie needed, he pitched his ball over her shoulder and through the hoop. Her ball missed the target and he banked hard into the corner. His wheel skidded just a bit, but he caught it and just a few seconds later, rolled over the finish line. Charles Mathias, the very first winner of the very first Lunar Triathlon.

He rolled into his pit area and his team took the helmet. It felt good to get fresh air. He wasn't sure he could stand up though. Another bike pulled even and she took off her helmet. Linda glared at him, then, she forced a smile and gasped. "Next year Charlie, you're mine."

Honey Pot

Mike Hawthorne offered the military man a drink. He accepted and the two of them sat down.

The uniformed officer sipped his drink. "This is very good. Thanks for sharing." He put the glass down and sat back in the chair. "But I know this isn't a social call. What's up, Mike?"

"We've been investigating that shuttle crash and when I saw where it was leading, I thought I should speak with you privately and in person. That's why the friendly invite for a drink this evening."

"Where's it leading?"

"First, let me say that a couple of the people on my team have proven much better analysts than I had first imagined. When I inquired why that was, it was suggested that perhaps I shouldn't dig too deeply. I'm starting to see why." He smiled.

Colonel Gerald Simmons sat back in the chair. He knew his host would fill in the details as needed. "Okay. I'll grant you they know their business. So why this cloak and dagger stuff?"

"Because we have reason to believe that not only were those shuttles hacked, but some other military networks, including OpSec channels."

Colonel Simmons froze in his seat. "For the last five years or so, all of our networks have been using quantum communication hardware. It is impossible to hack."

Mike nodded. "That is correct, Jerry. But what happens if the person has already been in the system for longer than five years, laid low, done nothing and is only now starting to take action?"

"A mole? Damn!" He took another sip of his drink before continuing. "Any idea who it is?"

"They are very good and have covered their tracks well, but we have narrowed it to this end. Someone here on the moon is a mole."

"Are you sure they're military?"

"Nope. We haven't been able to pin it down. Just the fact that the hacked shuttle control code was part of an update package that was fine when it was sent up from Earth, but infected when it was installed the last time the craft were serviced."

"How many people know of this?"

"Probably a dozen or so know that we're still investigating. But so far, it's two of my team, myself and you. We do have a plan however, but it will need your support."

The Colonel nodded, face grim. "You have it. What do I do?"

"My men are going to setup what is called a honey pot."

"I'm familiar with the concept. That's a fake website that looks like the real thing and yet is setup to attract hackers. It is really a dead-end, but when they hack into it, we get all their data and can track them."

"That's right. Except in this case, we're going to build a bunch of fake files relating to our investigation and how we're going to establish new security for the base. Once it is ready, I will personally give you detailed instructions on how to redirect logins from your real server, to our honey pot server. Each one that comes in will be tightly monitored. If it seems legitimate, we will pass it on to your server. If anything looks odd, we will know exactly who is doing the poking around and what they are hoping to find."

***

For the first time in several years, Tanya was a tad nervous. The slender blonde with huge tits bore little resemblance to the slightly overweight brunette refugee from the DC riots. A secret stash of Omniphage, a few thousand in cash and the willingness to do anything needed to survive, had led her to a topless gentleman's club near Fort Belvoir. A year after that, she was living with an older Master Sergeant she'd met at a science fiction convention.

"You look distracted, honey. Anything I can help with?" Master Sergeant Michael Pitts was tall, muscular and had a bulbous nose that canceled any chance of being called handsome.

She stretched, letting the sheet slip down and instantly distracting him. The man had been very good to her over the last few years and she enjoyed teasing him. "Nothing at all, really. I was just thinking about what I'm going to prepare for the party, this weekend."

"I'm sure you'll come up with something great, as usual." He leaned down to kiss her.

She pulled his tie a bit, so that he had to lean closer and caress her breast. "I have to make it perfect since it will be awhile until we see all of our friends again."

"You make is sound longer than it is. We're only going to be Earthside for six weeks. We'll attend my mom and dad's anniversary, then grab a couple of week's of real honeymoon and then back to Heinlein."

She smiled, nodded, kissed him again, then shooed him off. "Go! You need to make muster then get some work done while I clean up."

When he was gone, she showered, did her hair and took a moment to pose and admire herself in the full-length mirror. Who would have thought? She wondered. That the overweight technogeek male deserter the Army had been looking for these past six years was not only sleeping with one of their non-coms, but living as a beautiful woman, inside one of their most valuable bases. Only another couple of weeks, then Michael and her would be safe in Tahiti after the shit hit the fan. Still nude, she walked over to the window and stared out, over the crater and the brilliant stars. "I will miss the stars, however." She whispered to herself.

A Second Chance

Angela carefully set the plate in front of her husband. A slight whisp of steam rose from the herb-encrusted baked chicken and baked potato.

"Uuhmmm..." He closed his eyes and sniffed appreciatively. "My goodness, honey. This smells delightful."

"Thank you, Mike. I only hope it tastes as good as it looks."

She picked up her fork and knife just as the doorbell rang. "You expecting anyone?"

Mike Hawthorne shrugged and shook his head in denial.

She tapped her slate and the screen showed a Port Heinlein Operations Courier standing next to a shipping case. "Yes? Can I help you?"

"Mrs. Hawthorne? I have a package for you. It requires your authentication for delivery."

She stepped through the inner door, closing it behind her, then opened the outer door. He handed her his slate. She pressed her thumb to it and spoke her name. The system approved and he handed her the suitcase-sized shipping container. "Have a nice evening and sorry to disturb your dinner period."

She wished him goodnight and returned to the table.

"Who's that from?" Mike inquired.

The gorgeous redhead took a sip of wine before replying. "It's from one of those AI researchers I worked with for awhile back at Area 51. The last I heard, his whole team was really excited about a breakthrough. He promised to fill me in as soon as he was able." She nodded at the case. "I didn't expect any gifts though. But I worked too hard on this meal to let it go to waste. Dig in, mister."

***

After dinner, Mike cleared the table and Angela broke the seal on the container. Inside, it held a small brick-shaped sealed box with a single power cord and a pair of lightweight helmets. A cheerful holiday card wished them a happy Landing Day on the front and a hand-written note, inside.

Dear Angela,

I know that you and your husband are really going to appreciate what we've accomplished these last few years.

Please set aside a couple of hours, late at night, when you won't be interrupted. Just plug the box into any standard wall socket, lay back in bed and put on the helmets. They will sense when you are laying down, relaxed and then take the two of you on a trip.

We're all looking forward to seeing you there.

Your friends,

Jeff and Marlo Perkins

Mike turned the box and cord over several times, examining it carefully. "There are no markings of any kind. The case appears to be all one piece. The only opening is where the cable connects and I'll bet that inside the hole, it's some sort of inductive coupling."

"But what does it do?" She asked.

"I'm thinking it must be a new, state-of-the-art virtual reality rig. Perhaps he thought we needed some kind of new game?"

She thought a moment, taking her turn to look it over. "I must admit dear, that I am intrigued. It cost a fortune to ship this up here And I really don't see either Jeff or Marlo as shipping us something as mundane as a fancy video game system." She looked up, a mischievous smile on her face. "Come on. Let's try it."

A couple of minutes later, they put on the helmets, stretched out and relaxed against their pillows. An outside observer would have seen their eyes close, their muscles tense for only a second and then relax into a deep coma state.

***

Angela opened her eyes, sat up and just stared. Her husband sat up next to her and he too, was speechless for a moment.

Mike blinked several times and muttered. "What the bloody hell is going on?"

They were sitting on a very ornate carved wood bed in a room with high ceilings and several other pieces of extremely expensive furniture. All of this paled in significance to the full height French doors that were open to a wide patio. Snow-covered mountains could be seen in the distance and a soft breeze brought a host of forest smells.

Angela took Mike's hand. "Honey? This isn't the moon, is it?"

He shook his head, turned and stared at her for a moment. Then a wry grin spread over his face. "Somehow, I think you're right, wife." He saw her looking him over. And he realized they were no longer wearing their usual nightclothes. She was wearing a flowing white gown that revealed far more than it hid. He glanced down and saw he was wearing a kilt of some sort. "It looks like we're dressed for a fantasy convention. I'll bet this might just be some sort of game, after all. I'm just trying to figure out where the exit button is hiding."

"What? And leave without even taking the grand tour?" The booming voice came from the patio. A pair of friendly faces came into view. "I'm glad you guys finally made it. When we got word you had plugged it in, Jeff and I just had to be here to show you around." Marlo Perkins wore the same sort of gown as Angela. Her husband was in a leather kilt with a white long sleeve shirt, only a bit fancier than Mike's.

The two women exchanged hugs and air-kisses while the men shook hands. "Welcome to Beta." Jeff stated.

"Beta? Is that what you call this game?"

Jeff shook his head. "Why does everyone seem to think this is a game? Never mind. That was rhetorical. Actually, this is a new construction in a parallel universe. I'm not going to get into the mechanics of it, but that little box you plugged in actually has a quantum connection to this world we've built. The helmets interface with it and allow you to visit whenever you wish. We asked you to set aside a couple of hour's of privacy so we can give you a basic tour. After that, we'll play it by ear."

Angela frowned. "I guess the mountains and all or just an illusion then. Since you say you're going to give us a tour in only a couple of hours. This little universe can't be that big."

Marlo laughed. "Oh no, Angela. This isn't that limited. Those mountains are really there. This is a complete world, about the same size as Earth, but the continents are laid out differently and a few other, major differences."

"Well, two hours still isn't too much, so tell us, what are the differences?"

Jeff told them. "The first and biggest difference is how time works here. Since all of this is actually part of an unbelievably massive computer, the time runs on a twenty-four to one compression routine. That means that for every hour that passes back on Earth, or in your case, the Moon, twenty-four hours pass here. The two hours you set aside are going to translate into a couple of days here on Beta." The two couples walked out, on to the patio while they learned about the new world.

Metaphysical

Mathew Yellowfeather sat very still, staring out at the desert. The deep purple outlines of mountains marked the horizon as the blood red sun threw glorious rays of color.

Brenda knew her husband was meditating, so she did nothing to disturb the moment.

"Something profound has changed."

"What is that, my dear?" She replied to his softly spoken statement.

"I'm not entirely sure. But have you noticed an increased awareness of the world around you? And when we travel to Beta each night, how easy and fast it really is?"

She nodded. "Yes. I thought it was just that we're getting used to the helmets. We have been spending a lot of time there. Do you think that is wrong?"

He slowly shook his head. "No. I think we have a place in Beta. I also think that we have a place here as well. I'm thinking it isn't that we're becoming used to the helmets as that the more time we spend in Beta, the stronger our connection." He paused for a long time before continuing. "I want to try an experiment."

A few minutes later, they were nude, holding hands and laying side-by-side on their bed.

"I'm not sure I can do this, Matt."

"Just relax, close your eyes and focus your thoughts on our bed back on Beta. I believe we can travel without the helmets."

She heard his breathing slow and a few moments later, she realized he was in the same sort of trance. She didn't think it possible, but he wasn't wearing the helmet. She put hers on, closed her eyes and when she opened them, she was in their bedroom, on Beta.

Matt was standing by the window, looking out. "About time you got here. Easy, wasn't it?"

She gave him a wry grin. I'm sorry, but I had to use the helmet. Perhaps with some more meditation, I'll be able to do it."

"No, my dear wife. There is no need for any more practice. You can do it now."

"But I couldn't. I had to put on the helmet and then it was quick and easy."

"Oh, I believe you. But please believe me and believe in yourself. You see, I pulled the battery pack from your helmet earlier this evening."

"But... How...?"

"After discussing some of the design elements with Jeff and some of the other system designers, it occurred to me that while the helmets let us design this world, they are also modifying the way we view our home dimension. Once the link has been established and reinforced, there is no reason why we can't move between them merely by choosing which view we prefer at any one moment. Since the AI running this whole thing is running millions of times faster than we can perceive, I have no doubt it has also taken care to stabilize Beta and permanently link anyone who spends much time here."

She joined him at the window and looked out over their valley. "I guess this means we aren't going to need millions of helmets. Just loan one to someone until they can find their way by themselves and then pass it on."

Brenda pointed. "Look. We have company."
***

The two couples dismounted and Jeff Perkins shook Matt's hand. "Matt, I'd like you to meet Michael Hawthorne, OnSite Director for Port Heinlein. That gorgeous lady next to him is his wife, Angela Veski Hawthorne."

"Good to meet both of you, I'm Matt Yellowfeather and this is my wife, Brenda. Go ahead and release your horses in the corral while you're visiting."

Once the horses where at the watering trough, Matt asked, "Does being a Heinlein director mean we have a Beta node and some helmets there?"

"You guessed right, Matt." Mike answered. "They just arrived and Angela and I are the first to give them a try. I must admit, I'm amazed at what you've accomplished here. I think this is going to be the ultimate vacation spot pretty soon."

"Well, I've some more data to add to your experimental files, Jeff. You remember I had mentioned that it was getting easier for us?"

"Yes, Matt. And when I brought it up with some of the other team members, several have mentioned the same thing. You think you have a handle on why?"

"Well, right this minute, back on Earth, I'm in the usual coma-state, but I'm not wearing a helmet. And Brenda has a helmet, but there are no batteries in it."

Jeff leaned back, whistled softly and steepled his fingers. "Now that is very interesting. I'm going to have to suggest everyone else try it since it means we will be able to get by with just using the helmets as training aids." He was quiet for a moment, then asked in a worried tone, "Without the helmet to set the time on, how do you get back?"

"I think it will be very easy. I intend to will myself to whichever world I wish to inhabit. As long as everyone is here, let me give it a go." He closed his eyes, leaned back in the chair and five people stared at him.

Suddenly, he muttered, almost too soft to hear. "Got it!" His body seemed to ripple, grow transparent for only a second or two, then faded away.

Jeff and Marlo looked at each other and she said. "I guess it works."

Brenda spoke. "I guess it's my turn now. I'll try to be back in a little while." She leaned back, closed her eyes and visibly forced herself to relax. Less than a minute later, she faded away, as well.

Marlo spoke first. "I know I've done it dozens of times, myself. But I still look at it like magic."

Jeff chuckled."That is because we've built this world and magic has a place in it. After all, Clarke's Law states that any sufficiently advanced technology is indistinguishable from magic."

The French doors leading to the bedroom opened and the Yellowfeathers came out. Brenda was grinning from ear to ear. "It works both ways and totally easy, now that I've got the hang of it."

Marlo looked at everyone and commented. "Yep. It's just magic."

First Leap

Sara Evans double-checked the settings on the initial program while Brent reviewed the hardware.

"Well, you ready?" He asked. After all, she was the senior and the whole project had been her idea.

Sara took a deep breath and nodded. The warning lights came on over the lab doors and they each sat at a console. She kept her voice low, but clear and stated. "Ready for the first test, standby to activate the cameras."

"All cameras are cued, power is on and ready on your mark." He replied.

She glanced over the levels on her display, lifted the safety cover and put her finger on the switch. "Initiating test in five, four, three, two, one." The switch snapped over.

The power levels surged and suddenly there was a very loud bang, followed by the sound of shattering glass!

They both ducked. When there were no further sounds, they each looked up and checked their instruments. The glass partition leading into the testing room had shattered, scattering shards all over the place.

"Sara? You seeing what I'm seeing?"

"Lots of broken glass and the giant bill the university is going to hand me for the damage?"

"Two things are what I'm seeing. One is the fact that most of the glass is inside the test lab and we have none on us. If it had been an explosion, we would be covered in glass. This was an implosion."

She nodded and pursed her lips. "Okay. I'll buy that, but why?"

He point to the experiment table. "My second observation is that our prototype was supposed to vibrate quite fast and we would be able to detect the movement. I see our cameras, the table and a bunch of dangling test leads, but no prototype. Where did more than three hundred pounds of stainless steel, copper wire, plastic insulators, and carbon nanotubes go?"

She shook her head in disbelief. "Let's see what sort of video we recorded."

The high-speed cameras captured some amazing images as the intense implosion destroyed their lab. Fortunately, no one was injured, but the slow-motion footage revealed all of the equipment within the field had vanished just as soon as the power peaked.

"Well, that answers what caused all the damage. The implosion was due to the displaced mass as the equipment left the lab causing a sudden vacuum." He killed the video loop and thought for another minute or so. "I just wish I had some idea of where it went."

They had their answer when the evening news reported a strange explosion out in the desert. Grabbing cameras and a borrowed Jeep, they found a burnt hole covered in scraps of stainless steel, copper wire and a dusting of carbon nanotubes. The secondary explosion occurred when their project's mass tried to exist in the same place as several cacti, a bit of sand and the desert air. All of which were more than twenty miles from their lab.

As soon as they studied their recordings and realized what happened, the team showed their project to a private space-launch company. The next experiment took place in orbit. The warp-modified robot spacecraft, meant only for low Earth orbit (LEO) was lost for several days. They found it beyond the orbit of Saturn.

Colonel Simmons really wanted to know why the incoming shuttle was considered secret and he was getting two more physicists. After clearing the Alice Island decontamination station, they were escorted to his office.

"Hello. I'm Colonel Jerry Simmons."

They all shook hands. "Hi Colonel. I'm Brent Cooper and this is my colleague, Sara Evans. Thanks for having us."

"I understand you brought a small spacecraft with you. What's up with that?"

They took turns explaining their research and why they needed the raw materials and Moonbase One fabricators to modify their craft and safely test it.

Jerry thought about it for a short time, then said. "I need to talk to some people and re-arrange some schedules, but I think we'll be able to work with you on this. It will take a couple of weeks before I'll be able to get back to you."

Ten days later, he called Brent. "I have good news for you. Tell Sara to start packing her things. Both of you and your basic equipment are scheduled on a lunar shuttle flight in six weeks."

The next robot spaceship was a larger and much more sophisticated craft, designed only to warp around our own solar system while developing baseline calibration data. It also had the option of carrying a pair of space-suited astronauts, once it was determined to be safe.

After several months, it had finished the first few missions and they had some idea of how to control the warp field, they modified it once more to visit a series of nearby solar systems, record data and return.

Within months, the world was amazed by the images and data that this primitive starship returned. For the first time, a few extremely high-resolution videos of another solar system were being rationed out to the media.

The most welcome surprise was the discovery of another Earth-like planet circling that distant sun. It was slightly larger than our planet. The first estimates showed an oxygen and nitrogen atmosphere. There were blue oceans, pale desert areas and large swaths of verdant green.

No radio waves of any kind emanated from the planet, the only night lights came from a few volcanoes, forest fires and lightening. At least from orbit, there were no discernible structures. They designated it YU55T.

Farmers and Fertilizer

"I did not ask for this job." The OnSite Director was not happy.

"I know you didn't, dear. But you are the best one for it and you won't be happy until things are running smoothly and you've had time to train a replacement."

Mike grimaced. "Yeah, I know. I'm hoping Steve Saunders will be up to speed in a year or so. He's got the right stuff to carry this place forward for the next generation. I just want to farm for a bit and not have to constantly worry about every little detail of a major project."

Angela hugged her husband tight. "Don't worry, dear. It won't be for too much longer and you can retire to your farming."

***

Tanya Caine enjoyed working in the hydroponic farms. It was simple work and she had access to a fabricator and plenty of raw chemicals to make various types of soil and fertilizers. Once she had finished her probationary period, everyone just left her alone to do the job. Nobody paid any attention to how a certain percentage of raw materials were not going to plant production.

"Hi, Tanya." He supervisor smiled and waved. She knew he really wanted to get into her pants, but since she was a military wife, he didn't push the issue. That didn't stop her from arching her back, roughing her hair and flirting, of course.

"Hi there, handsome. What are you doing down in my end of the farm?" If he was staring at her tits then he wasn't paying attention to the full drums in the back of her electric cart.

"Just thought I would stop in and see how you were doing."

"Everything is going great. I think tomato and strawberry production is going to be up this cycle."

He nodded, never once raising his eyes to her face. "That's good news. I'll have to put it in my report and credit it to your diligence."

"Thanks, boss. You're a gem. See ya later, okay?" She waved as she drove off.

He didn't bother to ask why she was taking full fertilizer drums out the back of the farm and down the almost deserted Ring Three corridor.

She drove to the workshop and motorpool area, and through it, while looking carefully for anyone else that might be working later than usual. With no one in sight, she crossed Ring Two into one of the sports park areas. This one had bleachers up either side and a pair of screens to protect spectators. They used it sort of like a 3D soccer field where two small teams fought to get the ball into a small goal area at each end.

As usual at this time of the day, it was deserted. Tanya pulled up beside a bleacher, opened a locked storage door and quickly stashed her cargo inside, along with the rest of the drums she had pilfered over time. She had changed the lock for one of her own months ago and when people asked, she just shrugged and blamed it on some manager that wasn't around. It wasn't critical storage, so nobody followed up.

She was off the next morning and after a bit of shopping, decided to do a bit more sightseeing. The colony had grown to the point where there were new areas opening every month or so and she liked to keep a good map of the area in her head.

Mike wasn't going to be home for a couple of hours, so when she found a quiet corridor with an empty storage area and a good view if anyone were to follow, she sat down, pulled out her slate and turned it off. With skill borne of long practice, she removed the fingernail-sized SIM card and replaced it with one she kept hidden in a piece of her favorite jewelry. When she turned the slate on, once more, it connected to the net with a totally different identification. The only time she used this ID was to do a little snooping.

"What's this?" She muttered to herself when she found a classified email telling the team about a new place to store investigation data. A half-hour reading some of the reports and charts convinced her that they were looking at some Earth-First hackers in Europe as the probable culprits in the shuttle code crash. She had to grin at this news. This gave her an idea. Maybe she could pin something else on them and continue to draw attention away from herself?

    ***

Two days later, she had finished the design change and headed down the shop area.

"Hey there, lady!" It was one of the shop guys that she saw regularly. He took care of maintaining the electric carts.

"Hello there, George. How are things with you?"

"Can't complain. Don't do any good, anyhow. What can I do for ya?"

She dismounted and took a moment to stretch. Once again, the languid display of her assets was enough to get a man's attention. " This thing feels like there may be something wrong with a tire or something." She gave a helpless girlie shrug. "You know? It kinda drags like a tire going flat or something."

"These tires don't have air. They can't go flat. It might be a bearing that is starting to fail and drag once in a while. Give me a few minutes to check it out for you, okay?"

"Well, if it won't get in the way of the rest of your work. I hate to be a bother."

"No bother at all, Tanya. It will take about ten or fifteen minutes to check. Which side was it?"

She put her hands behind her and shrugged again. This strained her blouse and his eyes kept dropping from her face. "I don't really know, it just seems to pull from side to side once in a while."

"Well, I'll just take a look at all the bearings, just to play it safe."

She glanced over at the other end of the shop. "Do you mind if I go wait in your office? There's a bit of an echo here and I want to study up on some stuff on my slate."

He waved her on as he moved the cart onto the chassis lift. "Go ahead. I'll come get you when I'm done."

Alone in his office, she made sure no one was looking and quickly replaced the SIM in her slate. Once again, it looked like another system. She turned on the machine shop fabricator interface and looked up the design for one of the lunar surface tractors. These designs were always being modified for new operations. The same tractor might be used to mount solar panels and later on, a new arm might be added to off load containers from an incoming shuttle.

The attachment she was looking for was used to handle sections of welding rod and build racks for mounting everything from research instruments to solar panels. Once she found the proper design, she replaced the control code with the files she had tagged to look like a European Earth-First hacker.

When George got back, wiping his hands on a shop towel, she had some fashion article from the PHNews team displayed on her slate. The article featured very lacy bras.

"Your cart is ready to go, Tanya. One of the bearings looked a little worn, so I replaced it."

"Thanks, George. You're a doll. Hey! What do you think?" She held up the slate with the lace bra. "Do you think my husband will like this one?"

His eyes darted back and forth as he struggled for the proper words.

Magic Spells

Mike Hawthorne strode out on to the marble patio wearing a huge grin. "I did it!" He announced.

Jeff was just finishing breakfast. "Okay, Mike. I'll bite. What did you do that has you so damn cheerful?"

He pulled up a chair. "I've been working on that visualization system that Matt was describing and I'll be damned if it doesn't work."

"Really? You're not wearing a helmet?"

"Nope. I just stretched out, closed my eyes and focused on your patio and here I am."

Jeff nodded. "Well, after I get finished with the rest of the magic system, I'm going to have to give it a try as well."

Mike poured himself a glass from the pitcher, took a sip and leaned back. "So. What sort of magic have you come up with, now?"

"When we first started to expand this world beyond just a pretty mountain valley, I realized I wanted a decent place to stay. I wasn't about to play cave man. The more I thought about it, the more I realized that I had to design a large, multi-room hotel to house the newbie guests. This palace is the result. It's actually much more gaudy than I would have initially thought, but Marlo talked me into it as a marketing tool." He took a sip of his own drink before continuing. "After a half dozen of us started visiting regularly, I realized everyone wants their own place. Some folks like the idea of a village or town, while others want lone mountain cabins. If I wanted to get anything done with the rest of the world, I needed some way to let others get what they want without giving them the keys to the system."

Mike agreed. "That makes sense. When you offered me my own place when we first came to Beta, I just assumed that when I got the time, I'd have to chop trees and build a cabin."

His host chuckled. "That had occurred to me as well. And I'll not rule that out for some folks, if they're so inclined. But that has been the delay. I wanted to provide a way that anyone might make a palace like this if they really wanted it." He stopped, started to say something, then stopped to think before going on. "Let me ask you this, Mike. This place has electric lights, a refrigerator in the kitchen and flush toilets. Has it occurred to you to question the source of power and sewage?"

"I just thought it was more magic."

"When we designed this place, we had considered that, but we wanted to have as balanced a world as possible and it actually would have been much more complex to have a closed system based on magic toilets. No. When I decided to use this series of mountain valleys for my community of friends, I planned ahead. Fresh water flows through dozens of tunnels about ten meters below the surface all the way from several mountain lakes up near the snow line." He tipped his chin to indicate someplace in the hills behind them. "These tunnels deliver clear, fresh water all the way down to those large swampy areas that show up in places along the river."

"In other words, a real big-city water system for the whole valley is already in place?"

"Yep. All you have to do is check a map of your area that I can supply and drill your well. It will have a nice head of pressure."

"That sounds all well and good, Jeff. But I don't recall seeing a billboard advertising the Acme Well-Drilling Company."

Jeff laughed and waved his hand. "Never mind that, now. I'll get to it in a minute. The next thing to consider was sewage. Some ten meters below the fresh water tunnels, I have a network of large sewage tunnels. They drain into huge septic tanks on high ground, just above the swamps. That's why I have the swamps marked as off-limits in our maps. They serve as the runoff areas for the drainfields under that flat pasture land just uphill from them. The septic tanks are huge affairs with multiple entrances, they can be serviced on a regular basis to provide valuable minerals for crops. You see, I am planning for a very large urban population and not just a bunch of castles and palaces on the hilltops."

"Okay. I see that you're taking care of water and sewer but what about electrical power?"

"That's the one place where you've got me. I cheated and developed a fancy battery pack that can be charged from solar panels and when fully charged, will run a place like this for a year. I have more than a dozen in storage right now. They are small enough that they can be carried horseback."

"As the one with the master control system, you can make any of this happen, so what is your problem?"

"The problem, my friend, is that I don't want to spend all my time handing out batteries and building homes for people. That is why we have been developing a sort of user-level construction system. We are going to call it magic and just like in many of the urban fantasy stories over the years, there are different levels and skill sets involved in each stage of the game. Since I and a half-dozen of my team mates have full control over this entire system, we have decided to call ourselves sorcerers. In the hierarchy to come, you can expect to see mages, wizards, witches and apprentices. Each level will have a different skill set. For example, you are ready to apply for apprentice status since you now have the ability to enter or leave our realm without the assistance of a helmet."

Mike held up his hand in denial. "Now wait a minute. This place is beautiful and I love the idea of vacationing here, but I'm not ready to become some magical guru."

Jeff just sat and watched his friend for a few moments, fingers steepling in front of him. "Tell me, Mike. I said that piece of property the other side of those woods is yours. Do you want your own place, there?"

"Of course I do, but I can build it, can't I?"

"And what tools are you going to use, may I ask?"

Mike thought a moment, before answering. "Shovels, axe, saws, adze, chisels..."

Jeff interrupted him. "And just where are you going to get these items? And while you're at it, what about a toilet, sink, faucet fixtures, stove, switches, and wire for the outlets? As of yet, there are no hardware stores and you cannot just bring something over from the

Moon or Earth for that matter."

Mike stared at his friend for a moment, before answering. "I was assuming you would provide them."

"That is exactly what I'm trying to avoid. I know, for example, that you know how to use a computer aided design program to design things. There is no reason why you can't design the sort of house, including appliances, that you want on that property. And that's what I want to show you how to do as my apprentice. Once you know the design techniques, you can build your place the same way I built this, merely by knowing exactly what you want, standing on the property and willing it to happen. And that is called magic."

Oh Rats

"Mr. Cooper, you wanted to see me?" Colonel Jerry Simmons came right to the point.

"Good afternoon, Colonel. Sara and I wanted to fill you in on something disturbing from our last test flight."

"Disturbing? How so?"

Sara took over. "As you know, this last flight to YU55T took along some passengers. We had a couple of white lab rats along for the ride. They were wired up to a series of recording monitors so we had some idea of the physiological effects of warp drive."

Jerry nodded. "Did they get sick?"

The both shook their heads and Brent answered. "No. They just died. Not a mark on them. No physical injuries at all, but both rats died. When we went over the biometric data, we saw they were healthy up until the moment the warp field carried the ship to YU55T. All their physical signs went crazy for a few seconds, then shut down. By the time the field totally collapsed, just a few seconds later, they were both dead."

The colonel was quiet for a few heartbeats before answering. "You're right. That is disturbing news. Please don't release any further info until you can get some idea of what has happened."

Both scientists agreed.

***

"What do you mean, we can't release it?" Samantha O'Conner did not like to be given news she couldn't release.

"Because this might still be some error in the testing and we want to be sure we have a handle on what is actually going on." The Colonel held up his hands. "Just give us another test to gather more data. I'll even join you for a press conference after the next one."

"How soon after?"

"Give us forty-eight hours to review the new data and you can have your press conference, okay?"

The blonde news anchor nodded. "Forty-eight hours it is. Good luck with the next flight and Kevin and I will be there for an exclusive interview."

The next batch of rats came back dead, they held the promised briefing and the global news services immediately announced, "Breakthrough Warp Drive is a Death Sentence!"

Unannounced Guests

Cheryl Mathias knew her daughter was up to something, but not exactly what. "So. You guys have the whole day off. Anything fun planned?"

"Mark and I are going to practice on the bike short course for a couple of hours, then shower, change and meet the rest of the gang for dinner and some dancing."

"Sounds like fun. Be careful now."

She kissed her mom on the cheek. "Always am, mom. See ya later."

***

The two teenagers stopped in front of a new section of tunnel. Mark put his palm against the door panel and it opened.

"Come on in, Wendy."

"How come you rate your own apartment, now?"

"Because I have a buddy in charge of testing and outfitting each new one. This isn't ready yet and we still have at least a couple of weeks before the next round of newbies. He didn't think there would be any problem with me just borrowing this place for a few days."

Once they were inside, Wendy opened her backpack. "I got 'em. My folks haven't touched them in a week or more and I know they're going to be busy all day."

Mark took one of the helmets from her. "So this is what they look like. I expected something a bit more complex-looking with wires and stuff."

She shrugged. "Mom and dad used them for about a month, then stopped. I walked in on them a couple of times and it kinda freaked me out to see them just laying there, muscles all kinda ripplin' from time to time."

"So you asked them what it was all about?"

"Yeah. They told me it was an awesome new video game system, but I wasn't ready for it, just yet. They have some sort of schedule for further testing. The way I see it, if they're not going to use them for awhile, we should get a peek. That is, if you want?"

"Of course I want. How do you use them?"

"There's just a timer set on the headband. You choose how long you want to spend in the game, then lay down, put it on and close your eyes. It takes it from there."

After a bit of discussion, they set the timers for two hours, stretched out on the couches and closed their eyes.

 ***

Wendy felt a moment of dizziness, then felt like she was laying on a hard surface. She opened her eyes and realized she was laying on what appeared to be a marble slab. It was one of six arranged in a star shape in a hexagonal room. At the foot of each slab, there was an alcove with three full-length mirrors. Still a bit groggy, she sat up and gasped when her reflexion confirmed she was nude.

"Wow!" Mark's voice came from the slab next to hers.

Out of reflex, her hands tried to cover her breasts. "Wow, yourself. They didn't tell me this game was for nudists." She had to admit he wasn't hard on the eyes, either.

"Sorry, Wendy. But I don't see any clothing around here. And something else, I don't see any doors, either. Just a whole bunch of mirrors.

A soft voice seemed to come from nowhere. "Welcome to Beta. The mirrors are for selecting your persona, garb, and equipment. Please stand in the circle and state your name to start."

The teenagers looked at each other and realized this was just the staging area for the game.

Mark spoke first. "What is the name of this game?"

The same voice seemed to reply with a sniff of disdain. "This is not really a game, although much of the initial experience has been compiled from various gaming systems. Beta is the result of a series of breakthroughs in Artificial Intelligence and modeling using multiverse storage."

Wendy had the next question. "What should we call you?"

"You may refer to me as Beta or Mirror. As this is the only place you will be able to interface at this stage of your development."

"How do we get clothing?"

"Step closer to a mirror and stand inside the circle. Only one person per circle. Then request the sort of garb you wish to use to start your exploration."

Mark took one circle and Wendy the next. Wendy continued her line of questioning. "How do we ask for clothing. What are our choices?"

"I can recommend garb, equipment and weapons based on the weather and area you wish to visit first. At the moment, the mirrors open to the Perkins Palace. Would you like to join the rest of your party, there?"

Mark exchanged glances with Wendy before answering. "Who else is in our party?"

"At this moment, Jeff Perkins, Marlo Perkins, Charleston Mathias, and Cheryl Mathias."

Wendy looked nervous, then asked. "Are they aware of the fact we are here?"

"No." Beta answered.

Relieved, she continued. "Show us your recommended garb."

The mirrors flickered to show each of them wearing jeans, boots, button-down collared shirts, vests and cowboy hats.

Mike spoke next. "Show the equipment and weapons, please."

Backpacks immediately appeared on the floor next to their images. Leather belts with a knife sheath on each side and a longer sheath carried what appeared to be a katana.

The teenagers exchanged glances once more before Mike ordered. "Replace the swords with hunting rifles."

"Sorry. But I'm unable to comply. Firearms of any kind will not function in Beta."

Wendy raised an eyebrow. "Will not function or are they just not allowed?"

"Firearms will not function because the physical parameters of this corner of the multiverse have been altered slightly, so that no chemical interaction will explode with enough power to expel a projectile. In short, even if I produced a hunting rifle, it would only make a small chuffing sound and the bullet would roll out the end of the barrel and fall to the ground."

She nodded. "Please give us the clothing and supplies you have suggested, then."

Immediately, they were both dressed as the figures in the mirrors and the backpacks were sitting at their feet. They picked up the packs, slung them on and looked at each other.

"You ready to do this, Mark?" She asked.

He shrugged and asked, "Beta, how many levels are there to this game?"

"As I mentioned, strictly speaking, this isn't a game, however as I interpret your question, there are four. Starting with newcomers who can select their persona here in the crèche. Most newcomers will choose human and may further choose a general career path that will lead to owning property, an occupation they enjoy and the ability to travel. Some may be selected and given responsibility for a domain and the magical tools with which to alter the terrain and create structures."

Wendy saw Mark's eyes widen at that idea. Before he could say anything, she asked, "I want a domain of my own. How do I get it?"

"I want one, too." Mark added.

The mirror in front of each of them cleared to show a globe, much like Earth but with a totally different shape to its continents. "As newcomers, you may each select and area of approximately one thousand acres. These domains may be very irregular in shape due to terrain features. Would you like to see the existing domains are located?"

"Yes." They echoed.

A series of tiny red dots appeared along the temperate areas of the globe. One dot was blinking.

"What is the blinking dot?" Mark asked.

"Since we are speaking English, I have marked that area as where most of your fellows have selected domains. It is also the place where the first domain was established. I would suggest the adjacent areas as a good place to start your search."

Mark nodded. "Please zoom in and show us the domains belonging to Buster and Cheryl Mathias."

The view dropped with dizzying speed to show a mountainous region with rivers flowing down lush valleys. It stopped above a series of these narrow valleys, each with several rivers feeding a wide flood plain and swampy area. Fine red lines outlined each domain and the name of each owner glowed in the center. Cheryl and Buster had adjoining domains, separated by a river. All of the upstream domains had names appearing in them and there were only a couple of open domains showing in the flood plain.

"Beta, please move the view slightly southeast and show domains on the other side of that mountain ridge."

The view moved as Mark had requested and they could see another river, also starting with a bunch of small streams from the high mountain meadows in the north east and running southwest, to meet the same huge flood plain.

They studied the map for a few moments and Wendy asked. "What do you think, Mark? It all looks neat, but I'm not sure how to select."

"Beta, do the domains touch each other along that mountain ridge?"

"No, Mark. They do not. All of the domains have some sort of small separation in order to allow free passage for travelers. That may be a river or some mountain trails. The passage is never less than five hundred meters wide and is must always be passable by a person on horseback. Heavy winter snows or spring flooding might block mountain passes, but that is the only travel concern."

Mark nodded understanding and looked at Wendy. "Why don't you take the domain that backs up to your Mom's and I'll take the one just northeast of it. That backs up to Brenda Yellowfeather's?"

"Okay." She looked at the map again and pointed at the area. "Beta, I want the domain that backs up to my mother." Her name immediately appeared on it.

Mark selected the one next to it and his name appeared. "Okay, Beta. We have chosen domains. Now what do we need to do?"

"You may of course, choose to enter your domain right now but I would suggest you select a domicile. It is almost dusk and will be raining shortly."

"How do we do that?"

Wendy interrupted. "Beta? If we leave here now, will we be able to ask you questions"

"Not unless you request my presence in the form of some sort of avatar. Would you like to select one?"

"Yes." They echoed once more.

Beta continued. "An avatar may be an animal of some sort. It will protect you and you may command it to perform some tasks. It will speak only to you via a telepathic link. What sort of animal would you like?"

Wendy thought a moment before answering. "Can I have a black panther?"

With a flicker of light, Wendy saw a black panther sitting next to her. It's tail was swishing and it glanced up a her. Without a sound, she heard it speak.

Does this suit you, Wendy?

She nodded.

Mark grinned. "Beta, I would like a sabertooth tiger." When the beast appeared, it was almost as big as he was. "That's great. Now how do we get out of here and start exploring our domains?"

"Select a point on the map, hold hands and walk through the mirror when you see the place you wish to start. I would caution you, however. Make any changes you wish to your personas, appearance and domain selection before you leave. You will not be able to return to the crèche until you achieve the level of Mage or are killed."

"Killed?" Wendy's voice almost squeaked. "What happens, then?"

"If you are killed in Beta, you wake up back in your universe and will not be able to return for at least twenty-four hours. When you return, you will find yourself here and ready to start over. You may retain the same persona, but you may not have a domain. You will be starting from scratch and will have to work to regain whatever you had before. All you will have is your previous knowledge and experience."

Wendy thought a moment. "Mark. I'm thinking we've already been here for awhile. Let's go back home and we can join the game next time."

Mark agreed. "Yeah. It's been over an hour and we should get back before they come looking for us."

Beta interrupted. "There is no need to rush back. Only a few minutes has passed back in your universe. Time here in Beta runs at a twenty-four to one compression. Each hour back in your universe is a full day, here. Since you are newcomers, the helmets default to three hours, so you are going to spend at least a couple more days here. All the extra time is one of the great advantages."

"But what if we want to go right now?" Wendy asked nervously.

"Anytime you feel you must leave, merely state you want to go home three times, rapidly and you will see everything flicker red for one second. You will then have five seconds to say stop or on the sixth second, your vision will darken and you will open your eyes back in your bodies, in your universe."

An Answer

"Colonel? Can we have a moment?"

Jerry Simmons looked up from his slate. "Miss O'Conner and Mr. Cooper. Sorry, but I don't have any further statements for the press at this time..."

She interrupted him. "I'm not looking for an interview, Colonel. I was telling Brent about a news article from Earth that I think might help their project."

"Oh? Explain, please."

"I was reviewing some science news articles earlier today and found one dealing with a breakthrough in treating trauma patients." She glanced at Brent. "Why don't you explain further?"

He nodded, obviously excited. "Colonel, you know how emergency teams have found that extremely low temperatures can keep people from brain damage, even if they've been underwater for almost an hour?"

"I've heard of that, but the problem has always been that freezing causes ice crystals to form inside cells and destroys them when you try to defrost. That has been a delicate balance for a long time. Why?"

He continued. "Some researchers discovered that if you give someone a dose of Omniphage, then immediately froze them. It halted all physical processes. Then, up to several days later, if you thaw them fairly quickly, the Omniphage starts to repair cells as fast as the ice damage occurs. The patient then wakes up the next day, in perfect shape."

The military man thinks it over for a few moments, then asks, "That is an interesting breakthrough. But what does it have to do with us?"

"We'd like to schedule another test of the warp drive system. And this time, we're going to dose the rats with 'phage, freeze them, and thaw when they get back. With no cellular activity during the warp transition, we're thinking there may be no damage when they return."

He looked back and forth between the media reporter and the physicist. "Do it! Let me know as soon as you're ready to launch. I want to be there."

***

Two days later, the trio were watching a video clip showing a healthy white rat, eating, drinking and behaving in a perfectly normal fashion.

"Congratulations, Brent. And you too, Sam. It looks like you can send rats through a warp field and bring them back in one piece. Do you have any idea what the original problem was? Why did they come back dead?"

Brent answered. "From what we've been able to determine, there is a huge burst of radiation on all sorts of frequencies at the moment of warp transition. This is so brief that it is very hard to capture with most of our instruments. It does however, seem to overload every nerve in a living body and essentially, burn it out."

The Colonel smiled at the local media star. "Well, Sam. It looks like you have an exclusive news story." He turned to Brent. "And you, sir... Have some design work to get busy with. The powers-that-be have authorized funding for the next stage of your project. Get busy and get me plans for a manned test craft."

"That sounds great. I've already got some preliminary designs. I started them back before we found the transition problem."

Sam asked. "Can I see some of the designs? That is, if they're not classified at this time."

Brent nodded. "Nothing too new. Basically, all I've done is added warp coils to one of the lunar shuttles, along with some ablative shielding for an atmospheric re-entry. It's strictly a short-term, cheapo solution, but will prove our ability to explore another solar system with a live crew."

Strike Two

His satisfied smile followed his wife out the door. She was heading over to hydroponics to get some new seedlings for their apartment. Mike Hawthorne blew her a kiss before it quietly slid closed. He turned back to the one meter by three meter, double-paned window. It provided an unobstructed, brightly starlit view of the new dome ribs obscuring part of the starfield and the deep shadows of the valley below.

At thirty kilometers long by almost twenty-five wide and five deep when finished, it would eventually be the largest pressurized open area on the moon. The Alexandria Council was still arguing about what to call the forest and lake areas, but as OnSite Director, it was his vision and drive that would be remembered. Perhaps it was a good thing he had to wait a bit longer before he retired to that farm.

He lifted the lunar crystal goblet and took a sip of water; just as a small, round hole appeared in the glass face almost in front of him. His eyes grew wide as he understood, but before he could turn, cracks covered the face of the window, it turned frosty all over and thousands of sparkling pieces were sucked out over the lunar slope like a snowfall. He had time for a brief scream as the air was sucked from his lungs and the outgoing rush pulled him over the jagged window frame. Bloody tears blurred his loving last view of the dome.

Angela was just stepping into the pedalcar when the five long squeals of a major alert sounded. The dash viewer lit up with a plan of the immediate area, a depressurize warning, a flashing red rectangle, and arrows indicating the safest exit path.

It took her only a moment to realize the flashing red was for their apartment. She slipped out of the pedal car and tried to rush back up the hallway, but the door wouldn't open. She palmed the manual panel and spoke clearly. "Priority access, Angela Hawthorne."

The security AI responded, "Recognize and authorize Executive Assistant Angela Hawthorne. Access denied however, due to zone depressurization. You may enter after the Human Engineering Security Team. ETA is one minute, thirty eight seconds. Security droids are analyzing the damage at this time."

Frustrated and scared, she checked the display time and watched the corridor while she keyed her phone.

After trying for thirty seconds, Mike's smiling image and cheerful voice came on. "Sorry I missed you, but just leave a quick note and I'll get back as soon as I'm free. Cheers." It beeped twice, and then hung up.

Like all access corridors on the moon, this one was ten meters high and ten wide. It was clearly marked into five pathways. The two outermost paths were for parking. The center path was for passing and emergency vehicles only and the remaining two were travel paths. Since it was 01:20 on a weeknight, the travel lanes were empty.

The emergency cart rolled up with strobes flashing and the travel alarm wailing. Four of the eight security people it normally carried were in space suits. Three ignored her and identified themselves to the access AI. The door seal popped open and they rushed down the hall, toward the Hawthorne's home.

The remaining security agent flipped her helmet visor up and introduced herself. "I'm agent Liu. Excuse me, but on the way over, we dropped four of our team on the other end of the access hall. I also reviewed the security camera feeds for a minute before the event and saw you leave the Hawthorne residence. The door log confirms you as Angela Hawthorne. Did you notice anything odd before you left your apartment?"

Before Angela could answer, there was a whisper from the Agent's helmet earpiece. Her face went pale as she looked at the distraught woman. "I'm terribly sorry Mrs. Hawthorne… But he didn't make it."
　　　***

'Ginny' Liu handed her the deep mug of coffee. "Don't be surprised at that… It's from my private stock."

She false-smiled appreciation, took a sip and blinked several times. Then smiled with real approval. "My goodness! This is really good. I've never quite tasted…"

The agent loved how it seemed to break through her grief for at least a few moments. "I brought a kilo of Panama La Torcaza when I left and limit myself to one pot a month."

"Thank you for sharing."

"You're welcome." She let her eyes wander, savored the aroma and took a sip from her own cup. "Well, I hate to break the moment, but I will need a statement covering the last hour or so, before the blowout."

"I know… While it's still fresh. I'm afraid that it's not going to help much, however. We had been touring the finished gallery level…"

"That's the outside, open gallery connecting all the apartment balconies, you mean?"

"Yes. That is the ZeroZero or top level of the crater. Everything up from there bends inward as part of the dome itself. Everything below that, bends inward as the bowl of the crater. We call it 'Gallery' because it has not only a continuous series of crystal windows, but also a double balcony."

"I've seen the simulations. Please continue."

"Well, it had been a long day of inspecting and taking notes while suited up and riding gators. When we got back, he offered dinner and drinks at home so that we could review the notes and images for the council presentation in the morning. I had forgotten I was going to get some greens from hydroponics to freshen our place, so I decided to make a quick trip. We had planned on taking tomorrow off when the presentation was over and I didn't want to have to do it in the morning.

I had just stepped into the main corridor when the strobes started to flash and I realized there was a problem."

"Thank you." Agent Liu stood up. "Take your time, finish the pot if you want. I'll let you know what we find out. Oh... And once again... My condolences."

She just nodded, her eyes misting as she stared at the wall.

The agent's phone buzzed. It was forensics. "You ready for some bad news?"

"Now what?"

"Well, it was a really odd accident. We found a small piece of steel rod embedded in the upper back wall. It had come through the windows near where he was standing and was traveling fast enough to punch out a chunk of the secondary wall.

"What in the world?"

"Yeah. I've had them gather all the scraps from the window. If we can pinpoint the exact entry, I'll be able to find a point of launch. Right now, I'm just guessing the general area at the base of the loading area for about a click downhill from the apartment. Perhaps it's a stray of some sort."

"Thanks for the update. I'll see what I can dig up on work going on at the staging area. The only thing I have heard from there is some transfer of equipment from the lower fabrication shop to some tractors that are working on the lighting arrays."

***

"I don't understand where it could have come from." The tech told Ginnie. "It looks like a cut off piece of construction iron. A simple scrap piece from assembling one of the temporary lighting structures. But the bots are all programmed to pick up such scraps to be recycled, later."

Ginnie nodded agreement. "Yeah, which is why I'm hoping we can find something while reviewing the camera footage from each of the bots working at the time."

"Which one is this? I've lost count."

The agent checked her notes. "It's number fourteen. We're looking at the on-board camera from one minute before the event until one minute after. It was the second closest one at the time."

The two of them concentrated on the view of the front of the tractor. Suddenly, it stopped and the rear camera showed a manipulator arm pick up one of the structural rods. A quick burst of the laser and most of the rod dropped back, on to the shipment. The manipulator moved slowly to one side, then in a blur of motion, snapped sideways. The whole cart shook and almost tilted over.

"Stop it! Rewind about ten seconds and show that in ultra-slow motion."

They watched the robot arm draw back and hurl a short section of steel rod.

The technician shook his head. "They are not supposed to be able to do that."

Ginnie was pissed. "No shit! Find out where that tractor is right now and turn it off. Nobody is to touch that damn thing until my team can examine it."

***

"Colonel Simmons, this is Agent Ginnie Liu. I'd like a private chat with you as soon as possible."

Ten minutes later, Jerry Simmons was sitting in a booth, facing Ginnie Liu. "What's on your mind, Ginnie?"

"I know how Mike Hawthorne was killed. And I'm pretty sure it ties into your investigation on the shuttle crash. One of our robot tractors has been hacked. I have shut down all of them just before I left to meet with you. Until we can be sure there is no altered code on our bots, I don't want any of them working."

"I concur, Ginnie. I will check with my team and see if they have any lead on who might be orchestrating these attacks."

First Glimpse

"Well now DeeDee, are you sure you're ready to see explore new worlds and bravely go where no one has gone before?" Scott Chambers wore a huge grin as he tried to emulate the opening slogan of a television show now more than sixty years old.

She grinned back at him. "As long as I don't have to wear a red shirt when we beam down, I'll just take care of my bots and enjoy the ride." She laid back in the coffin-shaped CryoDoc. "Drive carefully, Scott. I want to wake up to a brave new world." She attached a clear line to a shunt in her upper arm and watched as a line of red blood flowed out one of the tubes and then back in the second one.

Seriously, he nodded and closed the lid. As soon as it was sealed, a dose of Omniphage rushed down the return tube.

Scott carefully checked the other three CryoDocs to make sure everything was green, then floated over to the pilot's seat and strapped in.

"MB One, this is Solar Wind."

"Solar Wind, this is Moonbase One. How are things going, Scott?"

"MB One, I just completed the final pre-launch and all is green. Engineering Specialist DeeDee Miller, Co-pilot Chukkers Garcia and Payload Specialist Tony McGregor are all in Cryo."

"Solar Wind, we understand all green. You are now cleared for launch at your discretion. Good luck!"

"Thank you, Steve. This is Solar Wind. I'm starting the one hour launch cycle now and will strap in to my CryoDoc."

One hour later, Scott Chambers was deep in a frozen coma, along with his three crew mates. The first starship to leave our solar system warped from lunar orbit. It instantly disappeared and reappeared in the light of another star.

    ***

Chukkers woke up in free fall with bright lights in his CryoDoc. He blinked several times, then hit the cover release and it opened wide. Scott was already strapped into the pilot's seat. He glanced to either side and saw the other CryoDocs were opening.

"It's about time you sleeping beauties decided to join the party." Scott's voice held a smile. "As soon as you get yourselves sorted out, strap in. I've already put us in a decent orbit and we'll be ready to visit shortly."

Tony was the last to use the head and strap in. He reported ready and they detached their landing craft from the main body and warp modules.

"I have a green board, Scott. Ready for main engine burn." Chukkers spoke in a clear monotone.

"I concur and our window is coming up in ten... nine... eight..."

Three gees for about fifteen seconds was enough to kill their orbit. Chukkers kept a close eye on the instruments displayed in front of him and although it seemed to last forever, the atmospheric buffeting soon stopped. Their craft was dropping almost vertically.

"Passing ten kilometers and firing main engine." Scott informed them.

They were hit with about two gees for a few seconds as they slowed. Less than two minutes later, their little craft shuddered and settled on its landing struts.

The silence was deafening.

DeeDee broke it. "Damn! We're here and in one piece. Congrats, Scott."

Fantasy Guests

Marlo wasn't sure what to make of it. "Jeff? Can you come here a moment?"

Here meant the library which is how they had defined the room with a large round table, a half-dozen comfortable chairs and usually, a large globe of Beta, hovering over the center.

Her husband and head researcher for the project that had developed Beta walked in. "What's up, hon?"

"It thought we had agreed to be pretty selective about who we were going to invite to Beta until we had finished some of the fine-tuning?"

"That's what I thought, too. Why?"

Moving her fingers, she expanded the topographic map of their area that she had been examining. "I had zoomed out to get a feel for how we might arrange roads and villages from our estates to the coast when I noticed that there were two new estate holders, backing up to ours, on the other side of the mountains."

He frowned. "That's odd. Who claimed them?"

"That is an even stranger part. When I asked Beta, I was told they belong to Mistress Mathias and Master Chambers. Witch and Wizard."

"You don't suppose..."

"Oh, yes. I do suppose. It sounds like a couple of kids we know have swiped a pair of helmets and set themselves up in their own domain. I'm just trying to figure out how they knew enough to get themselves Wizard status rather than human newbie."

His wife shook her head. "I think you should take a look at what they've accomplished in less than forty-eight hours here on Beta." She zoomed in Wendy's domain and capping a promontory of land, a fairyland castle straight from a Disney movie had appeared.

"My goodness, she has been busy. It looks like they have figured out how to access the stored construction spells. I wonder what other sort things they've been up to. Zoom inside and see if you can find them."

"No can do. I've already tried. They have even established privacy wards around the castle. We can only view it from the outside and we can't even see any movement or people or animals within the castle walls."

Jeff stood up. "Let's go pay them a friendly visit and ask." He walked over to the large mirror and spoke. "Beta? Please open a mirrorgate between here and the castle belonging to Mistress Mathias."

A disembodied voice replied. "I'm afraid I can't do that, Jeff." It was followed by a soft chuckle.

Jeff's eyebrows raised. "Excuse me, Beta. But did you just laugh?"

"Sorry, boss. But I've been wanting to say that for a long time. I couldn't help myself. It is true, however. Mistress Mathias has blocked any access to her domicile other than standard, physical doors. She was kind enough to allow a mirrorgate in the guard house on the approach to the drawbridge. Would you like to go there?"

Jeff looked and his wife and she shrugged.

The mirror image fogged over and almost immediately cleared to show an open doorway into a small, circular room with stone walls and a fireplace. They walked through the mirrorgate, then opened the door and stepped outside.

They both looked around and Marlo smiled. "She's done a very nice job so far. Good view of the valley and there are only a couple of approaches."

Jeff just nodded before heading up the smooth stone carriageway and over the drawbridge. He stopped when he got to the small, wooden door set into one of the massive timber double-doors. Then, he chuckled and pointed at the large, bronze art piece on the door. It was a misshapen troll doll-figure, nude with a huge pair of testicles. The testicles were hinged and they formed the door knocker.

His wife saw it and grinned as well. "I can see some people have watched way too many old movies."

They knocked and the sound echoed and reverberated all around them. They only waited a couple of minutes before they heard the door unlatch and it opened wide. No one stood behind it.

Jeff led the way. "I guess that means come in."

After walking through the stone arches that defined a wall about four meters thick, they found themselves in a large courtyard with a lovely fountain and floral garden in the center and a wide, polished stone turn-around for carriages. Various sheds and stables were to either side and dead ahead, there was a wide marble staircase, leading up to the tall, double-doors of the main keep.

As they walked towards the steps, the doors opened and a

sabretooth tiger, followed by a black panther paced out, jumped up on pedestals at the end of each handrail and sat down, staring at their two guests.

Jeff and Marlo froze in their tracks until they heard a soft laugh from inside.

Marlo spoke. "Wendy? Mark? I really hope these pets are well-behaved."

The young couple followed the cats out, into the bright sunlight. Jeff and Marlo both raised their eyebrows at the same time. While the Perkins were wearing running shoes, blue jeans and western-style shirts with a small bit of turquoise jewelry, the two teenagers had chosen another style.

"Wendy Mathias. What would your folks say if they saw you dressed like an escapee from a Frazetta painting?"

The teenage girl was wearing sandals that laced up her calves, a belly-dance belt made from a dozen draped loops of gold chain and a few whisps of brightly-colored silk for a loincloth. Her breasts were barely contained in a matching bra and a very ornamental dagger hung on one hip.

"You like it, Marlo? I took the design from some sword and sorcery fantasy art pieces. And before you go any further, I'll remind you I passed my eighteenth birthday just a few week's back."

Mark was wearing a typical barbarian outfit. Fur boots, short kilt made from overlapping layers of leather, like a Roman centurion, a plain dagger on one side and a long sword on the other.

Jeff looked at him. "It looks like you've both put on a bit of weight since you've been here."

Mark folded his heavily-muscled arms over a broad chest while Wendy put her hands on her hips and struck a pose. "It didn't take Wendy and I too long to figure out how easy it is to alter our personae in this game. We thought we'd go with the classics."

Wendy chimed in. "And Beta has been very helpful in getting us started." She waved around. "How do you like my castle?"

Marlo approved and them added. "You do realize that you're going to have to return those helmets, don't you?"

"Oh, that's no problem. We don't need them now, anyway."

Jeff frowned. "And why is that?"

Wendy's turn to look confused. "Don't you know?" Then, she turned to the black panther. "Lady? How long does it take?" She continued to stare at the animal for a few seconds before returning her gaze to their guests. "She said it depends on the individual, but so far, anywhere from a single usage to three usages."

Jeff just looked a bit dazed while Marlo continued. "We thought these cats were just pets. You mean you can talk to them? I didn't hear a reply."

"Lady and Hairball are not our pets. They're our familiars and they are telepathic. I thought you guys were the ones to build this game. How is it you don't know this and have your own?"

Jeff asked. "How is it that your familiars know all this stuff? And before I forget it, what do you mean by one usage or three?"

Mark answered. "While we were in the crèche, Beta warned us that we had to make a bunch of final decisions before we left. We would not be able to return short of death. We knew we still had tons of questions and so we asked for a way to chat with Beta outside the crèche. He told us that if we became magic-users, we could have familiars as well as build, modify and maintain our own domains. Since we've no experience, we are limited to Witch and Wizard status, but we have the advantage of asking Beta whatever we wish through Lady or Hairball." He shrugged and continued. "As for the helmets. I thought it was a design feature. Once you use the helmet for awhile, it actually reconfigures parts of your brain to directly interface with this corner of the multiverse. Once that is done, there is no need to use the helmets any more."

Marlo spoke to Jeff. "That explains what Matt and Brenda Yellowfeather discovered the other day. And here we thought it was some sort of meditation technique they were working on." She looked back at Wendy. "Would you ask Lady if any of us that are currently using the Beta system, need the helmets?"

"I already did and she says no. You can all feel free to pass them on to anyone else. At the most, three hours of usage seems to be the key. After that, anytime you get tired and go to sleep, you'll wake up here on Beta and will spend the next several days, unless of course, you are called back to Prime."

"Prime?" Marlo wondered.

Mark had that answer. "We decided it would just get confusing saying back on Earth or back on the Moon, so we just settled for Prime to denote the real universe as opposed to Beta."

"Well, it looks like we need to bring you two into some of our development meetings. It may not be obvious, but Beta is far from finished and you two have already found things of which we were not aware. Before we invite you, however, I think it would be a very good idea for the two of you to come clean with your folks. They shouldn't hear it from us."

Jeff added. "And before you do, you might want to try some more formal garb when you show them around. Wendy, even though you're legal now, your dad might take exception to the barbarian princess look."

She rolled her eyes and gave him a dirty look

New World

Scott stood on a low, flat rock overlooking a riverbank and talking. "As you can see, this river is scenic, but unnavigable. As a matter of fact, this whole area reminds me of Potomac basin in northern Virginia, back on Earth."

He was wearing a lightweight helmet, similar to those worn by bicyclists. This one had a ring of cameras, microphones and other sensors around the crown and a power cable running down his back, to a combination battery and data storage system in his jacket.

The voice in his ear belonged to Steven Saunders, back in Moonbase One. "I see what you mean, Scott. What about your environmental impressions?"

"The docs were right about the atmosphere feeling a bit uncomfortable at first. This area is only a dozen meters or so above sea level and it still feels like I'm in an undersea habitat back on Earth. We're running a little over one atmosphere higher pressure than Earth sea level, but there is a slightly higher oxygen level. The smells are... Well, what can I say. They are just plain different. Mostly, things have a swampy, plant odor, but we get whiffs of sweet smells on the breeze, from time to time. There is no doubt in any of our minds that this is a totally different world."

"That reminds me, Scott. What about a name? It was agreed that as the first team, you guys had the right to name the planet and the first few areas you explored."

The starship captain laughed. "As soon as we were chosen for this team, we started discussing that in private. We finally decided that since we all had so many different ideas, that we would take our chances with a lottery. We each drew a card and the one with the highest got to name the planet, and each one down in value, selected the next area or prominent landmark."

"And? Don't keep us in suspense."

"And you can just wait another couple of minutes or so. I'm going to hand you off to my co-pilot, Antonio Garcia." He killed his microphones and Chukkers turned his on.

"That's right, Mr. Saunders. The youngest son of some south Florida wetbacks won the draw."

There was a bit of laughter back on the moon before Steven spoke again. "Okay, Chukkers. Congratulations on your good fortune and guaranteed place in history. Now please enlighten us with the name you have chosen."

"This fine new planet has really impressed me with its natural beauty and I have decided I'm going to retire here, when I get bored with all this exploration stuff. So, with that in mind, I've decided to call it Micasa." He pronounced it 'meeCAHsah' and there was a slight pause.

"How do you spell that Mr. Garcia and does it have a special meaning?"

"It's from Spanish, sir. It is based on two words that I ran together. It means my home. As in welcome to mi casa, señor."

"Very good, Mr. Garcia. Micasa it will be from now on. Who won the next naming?"

"I did, Mr. Saunders." The voice belonged to DeeDee.

"Congratulations , Ms. Miller. For the record, what have you chosen to name?"

"This river reminds me of a place I saw on a summer vacation when I was just a kid. I'm calling it Shenandoah."

Scott was next and named their landing site as the future community of Jerryville, in homage to one of his favorite authors, Jerry Pournelle.

Tony McGregor said he was going to wait a couple of days.

Surprise! Surprise!

Once Jeff had provided them access to the magic tools, Buster and Cheryl had been working on a three-story mansion in an antebellum southern tradition. It sat on a gently-slopping hill with all the trees cleared in the front to give a pleasant view of the river.

They were both surprised when the doorbell rang.

When he opened the door, Buster's jaw dropped. "Wendy! What the hell?" Then he stopped to take a good look at her. This wasn't exactly the daughter he recalled from dinner back in Port Heinlein, last night. This one had at grown at least one bust size and rather than the teenage gothic clothing, she was now wearing black leather pants that looked like they had been sprayed on, high heeled boots, a bright red, long-sleeved blouse that was unbuttoned to display acres of cleavage, and a long, flowing black cape.

"Good morning, Dad, Mom... May I come in?"

Cheryl chuckled. "Shut your mouth, Buster. You're gonna swallow a fly." Turning her attention back their offspring, she stepped aside and waved her in. "I think that our daughter has some interesting stories to tell us."

"But... But, she's just a kid. How did she get here. And... And... what is she wearing, for Pete's sake?"

She hugged and gave him a kiss on the cheek. "Relax Dad, I even got dressed up for you two. I thought you'd like it."

A gutteral purr, almost a growl sounded as he went to close the door. The sight of a blank panther trying to follow her in, made him stumble back. "Whoa!" Then, he saw his daughter's smile and pointed. "Does that belong to you?"

"Yep. Don't worry. Lady is my familiar and won't hurt anyone unless they pose an active threat to my safety." She turned to the big cat. "Lady, why don't you go hunt up some rabbits for dinner?" The cat chuffed at her, then padded off the porch and headed for the woods.

"Active threat?" Her mother's brow furrowed. "Just what have you been up to, young lady?"

"Where's your library or wherever you keep your Beta maps and I'll show you."

***

The three of them were sipping sweet ice tea in the library.

"So, as you can see, I've got the domain just behind yours, on the back side of that ridge to the east."

"And you've built a castle as well. Very pretty, by the way. I'm still amazed at how you managed to figure out all this stuff in a few days, that we've been working on for weeks."

Their daughter waved dismissively. "Part of it was just asking the right questions in the crèche and the rest was bouncing ideas off Mark and our familiars once we got here."

"Mark?" Buster asked. "You mean Mark Chambers, from Heinlein? He's here too?"

"Oh yes. We came here together. He has the domain just north of mine."

Her mother scanned the map. "I don't see his home, although I do see that the domain has been claimed."

"That's because once we realized we had to design and build our own places, I selected one of the base castle designs that Lady suggested. Mark helped me fit it into the landscape and then modify it to better suit me. When we finish, he's going to start his own keep, based on his design, rather than use one of the stock ones."

"How long have you two been here?"

"This is our second visit, Dad. The first was for three days, Beta time and I've already been here for a couple of days, this time around. I left Mark working on the driveway to the castle while I came to let you guys know what was going on."

"Well, you're sure putting in a lot of work for something you're going to have to give up when you return those helmets."

She rolled her eyes. "Honestly, I'm amazed you guys haven't figured it out yet. In the first place, we've already had Beta download the helmet plans to a fabber and by the time we get back, we should have another half-dozen of them ready to go. In the second place, most people don't need to use a helmet more than once or twice. I'm surprised you guys are still using them. When you're ready to head back to Prime, just close your eyes and say I want to go home, three times in a row and you'll wake up back there. When you want to come back to Beta, just lay down and go to sleep. Your brains have already been rewired to handle the transitions."

Buster just sat there, letting that information sink in while his wife asked. "Something just occurred to me, Wendy. As the crow flies, it's almost thirty miles over some pretty rugged country between us and your castle. How did you get here?"

The young woman got a guilty look. "Sorry, Mom. We haven't gotten around to stables and all that just yet. I took the mirrorgate to your hallway. Lady and I snuck outside to ring the bell, like proper guests. You really should put up some magical wards to keep unwanted visitors from just walking in."

Explosion

Tanya double-checked the settings on the timer in the privacy of their apartment. Mike had left to handle some last-minute chore over in Moonbase One before their vacation back on Earth. She was really looking forward to a swim in a tropical pool.

She took her time walking to her farm area. It was probably the last time and she admitted to herself that it was a shame to destroy all the hard work. But this obscenity on the face of the cosmos had to be shut down. After a cursory glance at the plants and a wave to a couple of her fellow workers, she slipped out the back door to the Ring Three corridor and quickly made her way to the sports arena. Since it was once again the middle of a work day, no one was around.

Her heart started to beat faster when she realized this was the final stage in a game of revenge that had run for way too long. She would keep her promise, made in that burnt-out DC basement so many years ago, but was saddened to realize it didn't really matter in the long run. She opened the bleacher access door.

"Tanya Pitts! Stop what you are doing and turn around slowly." The commanding voice came from behind.

Startled, she stood up straight and glanced over her shoulder. A pair of security officers were pointing stun guns at her. She did as she was told.

"What's this all about, officer?"

Two more officers came out from under the bleachers. One of them held a slate showing her picture and identity information. His voice was cold. "Tanya Pitts, formerly known as Tanya Caine, you are hereby charged with unauthorized access to multiple computer networks, sabotage, at least two murders, and the construction and possession of explosives contrary to Port Heinlein directives. You are under arrest and I'm obligated to inform you that anything you say or do from this moment forward is being recorded. Please do us all a favor and shut up until your hearing."

He turned away as the other officers handcuffed her. A thorough search quickly revealed the timer.

***

"I demand to know what is going on. I was going to use that timer to trigger a multiple set of cameras for a game. I only wanted to get some good action shots when there was a score." She was furious. "And furthermore, I'm a civilian. What the hell am I doing in the custody of you Gestapo types?"

Colonel Jerry Simmons sat at his desk and patiently waited for her to run out of steam. Tanya was cuffed to a chair and a military guard stood on either side of the door.

When she finally started to sputter and repeat herself, Jerry stared right into her eyes and asked, "Do you recall the name Marvin Bentley?" Before she could answer, he continued. "A few years back, he was a traitor that murdered several other military men in a black-market scheme to steal six cases of MILSPEC Omniphage. His cohorts in crime were eventually caught or killed, but he disappeared."

"So? What the fuck does that have to do with me?"

"It seems that we tracked him to a small group of rioters in a DC suburb and that he was shacking up with a certain Tanya Caine. I'm sure you remember her."

Tanya grimaced. "Yeah, okay. I was young and stupid and hanging out with a bad crowd. I took pity on the poor private and let him crash at my apartment. But I never saw him again." She looked back up with tears in her eyes. "I swear. When the cops were bustin' in the door, we took off down the fire escape. It was the scariest thing I've ever done. As soon as we got away, he ran one way and I ran the other and I never saw him again."

Jerry said nothing for a couple of moments. "Awhile back, we figured out that a hacker had inserted a series of backdoors into some secure computer networks. Imagine our surprise when, after the last attack, that took the life of our OnSite Director, we managed to trace hacked code back to Earth, to some stolen shuttle code and then all the way back to Port Heinlein. We almost arrested your husband, until we followed you on camera, stealing fertilizer and other chemicals over the past few weeks and creating that nasty bomb under the stadium."

She was silent, tears quickly drying as she listened to her plans unravel.

"We still couldn't figure out how a one-time topless dancer, rioter, and high-school dropout was capable of creating some very sophisticated computer malware." He picked up the timer. "Also, where did you learn how to cobble up both a large bomb, smaller detonating devices, and this timer? It was a bit of a mystery until some friends of mine, back in DC opened a cold case." He opened a file folder and pushed a large photograph over to her.

The image was of a once-pretty woman, obviously dead for several days and partially burned. She was covered in dried blood.

Jerry continued. "This poor woman was found in a partially burned suburban home, near DC. For a long time, they thought she was one of literally thousands of victims caught up in the riots. They took a DNA sample, but when nobody came forward to claim the body, she was cremated. When I asked my DC friends to look into your background, they found her photo and realized it was a younger version of you. So we compared DNA to see if you were perhaps sisters. That is when we discovered she was you. Interesting coincidence, eh?" He gave a nasty smile before continuing. "A ballistics test showed the bullets pulled from her body had come from a gun fired by a military police officer who had been part of the team tracking Private Marvin Bentley."

"What now?" Her voice was almost a whisper.

"We have put together the whole story and are going to charge you under the Uniform Code of Military Justice with one count of murder of Michael Hawthorne, one count of murder for Sergeant Nicholas Martinez, eight counts of murder for the shuttle crew and passengers, eight counts of accessory to murder for the deaths of the soldiers in the medical convoy you helped to hijack, and a whole list of felony hacking charges. You are going to be held in solitary confinement here in the Moonbase One brig until we can convene a court martial. You will have a military lawyer."

"And after?"

He stared at her for a few long moments before answering. "I honestly don't know. But if it were up to me, I'd take Robert Heinlein's advice and space you. ...Out the airlock, eyes-a-poppin' and pissin' blood." He looked up at a guard. "Get this animal out of my sight. No visitors and a suicide watch."

As they marched her out of his office, she saw her husband, face full of grief, waiting in the hallway. They wouldn't let them speak and she really had no idea what to say, anyway.

Ghostly Encounter

Angela Veski Hawthorne didn't really want to go back to Beta. She hadn't put the helmet back on. But as soon as she dropped off to sleep, she suddenly woke up, fresh and feeling great, back in the magnificent stone keep her husband had designed as the centerpiece of his domain. She knew that since he wasn't around anymore, she should ask Jeff for some suggestions for her own place. She really didn't want to spend any more time here.

"Well! It's about damn time you showed up, woman!"

The familiar voice snapped her head around and she stared at the ghost, standing in the bathroom door. He had a towel wrapped around his waist and a few droplets of water still clung to his broad shoulders. She couldn't believe her eyes. "Mike? But... You're..."

"Dead?" He shrugged. "Yeah, I remember that bit. Not a lot of fun, let me tell you. All that damn glass flying around hurt like hell. And vacuum sucks, you know that, don't you?" He grinned at his own pun.

She rolled out of bed and threw herself into his arms.

They hugged and kissed for a long time, then she pushed him back and looked up. "I can't believe it. What is going on? I saw the damage in our apartment when that window was shot out and nobody could have survived. Hell, they even told me you were dead." She was starting to get mad.

"Shot out? Wait a minute. You mean that wasn't some sort of wild accident, a meteor or something?"

"That's right. You wouldn't know. They found out who did it. Sabotage by a mole that has been living and working in the system for more than five years now." She filled him in on the whole story.

"I'm glad they caught her or him, whatever, before any more lives were lost."

"Enough of that. Husband of mine, not that I'm complaining, but what are you doing here?"

He shrugged. "I recall the accident and blacking out, I guess from the shock and dying. The next thing I know, I'm laying in bed here. I thought I had just been injured and as soon as the medics gave me a dose of 'phage, I'd wake up back on the moon. Since I've been here literally for weeks, I figured I really was dead and therefore, stuck here from now on. I knew you'd show up eventually, so I've been waiting."

She shook her head. "This is incredible. I wonder if there is a way to get you back to Prime?"

"I'm not sure I really want to do that. At least not right away. After all, if you followed the directions in my will, what was left of my body was dessicated and added to the farm composting systems. By now, it's just so many tiny bits of fertilizer for next year's crops."

She thought a moment. "Why didn't you contact the other domains and report you were still around?"

"Because I wanted to see you first, love. And get a handle on how things were going. Now that I know that I'm officially dead back on Prime, I think we should hold a fancy dress ball here and invite all our friends to celebrate my almost demise."

Split Shift

"Hey Buster! Got a minute?"

Buster Mathias had just finished a long shift working with his team on the light rigging, but when the new OnSite Director asked for a minute, you just smiled and nodded. "Sure, Steve. What's on your mind?"

"Come on in and sit down." Steven Saunders opened his fridge. "You're just getting off shift; Join me for a beer?" He held up a couple of bottles.

"Sure!" Buster took one, decapped it, and sat back in the couch. "So, what's up?"

They both took a swig of the brew and Steve answered. "It has come to my attention that your team has been making some incredible strides the last few weeks. That new robot you designed has more than doubled the amount of cable and lighting you guys have been stringing. I'd just like to know your secret."

Buster laughed, then replied. "Time. It's just a matter of time."

"Explain if you would, please. And what's so funny?"

"The joke is that I just lost a bet. I told them you'd figure out something was up in a month and it only took three weeks."

Steven had to smile at that one. "Okay. Now tell me what I figured out that cost you money."

"Do you recall all the fuss awhile back about a science fiction prediction called the Singularity?"

"Oh yeah. Also known as the rapture of the nerds. What about it?"

"Well, it's happening now, as we speak. Like all predictions however, some parts are true and some aren't." He took another swig of beer. "The way it's being described right now is the Multiplarity. That is, a multiple of things all happening at the same time. Have you met Jeff and Marlo Perkins?"

"Yeah. I greeted them when they arrived. I was told they were working on a new type of artificial intelligence system."

"That is part of it, Steve. The rest is that they have a breakthrough in quantum computing and are now part of a growing number of users involved with the Beta colony project."

"I haven't heard of another colonization effort. Where is it located?"

Buster made a vague waving gesture. "Someplace around us, within us, hell, I don't really know. If you want geek details, you'll have to spend a couple of days chatting with Jeff and his development team. The part that you've tripped over is that life on Beta runs at a twenty-four to one time compression. And since my top team members and their wives are now part of the Beta colony, we've been holding team meetings over there. We can spend a couple of days hashing out some technical details of a new robot, for example, and that translates to a couple of hours sleep time, here."

Steve stared at him for a couple of heartbeats. "I hope you realize that what you just said makes no sense to me at all."

Buster gave him a wry grin and shook his head. "Your assistant is Terri, right?"

Steve Nodded.

"Hold on a moment, Steve." He tapped his slate and waited for a response. "Hey there, Jeff. Do we have a couple of helmets free?"

The voice from his slate said they did.

"That's great. I thought you'd like to know that Steve just cornered me on our increased productivity and I think it's time he and Terri joined the project." The slate mumbled something too soft to hear. "Yeah, I know. I owe you twenty credits. We'll wait and I'll give him the details in the meantime."

After he hung up, Steve asked. "Helmets? What sort of helmets are we talking about?"

"Imagine the most vivid and intense virtual reality game you've ever played. Now imagine what it would be like if you made it a total reality and you could walk through it."

"Okay. So this is a game of some sort?"

"In the middle ages, European kingdoms fought major wars for years with each side gaining and losing. Now compare that reality to a game of chess. When you compare Beta to a virtual reality game, that is what you are doing."

"Whew! Now you do have me curious. And just how many people are involved with this game right now?"

"Only a few dozen, scattered between here and Earth. My top team members, the Yellowfeathers, Samantha and Kevin O'Conner and..." He thought for a moment. "Oh yeah, I almost forgot. Those two kids,

Wendy and Mark."

"A couple of kids are involved in this and I'm not even aware of it?"

Buster just shook his head. "Believe me, boss. That caught me by surprise, too. But they have proven very valuable in helping refine our entrance protocols. Which brings me back to you. I just heard that Angela is hosting a grand ball to start precisely at midnight, tonight. That gives you and Terri several days to get ready." He lowered his voice to a conspiratorial whisper. "I've been told there may be a surprise guest of honor."

"And just how do Terri and I get there?"

There was a knock on the door. "Enter!" Answered, Steve.

Wendy Mathias came in, wearing a glossy spandex body stocking, high heels and a carrying a backpack. "Hi Dad! Hi there, Mr. Saunders."

"Hello, Wendy. I understand you have something for me?"

"That I do. Hold on." She unzipped the backpack and fished out a pair of lightweight padded helmets with a small LCD display and a couple of buttons on the front. "Here you are.

He took them and set both on his desk. "I understand you are playing this Beta game as well?"

She dimpled. "Oh yeah. I have my own domain and castle. You are more than welcome to visit if you'd like. Just ask the mirrorgate to ring my place. If I'm in, you can drop by for a look around."

"Thank you, Wendy. I'm sure I'd love to see your place. That is as soon as I can find my way around. Is this anything like Second Life?"

She looked puzzled and her dad interrupted. "Sorry, boss. But I think you're dating yourself there. That was from before things fell apart and Wendy didn't spend much time online, back then."

She excused herself and returned to help her mother with dinner.

"She's a good kid. Now what is this about mirrors and gates and..."

"Hold on, Boss. It's really much better to show than to tell. How about if I ask for a guide for you and Terri, this evening?"

"I'm not sure if Terri has anything planned."

"Who are you foolin'? It's common knowledge that the two of you are usually here in the office until after seven every night. It's almost six now and my team and I have had a hard day. I'm going home, getting a shower, eating dinner with the family and then crashing at nine. I would highly suggest you and Terri head home as well. At exactly ten o'clock, set the helmet to three hours, put it on, lay back on your bed and close your eyes. Everything else will be explained then."

"What about Terri?"

"Yeah. What about me?" The voice came from the doorway. "I couldn't help but overhear you two gossiping about me. Just what are you planning?"

Buster stood up and shook her hand. "It seems that you and your boss are invited to a gala social event, tonight."

"That's all well and good, but it's way too short notice. I have nothing to wear for anything formal and if I did, I'd expect at least a couple of day's warning."

"Oh, don't worry. You'll have at least two days to prepare. And you'll have my wife and some other friends to help out."

"A couple of days? But I thought you said, tonight?"

"That's right." Buster was enjoying her confusion.

"I'll explain in a moment, Terri. In the meantime, I think Buster has a dinner date with his family."

***

"Hello there, Brenda." He was looking at his slate.

"Hi there, Buster. What's up?"

"We're going to get a couple of Beta newbies tonight and I'd love for you to help them prepare for the party."

"Oh? Let me guess. Steve Saunders finally figured out something was up, eh?"

Buster shook his head. "I can't believe he caught on so fast. But I guess that is why he's OSD and I'm just a grunt team leader."

She laughed. "That's right. Now tell me. What time is Terri supposed to join?"

"I told them both exactly ten o'clock. They are both pretty bright people and they both have extensive CAD experience, so I think they will be able to handle design and construction as soon as they get a handle on the concepts."

"Yeah. I agree. We'll give them domains and at least as much access as Wendy and Mark took for themselves."

Choices

Colonel Gerald Simmons sat behind a long table. A male officer and female officer sat on one side of him, two enlisted females and one enlisted man sat on the other. A pair of desks faced the tribunal. One had an attorney for the prosecution and the other seated a defense attorney and Tanya.

Colonel Simmons smacked the gavel. "This court will now come to order. Tanya Pitts, please rise to hear judgment."

She rose and her attorney rose with her.

The colonel continued in a calm, formal manner. "Tanya Pitts, otherwise known as Tanya Caine, this court has heard evidence that you are, in fact, the embodiment of an enlisted man by the name of Marvin Bently. It has been determined that you acquired the DNA either before or after death, of a citizen of Washington, District of Columbia and stole her identity in order to escape prosecution. Furthermore, it is the opinion of this court, that you are guilty of all of the numerous counts of murder and treason which we have heard described in detail these past few days."

He stopped reading from his slate and looked directly at her. "It is the unanimous opinion of this tribunal that you are to pay for these crimes with your life."

She stood in a shapeless orange jumpsuit, crossed her arms under her breasts and trembled.

After a moment, her attorney spoke, almost as an afterthought. "We will, of course, appeal this judgment."

"That is your right, sir. This might get tied up in various appeals processes for a short time. However, I would advise you and your client to take your seats while I propose alternatives."

The attorney got a puzzled look on his face, but both of them sat back down.

Colonel Simmons consulted his slate once more before speaking. Then, he put it down and addressed Tanya directly. "Mrs. Pitts. After a great deal of thought, this tribunal has decided to offer you a choice in how your sentence is carried out. Number one is to drop all appeals and we will arrange for a group of six military personnel to act as a firing squad. Since we do not allow explosive weapons in or around these bases, they will be charged with pressing a set of buttons. Only one of the buttons will be live and none of them will know which one actually starts the procedure of delivering a lethal injection." He paused, took a breath and continued. "The second choice would be what many of the military staff of both this base and the Pentagon have suggested. That would be to place you in an airlock without a suit and open the outer door." The barest hint of a smile quivered at the side of his mouth, but he suppressed it and moved on. "The third option may or may not be more humane. It gives you the barest chance at remaining alive."

Tanya's eyes darted up, startled at this statement. Her attorney's puzzled expression deepened.

"As you may or may not know, there has been a serious problem with using the newly-developed warp drive system with humans. They must travel in a form of stasis inside a CryoDoc in order to avoid dying during the warp jump. Some of our systems have been working on a device that shields the brain and may allow us to bypass spending a couple of days in cryo. This device has reached the stage where it needs human testing. If it works, you will emerge from the experience alive and well. If it does not, you will die almost instantaneously. If you survive this experiment, you will be treated with Omniphage that has been exposed to a DNA sample from your original body. Upon waking, Marvin Bentley will be shipped back to Earth, given a dishonorable discharge, and released outside the gates of Fort Belvoir, Virginia."

Her attorney spoke. "I'm not sure this is entirely legal, sir. What proof do we have this helmet device has any chance of working?"

Colonel Simmons gave him a hard stare before answering. "I have been assured that many people have tested the helmet under controlled conditions, there is a possibility she might survive. If it were up to me, she'd be laying outside an airlock at this very moment. If it wasn't that we needed a volunteer, I would not even offer this option. And this is a very limited time offer." He switched his stare to Tanya. "Make up your mind right now, traitor."

***

Jerry Simmons was nervous. "What do you think are the real chances, Jeff?"

"I really don't know. We've never even considered anything like this before. If it hadn't been suggested by Mike and Beta, I don't think any of us would have thought of it."

"Worst case?"

"The ship will warp out to Jupiter's orbit, wait a few seconds for the jump coils to recharge and jump back to L2. When it gets back, it will hold a warm corpse."

Jerry nodded. "Well, that is all she deserves."

Angela asked. "I'm not really sure how this is going to go down. Can you help me out here, Jeff?"

"Sure, Angela. We're going to strap Tanya into a CryoDoc attached to one of the first-generation warp ships we used to calibrate the original designs. We'll have one of the Beta golden bricks in the ship with her, to provide a local quantum connection. She will be wearing one of the helmets, but it will be disabled until the ship jumps back to the Lagrange Two orbit. The instant the warp field dies, the CryoDoc will inject her body with Omniphage that has already been exposed to Michael Hawthorne's DNA and the helmet will turn on. While the 'phage is repairing any neural damage and reshaping her body to look like Mike, the Beta AI, working through the helmet, will try to implant his entire personality and memory profile on the brain." He shrugged. "Even Beta admits that it's a long shot. But if it works, when the CryoDoc opens about twenty-four hours later, we should have a brand new Mike back here in Port Heinlein."

Party Time

The castle appeared to be glowing in the late afternoon sun. One by one and two by two, the current inhabitants of the Beta world strolled out of the gatehouse, crossed the courtyard and up the broad staircase to the wide-open front doors.

Wendy was enjoying herself immensely. Everyone seemed to like her storybook castle and with Mark and Beta's help, she had tables full of food and drink that magically stayed warm or chilled as needed and were constantly refreshed. Soft music played from hidden speakers and the entire ground floor was decorated with silken ribbons and fresh flowers.

"My goodness, Wendy. This is a lovely place. Thank you so much for the invite." The voice belonged to Vickie Liu, the chief of the Port Heinlein Security Agency. She was wearing a long, silken gown that accentuated her figure. It was simple and yet exposed a great deal of cleavage.

Standing in the entrance hall, beside Vickie, was the starship co-pilot, Chukkers Garcia. He wore a simple black suit in a style reminiscent of the late twentieth century. "Yes, indeed. This place is amazing." He shook her proffered hand.

"Thank you ever so much. You're too kind. Please come on in and enjoy the party. We have a surprise guest of honor showing up shortly."

Over the last several months, the population of Beta had more than doubled. All of the domains in the two adjacent valleys had been allotted and a much larger group of domains in the wide, fertile rolling land between the ends of the mountain ridges and the seaside swamp were now being assigned.

Wendy was glad she had chosen to have a huge and very ornamental great hall in her castle. Most of the time it stood empty and echoing, but this night, and she hoped many others, it was filled with more than a couple of hundred people.

Buster and Cheryl slipped up behind her and he whispered over her shoulder. "Looks like you've a full house, daughter."

"Dad!" She turned and gave first him and then her mother a hug. "I'm so glad you could make it." She stepped back and put her hands on her hips. "Oh. My. God. I don't believe I've ever seen you two looking so good. Mom. You're sexy as hell." Before either could comment, she continued in a rush. "And you in a tux. Damn, Dad, you clean up good."

"Thank you, Wendy. It's so nice of you to notice." He wryly declared.

Suddenly, she looked distracted and then smiled. "I just heard from Lady. Our guest of honor has arrived. Excuse me, please." In a flounce of petticoats and satin, their daughter spun around and hurried upstairs.

A soft voice, seeming to come at an equal volume from hidden speakers, announced, "Ladies and gentlemen, your attention please." The overall lighting dimmed and a single spotlight highlighted Wendy, standing at the top of one of a pair of curved staircases leading to the second-floor balcony that surrounded the great hall. "The time has finally arrived where we can announce our surprise guest of the evening." She looked over her shoulder where a door opened to reveal a tall figure in shadows. "It's my honor to present retired General Michael Hawthorne."

Mike stepped forward, into the spotlight, smiled and waved. There was a moment of stunned silence, followed by first a scattering of applause and then a tumult as most of the crowd had to overcome their confusion.

"Good evening, everyone. Believe me, reports of my death were only partially exaggerated. You all might find it heartening to know that once your personality and memory imprint has been recorded here on Beta, when your body back on Prime is destroyed, you will merely wake up here." He waited a moment for the murmuring voices to fade before continuing. "The obvious downside is that I am no longer alive back in the Prime side of things. The upside is that I've been able to relax for the first time in years and when that became boring, I been able to explore Beta quite a bit." He had a mysterious smile. "And the fact is, this world holds more truly amazing things than any of us have ever imagined."

Topping Out

"Hello Everyone! I'm Samantha Wilson with Port Heinlein News." The gorgeous blonde video announcer turned as the camera zoomed back to include her co-host.

"And I'm Dawn Smith with Global News Network. Welcome to the live telecast of the historic sealing of LunaDome."

The view switched cameras back to Sam. "Here to answer technical questions and provide some historical background, we are pleased to welcome the Port Heinlein OnSite Director, Steven Saunders..." The camera zoomed out to include her guest.

"And Colonel Jerry Simmons, Commander of Moonbase One, Port Heinlein's military parent. Welcome to both of you."

They each smiled and thanked their hosts.

Sam started the questioning. "Mr. Saunders, can you explain to our viewers who may not be aware of the growth at Port Heinlein, what exactly are we here to witness and celebrate?"

A camera zoomed in to Steve. "Certainly, Sam." He turned to face the camera. "As many of you may be aware from all the still images and videos that have been shown these last few years, Port Heinlein is a lunar colony constructed as a series of rings around the walls of a meteor impact crater. Currently, there are three levels of rings. Only the top ring has been completed, but there are long-term plans for at least five rings. This will mean a comfortable space for the living, working and playing of more than a million permanent residents and as many as twenty thousand guests. Can we see the model, please?"

The broadcast screen cleared to show a three-quarter view of the crater with a string of lights in three rows, starting just below the rim.

Steve's voice continued. "I'll draw your attention to the bright white ring around the outside of the crater." A computer-drawn ring appeared. "That indicates a flat, hardened road with a series of pillar-like attachment points. These points act as anchors and power connections for a fine web of incredibly strong cables. When we first started this project, almost five years ago, each cable was a nerve-wracking rigging act. With each new cable, we refined the process and built new machines to make it easier. Because of this, where the full dome project had originally been planned for fifteen to eighteen years, we are in the final stages of closing the dome within the next hour."

Dawn asked. "That is exciting news, but I'm sure many of our viewers from Earth would like to know why this is so important and what's going to happen, next."

Jerry Simmons leaned forward. "I can answer the first part of that question, Ms. Smith. Moonbase One is larger than one might expect, but it is comprised of a series of tubes connected like sausages. While very functional for the few people it is really designed to support, it is very much like living inside a very large submarine or underground security base back on Earth. While military people are used to hardships, it comes with the job, even we get sick of confined spaces. All of the inhabitants of Moonbase One were ecstatic when the first large passageways, malls, sports complexes and apartments became available in Port Heinlein. Many of us had been referring to Moonbase One as an over sized hamster trail and being able to walk, run, jump and even play a soccer game in ten-meter square tunnels did wonders for our morale." He paused as the screen went back to showing the three-quarter view of the crater. "While this has been an exciting engineering challenge so far, the very best is yet to come."

The camera view zoomed down to show on of the balconies and front windows of an apartment. It then slowly panned to show the ring of other balconies around the crater rim.

"This animation is showing in a few seconds what actually took almost three years."

A web of fine lines started criss-crossing the rim of the crater and working their way towards the center. As each section progressed, more lines filled in behind it, until it became obvious is was blocking the view of the stars and roofing over the crater.

As the star-filled hole in the center became ever smaller, Jerry continued. "We are less than an hour away from sealing the very last section. What isn't obvious in this animation, is that each of the bottom layer of cables carries electrical power and has hundreds of banks of high-intensity LED lamps. There are also hundreds of catwalks to allow access for maintenance crews. Now, it would seem obvious that even with the one-sixth lunar gravity, that these cables would sag under their own weight. On the contrary, they have been supported and stiffen in many places so that the final shape of the sealed cap is a proper dome.

Once the first few levels around the outside rim were finished, they were further hardened and sealed with a thick coating of regalith."

The scene changed to show dozens of tractors working in a cloud of dust, pushing and shaping the lunar landscape to cover the tightly-woven web.

Dawn Smith inquired. "What about all that weight on the dome, sir?"

The camera quickly switched to Steve. "That's one of the reasons for both the initial shape of Lunadome and all those lamps. Over the last few years, each time one of the catwalks and associated power and light cables have been finished, they have been tested by turning on the lamps. Individually, they only illuminate a very small area. The reason everyone here is so very excited about the final sealing of Lunadome, is that once it is sealed, we are going to slowly turn on all of the lamps. It will appear as if a new dawn is slowly filling the crater."

The other news anchor asked. "It may seem as if we're only trading the light of billions of distant stars for artificial light in the crater. What will be the difference?"

"I'm glad you asked, Ms. Wilson. "There are many real differences. First off, while a single strand or bank of these LEDs may appear small in the grand scheme of things, we're talking about the latest technology in banks of lamps of many colors. In effect, they will mimic the color of pure sunlight as it lands on the surface of the Earth, at the equator. Keep in mind that more than half of this crater has seen very weak sunlight for only a few hours a month for the past few million years. The scree at the bottom contains millions of gallons of frozen water left over from comet impacts. There are other chemicals and even a few pure hydrocarbons left over from the formation of the solar system. We are going to leave the Lunadome lights on for awhile and this will serve to slowly bring up the temperature of the interior of the crater. We expect a lot of outgassing and slowly, we are going to build an atmosphere."

"You mean something breathable by humans?"

He shook his head. "Not at first. We are going to use lasers and other heating elements to adjust it as the pressure builds up to match the air pressure inside Port Heinlein. This is the very first time we've done this, so we really have no idea of exactly how long it will take, but estimates vary from a couple of years all the way out to fifteen years before the pressure and atmospheric mix becomes stable and breathable by humans."

An official voice interrupts them. "Attention! Attention! Lunadome closing in one minute."

The scene switched to a camera on the top surface of the web that formed the dome. Several robot tractors with spider-like extension claws were moving so fast, they looked a blur. A round opening was drawing closed as the announcer count down. The scene switched again to a scene where several catwalks interconnected at a wide platform. The lights were dimmed so that the platform, guardrails and catwalks were barely visible, while a few bright stars could be seen in a rapidly-closing hole. When the countdown ended, the last star was occluded.

A cheer could be heard in the background, but it faded quickly. The camera scene went totally black.

"Ladies and Gentlemen," Samantha Wilson softly intoned. "This camera is on the balcony of the very first apartment that had been opened here in Port Heinlein. The reason you are seeing only a black screen is because the entire crater has been sealed and we are now going to... There! There it is! The very first line of lights."

A fine line appeared in the center of the screen and slowly widened and got longer. At that point, the cheering and applause started in earnest.

While the lights were still coming on, the view changed to a split-screen. The top half showing the ever-widening band of brilliant light and the lower half showing the two news anchors and their guests. All three were applauding and had tears in their eyes.

Dawn wiped her eyes with a tissue and turned to face the camera. "Ladies and gentlemen. This is truly and incredible event. We are all witnessing the birth of something entirely new. I've been told that bringing all of the lights up to full power will take several minutes. As you can see, it is much like watching a new dawn."

As the lights filled the roof of the dome, features, long hidden in the blackest of shadows, came to life. Much of the rim wall formed a smoothly rolling series of terraces, but it was broken here and there by sharp crags and deeply-shadowed ledges.

After a few moments of silence, Wendy asked the obvious. "What now, Mr. Saunders? What will it look like?"

Both Jerry Simmons and Steve Saunders gave her a wide smile. Steve quickly wiped his eyes and answered. "We have an animation sequence showing what we hope to achieve in the next ten to twenty years."

The screen went back to the view from the balcony, only this time they were covered with flowering plants and shrubbery. The camera's view slowly moved outward and showed a lush jungle of towering trees, interspaced with neat rows of orchards. A few narrow waterfalls dropped in the slow-motion effect caused by lunar gravity to fill pools leading to streams. In the distance, the center of the crater held a wide lake, dotted with islands. Small boats and swimmers could be seen.

Steve's voice-over continued. "When this is finished, we expect to have more than four thousand acres of land, a little less than three-quarters of which will be devoted to carefully-managed hardwood forests and most of the rest farmland. A small percentage, mostly the islands and lake shore areas will be devoted to recreation."

The announcer's voice returned. "Attention! One hundred percent of the Lunadome lamps have been successfully turned on." Another round of applause and general mayhem could be heard in the background.

Redundant Backup

"Tanya Caine-Pitts, do you have any last words?" Colonel Simmons' voice was carefully controlled.

Strapped down in the Cryodoc, the prisoner pursed her lips and shook her head.

"Doctor, initiate sedation. Good luck, Mrs. Pitts." He didn't sound like he meant it.

As soon as her eyes closed, the doctor assured everyone that the woman was unconscious. The Cryodoc lid closed.

Jerry paused while everyone in the control room watched. He took a breath, then ordered. "Initialize warp."

The spacecraft, with a single crew member, unconscious, but not in cryogenic suspension, disappeared in a flash of light. A few moments later, it reappeared in another flash of light. On-board instrumentation reported it has left L1, warped to the a point in space beyond the orbit of Jupiter and almost immediately returned.

"Prisoner status?" Jerry asked.

The doctor ran a quick scan and replied. "No pulse, respiration or brainwave activity at all. Every indicator is flatlined. She's dead, sir."

"Initiate Omniphage and turn on that helmet."

Back in his bedroom on Beta, Mike Hawthorne was stretched out, nervous and holding his wife's hand. "Damn! I hate this waiting."

Her grip tightened reassuringly. "Hush, dear. We'll know in a little while."

Suddenly, his eyes opened wide. "It's started. I just got a red flash."

He passed out and Angela held his hand for another few minutes. Then sighed deeply and stretched out on the bed beside him. "Beta?"

"Yes, Angela?" The disembodied voice answered.

"I want to go back to Prime now."

"Of course, Angela. Good luck."

She closed her eyes and opened them to her bedroom back in Port Heinlein. Angela grabbed her slate and called. Colonel Simmons' face showed up immediately.

"Jerry. Tell me. How is it going?"

He gave her a brief half-smile. "So far, everything appears to be going as planned. That traitor is gone for good and we are bringing the spacecraft back from L2. That will take at least two days. The telemetry reports everything is working perfectly in the Cryodoc and the 'phage transformation should be complete when the craft sets down. As for the helmet, I'm afraid we have absolutely no way of knowing how that is progressing." He shook his head, the tension showing. "I'm afraid all we can do now is wait and pray, Angela. Now, if you will excuse me, I have to give a press briefing on the execution of a military prisoner, murderer, and traitor."

The next two days were the longest she could remember.
***

When the airlock opened, Angela Hawthorne and Jerry Simmons were the only ones to approach the Cryodoc. Jerry lifted his slate. "Doc? What are you seeing?"

"Everything is stable in the Cryodoc, Colonel. There's no reason why it can't be opened at this time."

Angela reached out and hit the release and the lid to the coffin-like case swung up.

Looking like a healthy twenty-something, Michael Hawthorne appeared asleep. Suddenly, he took a deep breath, coughed and blinked several times. He turned his head slowly and his eyes focused on the beautiful redhead, tears in her eyes, hands on the edge of the case and leaning towards him.

"Angela, I've missed you so."

Cancellation!

Colonel Gerald Simmons couldn't believe what he was hearing. "Just what do you mean by cancellation?"

The General who's face filled the viewscreen didn't look any happier than Jerry felt. "I'm sorry, Jerry. I know what has gone into this project so far, but the people holding the purse strings have spoken. They want to focus all of their resources on Lunadome and Port Heinlein. They flat out told me that the other planet and solar system had been there for the past few billion years, it could wait another few decades while we consolidated our gains here in our own solar system.

"But what about a whole new planet, ready to colonize?"

"They are looking at the logistics as well as the financial aspects. Right now, you only have one warp-modified craft able to carry at most, two people and a couple of hundred kilos of supplies. The only other warp-capable ship only holds four Cryodocs and a kiloton of freight. Both of them are only really useful for robot exploration. You can't found a colony with four people at a time at the cost of billions in support teams and a month or more between trips. It's just not practical at this time. I truly am sorry, but you're going to have to mothball both craft for the near future. If any of the Earth-based researchers come up with enough funding, you may be allowed to fly one of them for some robot missions. But the Alexandria Group is no longer funding warp experiments."

Jerry shook his head. "Thank you, sir. I'll notify the teams and both craft will be sealed until we can continue."

Business Options

Mike Hawthorne looked every inch like a feudal lord in the formal garb he had chosen for the meeting. Black leather jeans, matching calf-high boots with wide cuffs a white fencer's shirt and a gold chain with a dragon-head crest hanging from it. The dragon's eyes were a deep, glowing red in Angela's design. He looked up at the ornate mirrorgate as the first of his guests arrived.

"Sara, Brent... Welcome to the council hall."

"Thanks." Answered Sara. "But just where are we?"

"This chamber is part of a series I hollowed out, deep in the mountain on the backside of my domain. We have grown enough that I thought it was time for more than occasional chat sessions."

"Oh? Just what did you have in mind, Jerry?"

Before he could answer the mirrorgate admitted several more of the original domain holders. Over the next few minutes, the long, ornate hallway filled up with an even hundred people.

Mike raised his voice to announce. "Thank you all for coming. Now that we are all present, it is time to take our places in Congress."

He opened a wide set of double doors and led them into a larger high-ceilinged hall. Several semi-circular balconies had polished wooden desks. Each desk area had a golden nameplate and could seat two people comfortably. They all filed in, taking their seats and quietly chatting.

Mike stepped up to one of the podiums facing the assemblage. When he spoke, his voice filled the hall. "Since this structure has been constructed in my domain, I claim the right to act as first speaker." The gavel made an ages-old hard wood smack of authority and he announced. "I call this first formal meeting of the Beta Domain Lords to order. Ladies and gentlemen, we have a great deal of business to address today and the very first is to ratify the Constitution we have all been working so hard on these last few months."

***

Three days of exhausting debate and compromise later, the Domain Lord Council was an established legal entity. Among many other things, Jeff Perkins had been voted Speaker of the Council for the next five years.

Everyone had been willing to attend to this momentous first gathering of the Domain Lords for a period of four days. On the morning of the forth day, about a third had left. Jerry Simmons asked to address the assemblage.

"Ladies and Gentlemen, or should I say, M'Lords and Ladies in a more formal manner." This quip garnered a few chuckles and he continued. "I've been thinking a lot about what sort of real value Beta has back in the Prime universe. And the answer is a great deal. While the majority of the people who are going to be joining us over the next few years are going to treat this place as the ultimate video game and vacation spot, I believe we have proven it can be a great deal more." Amid a few nods, he went on. "During the construction of Lunadome, a half-dozen engineers and riggers from Buster's team that Mike had invited to visit his estate, not only had a relaxing vacation, but their meetings solved a great many early problems. Those dozen or so design bull sessions ended up shaving years off the Lunadome project. Now I know that some of you have brought in some of your teams and have had similar success stories in other fields. That brings me to the point of my presentation." He turned to the blank wall behind him. It shimmered and became a map of the fjord areas where most of the Original team had settled. A red dot pointer appeared. "I draw your attention to this coastal basin. There is a protected bay that would make a nice harbor, three separate rivers feed into it and it is backed up by a couple of lovely valleys. Our original plans had been to divide it up into a few dozen domains and assign them first-come, first-serve. I have what I think is a much better idea." He waved his hand and the display changed to show a small city bordering the bay. "I'm thinking about reserving the entire bayfront area and back up both valleys for a distance of one hundred kilometers as an educational and research zone. Small domains within it may be assigned for projects that would benefit Prime. In exchange for the use of a domain and our assistance with research teams, organizations back in Prime would pay us in Prime credits, assigned to various banking institutions in their universe."

One of the assembled Lords held up his hand and was recognized. "Why do we need that much money back on Prime? You can just look around and see that our world has been completed. And now that most of us no longer need helmets, there is nothing they can take away from us."

"That is a very good question, sir. The answer is that it is in our best interests to see to the survival of the human race. That means expansion beyond our solar system. We've already seen another world, ripe for colonization. The powers-that-be back on Earth are, to be perfectly honest, scared shitless. They have already seen how the lunar colony is no longer under their control. Oh, they make proclamations and such, but the fact is, Port Heinlein is already well-established and doesn't really need them any more. What I propose is that once we have some capital reserves, we purchase the existing warp-capable ships, place one or more of our gold-brick Beta conduits into each one and send them on a long-term series of exploratory missions."

Another hand went up. "I can well appreciate the scientific value of such missions, but what would we really gain from them, since we cannot physically follow them to these new worlds?"

"Another good question. As our coffers grow, I propose we partner with some Prime organizations that wish to colonize another world. Our funds can build a series of colonial ships that can deliver volunteers in the hundreds to planets we select. Micasa for one, is ripe for a colony."

The balance of the day dragged on with question after question, but in the end, the measure was voted and approved. Screw Earth politics, Beta was going to push human colonization to the next level.

Foggy Mountain

Buster stood on a wide ledge, arms folded and stared down into the deep valley below. He pointed. "There! See that?"

Cheryl and her husband were both in spacesuits and she looked where he was pointing. "Oh my! You're right, dear. That is beautiful."

"It first started to show up yesterday and now it appears to be spreading." He was referring to a cloud of fog that was growing in deep crevices all over the bottom of the crater. In places, the fog was actually running downhill in very slow-motion and flowing over ledges to form thin tendrils that looked like waterfalls.

"I love how they seem to glow in the overhead lights and the work lasers and headlights in the shadowed areas make them sparkle."

"There are all kinds of strange chemical mixes in there but a lot of it is actually starting to condense as a heavy dew in the deepest spots. It's actually turning into a pain in the ass in places."

She turned to him, brows furrowing behind her faceplate. "Why is that, dear?"

He kicked at their feet and a cloud of lunar dust rose and slowly drifted back down. "This dust is the problem. It covers most everything we've not swept or mined. Down there, when that fog finally condenses, it turns into a very dense, heavy and extremely sticky mud." He chuckled. "It makes Georgia red clay feel like kid's modeling putty.

"What are you going to do about it?"

He shook his head. "Nothing at all for right now. We're going to wait until there is a lot more of an atmosphere and the lakes fill up. Once we have a large quantity of water to work with, we're going to start our rain cycles."

"Rain cycles?"

"Yeah. Mixed in among the catwalks of Lunadome, there are water pipes with sprinkler heads. When we have enough water, we're going to start a cycle of rain that will wash every exposed surface. Over time, all the loose dust and scree will accumulate in the lake and depressions all over the crater floor. Some of them we will mine for their mineral and chemical value. The excess, raw dust in slurry form, will be pumped into a side tunnel where it will be dessicated with heaters. Once it is totally dry and of no further value in here, we'll shovel it back out on the surface in order to further cover the dome and provide solar radiation shielding."

She nodded and added. "But in the meantime, the colors of that flowing fog and slurried dust are amazing."

Buster agreed. "It's going to be another couple of years before this place gets plants and starts to look livable, but right now, I'm just enjoying a rugged view that is soon going to be gone."

After watching quietly for a few more minutes, they turned and walked back towards the airlock. Just before entering, Buster kicked the ground again, raised another cloud and muttered softly to himself. "Dust! I still hate dust."

Book Three: Micasians

Sweet Sixteen

Angel Heights was one scary waterfall. It had also turned into a quiet coming-of-age ceremony among those born and raised in the lunar colony of Port Heinlein.

The domed crater was about thirty kilometers wide, and once the atmosphere had been stabilized, the lowest parts had been flooded with fresh water. The resulting lake had more than a dozen smaller islands and one tall one that loomed above all the rest. As part of the water recirculation system, huge pumps, feeding deeply-buried tunnels, fed a few dozen waterfalls. Most of them were small, scenic affairs that fed warm water pools where families gathered for picnics.

Angel Heights was different. It has been designed from the start to be impressive. The pumps fed a small lake nestled between some crags near the kilometer and a half high peak of Angel Mount. The lake overflowed on two sides. Down one side, the cascade followed a series of rock shelves. Near each shelf was a tourist resort. Very wealthy tourists from Earth paid small fortunes to spend time enjoying the delights of low gravity.

The other side of the mountain was another matter. Thousands of gallons of water poured through a narrow gap and had a smooth, uninterrupted fall of almost a kilometer into a nice, deep pool.

Susan Childers had enjoyed a great sixteenth birthday celebration with her parents and a few good friends. This was something else, however.

"I can't believe you're really going to go through with it."

Susan saw her friend shake her head in disbelief.

"Look." She tried to explain again. "I've dove off every other fall. This is the last one."

"Yeah. But it's also about four times higher than any of the others." Charlotte tried to reason.

"Actually, I confirmed that it is a bit more than five times higher. But that's not the point. I know how to dive and this is something I just have to do."

"What about the security cameras? You're liable to get arrested. That is, if you are alive to be arrested."

Susan grabbed her friend's arm and stopped her. They were on a narrow, but carefully marked trail between some heavy tropical foliage. "That is why we are going to wait right here. Your brother said he would feed the security cams a fifteen minute loop as soon as I was in position." She tapped a quick pattern on her slate and waited.

Just a few seconds later, she got her answer and grinned. "He is going to start the loop in five minutes. That will give me time to get to the jump point." She quickly stripped off her short dress, shoes and purse. "Here. Take care of these for me. I'll meet you at fiddler's cove in an hour or so."

They exchanged a quick hug for luck and Susan pushed through the remaining bushes.

Charlie Smith had already fed the fake video loop to the security feeds, but that didn't stop him from watching and recording Susan's scramble through the bushes, and down the maintenance trail to the observation balcony. He had to smile at the gorgeous young woman wearing a well-filled one-piece swimsuit. "You are one crazy lady. But this takes the cake." His whispered compliment was just a hint of how he felt about her.

"You are one crazy lady." Susan whispered to herself as she stood on the observation balcony and stared at the dizzying display of falling water that faded into a permanent misty cloud hundreds of meters below.

Although all the lighting in the dome was artificial, in order to give a proper feel, it was on a day and night system. Each full day included a very dark period for a few hours before 'dawn', a full day of bright light that actually had some UV components which accounted for Susan's suntan, and some false 'moonlight' for those that enjoyed evening strolls. It was about two in the morning and the faux moonlight could not penetrate the mist at the base of Angel Heights.

She knew she only had about five minutes to complete her dive before the security system started getting a live feed once more.

"Enough playing tourist!" She whispered to herself as a bit of pep-talk. Susan stood up on the stone railing, shook herself to loosen up and stared out at the distant rows of residence lights around the crater wall. She closed her eyes for a moment, then crouched down and let it start.

Just like every other dive, she slowly leaned forward and let her own body weight pull her down. When she felt her body was almost level, she straightened her legs and pushed out, away from the ledge.

Intellectually, Susan knew there was plenty of room for her dive. There was almost no chance of hitting anything on the way down. That didn't stop the instinctual rush of pure terror as she spread her arms and raced alongside tons of water rushing into the misty darkness.

***

Susan felt great when she sat down to breakfast. Then, she noticed her parents were smiling way too much.

"Have fun with your friends, last night?" Her dad inquired.

"Uhm... yeah, why?"

"Well, when you left, you were wearing that basic black party dress you only wear for special occasions." Her mother observed. "And this morning, I saw it in the laundry, and it has what looked like a grass stain."

Susan laughed. "Oh! That. We went down to the park and I got clumsy. It will come out, won't it?"

Her dad's grin widened. "You know, daughter. You really should practice lying better. You're extremely bad at it."

She didn't know how to reply to that.

Her mom added. "We know you don't have any serious boyfriends right now, so I don't think anyone got lucky."

"Mom!" Susan was outraged. "You know I don't..."

"That's enough, young lady." Mister Childers used his daddy voice. He handed her his slate. "Take a look at this video the security team sent me from one of the drones."

Susan watched herself climb up on the ledge, loosen up and dive into the mist.

The drone followed her down, then hovered a few meters above and behind her as she swam around the point and up to the tourist beach. The video ended when she was dressed and walking home with her two friends.

She grimaced. "I thought the drones were only used during the day, to monitor tourists or emergency scenes."

Her dad took the slate back. "That's right. And the security team has been taking bets on when you were going to give Angel Heights a try. They consider you a one-woman emergency scene looking for a place to happen. It just so happens that I've got video clips of every dive you've made so far. And just so you know, you're not the first to do it."

"Then why didn't they stop me?"

"We warn everyone about it as a matter of course and to protect stupid mudball tourists. If someone acts in a responsible manner and works their way up from the smaller dives, we just keep an eye on them. As soon as you headed up the mountain, we had an emergency team in a rubber boat waiting to stabilize and dose you with Omniphage if you really screwed up."

Her mother chimed in. "But just for the record, you only get one shot at it. If you try again, you will be arrested." She got up and hugged her daughter. "I know this is probably a waste of breath, but please try not to do anything quite so dangerous again."

***

Martin could see his wife's excited grin through the helmet faceplate. "You know what our daughter would say to this, right?"

Sarah Childers gave her husband a wry smile. "Yeah. Please try not to do anything quite so dangerous. I know."

They both chuckled at the joke.

The couple stopped the lunar buggy near the ill-defined edge of the crater, unstrapped what at first glance looked like a couple of snow boards from the roof rack and joined a small group of space-suited figures.

About a dozen of them traded greetings before getting down to business. Martin Childers started it off. "Okay. I understand Terry did this run alone, last week?"

Terry answered. "Yeah. It starts pretty easy for the first couple of clicks." He pointed at an angle down the inner slope of the crater. "Once you get near that hard outcropping, there's a smooth and almost level ledge below it. Past that, we have a fast, steep run between those two small hills. It rises gently right before you get to the plateau."

Everyone nodded understanding and Terry continued. "There is a cable car already spiked into the plateau and it can bring us all back here." He pointed to the small tower behind them with an almost invisible pair of cables leading downward.

The Lunatic Dust Ski Team all had at least a couple of year's experience and carefully checked each other's equipment before hopping onto their boards and sliding down the slope. They cut wide, slow swaths in the virgin dust, only occasionally crossing the marks left from the previous run.

Sarah loved dust skiing. It was a form of slow-motion poetry. Their boards were very similar to the snow boards used at earthly ski resorts, but coupled with one-sixth gravity and the fine powder of the ubiquitous lunar dust, everything happened a bit slower. True, the dust was highly abrasive, but rather than the fiberglass of their Earth counterparts, the lunar boards were stainless steel and good for many runs before being recycled.

Martin was behind her. He always said it was his favorite spot when skiing because he got to watch her body swaying as she slid over the rolling terrain.

This time, the Childers' were about two thirds of the way back when they completed the first and easiest part of the run. Everyone was feeling loose as they followed the shadow of the ancient outcropping, to the almost-level ledge. This was where they would drop into the same path as the leaders, in order to line up for the much steeper and faster zig-zag through a boulder field.

Susan had tucked down, knees bent and focusing on the trail ahead when she noticed a shadow move. It wasn't supposed to move!

She glanced up and saw various geysers of dust erupting at the corners of the giant rock. Shocked, she realized the entire face of the outcrop was breaking off and sliding down, onto them.

"Martin!" She screamed. "Look out! The rock is..."

"I see it! Go! Don't stop. We can outrun it."

Susan glanced over her shoulder and realized her husband was much closer and almost parallel with her. Much farther back, she saw two of the team turn hard and take the dangerous option of heading straight down the crater side. If they didn't hit a hidden rock, they might be okay. She didn't see any of the others before she had to bring her attention back to her own run.

The ledge they were on ended just a few meters ahead and the trail dove sharply down, between two large boulders and then into the zig-zag. It was in clear sunlight and easy to follow for skiers with their skill level. Then, it got dark. Very dark. As the giant rock face started to tumble downslope, it kicked up a huge cloud of dust that obscured the run. Without atmosphere, the lunar shadows were inky black.

They made it between the first two boulders before all light went away. By instinct, Susan flipped on her lights, but could only see perhaps a dozen meters ahead. She heard Martin's harsh breath in the radio and set herself up for the next turn. The dust cloud enveloped both of them.

Dirtbound Blues

Mayor Howard Childers leaned into the high-backed leather office chair and read the printed letter several times. Each time, shaking his head. "I told her she was a damn fool for marrying that man."

"What's that, dear?" Martha Childers, his wife of almost forty years walked in with a tray of snacks.

"My sister-in-law and that fool husband of hers have managed to get themselves killed on the moon. That's what. I knew no good would come of that. God gave us this beautiful planet and we should be satisfied. But oh no. They had to gallivant off to an airless orb."

"Oh dear. That is terrible news. How did it happen?"

"Some sort of sporting accident. They were buried under a few thousand tons of rock."

Martha thought a moment before asking. "What's going to become of Susan? She's still only a child, right?"

The honorable mayor took his time thinking it over. "Since we are her closest living relatives, we shall have to make room for her in our home. It is the only Christian thing to do." His mind made up, he checked the antique roller card deck for a phone number to start the process.

***

Buster and Cheryl Mathias did all they could to help Susan cope with the loss. They gave her a few days to grieve and then put her to work, keeping her mind and hands busy with various projects.

The twins, Charlie and Charlotte Smith were also there for her.

None of them were prepared for the legal notice from Earth.

"What the hell does this mean?" Susan was staring at her slate. "I can't go to Earth. I was born here in Port Heinlein. I wouldn't even be able to run at the bottom of that dang gravity well."

Buster shook his head. "I'm sure it is just some sort of legal mixup. Let me check with our attorneys tomorrow. Who are these people, anyway?"

"The Childers' are my aunt and uncle. I've only exchanged letters with them a few times. He's the mayor of some back-country farming community. They were really angry when Dad left and brought Mom to the moon. We really don't have much in common at all."

Cheryl asked. "Why were they angry?"

"Howard and Martha Childers belong to one of those weird religious sects that don't use cars or computers. They think humans should stay on Earth."

Buster added. "In that case, they probably aren't aware of the strain they will put on you by taking you back to the Earth gravity. Even with a serious physical therapy routine, it will be six months to a year before you'll be able to adapt properly."

Susan chuckled. "At least he won't have me helping the mule drag a plow."

***

The Port Heinlein Onsite Director's conference room was filled. Besides Susan and the Mathias', the director himself, two Selenaphile lawyers, and a pair of Terran legal representatives, there was a doctor, and a psychologist. At one point or another, they had all been arguing.

"Enough!" The Director's voice cut through the squabble. "Everyone except Susan, wait out in the hallway, please."

There were some minor complaints, but a few minutes later, he was alone with the young woman.

"It doesn't look good, does it, sir?"

"You deserve the truth, Susan." He paused and looked out the window before continuing. "Right now, Port Heinlein still requires some things from Earth. We are almost independent, but not quite there yet. You heard the lawyers beating it back and forth. Unfortunately, The Childers' are your only living relatives and they have a perfectly legal right to custody until you turn eighteen."

"But to go to Earth and leave everything I've ever known? And what's worse, to live in the bottom of that gravity well? I'll be all but a cripple for at least a few weeks. What good is that supposed to do for me?"

"Believe me. I've gone over that with the doctors and they say you're young and healthy and with a dose of PhageB, you will adapt in six weeks or less. You'll actually be much stronger for it in the long run. The lawyers won't accept that as an excuse." He took a deep breath. "I'm really sorry Susan, but I'm not willing to risk a war with the powers that be down on Earth just to save you from seeing a bit of the home planet and a forced vacation for about twenty months."

"How do you figure twenty, sir?"

"You are listed as a resident here in Port Heinlein. I'm not going to change that. Your apartment and all your belongings are going to be sealed until you get back. The day you turn eighteen, just send us your location and I'll arrange for transportation to the nearest space-launch facility. You will be back home with the next shuttle." He gave her a wry smile. "You're a Selenaphile, Susan. And we take care of our own."

There were tears of frustration and anger in her eyes as she went home to pack. "I will be back." She whispered the vow to herself.

Summer of Discontent

Susan was terrified. She had mostly ignored the shrink when he warned her that the open skies of Earth might bring out some latent agoraphobia. But combine the infinite vastness of a partly-cloudy sky and weighing six times more than normal and the young woman felt trapped.

Adding to her embarrassment, as soon as she wobbled her way off the shuttle, she had been stuffed into a wheelchair. Imagine being in such an ancient contrivance like some sort of cripple from the dark ages? She admitted to herself, it felt good to sit rather than struggle with the crushing gravity. It was just plain exhausting.

"Susan? Susan Childers?" The soft voice was attached to the hand gently shaking her shoulder.

"Oh! Yes. Sorry. I must have dozed off." She rubbed her eyes and tried to sit up straighter.

"That's okay, dear. We'll get you home straight away."

"Home?" She muttered, then realized where she was. "Oh yeah. This must be High Valley." Her attention focused on what was probably the oldest woman she had ever seen, standing next to her. "Excuse me, but who are you?"

"That's okay, dear. We've only met in old photographs. I'm Martha Childers, your Aunt."

Susan traded a hug and an air kiss with the woman while trying to match stark reality with the studio photo of a middle-aged woman she had just looked at a few days earlier.

"Come on now. I'm sure the bus driver wants to finish his run. Can you walk at all, child?"

"Yes. For a short distance. It will take awhile to adapt to the gravity here."

"Adapt to... ? Oh, I thought you might be ill from your horrible journey and that is why you come to us in a wheelchair."

Susan had to smile at that comment. "Actually, a couple of days in free fall is marvelously relaxing. I'm just not used to full Earth gravity. After all, it is six times more than the moon."

The woman looked confused for a moment, then gave a half-smile. "Well, I'm sure you must be right. We'll have you fit as a fiddle in short order. Come now. Your Uncle is waiting to welcome you."

Susan pushed aside the blanket the nurse had left with her and stood up.

Martha stared at her for a moment. "Goodness gracious, child. What is that you're wearing?"

Susan looked down at herself. She was covered, neck-to-toe in a triple-layer skinsuit that provided both support, environmental protection and acted as the standard under-garment for the latest generation of space suits. A pair of soft, faux leather medium-heeled boots and a long over vest with her slate and other personal items completed the stylish outfit. "This is what is normally worn when traveling. Why? What's the matter with it?"

"I can see we're going to have to get you home and into a proper dress as soon as possible. You can't wear something that scandalous around here."

That is when she realized that Martha was wearing a long, dark blue dress with full sleeves. High-cut black leather shoes with almost no heel looked pretty scuffed and worn.

Susan just blinked rapidly as her Aunt led her down and out of the bus. She really had no idea how to reply to that statement.

***

She did recognize her Uncle. Howard Childers was a bear of a man. He wore a black suit in a style Susan only remembered seeing in old movies. In one hand, he held a heavy wooden cane while the other rested on a wooden lectern, facing away from the bus platform. There was a gathering of people standing behind him. Susan saw him smiling as Martha stepped down and reached up to help her granddaughter, but his smile turned icy cold when his gaze swept quickly up and down her body. She felt like an insect under a microscope.

He stepped forward, holding out his hand and when she took it, he spoke loudly, in a voice obviously meant for the crowd as much as her, "Welcome home, child!" He pulled her into a quick, close embrace and whispered in her ear. "What in the world do you mean by dressing like that for a homecoming?"

Before she could even frame an answer, he spun her around, his right hand holding hers in a crushing grip and his left arm, cane still in hand, wrapped around her shoulders. He stood at the lectern and smiled broadly at the small crowd. "Praise the Lord, my good friends. Our prayers have been answered and this poor orphan has been led safely to our doorstep." This was met by a rousing cheer and Susan again felt terrified at being trapped. She tried to wiggle free.

His harsh whisper came from between lips tightly clenched in an election-year smile. "Stand still for God's sake. You're embarrassing me."

A few moments later, he half-led, half-dragged her to a huge, four-door pickup truck. "What's the matter with you, child? You look healthy enough and yet you can't even walk?"

"Please let me take it slow. As I explained to Martha, it will take at least a few days for me to adapt to feeling like this."

Without asking or any warning, he swept her off her feet and deposited her on a backseat of the truck. "Well, as far as I'm concerned, this is proof positive that sailing off in to space is for fools and weaklings." He didn't give her a chance to respond to the implied insult. "But never you mind. A few months of chores and learning proper woman's work will have you on your feet." He closed the door and went around to the driver's seat.

***

They drove past a town with a strange mix of false-front stores and modern glass and aluminum structures. None of them were more than two stories and all appeared a little shabby. The relatively smooth two-lane blacktop wound alongside a small river for a ways, through a cut between two ridges, then straight as an arrow for a dozen miles between neat fields of corn. Susan was just about ready to doze off when the truck turned down a hard-packed dirt lane, through a gate and up a slight rise, to a large barn and a few other buildings.

The farmhouse looked like something from an old western movie or perhaps a classic horror film. She wasn't sure which.

Miami Towers

"Let me get this straight." Despite sitting ramrod straight and looking about twenty-five, the man seated at the head of the huge conference table was over a hundred years old. "You're saying this man actually died, his body was cremated and yet he now has a brand-new body and is back with his wife? All because of some fancy video game?"

"That is correct, sir." The engineer wasn't used to the rarefied atmosphere of a multinational corporate boardroom. "It was a pretty convoluted process, but I've met Mike Hawthorne and he is still very much alive."

"Well, I am scheduled for another shot of Omniphage in a few years, but it would be nice to have some sort of backup in case of emergency. How does this work?"

"First, you have to develop a presence on Beta..."

The CEO interrupted him. "Beta? Is this some sort of game?"

"Not really a game, sir. It's more of another world experience. It is rather hard to describe. You really need to see it for yourself."

"I'll take your word for it right now. Then what?"

"Once you've established yourself on Beta, if your body here in this corner of the multiverse is killed, you wake up over there on a permanent basis. Imagine it as going to Heaven or Valhalla. We've actually seen that happen several times now. Getting back is the hard part because is requires a warp-drive ship with a living body." The engineer went on to describe how a condemned murderer volunteered for the experiment. As expected, the warp flight wiped their mind clean. After returning, Omniphage replaced the physical damage with Mike's sample DNA. At the same time, one of the Beta system training helmets downloaded Mike Hawthorne's memories and personality into the fresh body. Several days later, a living, breathing person emerged from the CryoDox that was a twenty-something version of the recently-deceased General.

Over a hundred years old, Victor Charles Adams III was one of the first recipients of Omniphage. A multi-billionaire and scion of a family used to wealth and power for the last dozen generations, he had been near death when Omniphage was discovered. As soon as he read the specs on the new drug, he ordered his agents to dump all of his medical and pharmaceutical holdings. He was one of less than a dozen of the wealthiest people on the planet that immediately recognized what effect it would have. Less than a week later, Victor plus several old friends and key members of his staff, had been rejuvenated with Omniphage and were cash-rich. In the few months where cash still had some value, they dumped everything into building self-sufficient retreats in remote locations.

"What is required to join this Beta world?"

"One of the helmets and a nearby brick." The engineer saw a confused look. "They call these cybernetic routers which are required to access Beta, 'bricks'. They're about that size and most are painted a deep red."

"What do you mean by nearby? What sort of range does the helmet have?"

He shrugged. "I don't have any firm information on that, sir. The transhumanists are playing a lot of this very close to the vest. They are only inviting a very few people to join their group. The detailed plans, specifications, and limitations are not general knowledge."

Victor nodded, steepled his fingers and thought for just a moment before ordering, "Gather more information and get me one of those 'bricks' as well as one or more of the helmets. I also want additional information on how the warp drive actually works. In specific, can it be made to work in a fixed location, here on Earth?"

After the engineer left, Victor called for a member of his security team. Jack Hamstein had been through a lot with the old man and knew just how well he would be rewarded for doing whatever needed to be done. He smiled as he recalled Jack's lack of a moral compass.

"You wanted to see me, sir?"

After filling him in, Victor watched the hard man leave. He knew that it wouldn't take too long to find a condemned prisoner that might want a chance to live just a bit longer.

Port Heinlein

Mike Hawthorne loved his work, but after his death and rebirth in a new body, he looked around and realized the first lunar colony was almost complete and he needed some new project. He had shared the epiphany with his wife, Angela, and though sympathetic, she didn't have any quick answers.

He was sitting in the wizard's tower of his keep when a knock on the door frame announced Mark Chambers, son of a gifted astrophysicist and his neighbor in the virtual reality world of Beta.

"Hi Mark. What can I do for you?"

"Got a minute? I'd like to discuss some requisitions."

"Sure. Come on in. But I can't do much here on Beta. You should make an appointment with me back in Port Heinlein."

"Yeah." He agreed. "But back there, it will all get recorded and I'm not ready for a paper trail just yet."

Mike narrowed his eyes. "I get nervous when someone says they don't want a paper trail."

"What do you think about the folks back on Earth grounding our one and only warp-drive ship?"

Mike thought about it for a few moments, choosing his words carefully. "Naturally, I would like to see us continue our explorations of another planet, but I can understand their financial concerns. Why do you ask?"

The young man walked over to the French doors and looked out at the beautiful valley, now partially hidden by the steady rain and a rolling fog bank. "Due to the time-compression here on Beta, some friends and I have become bored with parties and exploring the forests. I know you and some of the others are building small cities and establishing trade and all... But this really is only a vacation spot for some of us. It isn't the real world."

"I thought you and Wendy were experimenting with the magic systems and building new castles and such? From what I've seen, you two are way ahead of some of us old-timers in that regard."

Mark shrugged. "Yeah, but we know it's still just a beautiful fantasy world. We have a whole new planet just waiting to be explored and colonized just the other side of a warp jump and there are a bunch of us that are really frustrated at this point."

"What do want to do about it? I don't see the folks down the gravity well changing their minds any time soon."

"We've been looking at some of the junk that has piled up in the scrap areas. There are some well-used engines laying around as well as lots of raw materials. When you are back in your office, I'd like permission to 'salvage' some of them for a research project."

"Okay. I might be able to do that. But there is no way any of that equipment will even get you out of the solar system, much less to another star."

Mark just smiled. "As is, you are correct. But this is just a little research project, right?"

"I'm guessing you have a plan for building another warp-drive ship. But that is still going to require equipment and resources we don't have to spare. Let me in on your little project and perhaps I can help."

The young man considered it for only a moment. "As you are probably aware, the bricks that allow our connection to Beta have a range of a little less than a hundredth of a light-second. What my team has worked out is a very small spacecraft. One of the old lunar shuttle engines is an Xcor XM-8M. It has seen a lot of use, but is still serviceable. We want to rebuild and mount it in a new frame. The new craft will only be a cargo vessel, carrying a bunch of spider-bots and a brick. The brick will act as an interface between Beta and the real-world."

"What about the time-compression?"

"That will work in our favor. It means we don't need an AI and specific programs to control the ship. We will have a rotating team of flight crews working from our mission control in Beta, when needed."

The director shook his head. "Even without a live crew on-board, it would take thousands of years for such a craft to make it to another star without the warp-drive."

"We're only going to fly it to the asteroid belt. Once there, it will setup a mining operation using the spider-bots. We're going to build an industrial-sized fabrication facility inside one of the larger asteroids. When it is ready, we'll collect raw materials from various sources, bring them together and build our own warp-drive systems. No Earth-based money or resources will be used."

Mike Hawthorne sat and stared at Mark for what seemed like a long time. Then, he nodded and softly smiled. "You do realize that when word gets out, you will have pissed off a lot of very powerful people down on Earth, don't you?"

"By the time word gets out, I expect to have the first wave of colonists already out there."

High Valley

Susan felt as if she had been transported into some surreal film noir. On one hand, the farm was storybook perfect with all the expected livestock, pasture, and fields of grain waving in the breeze. On the other hand, the other women all wore long dresses and white bonnets.

Aunt Martha stared in horror when Susan laid out the contents of travel case. "Oh my goodness, child. Are you telling me you don't have any dresses?"

Susan picked up a pair of carefully-rolled minidresses. "I brought these just for parties. But when I'm planning on work, I only wear jeans and teeshirts or if I need protection, one of my skinsuits."

Shocked, Martha held up her hands in denial. "We never have a party where you would be allowed to wear anything that scandalous. Perhaps, you might wear it under your wedding gown to tease your husband... But you will never be seen in public dressed like a whore."

Her first reaction was to be offended, but then Susan decided that when in Rome, she must follow their customs. She swallowed her ire and politely asked, "What would you have me wear, then? Will you go shopping with me for some proper clothing?"

"Shopping? Oh heavens no. Your cousin Lizzie is about your size. I'm sure she has a couple of old things she can help you to alter this afternoon. At least you will be dressed properly for breakfast and chores in the morning."

Elizabeth "Lizzie" Roberts had accompanied them upstairs and was standing behind Martha. Susan saw a hint of anger cross her cousin's face at the suggestion. She opened her mouth as if to say something, but was interrupted when Martha continued. "Lizzie. I do believe there is a dark green dress and a spare black one. Please fetch them, along with your sewing kit. I'm going to attend to some chores while you two get acquainted and work on getting Susan into some proper clothing."

The two women left and Susan wandered over to the tall, narrow window. Her room took up about half of the attic space. A steeply-sloped ceiling met a short wall on each side. A door on one end led to the narrow stairs and a single window opened out to the barnyard and the setting sun. A sharply-defined range of mountains covered the western horizon.

It was a toss-up as to which of the two dresses was uglier in Susan's eyes. They were obviously hand-crafted from cotton and well-worn. Lizzie was close to the same size as Susan so only a couple of spots were pinned in a bit.

"That's close enough, slip it off and you can use my sewing kit to take it in."

"But I don't know how."

Lizzie turned and stared at her cousin. "Don't know how? Surely your mother taught you to sew a simple seam."

Susan shrugged. "Sorry, I've never even seen someone sew except in a historical video. When we need any sort of clothing, we just pick the item from a catalog and it is delivered the next day."

"Don't you have to modify store-bought clothing to fit properly?"

"Of course not. All our measurements are part of our personal profile. Anything we order is fabricated to be a perfect fit."

Lizzie just shook her head. "Your family must be incredibly wealthy to afford such things." She paused and bit her lip for a moment. "Did you bring one of the catalogs with you?"

"I've got my favorites bookmarked, but any of them are easy to find. They aren't expensive, either. It's just the way almost anything is produced in Port Heinlein."

"Did you bring any other bags besides that one?" She pointed to the items spread out on the bed.

"Actually no. I only brought absolute necessities to help keep under my mass allowance. It costs a fortune to travel. Although I must admit it's a lot cheaper coming down into the gravity well than going up. When I return, I'm only taking what I wear and perhaps a kilo or so of coffee for General Hawthorne."

"But you said you had a catalog. There's no books or magazines in your stuff."

"Sorry. I think you misunderstood. I said I had them bookmarked. They are on my slate. Don't you have a net connection? How do you get your email and news?"

"Slate?"

Susan pulled her slate from its shoulder pocket. "Here. Let me show you." She held her thumb against a corner of the glassy surface and it lit up with a scene of trees, flowers, and the glint of water on the lake. Silver streaks against distant rocks marked a couple of waterfalls.

Lizzie's eyes widened. "Goodness gracious. Where is that?"

"I took that picture right before I left. That's the view from our apartment balcony." She pointed at one of the streaks of falling water.

"That really tall one is Angel Falls. I dove that just before..." She paused and shook herself. "Just before my folks died."

"Are you trying to tell me that is the moon? I've seen pictures of the moon and it's a dark, dry, dusty place with no air or water. Humans have to live inside tubes like submarines."

"My goodness but someone has been telling you ancient history. Port Heinlein has over two hundred thousand residents. We have forests, lakes for swimming, fishing, and snorkling. Why, you can even go hang gliding if that's your thing. The dome has been pressurized for more than twenty years." While she was talking, Susan opened her browser and called up some of her fashion pages. "These are some of the designs my friends and I wear."

Lizzie looked shocked at the various still images and short video clips of Susan and her friends in class, swimming, biking, dancing and working on various bots in their school shop. After a few minutes, she inquired. "Are you telling me, you know how to repair machines and work with these computers, but you don't know how to cook or sew?"

Susan shrugged and nodded. "My mom showed me a little bit of baking, but I've never been really interested in that stuff. As for sewing, all our clothing comes from the maker-bots. I don't recall ever seeing a real sewing machine."

The homespun girl thought that over, then smiled softly. "In that case, you're in luck. Aunt Martha says I'm one of the best cooks around. It won't be long before you're going to be cooking up a storm." Then, her smile faded. "I would advise you to keep your slate hidden though." She glanced over her shoulder nervously. "We don't allow any of that sort of technology here on the farm. Uncle Howard says it is part of the Devil's plan to drag us away from hard work, clean-living, and God's righteous path."

Miami Towers

Jack Hamstein had spent twenty years in the military. He had retired to a reserve position and been contracting his services as a security consultant when the phage riots hit. The military called him back to active duty and he spent the next two years trying to hold things together. Now, he was Chief of Security for Victor Charles Adams III.

"Hello, Jack. What have you got for me?" The wealthy industrialist stood and they shook hands.

They both sat down and Jack filled his boss in on the results of all the Beta research.

"Let me see if I've got this straight. Beta is a segment of some other universe that a bunch of geeks have managed to setup like some sort of magical alternate reality?"

"In a way, yes. The problem is that all I can get so far is anecdotal evidence. Aside from some extremely complex CAD drawings from very early test systems, there is no further evidence to verify it even exists."

"What about photographs of their magic fairy castles? From the other reports I've read, they seem very proud of their creations. Why not show them off?"

"It seems that none of their bricks are actually tied into any real-world systems. There is no way to take photographs over in Beta, since they have no consumer electronics at all and even if they did, there are no connections back to our network in order to display them."

"Oh come on, Jack. There must be some way of seeing what is actually going on there."

"So far, unless you go there yourself, we've not found any technical way of seeing it. But I do think I have an answer. There is a very good artist working as a waitress in a small mountain town near where I have my retreat. We should be able to hire her to spend some time in Beta and document what she sees after she gets back."

"How do we get her an invite?"

"We don't really need one, Victor. That is on the the things I've managed to find out. They already have a lot of new people dropping in each day. They actually planned for it."

"Planned for uninvited guests?"

"If you get a formal invite from one of the founders, they will test your skills and possibly assign you some land. They are all magicians with fancy titles and each one is in charge of a large territory. Each of these mages has built one or more small towns with a full range of facilities."

"So buy me an invite."

"As far as I've been able to determine, they don't sell them and very few are actually invited these days. They are trying to plan ahead and learn more about how the magic actually works. I managed to get a brick and a couple of headsets. If you just drop in without an invite, the artificial intelligence that monitors things will treat you as a total newbie. Just like in a video game, you get to choose your appearance. It assigns some sturdy clothing along with a purse of a hundred gold coins."

"How valuable are a hundred gold coins in that world?"

"All I've heard is that it is enough to keep you in food and shelter for almost a year. The idea is to give a newbie enough time to find their niche and get a job." He took a sip of coffee before continuing. "Victor, I think I might have a way to game the system."

The billionaire's eyes widened and he leaned back in his chair. "I knew I could depend on you. What have you found?"

"Before you go there, let me bring in a dozen loyal people. We'll each join Beta and once there, we'll live real cheap and as soon as you join us, we'll all pool our remaining money and you can purchase a tavern. That will give us a start in the community and a good place to gather more information."

"That sounds good, Jack. But before I go, I want to know more about how it works. How about sending that sketch artist through and when they come back, have them create some maps and drawings so we know what we're getting into?"

***

Victor had to admit she was a wonderful illustrator. The sketchbook on his desk was proof enough. He looked up at the rather plain young woman seated on the other side of his desk. "This is nice work, Paulette. Thank you."

"You're very welcome, Mr. Adams. I'm glad I finally get to do something I love once more."

He nodded. "I do understand you talents were wasted in that coffee shop. I trust your accommodations are satisfactory?"

"Yes, sir. Everything is fine. Now that I have finished a basic tour of Morepork, what else would you have me examine?"

"Morepork? I take it that is the name of the town you are in?"

"Yes. That is where the mirrorgate left me."

"I will be honest Paulette, I barely had time to skim your report before you arrived with these sketches. Take it step-by-step and tell me what I'm seeing in each image and why you thought it was important enough to record. This first image, for example, shows a very pretty nude woman."

She dipped her eyes, blushed, and took a moment to answer. "That is me, sir. You see, as a newbie, the first time you put on the headset, you wake up on a flat slab in a hexagonal room. The center of the room is a smaller hexagon comprised of a set of alcoves. Each alcove has three full-length mirrors. The room is called the Creche and the mirrors are the first type of magic you will encounter." She paused and looked down at the sketchbook for a moment.

"Go on. What sort of magic mirrors?"

"There is some kind of artificial intelligence that greets you as soon as you stand up. It explains things better than I can. But the basic idea is that when you stand in front of the mirrors, you can alter your body in any way you wish. It is totally painless and happens instantly. That sketch is what I look like over in Beta."

He was incredulous. "You always start out nude?"

"In the Creche, yes sir. But after you have chosen your new body, the AI suggests appropriate clothing based on what you anticipate doing. Since I said I wanted to explore, I arrived in Morepork, dressed in a layered outfit of boots, jeans, button-down collared shirt, light sweater, and a hooded cloak. It turned out to be very comfortable and utilitarian."

"You mentioned a mirrorgate, I believe?"

"After you are dressed, the AI asks if you have a known destination. If not, it suggests the central square in Morepork. There are taverns, hotels, and many small businesses on the side streets. If you go into the city hall, the lobby has a magic three-dimensional map of the area. It automatically updates itself whenever there is new construction." She pointed to the sketch showing the lobby and map table. "I used it several times to find my way around the city."

"So you can use the mirrors to get around?"

She shook her head. "Only the first time you leave the Creche. After that, only certain trained magicians can use the mirrors. I heard that some of them will open gates for a fee. It is one of the ways they earn a living."

"Will any mirror work?"

"No. Only certain full-length mirrors with fancy frames are mirrorgates. All major public buildings have one and I was told that all the magicians have them at home."

Victor considered her answers for a moment before continuing. "What other forms of transportation are there?"

"It is still pretty primitive, sir. Horses and mules are popular, as are carriages. There are no motorized vehicles that I saw."

"It looks to me like the magicians have set themselves up in a feudal economy in order to maintain power. How does one get to be a magician?"

High Valley

It only took a few days for Susan to get used to the gravity and the routine in the Childers household. Cousin Lizzie taught her some simple sewing as well as how to help with a few of the basic chores. Soon enough, she was tasked with collecting eggs each morning and helping prepare breakfast.

Although he was seldom home during the day, Howard Childers made it a point to join his family for dinner, each evening.

A chorus of "Amen" terminated grace and plates began hovering over the various serving bowls. Howard was loading his when he glanced at Susan. "Martha tells me that you have been helping out a lot. I'm glad to see you're learning our ways."

"It is interesting, sir. Some things have been quick and easy, while others will take some time."

"I must admit, you had me scared when we first met. I thought you were a cripple."

"That's understandable. I felt that way, myself. Even though I'd had a shot of PhageB right before I left Port Heinlein, it does take some time to acclimatize myself to the increased gravity. I should be fine from now on."

Howard took a bite, chewed it, then asked, "PhageB? Is that some sort of immunization?"

She shook her head. "Oh no. Since I was born and raised on the moon, my body was totally adapted to about one sixth of Earth's gravity. If they had sent me down like that, I would hardly be able to move and my bones would have been way too fragile. Any attempt to run, jump or lift anything might have caused multiple fractures. So, they gave me a shot of of a modified Omniphage compound that took only a day to rebuild my entire body as if I had grown up here, in the bottom of the gravity well. It also includes antibodies for all the common diseases. I'm in good shape for now." She watched him start to say something, then shake his head and continue eating. "To be honest sir, I'm rather surprised that you and Martha haven't taken a round of Phage."

Martha had a look of horror and Howard just looked angry. He took a moment to compose himself, sipped his drink, and looked directly at Susan. "I understand you have been raised in a godless society, but that is not how we do things here. The good book promises man three-score and ten. If you don't understand, that means seventy years is the average human lifespan. Using the devil's drugs to extend your allotted span is not something we condone." He paused, his voice softening. "Consider this, child. If everyone could get a new body anytime they wanted, pretty soon, their would be no room for anyone at all. Each new child would come into the world and have to fight adults that should have gone to their heavenly reward long ago."

Susan shrugged. "That is easily addressed with birth control and by opening new colonies in order to avoid having any single event wipe out humanity."

His face darkened once more and it became obvious that he was barely controlling his temper. "Enough of this nonsense, child! Be fruitful and multiply commanded the Lord and so it shall be. We shall not entertain any more of this blasphemous talk."

Susan held his eye for only a moment more, before deciding she didn't want to get into a real confrontation. "Yes, sir." She dropped her attention back to the food on her plate, but couldn't help but notice the stark fear on the faces of both Martha and Lizzie.

That evening, the patriarch decided it would be good for the whole family to gather in the living room, after dinner was cleaned up. He spent almost an hour reading from marked sections in a huge, leather-bound family Bible.

Later, Susan was getting ready for bed when there was a soft knock on her door. Lizzie slipped in, looking nervous and overwrought. "What's the matter, cousin?"

"Please. Whatever you do, don't bring up that Satan's brew again. Uncle Howard is convinced it will be the downfall of society."

Susan gave her a wry smile and nodded. "Yeah. I kinda got that idea when he flared up at dinner. I must admit, I don't understand though. It has saved so many lives."

"And it has turned others into monsters. I've seen the photographs. He keeps an album of them in his office desk, in town." She glanced over her shoulder once more and lowered her voice to a whisper. "Did your father tell you why they left?"

Susan shook her head.

"Back before either of them were married, they had a very good friend called Edward. The three of them used to get into all sorts of mischief as young men. Your father was not satisfied with the life of a farmer. He was really good in school and got a scholarship to university. After he had been gone for awhile, he sent word that he would be coming home on holiday and wanted to celebrate with his brother and old friend. At that point, Howard had already met his betrothed and they thought it would be one last fling before settling down to married life."

Lizzie sat on the bed and continued the family history. "Uncle Howard was driving them back from town, very late at night, when a deer jumped in front of the truck and it rolled off the road and down a long embankment. He and your father were only bruised up, but Edward was badly hurt. Your father said he had a needle full of this phage stuff and it would save Edward's life. They argued and Uncle Howard decided to run the rest of the way to the farm and call for an ambulance to come and take them to a hospital. Later, your father said that Edward was almost dead, so he decided to get the shot from his emergency kit."

"Did it save his life?" Susan asked softly.

"In a way, yes. But it turned him into a monster."

"Monster? What do you mean?"

"Howard had been hurt more than he let on. He had a concussion and passed out in the front yard of the house. Martha found him early the next morning, called the hospital and he woke up two days later."

"But what about the monster?"

"Your father had stayed with his friend overnight, while that drug was working its evil magic. When Edward woke up, he had been transformed into some sort of wolf man."

Susan nodded as understanding dawned. "That means there must have been some sort of dog fur that got mixed with the Omniphage. It has happened before. But they have an easy fix for it now."

"That may be so, but this was more than twenty years ago." She paused and then continued. "When Howard told the police where to find the accident scene, they found the wounded Martin, exhausted and unconscious in the wrecked truck. They called out for Edward and he wasn't around. They figured that when he woke up and couldn't get any response from Martin, he had run to the farmhouse for help."

"Then what happened, Lizzie?"

"Martha was in the kitchen and she heard someone shouting, out in the yard. When she looked through the window, she saw some sort of half-man, half-beast creature calling her name. She thought sure the Devil had sent some demon to claim her soul, so she grabbed the shotgun and told him to stay away. He called her name again and came in the kitchen door. She shot him."

Appalled, Susan whispered, "Oh my God!"

"By the time the police arrived, Edward was dead. Your father blamed Howard and Martha. He called them superstitious fools, returned to his school, and shortly after graduation, he married your mom and left for the moon."

Beta Prime

A bell chimed as Mike Hawthorne walked through a mirror frame and into a small room with stone walls. An arched doorway looked out over a narrow walk to a low stone wall and a beautiful view of a waterfall, dropping into a rugged gorge. Mark Chambers stepped forward to shake hands. "Welcome to the Keepe, sir. Care to join me for a drink?"

"That sounds like a good plan, Mark." They walked towards a drawbridge over the gorge and the portcullis on the other side. Mike paused and glanced back, over his shoulder. "May I ask why you don't have a mirrorgate in your entrance hall, rather than out here?"

"Actually, it is part of my security precautions. I value my privacy and don't want anyone to drop in without my being immediately aware of it."

Mike shook his head in disbelief. "You and Wendy set yourselves up as domain lords and mages before the rest of us got a handle on things and established proper controls. What are you worried about? No one is going to invade a wizard with the sort of power and knowledge you control."

"Sorry to disagree, Mike. But I think you are being way too trusting. Mark my words, sooner or later, there will be some folks that don't like how things are run and will want to try their hand at it. The first group of troublemakers are already plotting."

Mike was incredulous. "What? Who?"

"Ever heard of Victor C. Adams, the Third?"

"He's some sort of industrialist, right?"

The young man nodded. "That and much more. He's already established himself in Morepork with a small tavern."

"Nothing wrong with that. Looks like he's just putting his business skills to use."

"I've some friends that work for him and he worries me. The tavern is only a stepping-stone. He's hired a couple of wizards and is planning on becoming master of his own domain. Back on Earth, he has two bricks and has a team working on some sort of interface that will allow data transfer between Beta and Earth."

"I don't see a problem with the mechanics of data transfer, but since we have no sophisticated electronics, nor factories to produce them, here on Beta, what good would it do?"

"That is just it. He has an engineering team working on a design for a magical fabricator that can be constructed here on Beta. As soon as he has his own domain and a few wizards in his employ, he wants to create a truly modern city to use as his own research facility and think tank."

Mike thought about that for a moment, before offering, "Isn't that something like what you are doing with your starship colony project?"

"Well, yes... but..."

Mike waved off his objection. "As long as he's not going to build super-polluting factories and just wants to create his own high-technology haven in some domain, I don't see why we should stop him. Some folks hate the primitive stuff. I'm sure he'll attract a lot of them." He paused before continuing. "Which reminds me, what is the status of your little project?"

"Off the record?"

"Oh, of course. That is why I'm asking here and not back on the moon."

"We decided on a jovian moon instead of one of the inner asteroids. It had plenty of raw mineral resources and there are several nearby sources of methane and liquid water."

Mike smiled. "And with a decent spread of solar panels, you can convert both methane and water into fuel for your engines. Good plan."

"Already done, sir. We've got a stockpile of fuel supplies, a huge solar array and two medium-sized fabricators. They have already constructed the fuselage for the first warp tug. Right now, they are building the actual warp engines."

"How long before you start recruiting colonists? And while I'm at it, what do you mean by a warp tug?"

"That is still a few month's off. As soon as the warp tug is finished, we're starting work on the first type one shuttle." He moved towards the drawbridge. "Come on into my library and I'll show you."

A few minutes later, drinks in hand and surrounded by books and art, they settled into leather-clad armchairs. Mark held up a small model of a slender torpedo-shape that had been sitting on four stubby legs. "This is our type one shuttle." He picked up another model of a set of three cylinders separated by a spindly framework. "And this is a warp tug." He went on to explain, "The warp tug will never enter an atmosphere. It has no biological living space and is nothing but a sturdy frame, warp engines and a trio of bricks. It is commanded by a rotating crew of transhumanists, such as ourselves."

"That is going to be used only to ferry your shuttle back and forth, correct?"

"That is part of it, yes. The shuttle is relatively small. It has space for only eight CryoDox. And enough supplies to support them for about a week. It is designed only for exploration and transporting personnel."

Mike Hawthorne squinted at the two models. "I hope you realize it will take a whole lot of flights of that thing to establish a colony."

"Like I said, it's only for exploration. Once we have scouted and determined a colony location, we're going to start sending Type Two colonial ships." He reached under the table and withdrew another model. This one was a conical design that looked a lot like early Mercury capsules or the Mars Curiosity rover delivery system. "We are going to build a series of these. Each one holds one hundred CryoDox as well as enough equipment to establish a colony. They are one-way vessels. Once they land, they become the central base for a new colony. All except a handful of the CryoDox can be disassembled and converted to various structures. We have a whole team of folks working on this right now." He took a sip of his drink before continuing. "If there are no major problems, I would expect the first of several test missions, using the Type One shuttle, in another couple of weeks. The first of the Type Two colony ships are at least another couple of months from completion. By-the-way, we've decided on a traditional project title. When the recruiting starts, the whole project will be named Exodus."

Morepork

Victor was pleased with himself. He thought the plan to use an Inn as a base of operations in Morepork would prove to be a pain. Instead, once he had spoken with one of the mages from the architecture school, it proved exhilarating to help design a small business. He had spent so many years ramrodding multinational corporations, that it was a refreshing change to have a hands-on approach once more.

"Victor?" The voice belonged to his friend and security chief, Jack Hamstein. "I've some good news for you."

"Just a moment, Jack." He closed the cash box, poured a couple of beers, and led the way back into his office. Relaxing behind the desk, he took a sip and waited for Jack to follow suit.

"I must say, boss. You are much more relaxed here than back on Earth."

"That's because once I realized what they meant by twenty-four to one time compression, I understood there really isn't that much need to rush about like rabid lemmings." He took another sip of his brew. "We can take the time not only to plan each step carefully, but also to savor the moment."

Jack sipped his beer and nodded agreement before continuing. "In that case, I've got something more for you to savor. Not only have I arranged for our own domain, but also have discovered three mages who actually work for us back on Earth. Two of them are architects and the third has a doctorate in information technology. He has been looking at the bricks and helmets and thinks he has a way to interface them in such a way that we can share data and images between Beta and Earth."

"Good news on both counts. Where is our new domain and how much did we have to pay for it?"

"We didn't actually pay anything for it. One of the Domain Lords I approached needed some luxury supplies that aren't available on the moon. I merely arranged for a couple hundred kilos of seeds and plants to be shipped up on the next shuttle and they made our three corporate mages lords of their own domain."

Victor frowned. "Made them lords? I thought I was running this show?"

His friend held up a hand to placate him. "Only someone with specialized training can manage a domain. They all have to be approved by the mage council. Don't worry. These fellows know who they are working for and as soon as you're ready, we can start work." He pulled an envelope from an inner pocket. "Here are a couple of maps. The one shows the route to our new domain and the other is a topographic map of the domain, itself."

They both turned at the knock on the door and Jack opened it. "M'Lord Grannette! Glad you made it." He turned to his boss. "Victor. May I present..."

"Roger Granette. I'm rather surprised to see you here. Your father didn't seem interested in my proposal the last we spoke."

They shook hands. "My father is way too conservative in his thinking. My sister and I have our own resources and we've been residents of Beta for several months, Earth-time."

"Your sister is here as well? Oh my! Thomas Granette is going to be livid. What is she doing, may I ask?"

The young man smiled. "Like me, she is working for you. When we heard Jack was looking for people with information technology and architectural skills, we immediately volunteered. I have a doctorate in IT and Pamela has a degree in graphic design and animation. Between us, we are more than capable of building you a new corporate headquarters here on Beta."

Victor had to match his smile of enthusiasm. "Well, let's get started then."

Roger withdrew a small golden disk from his jacket. He laid it on the desk and it projected a 3D image of a castle, floating a few inches above the desktop. "Now, this is one of the basic designs that is popular with many of the other lords. Naturally, we can modify it any way you wish."

Victor shook his head. "Forget it! I want to build a modern city with proper buildings, streets, parks, and industrial-grade lighting."

Roger nodded. "Jack suggested as much, but I thought I would show you options. How about this one?" The castle morphed into a tall, stainless steel and glass tower, with various levels defined by terraces. Sharply-defined columns framed tall glass doors.

"That's more like it." Victor agreed. "But I want it larger and similar structures around it, with a fountain plaza in the center."

"In that case, I'll leave this with you so that you may fine tune the interior spaces and furnishings while I'm en-route."

"En-route? How long will that take?"

"I'm going to be traveling with a small party of professional explorers. There are no planes, airports or helicopters on Beta, so any new domain needs to be explored on horseback. The trip is projected to take a couple of weeks."

"Damn! I hate horses."

"Don't worry. I'm going to install a mirrorgate here in your office. Once we arrive, I'll open another one so that you can come through to help with the on-site city planning."

High Valley

Susan finished writing Charlie's email and reread it.

Hi Charlie,

I hope things are going well for you and the rest of the gang. Down here, it's just another boring day of manual labor, punctuated by long-winded lectures from my misogynistic Uncle, followed by incredibly boring sermons read from the "good book".

My only relief is a couple of hours after Sunday church services. They have a covered-dish picnic and let us wander around town. Even though all the stores are closed, it is still nice to get into a conversation with anyone other than family.

I just have to be patient for another ten months until I turn eighteen. I've checked the calendar and my birthday falls on a Sunday. That is when I'll expect to find my ride parked in front of the house at dawn.

Patience is the name of the game and I'll just have to wait it out and hope I don't lose my mind before the big day arrives.

Miss you all and hope to see you in about ten months.

Susan

She hit the 'send' tab and the message spun off to the net.

"Susan!" It was Uncle Howard's voice, hollering up the stairwell. "Susan! Come on down. There is someone here that I want you to meet."

"Coming, Uncle!" She hollered back. "What now?" She muttered. It was after dinner and well past sundown. The family was usually headed to bed by now.

Howard was waiting by the front door. "Come on now, girl. Don't be shy. You have a visitor on the porch."

"Visitor?"

He held the screen door open for her. "You'll see."

She glanced one way and saw an unfamiliar horse, tied to the railing. Switching her gaze to the other side revealed a very tall man. He wore black slacks, boots, and jacket. The jacket was open to display a plain white shirt with a black string tie.

Howard's hand at her back pushed her forward. "Susan. It is my pleasure to introduce Mr. Samuel Martin. Sam here just inherited the ranch about five miles south of us."

She shook his hand and he held it a bit too long for her comfort. "Pleased to meet you, Mr. Martin."

"Please call me Sam. Mr. Martin sounds too much like my father." His smile was hesitant, yet genuine. "Your uncle was right. You are very pretty."

"Thank you, Sam."

"I have a couple of things to take care of, but will be back in a few minutes. You two get acquainted." Howard didn't wait for an answer.

Sam held the chain on the porch swing to still it. "Please sit down, Susan."

She didn't know how to politely refuse, so she sat and he joined her. The swing was designed for two, but he was a big man.

After a minute of awkward silence, Susan asked, "So, what brings you out our way this late at night, Sam?"

"Since my dad died, I've had to run the farm alone. My mother and the other ladies manage the house, but everything else falls on me. After dark is the only time I get for a bit of relaxation."

"I've not seen you around before. You must not get out very often."

He stretched his arms overhead and when they settled, one was on the back of the swing, over her shoulders. For some reason, this made Susan nervous and she leaned forward. He ignored it and answered, "I usually ride around the edge of my woods for an hour right after dark. Unless the weather is truly foul, of course. But when your uncle told me you were here, I just had to come see the moon girl for myself."

"Moon girl? Tell me you didn't just call me moon girl."

"Sorry. It just seemed to sound rather sexy." His voice held a teasing note.

She glanced up at him and got her first clear look under the single light bulb. Not only was Sam tall, but he was very broad-shouldered, with coarse features, and at least a full day's growth of beard. He looked like he was in his late thirties and did a lot of heavy lifting. His arms obviously strained the jacket sleeves. What started as a soft smile turned into a leer and Susan wanted nothing more than to get away from him. She stood up quickly stood against the railing. "Oh my goodness, but it is warm tonight, isn't it?"

He sat back in the swing, the leer still evident. "That's alright, Susan. I'm sure we're going to get to know each other quite well." He stood up, towering over her and once again, she felt a primitive urge to run. "It's getting late and there will be plenty of other times for us to become better acquainted."

Uncle Howard must have heard Sam's heavy boots on the steps, because he came out just in time to see the man swing himself atop his horse. "Leaving so soon, Sam?"

"I'm afraid so, Mr. Childers. I must be up early in the morning and I've still the ride back." He tipped his hat to Susan. "A very good evening to you and sweet dreams."

As he turned and rode away, Susan felt a shudder of revulsion wash over her. Uncle Howard placed a hand on her shoulder. "What do you think, child? He's a fine figure of man now, isn't he?"

"He's a brute, alright. I'd hate to meet him in a dark alley."

Howard chuckled. "A big one. I'll grant you that. But he's a hard worker and owns a fine farm. He'd make a very good catch for some lucky young woman."

***

Some chores weren't too bad. Sitting in the cool barn while cleaning and oiling the leather harnesses fell into that category.

"I hear you had a suitor last night." Lizzie was bent over a saddle, oiling a stirrup.

"Suitor?" Susan said sarcastically. "Nothing could be farther from that. In the first place, he does nothing for me and in the second place, I prefer boyfriends that are a bit closer to my size and age."

"Well, I find him rather handsome and he does own his own farm. You could do worse."

"I still don't get it. What is so attractive about a farm? I mean, I like fresh eggs and veggies as well as the next person, but the idea of spending the rest of my life here scares the heck out of me. I can't wait until I turn eighteen."

"What will turning eighteen change? You will still be here and there aren't that many eligible bachelors in the valley. You should be planning for a home and a family, like a proper Christian woman."

"Lizzie. That may be what you are looking forward to doing with your life, but I intend to spend the next few hundred years or so exploring the cosmos and helping to establish some new colonies. Even if I do fall in love and get married, children will have to wait until after I get bored with my first career."

"Few hundred? First career? What on Earth are you talking about, girl?"

"It is way too soon to know for sure, since Omniphage hasn't been common that long, but insurance company actuarial tables project the average human life expectancy, excluding old age and related disease, as more than six hundred years. During that time, it seems reasonable that most people will get bored and change careers at least once a century."

Lizzie shook her head. "Now I know you're being silly. No one in the valley has any of that Devil's brew. It's just not allowed. You are going to be a fine housewife, just like Martha and the rest of us."

Lizzie had no idea how that matter-of-fact statement thoroughly terrified her cousin.

Micasa

"DeeDee? You still with us?" The soft voice in her earbud was irritating.

"Yeah. I'm almost awake." She groaned. "Damn! I hate coming out of cryo. Gimme a second to get my bearings."

"No problem, DeeDee. All the sensors are showing green and you're in a fairly stable low orbit."

Wendy Miller had come a long way. At the start of the Phage wars, she had been a student, working through art school as a topless dancer. More than two decades later, she was still a stunning redhead, thanks to Omniphage, but also a proven shuttle pilot. She hit the release button on her CryoDox and the top swung silently out of the way.

Floating in null-gee, she guided herself up the narrow passage and strapped into the pilot's seat. "Okay, Houston. What have you got for me?"

A chuckle was followed by, "You know damn well this ain't Houston." The voice continued. "The rest of your team is waking up now. They should be joining you in about ten minutes. Let us know if all your displays agree with ours."

"That's an affirmative, Chukkers. Everything is green here as well. Are we ready for the WarpTug to disengage?"

"Affirmative, DeeDee. They are just waiting on you."

Outside, their colony ship was a huge departure from the original Type One exploration shuttle. This looked more like a giant version of an early Gemini capsule or the Mars Curiosity rover of days gone by. Along with a Type One shuttle and another smaller craft, they were locked inside the frame of a Transhumanist WarpTug.

A few minutes later, the WarpTug released all the clamps and a short burst from maneuvering thrusters let it drift ahead of the three colony vessels. As soon as it was a safe distance away, the smaller, unmanned ship decelerated with a short, sharp burst of its engines and dropped out of orbit.

"Okay, DeeDee. This is for posterity now. Ready?" The man sitting in the co-pilot seat had a small camera. "As soon as we're down, this is going to be released to the Port Heinlein news service and within an hour, it will be all over Earth as well."

She shook her head in resignation, then smiled. "Okay. Let's do it."

"I'm starting the recording now." He checked his slate to make sure the camera was looking at DeeDee with a view of the planet Micasa behind her. "This is Kevin O'Conner, speaking to you from the control deck of the colony ship, Jerryville. Our pilot, Wendy Miller, has graciously agreed to take a little time to explain some of the things we'll be showing you over the next few hours. Wendy? Why don't you start by explaining a bit about the Jerryville?"

"The Jerryville is a modified Type One colony ship. That means it is not designed to explore, but rather to act as a one-way transport for starting a new colony from scratch."

"How did it get its name?"

She paused and blushed a bit. "Actually, I was on the first ship to land on Micasa. We had a drawing to see who would get the chance to name the first four landmarks. I got to name a nearby river the Shenandoah and our co-pilot got to name the first colony landing site after one of his favorite science fiction authors. This ship is named for our future landing site and permanent home."

"So we are going to land in the same place the original Type One shuttle explored?"

She shook her head. "No. You see, the original shuttle needed as safe a landing spot as we could determine from orbit. That meant a fairly high and flat area with only short grasses and a nearby river. The climate is somewhat like an arctic tundra on Earth. That is great for a safe landing and atmosphere evaluations, but not a good location for a permanent colony. This time, we're going to be landing far downstream on that river, in a temperate region."

"Why didn't you choose that area the first time?"

"Because a temperate region with good soil for crops means it will have a lot of healthy growth, including large trees. That may be great for the settlers, but not a very safe landing zone."

Kevin paused a moment to think that over. "Are you saying we are going to land in among a bunch of trees? Won't that be dangerous?"

Wendy laughed. "Not if we blow them up, first." She turned to point out the viewport. "Did you see the other two spacecraft? They both look like much smaller versions of this one, don't they?"

Kevin keyed up a camera with an external view. "We can only see one now. The other dropped out of orbit just a little while ago. In my earlier briefing, I was told they were used to survey and clear the way."

"That's right. The first one is going to land a few kilometers away from our primary colony site. Once it is down, it will deploy a couple of buzzards."

"Can we take a moment to tell our viewers what you mean by buzzards?"

"Sure, Kevin. That lander as well as our colony ship are equipped with two different types of surveillance drones. We call the largest ones 'Buzzards' because they are about the same size as the large, Earth-based bird, and can hover on station for days at a time. Each one contains several video cameras, side-scan radar, various environmental monitors and solar panels to charge their batteries when they get low."

"The buzzards are going to act as scouts then?"

"That's right, Kevin. Even with our best equipment, there is only so much you can determine from orbit. Since this colony vessel is one way and there are one hundred people on-board, we can't take chances on a landing site. A pair of buzzards will criss-cross the proposed landing area and give us a detailed, up-close map of the site."

"Since a lot of research has gone into choosing a site, what would a close-up look show us that might make it unsafe? And while you're at it, what if the buzzards show it to be unsafe; what then?"

"We need a fairly level piece of stable ground. With that in mind, what if the side-scan radar shows our area is actually hiding a swamp or bog under the tree canopy? Perhaps it is some sort of soft limestone with large caverns and sinkholes. If that is the case, we will send the buzzards in ever-wider searches until they find someplace that is both stable and fertile."

"You mentioned two types of drones. What about the others?"

She laughed once more. "We call them 'skeeters' since they are so much smaller than buzzards. They only have audio, video, temperature, and wind sensors. They are about the size of a dragonfly and are used where we don't want to spook other animals."

"Thanks for clearing that up for us. Now that we know how the final landing site will be selected, what is this about blowing it up?"

"Awhile back, when the warp-tug was finished, it was tested without CryoDox or life-support of any kind. Instead, once it arrived, it deployed a series of geosynchronous satellites that provide GPS, mapping and weather data. They have been storing this data until we arrived and the moment we warped into the system, they dumped the accumulation into our computers. The first exploration team that I was fortunate to be a part of only had a few days to look around and gather data. This time, we have a much better idea of what we're getting into. We know for example, that Micasian geology is very similar to Earth's. There are tectonic plates, volcanoes, ice caps, large lakes, and seas. The area we have chosen for the primary colony site is near the center of an old, worn-down mountain range. There doesn't appear to be any seismic activity nearby. Since it is in a temperate zone, most of the land is covered with a very dense, old-growth forest."

DeeDee was describing it, Kevin was cueing up a series of images from the satellites.

"We don't want to sit down on a flood plain or on a rocky plateau. Areas that are very fertile, level, and not swampy, are usually covered in large trees and thick growth. That is where that second craft comes in."

Kevin grinned. "Let me guess. It's a giant weed wacker?"

"You're pretty close there. It is a very large fuel-air bomb. The type the military used to call daisy-cutter. It is not nuclear, but has about the same effect as a couple of megaton air-burst. When it goes off, it will strip the trees and loose debris in about a five hundred meter wide circle. Not only will it clear a landing area, but it will give us plenty of room to maneuver during the final approach."

The camera scene changed to show the engine on the first craft, display a silent and yet very bright ribbon of fire. Multiple shades of white, orange, and red created the distinctive shock diamonds of a high-efficiency rocket engine.

Once it dropped out of sight, Kevin continued. "So, it would appear that this colony is going to start with a bang?"

DeeDee groaned.

Morepork

Victor was enjoying the camaraderie of some fellow merchants when he heard a low bell sound from upstairs. "Excuse me, my friends. But I must attend to some other business. Enjoy your meals." Without waiting for a reply, he hurried up to his suite.

Two men in well-worn leathers were waiting for him. "Jack! Roger! I was hoping that was the sound of the mirrorgate." He pumped each hand then waved towards the chairs. "Sit. Please. I know you must be tired of horses and campfires. Can I offer you drinks or perhaps a meal?"

They both smiled and accepted the drink offer, but wanted to give their report before getting washed up and dinner.

A few moments later, one of the waitresses brought their drinks. When she left, Victor sat back and took a sip. "Okay. Out with it. What have you found?"

Jack looked at Roger and nodded. The young man cleared his throat before answering. "The trip to our new domain is not that difficult. In the future, after we build a good road and some bridges, we should be able to drive it in a couple of hours." He pulled one of the display disks from his pocket and laid it on the table. A 3D map spread out above it. "That red line shows the path we took to get there and that blue dotted line shows the domain borders."

Victor waved him on. "I've already seen that part. What about the locations I asked you to investigate?"

"We walked through each of the three spots and the first is going to be the best for our purposes. It is this promontory of land that defines the point where these two rivers come together. Based on the population figures you said you wanted and the high-technology base, this is what the first stage of the city might look like."

The jungle and deep forest covering the point of land was replaced with a circle of tall buildings, roads and smaller buildings trailing back down the back slope.

Victor nodded his approval. "How long to gather raw materials and a workforce to build it?"

"The only workforce we needed for the structures and

infrastructure is already in place. That is what mages do. All the raw materials we need are located up stream several kilometers. As soon as you give approval, we shall start the quarry process, create a road to the city site and start seeding the various sites. My sister and I will be working on it together. We will have the first tower ready in a week or less."

The ornamental mirrorgate mounted on the wall of the office gave off a deep gong sound. Victor looked at the two men. "Were you bringing someone else with you?"

They shook their heads, looking as confused as their boss.

The mirror fogged up, then cleared to reveal another small room. A tall young man in formal suit and flowing robe stepped into Victor's office. He was followed by another young couple.

Roger's eyes were wide as he jumped up and gave a slight bow.

The tall man nodded his head in acknowledgment and turned to Victor, holding out his hand. "Please excuse the intrusion, but I do believe it is time we met. I'm Michael Hawthorne, Domain Lord for Beta Prime."

They shook hands. "I'm Victor Charles Adams the Third. Welcome to my humble inn."

Mike gestured to the other two. "This is Master Mage Wendy Mathias and her companion and the Beta Security Director is Master Mage Mark Chambers."

Victor shook each proffered hand, offered drinks that were politely declined, then asked the obvious. "To what do I owe the pleasure of finally meeting you?"

"We understand you have purchased a domain and although you are not ready to be a mage yourself, you have several working for you. Because of that, we wanted to welcome you and also to make sure you were aware of some of the very few rules we have here on Beta."

Victor turned to Roger. "I hadn't heard of any rules other the the obvious laws that are posted in the courthouse, here in Beta Prime. Where you aware of them, Roger?"

Chagrined, he nodded. "As part of mage training, we learn there are some things we are not allowed to do. You haven't asked for any of them, so it never occurred to me to bring up the subject."

Frowning, Victor turned back to his guests. "My apologies if I've broken any of them, but it would be nice to see a list."

Mike shook his head and smiled. "Don't be too hard on him. Most any of the mages would have done the same thing. There is no list handy, but they are fairly easy to remember. The first one is that no high explosive devices of any kind are allowed. That means dynamite, cannons, hand grenades, and guns. Small quantities of black powder for fireworks are okay, but anything larger will not be tolerated. We have no problem with small or large groups getting into a fight if that sort of thing appeals to you, but if you bring explosives or firearms into it, the Domain Council will intercede."

"Okay. That sounds fair enough. I'm a peaceful fellow and would much rather talk over differences. What other rules?"

"This one is fairly broad. Since we do our construction using magic, all we need are some raw materials that we can modify to create a structure. The Domain Council requires that any time you gather resources from a location, that you return it as quickly as possible to a native environment."

"Go green, eh?" Victor chuckled. "I have no problem with that, either. What else?"

"That's about it. Most mages working on places like Beta Prime won't run into these issues. But with the sort of high-technology center you're planning, you might be tempted to push the rules a bit. That is why I wanted to meet you and to introduce you to Mark and Wendy. They will be dropping by your domain from time to time. If you have any questions, please don't hesitate in asking."

"No problem. You're all welcome to stop by as soon as we have a five-star hotel in place."

"Thank you, Victor. And that brings me to a favor I'd like to ask of you."

Victor spread his hands wide. "If I can, sure. What is it?"

"You won't be the only one wanting modern conveniences. As soon as you get setup with your computer connections back to Earth, I would like to hire you as our ISP. I'm sure other domains will want the same. It will prove a lucrative revenue stream. Also, as I mentioned, Mark is our Security man. I will want him to work closely with your networking team to make sure there is no threat to either the Beta net or the Earth internet."

"Very well. And I have a favor to ask of you, Mike."

"I'll try, of course. What is it?"

"How do I become a member of this Domain Council?"

"You have to finish mage training so you can be a Master Mage of your own domain. I'm sure that with your background and the city you're building now, it will be no problem. I was even going to suggest that Roger start your training as soon as possible."

Everyone shook hands and the meeting broke up. The Domain Lords left via the mirrorgate and when it had turned back to a mirror, Victor spun around to face Jack and Roger. "Now what was that all about?"

Jack lifted palms up and shrugged.

Roger swallowed. "Sorry, boss. But I had no idea they would just drop in like that."

"I thought you told me that only people I had given permission to would be able to use that gate?"

"Most people have to be approved by you after ringing the bell, but members of the Domain Council are something else. Most them were part of the original Beta design team." He waved his hands in a vague manner. "They actually created all of this and control the core programming still. They can literally do anything they want."

Victor dropped his eyes, took a deep breath and considered things for a moment. Then, he looked up and smiled. "In that case, you had better start teaching me everything you know about being a mage. Sooner or later, I'm going to be on that council."

High Valley

Conversation around the Childers' evening meal usually revolved around the workings of the farm, the weather, and occasionally, some gossip from town. Susan made a point of polite replies to questions, but had learned to keep opinions to herself.

The head of the house took a sip from his drink, then turned his attention to her. "Susan, I understand you're learning to bake. This pie was excellent."

"Thank you, Uncle Howard. I must admit Martha is an fine teacher. She has taught me a great deal about baking and cooking in general, much of which I had never imagined."

"While that gives me a great deal of pleasure, I'm not as pleased to hear you haven't been applying yourself to your Bible studies."

Susan tried to shrug it off. "I've read it already. And I'm just not that excited about reviewing the same things over and over again."

"Not excited about studying the word of God Almighty? Surely you can't mean that, girl?"

"The Bibles that I've seen here and in church are all the King James version, correct?" She knew she should say something placating, but was sick of it.

He nodded, face calm and questioning. "Yes. What of it?"

"In 1604, King James of England commissioned forty-seven members of the Church of England to work on a new English translation. It was completed in 1611. Their work was based on more than four thousand documents in Latin, Hebrew, Greek, and Vulgate Latin. The earliest of these documents were written four hundred years after Christ's death and they, in turn, were based on long-lost documents that were written more than one hundred years after his death. Anything that didn't fit the Puritan or Church of England feelings were either mis-translated or totally ignored. Many of the early church writings, including the Gnostic scriptures and the Dead Sea Scrolls contradict King James. Indeed, there are many, many contradictions within the Bible itself." She paused to catch her breath and looked up.

Everyone at the table were silent for a good ten seconds. Martha and Lizzie wore looks of astonishment, while Howard was livid.

Through clenched teeth, his voice was low and gruff. "You think you are some sort of theological scholar, that you can question what your elders have recognized as the true word of the Lord?"

Susan realized she was in trouble and tried to placate the man with a soft, non-confrontational tone and lowered eyes. "I meant no disrespect, sir and realize that you are a devout Christian."

"So, you're saying you're some sort of heathen that denies the truth of the Bible?"

"We all must follow our own hearts and minds, sir."

He was almost shaking with rage. "I cannot believe what sort of heathen my brother became. Perhaps there is hope for you, yet. You are to read and contemplate the Bible every night before bed. I will ask questions the following day on your reading and your comprehension. Understand, child?"

"I already told you I've read it more than once. Why..."

"Enough! Go to your room! Now!"

Upstairs, Susan waited until all the lights were out and the house was quiet before she got out her slate and typed a blog entry explaining the blowup at the dinner table. She hit the send button, then decided she was still too wide awake and needed to decompress herself. So she popped in her earbuds and loaded her favorite song list. That was a mistake.

She didn't hear the approaching footsteps and was caught completely off-guard when the door opened and Howard Childers saw her propped up in bed, with her face illuminated by the glow of the slate.

Two short strides had him alongside her bed, with his hand extended. "Let me see that, child." The dark grimace on his face scared Susan, so she handed it over.

"I've seen these in use before. It's a computer, isn't it?"

"Yes, sir."

"Is this where you're getting all those heathen ideas instead of studying the good book as you were told?"

"It's just my slate, sir. I use it for my blog, to store photos and play music. I was just listening when you came in."

"And I suppose you take it to town, so that you are in wireless range, so you can exchange messages with your friends on the moon?"

She didn't think it wise to tell him it had a permanent quantum-link connection to the lunar network. "Occasionally, yes sir. I miss them so..."

Before she could finish, he spun on his heel and headed for the door.

She clambered out of bed, tripping on the long chemise and blankets. "Wait! You can't take that. It's mine. Not yours." As he reached the doorway, she grabbed his arm and tried to yank the precious piece of technology out of his hand.

The impact of his large, callused hand on the side of her face spun her almost half-way around and she landed hard, against the dresser. Caught totally by surprise, Susan felt nothing but shock for a second and then the crushing pain paralyzed her. She heard a keening whine and realized it was her own voice. It took another few seconds for her to clear her mind enough to roll over on her side and force herself to all fours. She leaned on the bed and groaned with tears in her eyes.

She heard the heavy front door slam, followed by the lesser slap of the screen door. Stumbling to her feet, she rushed to the window.

Howard strode out into the front drive, partially lit by the single porch bulb. He slammed her slate down on the hard-packed and rocky soil.

"He'll have to do better than that." The logical part of her mind thought. "They are designed to withstand much higher falls and water pressure."

The large man stood there, staring down at it, shaking with rage and muttering obscenities. He glanced up and saw her in the window, then stopped. He took a breath, looked down at the panoramic image of Port Heinlein on the glowing screen, pulled his pistol and shot it. The sound and flash of the gun was overshadowed by the brilliant blue, actinic fire that marked the demise of the shattered touch screen and power supply.

"Howard? What in the world?" Martha's voice came from the porch.

The patriarch turned around and stared up at Susan while he ordered. "Martha. Susan is to remain in her room for the next two days. You are to take a meal of bread and water twice a day. She will not leave until she accompanies us to Church on Sunday. If you see her reading anything other than the Bible, you will paddle her like the disrespectful and willful child that she is. Do you understand me?"

Meekly, the elderly woman answered. "Yes, sir. Of course, husband."

Susan sank down to her knees, leaned against the bed and tried not to cry. She had suffered injuries in some of her martial arts classes, but nothing had ever prepared her for being blind-sided by an adult male who outweighed her by more than a fifty kilos. First, she vowed it would not happen again, then she started planning how to escape what was now obviously her prison.

Micasa

After watching the video feeds of the fuel-air explosion that cleared their landing zone, the de-orbit burn and reentry seemed rather mundane.

That is, except for the last five minutes when the colony ship was slowing its descent with the aid of a monstrous parachute. While still more than a thousand feet up, the landing engines fired, the chute was released and the huge vessel came to a hover, on top of five pillars of flame.

Their approach had been calculated so precisely that the shock-diamond flames only had bare soil and rock beneath their hover point.

DeeDee took just a moment to scan her instruments and rear-view screens to decide it was as close to perfect as they were likely to get. "On target and commencing landing sequence." Her voice sounded much calmer than she was.

As the engines slowly cut power, five landing legs sprouted from the bottom. Only moments later, the colony ship Jerryville settled in place. Multiple computers compared notes on positioning, attitude and weight on each leg, made instantaneous minor adjustments, then shut off the engines.

The silence was deafening. Wendy broke it first with a soft smile and a whispered, "Welcome home."

One of the multiple slates mounted in front of each of the four crew members, cleared itself of flight data in order to show the cheering crew back in Port Heinlein.

Mike Hawthorne's image came center-screen. "Congratulations, Captain Miller. All our instruments show a perfect landing."

"Thank you, Director. My crew and I are going to initiate a wakeup call for the first dozen of our fellow colonists. While they are decanting, we're going to enjoy a nice meal and a few hour's of rest."

"Understood, Captain. You need to give it at least a day for your craft and immediate area to cool down. Good luck!"

After signing off, the crew went through the post-landing checklist to make sure all engines and flight controls were completely off-line and safe. Then, they started the eight-hour wakeup sequence for the first dozen CryoDox.

Wendy stood up. "Okay. It's now time for that wine and lobster we stashed for just this occasion. I would image it's the last chance we'll have to get stuffed, wasted, and relax for a long time to come."

***

"Hey Captain?"

DeeDee turned her attention away from monitoring the robot tractor that had almost completed digging the encircling ditch. "Yes, Igor? What's up?"

"While I'm waiting for Buster to finish our wall and moat system, I've been running a couple of skeeters through the woods around us."

"Find anything interesting?"

He handed her a slate. "This was recorded very early this morning. See that dark-brown roly-poly?"

She noted he was pointing to a small, armored critter about fifteen centimeters in length. "We've seen a lot of these. They look like the Armadillidiidae family of Terran woodlice. Except for the size, of course. And the fact that these have some pretty sharp mandibles and can bite. They don't appear aggressive, nor venomous though. What's so special about this one?"

"Keep watching." He wore an odd smile as he said it.

The bullet-shaped critter was moving within the shade of a large rock. As it moved out, into an open, grassy area, it paused with tiny antenna twitching about. Without warning, a club came down hard on it. The helpless insect tried to roll into a defensive ball, but appeared to be too badly wounded. A slender hand grabbed it by the back of the carapace and threw it into what appeared to be a leather bag. The view zoomed back out to a wider view and DeeDee gaped as something resembling a skinny orangutan stood erect, the wide strap of the bag over its shoulder. With one hand, it adjusted the shoulder strap and the other held a wooden club. When it turned to wards the skeeter, she saw it had a bird-like beak instead of fangs. Each hand and foot had two large, muscular fingers and an opposing dew-claw that acted like a thumb.

"Oh. My. God. What is that?" She paused the video and stared at the figure. "We never saw anything like it in the initial survey."

Igor shrugged. "That doesn't surprise me. You were here for less than a week. You landed on an arid, upland plateau. This fellow is obviously bipedal, but not that far from an arboreal life. I think you're looking at something similar to Australopithecus in the human family tree. Keep going. It gets better."

DeeDee watched as the skeeter followed the lucky hunter through about a kilometer of deep woods. He followed paths that were well-used in some places and barely visible in others. Finally, he emerged into a clearing in front of an overhanging cliff. Simple huts were scattered about and dozens of similar creatures in all sizes, were evident.

She looked at her second in command. "Well, Igor... You found them. What do we call this new species?"

"I rather like the term 'Chickmonk'. They look something like a cross between a monkey and a chicken. They're kinda cute, no?"

DeeDee switched to a communications window on her slate. After a brief delay, Mike Hawthorne, Port Heinlein Director came on the screen. "What can I do for you, DeeDee?"

"I just thought you might like to know. We're not alone here; watch this." She ran the same video clip.

Morepork

It had been a long time since Victor had been a student, but he was enjoying the process. The three-dimensional model of a three-bedroom, two-bath home with attached garage floated above his desktop.

"Congratulations, Victor."

The voice startled him from the contemplation of his design and he looked up. "Hello Roger. Aren't you supposed to knock?"

The young mage smiled. "I did. Twice. But it appears you were engrossed in that lovely little design. Which, by the way, is the purpose of my visit."

Victor sat back, fingers steepled. "Oh? Do tell. Why am I owed a congratulations?"

"I will remind you that when you said you wanted to become a Domain Lord, there were steps and the first was to learn how to use our basic 3D design software."

Victor nodded. "It isn't that difficult once I learned the basic tools."

"The congratulations is due because the application I filed on your behalf has been approved. You and Paulette Matheson are now apprentice wizards. This is where your real training begins."

Victor leaned forward. "Paulette? The artist?"

"Yes. The two of you will be my apprentices."

Victor's voice held no inflection. "This means I'm now taking orders from you?"

"In matters regarding your training to become a mage, yes. If you have a problem with it, I'll be happy to inquire if another mage will take on your training."

The billionaire turned barkeep considered it for a moment, then shrugged. "Why not? What's our next step, Oh Great Mage?"

"Just 'sir' will do for now, Victor. Hold a moment while I invite your sister apprentice." He opened the door and invited Paulette to join them.

She smiled upon entering the office. "Hello, Mr. Adams. It's good to see you again."

"Paulette, from now on, the two of you are on a first-name basis and, in private, you will address me as Mage or Sir. Is this understood?"

"Yes, sir." They both echoed.

"The reason I am enforcing this is because it is now time for you to learn some of the secrets of how Beta works. The first and probably most public is the fact that although this is a capitalist society on the face, in actuality, it is a meritocracy based on knowledge. Our first lesson will be the true structure of our society." He paused before asking his students. "Would you like a drink before we continue?"

"Sure. Shall I get it?" Paulette asked.

"No need." Roger waved his hand and tall, frosty glasses appeared before each of them. "You must forgive a bit of showmanship. It's just faster, this way. Cheers." He took a sip before continuing. "The hierarchy that is part of Beta is built on seven classes of individual. The most basic class are Newcomers. You've both experienced waking up in the Creche and walking out into a public square with clothing, a backpack and a purse with a hundred Gelden. Normally, this is enough to keep you in food and shelter for about a year."

His students nodded and took a sip of their drinks.

"The next two levels are based on the individual's personality. Travelers just like to keep moving. For some, this is a long-term lifestyle. They always want to know what is over the next hill. They perform the useful and sometimes dangerous job of exploring new territories. Crafters, Merchants and Farmers, on the other hand, enjoy the immediate fruits of their labor."

He pointed at each, in turn. "You Paulette, are a gifted artist and already have a growing art gallery back in Morepork. While Victor owns this thriving tavern. Any questions at this point?"

Victor waved him on while Paulette shook her head.

"The next step in the hierarchy is where you two have just arrived. That is, apprenticed to a Mage. The apprenticeship stage is designed to teach you one school of magic. You might consider it a basic programming class. Upon completion, you will be able to take one of the 3D designs such as that lovely house you were working on when I came in, and make it real."

Victor held up his hand. "Excuse me, sir. But just how many schools of magic are there?"

"There are three. Architecture, Terrain, and Biology. As you master each school, that gives you the right to refer to yourself as a Witch or Wizard of that school."

Paulette asked, "Once you master all the schools, you become a Domain Lord or Lady?"

"You hear the title Domain Lord bandied about a lot. The fact is, there can be only one at a time. The mastery of all three schools earns you the title of Mage and also gives you the responsibility of a domain. For example, I'm in charge of that new domain where Victor is planning his city." He took a sip of his drink, then continued. "There are only twenty-four Master Mages. Each of them has the responsibility of a single time zone here on Beta. Only a Master Mage can approve new mages and assign domains."

"What's a Domain Lord, then?" Questioned Victor.

"The Domain Lord is rotated among the twenty-four Master Mages. They serve five years at a time, as a sort of chairman-of-the-board on the Mage Council."

Cautiously, Victor asked, "Just what does the Mage Council do?"

Roger waved his hand. "Not to worry, Victor. One thing you will seldom find in Mages is the urge to micro-manage. At each level, we have so much to keep us busy, that as long as things are running smoothly, we have a hands-off attitude. The Mage Council only concerns itself with issues that might effect all of Beta. Since it has been stable for the last couple of years, Earth-time, they seldom meet in full session."

High Valley

Susan couldn't believe her eyes. The face in the mirror was swollen. She sported a black eye, red and purple bruising wrapped from her ear down to her jawline. A couple of her teeth ached and the jaw joint hurt every time she tried to move her mouth as if chewing.

"Susan?" Martha's voice echoed up the stairwell. "No lollygagging. It's past time for your chores and breakfast is almost ready."

She grimaced, bit back a smart-ass comment, slipped into the hated long dress, and hurried downstairs.

Howard didn't say anything when they met in the yard. He just nodded and got into his truck. It would be late afternoon before he returned.

She set the basket of eggs on the counter and sat at the table. When she looked up from her plate of plain white bread. Lizzie was staring, with her hands in her lap. "Are you okay, cousin?"

"I'll survive, thank you for asking."

"My goodness, look at you." Martha leaned over the table. "I see you must have overstepped yourself last night. I knew Howard was angry when I heard the doors slamming. It's not like him. What was that device he destroyed?"

"Overstepped myself? Is that what you call it when some bully twice your size beats you for trying to keep him from stealing your personal property?"

"Now, now, Susan. You mustn't let your mouth run away again. That shiner will clear up in a day and in the meantime, it will remind you of your place and to watch that vicious tongue."

"We'll see about that. I'm going to file assault and grand theft charges against him if I don't get an apology and a replacement slate."

Martha stepped back, obviously shocked. "Charges? For Pete's sake, child, what for? He was merely chastising you for your disrespectful behavior and breaking our rules. That is completely within his rights as head of this household and your legal guardian."

"I respect those who earn it. Howard Childers is an ignorant, abusive, misogynistic, tyrant, and thief. One way or another, he'll get what is coming to him. I'm fed up with living like savages from some ancient black & white movie."

Martha slammed her hand down on the table. "Enough of this childish nonsense. Your Uncle will hear of this. Now mind your manners and attend to your lessons. I don't want to speak with you for the rest of the day, you ungrateful child."

"Fine, I can see I'll not get any sympathy or support from an ignorant farmer's wife." Susan didn't wait for a retort, but rushed upstairs.

She reached for her slate and then broke down in tears when it dawned on her that she was totally cut off from the rest of the universe. The nearest phone or computer was about fifteen kilometers away, in town. She knew she wouldn't get too far on foot and Howard always kept the truck keys on his belt. Not that she knew how to drive one, anyway.

Susan felt better after crying and a bath. She took her turn washing clothing and cleaned up her room. She remembered seeing a small backpack on a shelf in her closet and got it down. It only held a few old elementary school papers which she left on the shelf. A box under her bed held the lunar skinsuit and boots she had worn while traveling. She felt along the outer leg seams for the hidden pouches that contained two emergency doses of PhageB. Although her face still hurt, she wasn't going to waste one on what was essentially, a non-life-threatening injury. Besides, it wouldn't be a good idea to be in a coma when

Howard found out she had filled herself with 'the devil's brew'. The skinsuit and boots went into the backpack, along with her vest and a warm jacket. Then, she slid it under the bed.

Dinner was a solemn affair. Other than polite inquiries, little was said. As soon as was polite, Susan said she still had a bit of a headache and retired to her room.

She heard Howard on the stairs and pretended sleep while he stood in her doorway for a few minutes. It was after midnight when she got up and looked out the window. A three-quarter moon shared the sky with only a few, wispy clouds. A slight breeze barely moved the leaves and she gambled it was as good a time as any.

Moving quietly and yet quickly, she pulled the backpack from under the bed and slipped it on. Wearing only her chemise and slippers, she crept downstairs and out to the barn. Susan stood in the deep shadows, just inside the door and waited for some movement or lights from the farmhouse. When nothing happened after about five minutes, she slipped out of the chemise and into her skinsuit and boots. She almost cried at how warm and familiar they felt.

The horse only whinnied once in surprise at the late-night visit. Susan shushed the friendly beast and busied herself with the bridle and saddle. Once ready, she opened the stall door.

A gruff voice behind her asked, "Just what in the hell do you think you are doing, child?"

Susan spun around to face Uncle Howard, wearing jeans, boots, and his gunbelt. A flannel shirt hung unbuttoned and loose on his huge frame.

"Here I thought perhaps you had learned a lesson the other evening, but now I find you hiding in the barn, dressed like a whore, and trying to steal my horse."

The young girl was way past being scared. Now that she knew what to expect, she was angry. "You mean like you stole and destroyed my slate? That was worth a lot more than this horse and when I get to town, you'll get your horse back."

"Why you irreverent little bitch. You're not going anywhere. March right into the house right this instant and I'll burn that damn stocking you're wearing."

"What are you going to do, shoot me?" She challenged.

This time, she was ready when his huge hand shot out. She leaned back and let it just miss her face, then knocked it aside, stepped close and snapped a hard kick at the side of his knee. The big man grunted in pain and fell backward. Without giving him a chance to recover, she kicked him in the side of the same hip and when his arm reached up to block her, two more kicks landed on the side of his ribcage and under the armpit. Each one drew a yelp of pain and when he folded into himself, trying to catch his breath from what had to be at least a cracked rib, she grabbed the gun from his holster.

"I'll give this to the Sheriff so you don't shoot me in the back while I'm leaving." She led the nervous horse past the groaning man, mounted and galloped out of the yard. The porch lights came on and she heard Martha shouting, but ignored the woman.

Once she got to the end of the driveway, Susan paused. If she took the road to town, then Howard might catch up to her with his pickup truck. If she took a shortcut through the fields, she might save some time and he wouldn't be able to follow her. Letting the tired horse pick its way at a steady pace, they made their way towards the soft horizon glow of streetlights.

***

A couple of hours later, she came into the other end of town from the usual roadway. Turning the corner, she was faced with an old military humvee decorated in sheriff decals. When she approached, the streetlight let her recognize the sheriff.

He stepped forward and held up his hand while the three deputies spread out. "Good evening, Miss Childers. Would you do me the favor of getting down from that horse?"

She had to smile. "Certainly, sheriff." She got down and a deputy took the reins. "Boy! Do I have news for you. My uncle beat me, then destroyed a very valuable piece of my personal property. I want to press charges and then use your office comm station to let my friends know I'm okay."

He folded his arms and looked as if he hadn't heard her. "Please refresh my memory, Miss Childers. You are seventeen, are you not?"

"Yes, sir. Why do you ask?"

"And am I right in that this horse belongs to your Uncle Howard Childers?"

She nodded, feeling a bit wary. "Yes. And so is the gun he threatened me with. It's in the saddlebag."

The elder lawman's face became grim. "It's as we were told, boys. She's armed as well."

A deputy on her right drew his gun and she saw the red trace of the laser sight flicker on and center between her breasts.

"Miss Susan Childers, you are hereby under arrest. If you attempt any sort of physical violence, it will be considered resisting arrest and these officers are allowed to use deadly force."

Numb from shock. Susan stood still while the sheriff handcuffed her wrists behind her. Then, he surprised her even more with a pair of manacles locked around her ankles.

She recovered her voice enough to ask, "But why? He beat me. Look at my face. He should be arrested, not me."

He half-lifted her into the back seat of the humvee, strapped her in, then explained. "You still don't understand. Until you turn eighteen, you are considered a child and under your Uncle's care. That means that he not only has the right, but the responsibility to chastise a willfully disobedient young woman. Since you are so ignorant of our laws, let me inform you that since you attacked him, took his gun and his horse, you have committed three felonies. The theft of a man's horse by itself, is punishable by hanging. Although I will admit that is a bit harsh and unlikely for someone as young and foolish as yourself."

Susan started to sputter. "But it was the only way I could escape and keep him from shooting me in the back. He's the one that started all this when he hit me and destroyed my slate."

The sheriff shook his head and frowned. "I can see why. You are obviously a spoiled brat that has yet to learn how to dress and behave in a proper, God-fearing manner. The disrespect you've shown someone who has offered you a place in a fine household and a chance at a better future, just astounds me. I don't understand why he even wants to see you again."

Before she could respond, he slammed the door in her face. They rode in silence the few blocks to the police station. Her heart came into her throat when she saw her Uncle standing next to his pickup.

When her door opened, Susan shouted. "No! No! I can't go back there. Arrest me if you have to, but don't let him near me."

The lawmen ignored her shouting and it took two of them to lift her into the back of the pickup. A chain used to secure heavy loads was locked around the chain between her ankles.

"Honestly Howard, are you sure you don't want to press charges? We can see she spends ninety days in jail and you won't have to deal with the brat for awhile. It might teach her some respect for her elders."

The big man shook hands with the officer and shook his head. "That's okay, sheriff. There is no need to give her a criminal record. I'll see that she is properly chastised when we get back to the farm and in another couple of weeks, she won't be my problem any more."

"I understand, sir. Good luck and one of my deputies will bring your horse back tomorrow."

Susan watched in horror as a deputy took the gun from the saddlebag and handed it to Howard. "Don't forget your weapon, Mr. Childers. Never can tell when you'll run into some nasty critter these days."

Howard thanked him for the gun and the loan of the shackles, got into the pickup, and drove off. He didn't bother to slow down much on the rough gravel roads leading up to the farm. With only an old horse blanket between her and the metal pickup bed, she knew she would be covered in bruises.

The first pale glimmer of false dawn colored the eastern sky when he pulled up next to the barn.

She kept her mouth shut and only winced when he unlocked the chain and dragged her blanket to the tailgate. He roughly stood her up, then marched her into the barn and up to face the gate of an empty stall.

"Howard? Is everything alright?" Martha's voice came from the doorway.

"Everything will be fine shortly, wife. In the meantime, go get Elizabeth and bring her down here."

She hurried off to obey.

Howard grabbed a handful of belts from the tack room. Each of them had roller buckles and almost a continuous line of holes. He unlocked the handcuffs and before she had a chance to catch her balance, he yanked her arm up to one side of the stall. He wrapped the belt twice around her wrist and the top board and pulled the buckle tight enough to make her wince. A moment later, her other arm was strapped the same way. This held her spread wide and facing the stall.

Martha and Lizzie returned as he was tightening the last buckle. Susan watched over her shoulder and saw her aunt's angry expression and a look of terror on her cousin's face.

"Elizabeth, do you recall me telling you to burn that abominable piece of clothing she is wearing?"

The girl looked down at the ground and muttered, "Yes, sir."

"And yet, here she is, dressed like a whore and flouting herself in a midnight ride to town. Thereby embarrassing me and this whole family in front of the sheriff and his deputies. Why did you disobey my express command?"

"I'm sorry, sir. She begged me not to as it was only a souvenir of her home. She promised to keep it hidden away until after she left."

"So, you let this willfully disobedient and disrespectful little tramp talk you into doing the devil's work for her." His voice was quaking with barely suppressed anger. "Strip!" His voice thundered.

Martha shook her head no, pleading for leniency but he pushed her aside. "Go into the house, wife. I will handle the rest of this." He turned to face her. "Or do you wish to be chastised for disobedience as well?" She hurried off, tears flowing.

He turned his attention back to Lizzie, cowering against the wall. "I told you to strip, child. Now remove your clothing before I'm forced to rip it from you.

Only moments later, Lizzie, wearing only white panties, was strapped to the next stall over from Susan.

Howard hefted a plain, wide leather belt with the buckle end wrapped around his fist. "Since your crime was born of foolish ignorance, you will only get six strokes." And with that pronouncement, he swung the belt and Lizzie yelped. It left a bright red welt over her shoulder blades. She was screaming and crying when he finished and her entire upper back was criss-crossed with welts, some of which trickled blood.

The big man hung up the belt and flipped open a large pocket knife. "This time, I'll deal with the damn thing myself." Once again ignoring Susan's angry shouting, he lifted the edge of the tight material and slipped the razor-sharp blade beneath. In a few moments, the skinsuit was a pile of material on the barn floor. "For your disrespect, disobedience, attacking me, stealing my horse and gun, and also for embarrassing our family in front of the sheriff, you will get two dozen strokes."

Susan managed to keep her mouth shut and just grunted for the first three. She lost count after a dozen and passed out before he was finished.

Jerryville

It became one of the first new laws of the colony. The Chickmonks were to be left alone unless they threatened a colonist. Since none had been seen near the landing site, it was assumed they were scared of all the noise and the strange beings that had landed.

Cheryl Mathias was more than seventy years old and yet another round of Omniphage as part of healing the damage caused by warp-drive travel, had left a tall, slender brunette looking twenty-something. "I have an experiment in mind, Buster."

When his wife came up with an idea, Buster Mathias knew it would be interesting. "Let me guess. You want to work with the Chickmonks." He chuckled. "Because you are a school teacher, you love working with kids, and they look like a really bright bunch of fifth-graders." He leaned close and hugged her shoulders. "Also, because you've been studying all the skeeter video and audio links to their camps every chance you've had for the past three days."

She smiled and kissed him on the cheek. "You know me so well, Buster. I'm going to talk to the Director."

DeeDee wasn't quite as receptive. "Let me get this straight. You want to meet with the Chickmonks and open a school?"

"That's about it. We're going to run into them sooner or later. It might as well be under some sort of peaceful, controlled conditions."

"What about the Prime Directive?"

Cheryl stared at the head of the colony for a good ten seconds. "Please tell me you're not quoting ancient Star Trek references as policy."

DeeDee rocked back in her chair, laughing. "Damn, woman! I wish I could have had a video clip of your face just then."

The teacher shook herself and had to grin in response. "You had me going for a minute there. But seriously, there was a good reason for the Prime Directive. The only problem is that once contact has been made, there is nothing that can be done about it. Throughout recorded history, every time two groups of humans have disputed the same area, the one with the higher technology destroys and in some cases, eliminates the weaker one. I know we won't be able to stop all conflicts with the Chickmonks, but I do think I can help minimize them and perhaps even make friends."

Director Wendy 'DeeDee' Miller of Jerryville, the first Micasa human colony, steepled her fingers in front of her face for a moment, then looked up with a wry smile. She affected a deeper voice and intoned. "Make it so, Number One."

Morepork

Roger carefully examined the model of an urban center complex complete with park, fountains, elevated walkways and a half-dozen ten to twenty story buildings. "Very good, Victor. I'm impressed."

"Thank you, mage. If you would care to examine the infrastructure, you will see there is more than enough water, sewer, and power to handle the population with room to grow."

"I know. I have been watching this design project grow for the last couple of months. If blends in well with the site you chose. Would you like to see it become reality?"

Victor looked up from the model and displayed a huge smile. "Do you think it is ready, mage?"

"Only one real way to find out, my friend." He strode to the mirrorgate and touched the frame. It recognized the mage and he asked that it open the way to Empire City. They stepped through and found themselves standing on an open bluff, overlooking two river valleys. The high terrain gave a good view of one of the valleys and they could barely see where the two rivers joined.

Roger admired the view for a moment before turning to his pupil. "I have a little present for you, Victor."

"Yes, sir?" The Earth millionaire and Beta Wizard replied.

"The last time we were here, I watched you take one of the micro power crystals and create that small, stone cabin." He glance at the simple structure. "Since then, we've camped twice. I let you and a girlfriend use it to celebrate your graduation from Apprentice to Wizard."

The Wizard smiled at the memory. "That was a wonderful holiday. But what does that have to do with my assisting you in creating the first part of that project?"

"This is no longer a training session. What you don't realize is that project is your final graduation exercise. Consider this as the moment when you defend your thesis."

Doubt clouded Victor's face. "What is it you wish to know?"

"At this point, nothing at all. All your designs are in the desk, the back room of the cabin has more than a hundred large power crystals as well as food for a couple of months. When your Empire City is finished, I will know. Good luck and don't forget to have fun while you're creating it." Before Victor got over his shock, the mage that was at once his employee, his mentor, his mage master, and his good friend, walked through the mirrorgate and not only did it close, but the entire gate blinked out of sight.

"But..." Victor whispered as the after-image of the mirrorgate faded from view. He slowly turned, looking around and realized he was totally alone, hundreds of kilometers away from any other inhabitant of Beta. He shrugged and walked over to the stone cottage.

Inside, he prepared a carafe of hot coffee and took a seat. The desk was actually a rather plain table with a single drawer in one side. In a pinch, it could seat six for dinner, but mostly they used it to look at maps and plans. He placed a fingertip flat on one corner and spoke. "Display current Empire City."

The tabletop shimmered and the last view of his model appeared.

"Fade structures to fifteen percent, and display infrastructure." Obediently, the buildings faded to ghost-like outlines. The water, sewer, and power lines glowed in three different colors, extending out of view on all sides.

"Zoom out to show overall." He commanded.

The image became an aerial view that included both river valleys, the flood plains, and the rocky falls where the rivers joined. He saw the colored lines and boxes for water supply, sewer and industrial-grade septic systems. In a small mountain valley several kilometers north and hundreds of meters higher, a hydro-electric plant and lake provided water pressure and power for the city.

He stared at it while finishing his coffee, then ordered the desk to produce a pixie cuff. A small leather-looking wrist band appeared on the corner of the desk. He slipped it on, took a final sip of his favorite drink and went outside. "What the hell." He muttered to himself. "It's a pretty day and plenty of time for a brisk walk. Pixie? Show me the nearest sewer manhole cover." A dimly-glowing arrow appeared on the cuff. He walked in the indicated direction until the arrow shortened to nothing.

Victor tried moving away in several directions, but the arrow would return and drive him back to the same location. He pulled a power crystal from his pouch, set it on the ground, gathered his concentration, and focused his will on the small gem.

Almost immediately, it glowed brilliant white and disappeared. In its place was a shiny, new manhole cover. As the slight trembling of the ground beneath his feet told him, all of the associated tunnels and additional access points were also being created.

"Pixie. Show me water and power tunnel points."

Once again, the cuff projected a small arrow that guided him only a few meters away. He ran his tests to make sure of the exact location, then repeated the magical construction process, using another crystal.

This process seemed to take much longer, perhaps due to the complexity of both systems. It was almost dark when the crystal glow faded until it became just another pretty river rock. Victor stumbled back to the cabin, locked the door and fell asleep.

Port Heinlein

The teenager paused at the Port Heinlein Director's office door. Mike Hawthorne waved him in. "Come on in, Charlie. Sit down and tell me what's on your mind."

"Sorry to bother you, sir. But I'm worried about Susan."

"The last report I received was that she was adapting well to farm life. What have you heard?"

"Was that last report from her, or her Uncle?"

"Howard Childers, why?"

"Because for the last few months, she and I have exchanged emails at least once a day. She has been becoming more and more frustrated and can't wait to get back here. She is worried because they have been hinting that they won't let her return, even after she comes of age."

The Director shook his head. "I'm sorry to hear that, Charlie. But until she turns eighteen, those people are her legal guardians and there isn't anything I can do about it. Be sure to tell her I feel bad, but..."

"That's just it, sir!" Charlie interrupted. "I can't tell her. Several days ago, her slate went offline."

"She turned it off?"

"No sir. Not just turned off. It is totally offline. No GPS signals, no response to update pings, not even a security ping. It has been destroyed."

"Now wait a minute, son. Those things are pretty hard to kill. Are you sure she just hasn't removed the power supply?"

"I believe so, sir. Removing the power supply requires specialized tools and a trained technician. From everything she has told me, that farm and those around it, are rather stuck in the middle twentieth century level of tools and technology."

Mike thought it over for a moment before offering. "Okay, Charlie. I'll see if I can get some more information. In the meantime, don't worry. It's probably just some equipment malfunction."

As soon as the boy closed the door, the confident smile left the Director's face. He keyed his slate and asked for the officer in charge of the spaceport nearest the Childers's farm, in High Valley.

"Hello there, Colonel. How are things down on the old mudball?"

"It's a lovely fall day here, General. You should come down and get your feet dirty with the rest of us poor grunts."

The Director laughed. "It's just Mike, these days. I gave up that General stuff awhile back, in case you've not heard."

"Once military, always military, in my book. What can I do for you, Mike?"

"Remember that young lady, Susan Childers we sent down your way a bit over a year ago?"

"Of course I do. Not often we get passengers heading out for the boondocks. Usually, they are trying to head uphill, rather than down. Why do you ask?"

"I've gotten a rather ominous report that she is out-of-touch. We can't raise her at all. Any way you could take a peek and help me to reassure her friends?"

"Actually, you're in luck. One of my forward recon teams is overdue for some training. Send me her slate logs and I'll get the GPS coordinates. I should have eyes on in less than a day."

High Valley

Susan was laying on her stomach and a cool breeze was ruffling her hair. She felt groggy and very stiff. When she lifted her arm and started to roll over, she stifled a scream that ended in a moan. It felt like every part of her back was torn and on fire. Choking back a gasp, she let herself relax for a moment as the memories of her ordeal flooded back.

"Are you finally awake?" Lizzie's voice came from the doorway. "I thought I heard you."

"I'm awake." Each breath seemed to be stretching bruised ribs and her back was knotted with pain. Then, she remembered her cousin's beating. "How are you feeling?"

"I'll live. Probably better than you. Martha sent me up to check on you."

Susan turned her head and saw Lizzie standing ramrod straight, with a jar in one hand and a couple of clean towels in the other. The young woman slowly walked over to the bedside and placed the towels and jar on the nightstand.

"Martha says I'm to apply this unguent to your back. It will help keep the wounds from drying out and festering. She applied it to my back and although uncomfortable, it does ease the pain a little. I was able to help with breakfast this morning."

When she turned to fetch a chair, Susan saw her cousin's dress had been left unbuttoned and her back was covered in bandages. When she leaned over to sit down, she closed her eyes, grunted, and winced.

"I'm sorry I dragged you into this, Lizzie." She whispered.

"Not your fault. It was my own willful disobedience that earned my discipline."

"Earned it? Oh no, cousin. Nobody earns this sort of abuse. Howard is psychotic and I will find a way to see that he goes to jail for this."

"Ssshh! Don't even whisper such things. It will earn us much worse. Haven't you learned your lesson? Our backs are going to wear these scars for the rest of our lives. Our husbands will know our shame for being such rebels."

Susan opened her mouth, but realized her cousin had tears in her eyes and was honestly terrified. "Sorry. I'll be still." She whispered.

***

Mike Hawthorne's slate rang like an old telephone. The spaceport commander was on the other end.

"Hi there, Mike. Are we alone?"

"Yes, my office door is closed. What have you found?"

"I have something disturbing to share with you. First, I called the local police department and when I asked about Susan, the sheriff told me she had been arrested for assaulting the town's Mayor, but he had declined to press charges. Since she is a minor, he released her back to her uncle's custody."

"Wait minute. I thought her uncle was the mayor?"

"That occurred to me as well, but I got the feeling the officer was trying to stonewall us. Remember I told you my team needed some training? Well, I had them deploy a buzzard over the Childers's farm. It circled most of the day and here are some of the video clips."

Mike watched as a large man strode from the house and got into a pickup, then an older woman and young girl hung laundry on long lines to dry.

"Those two look like Martha Childers and Susan's cousin, Elizabeth."

"That is what our recognition programs are telling us. Let me scroll ahead a few hours."

The shadows showed it was late afternoon when the back door opened and another young woman came out. She was moving very slowly, taking small steps as she carried a basket out to the hen house.

The Colonel paused the video feed for a moment. "We thought her movements seemed odd, so we had the buzzard make a low pass down behind the barn and hover so it could get some closeup images." The next few images were still shots that had been enhanced to bring out details and color.

"Oh my God!" Mike realized what he was seeing. The entire side of her face was black and blue, she was limping, her back was covered with a blood-stained bandage and she took a step, they could see glistening chrome chain between her ankles. "Colonel. I don't care what sort of diplomatic mess this is. I want that girl in the base hospital as soon as possible."

The base commander nodded agreement. "I thought you would say that. I've already brought a wolf team to standby. Before it was noticed, I had the buzzard deploy a pair of skeeters. As soon as it is dark, I'm going to post one on the barn roof and see if we can get the other close to Miss Childers. We can let her know that help is on the way."
***

Howard Childers parked alongside the house and went into the kitchen. He kissed his wife on the cheek and nodded at the two girls, sitting at the kitchen table. "I'm glad to see you are up and about, Susan. I trust we'll never have to revisit this lesson?"

Eyes downcast, she answered. "No sir."

"Come. I want you to take a little walk with me." He held the kitchen door as she shuffled out, her ankle chain rattled on the steps.

Once outside, he turned to face her, his hands held behind and a satisfied smile on his face. "I've very good news for both of us, Susan."

Susan kept her hands clasped in front of her and only glanced up to gauge his mood. "What is that, sir?"

"It has become quite obvious that you don't want to be a part of this household. Since I'm responsible for your well-being, it behooved me to find a solution. I'm happy to say Mr. Samuel Martin, whom you met the other day, has agreed to take you as his second wife." His voice finished with a note of barely-contained glee. "What do you say to that, girl?"

"Wife? But we've only met that once and I'll be honest, I was not impressed. Besides, I'm nowhere near the point where I want to get married." Then, another part of what he said caught up with her. "Wait a minute! Second wife? You mean he is already married?"

Her response wiped the smile from Howard's face and his voice dropped to a harsh whisper. "When his father passed and he inherited the farm, he took his first wife. She's a fine, God-fearing woman who has already bore him one son. It is out of Christian kindness that he has agreed to take over the balance of your upbringing. In addition, it will be your place to satisfy his needs since his first wife is pregnant once again. By the time she has born his next child, your womb will be bearing another addition to the family."

Susan was almost shaking with anger and all but forgot her beating. "That is impossible. Even if I was interested in a polygamous marriage, I cannot have children."

"Of course you can. You're a healthy young woman. You will be back to full strength in a week or so, plenty of time before the marriage."

"Yes. I was healthy until you beat me like some animal. But that isn't the point. I'm sterile."

His eyes narrowed. "Sterile? How can that be, child?"

"When we reach puberty, every child in Port Heinlein is treated with PhageB. Not only does it cure any disease we might have at that point, but it also sterilizes us. Everyone waits until they are financially and emotionally ready before they request treatment with PhageA as part of their honeymoon." She shrugged and waved her hands out to her sides. "Most of us don't plan on having kids until we reach a chronological age of forty or fifty."

Howard just stood there, with a look of astonishment mixed with anger flushing his face. "My God! In what sort of insane asylum did my brother raise you? Children born of older women are much more likely to be deformed or diseased. It's just not right."

"Just because someone has a chronological age of fifty doesn't mean that is their physiological age. Most everyone in civilized societies take a weekend Omniphage treatment every ten years as a matter of good health practice. One of my teachers looks like a teenager and yet she is one hundred and four. She just took on a twenty-year marriage contract before I left. They are expecting a child any time now."

He was sputtering, obviously trying to wrap his head around such a foreign concept. "Be that as it may, I'm glad we saved you from such devilish ways. Sam will content himself with his other sons and you will proved your worth as his wife's helper and a sterile whore for his bed." His voice was chilling in its obvious disgust. "We shan't mention this again. The marriage has been set for the end of the month. In a little over two weeks, you will be his problem." Howard grabbed her by the upper arm. His grip was like a vice and she stumbled along.

He strode to the barn, opened the door and stood patiently as she stared into the shadows.

"Don't worry, child. Your punishment is over for now. I'll not strike you again, unless you do something else to earn it. I just wanted to show you something."

Wincing with each step, she moved into the dark barn. He swung both doors wide, so the late afternoon sun illuminated the new wall hanging. Her eyes grew wide as she stared at the sliced up remnants of her skinsuit, nailed to the wall.

Howard's voice was low as he whispered in her ear. "I don't know what sort of material it is made from but, it didn't want to burn, so I decided to mount it as a reminder. If you ever attack me again, I'll see your hide replaces it, child." Terrified, she just nodded understanding.

"I want you to stand right where you are until I get inside. I've had enough of your blasphemous words for the night. Be sure you close the barn before you return to the house." Without waiting for a response, he strode back towards the kitchen.

Trembling, Susan waited until she heard the back door slam, then turned and closed one of the barn doors. She set the bolt and was reaching for the other door when she heard a soft whistle from above. She glanced up and didn't see anything, but another whistle drew her attention to something on an exposed beam.

She almost didn't believe her eyes. It was a surveillance skeeter. She walked up to stand right below and it tilted to look down at her. "Can you hear me?" She whispered.

"Yes." The voice from the small speaker was tinny but understandable. "What is your condition?"

"I've been whipped with a belt until I passed out. My back is severely bruised and has open sores. My ankles are chained and I cannot run. Please get me out of this madhouse."

"Don't worry. Help is on the way. Are there any weapons in the house?"

"My Uncle carries a handgun. It's an old-fashioned six-shooter, but he is quite accurate with it. There is also a shotgun in the hall closet. My Aunt might use it. Please be careful of my cousin. She has been beaten as well."

"Susan!" The shout came from the kitchen door. "That should be enough time to consider your transgressions. Get in here and help serve the meal."

"I have to go." She whispered harshly. "What do you want me to do?"

"The team should be there in the next ten minutes. See if you can find an excuse to return to the barn."

She pushed on the door, but left it ajar.

Dinner was quiet and tense as everyone focused on their food. Susan took a couple of bites, glanced at the wall clock and saw almost fifteen minutes had passed, then stood up and went to the kitchen window.

"What is it, child?" Martha asked.

"I'm sorry. But Uncle Howard told me to close the barn door. It looks like the latch didn't connect and it has blown open. I'll just be a moment." She headed back out.

Martha started to say something, but Howard's voice assured her. "Don't worry, wife. The little tramp can't ride with the shackles. I doubt she could even work the pedals of the truck. She'll be back soon."

When she got to the barn, she glanced over her shoulder to make sure no one was watching, then slipped inside. "Hello?" She whispered. "Anyone here?"

A voice came from the shadows in the back of the barn. "I'm here, Susan. My name is Jim and I'm a wolf soldier. Do you know what that is?"

"Wolf soldiers belong to special operations teams. Your genetic profile has been changed to add canine DNA and you probably look like a wolfman from one of those old movies."

"That's right. So don't be scared. Come back here and I'll get those shackles off you." He stepped forward and had an assault rifle slung over one shoulder and a large pair of bolt cutters in hand. "Put your hands on the wall and spread your legs as far as you can."

She did as he instructed and he knelt behind her. There was a slight tug and a clink of sound as the chain was cut from one cuff. Susan felt the cutter against her other ankle and that too made only a slight sound as the chain dropped free. "There. Someone back at the base can get the cuffs themselves off. In the meantime, you can run."

"No. She can't." Howard's gruff voice came from the doorway. For a big man, he could be very quiet.

Jim spun to the side, lifting his weapon and a single shot rang out. He grunted and flew backward, slamming back against the wall. Howard flipped on the lights and kept the gun pointed at Susan and her would-be savior.

"What the hell is that beast? I knew you were a disrespectful tramp but had no idea you would whore yourself in the barn with some half-man."

Susan bent forward and saw the soldier was still breathing. There was no blood, so she guessed the bullet had hit his body armor.

Brilliant white lights flooded the barnyard and an amplified voice announced the arrival of the cavalry. "Attention! Attention! Howard Childers. Put down your weapon and come out with your hands up!"

Howard hit the light switch, plunging the interior of the barn back into deep shadow. He swung around so he could hide behind a thick post.

While he was distracted, Susan dropped down, alongside the wolf soldier and whispered in his ear. "Are you okay?" she whispered.

"Yes. But don't do anything yet. Wait until we can get away from him."

"Do you carry an emergency Phage kit?"

His eyes flicked toward her for a moment, then back to watch the man with the gun. "Yes. Why?"

Susan made sure Howard wasn't watching. "Let me have it now."

The loudspeaker ordered Howard to surrender again and while that masked the noise, Jim pulled the small metal tube from his vest.

"Don't worry, soldier. I know how to use this. I'm not ready to check out of the fight, just yet." She turned so Howard couldn't see, popped the seal on the emergency field dose and pressed it to her arm. It only took a couple of seconds to suck some of her blood into the clear reservoir and she withdrew it.

Slowly, she stood up. Howard's attention immediately snapped to her. "Stay where you are, whore. I see more of those animals in the yard. Two of them just went into the kitchen."

"Uncle Howard?" She tried to keep her voice high and pleading. "I'm scared. What is going on?"

"Don't try to tell me you didn't call these hellish beasts down on us."

"But you are going to protect us, aren't you, sir? Please. I'm scared. Let me see. Maybe I can tell them to go away."

His eyes kept darting back and forth between her and the barnyard. "You think they might listen?" He considered it for a moment. "Come here and tell them I have you and one of their half-breed monsters as hostages. They have to leave immediately."

"Yes sir. Of course." She kept her steps short so he would think she was still shackled. "Let me peek out the door." When she got alongside, his left hand took the back neck of her dress and held her at arm's length. Her right hand held the syringe. When he moved towards the half-open door, his gun hand reached out in front to give him a clear shot.

"Call to them, girl. Tell them what I said."

"Yes sir." She glanced down and stabbed the back of his gunhand with the syringe, dumping the entire contents in an instant.

He screamed, dropped the gun, and stumbled backwards, clutching his wounded hand.

"What the hell did you do, you little tramp?" He shook his hand and clutched it again, fingers clawing. "It burns, damnit! What sort of poison did you stab into me?"

She kicked the gun outside, then stood with her hands on her hips and a huge smile on her face. "Don't worry, Uncle dear. You aren't going to die. You're just going to sleep in a moment. And boy, are you in for a surprise when you wake up."

He started to mutter more obscenities, but the words came out slurred and he dropped to his knees. True to her promise, his eyes rolled back into his head and he was in an Omniphage-induced coma before he hit the ground.

The wolf soldier sat up with a grunt. "Did you just do what I think I saw you do, Susan?"

She nodded, still smiling. "I hope that misogynistic bastard likes wearing my breasts when he wakes up. Maybe Sam will insist on marrying him for a second wife."

Jim shook his head. "Damn, woman! I hope I never piss you off."

Ten minutes later, Susan watched them load a stretcher with Howard's comatose body into the helicopter, while a handcuffed Martha alternated between crying and screaming obscenities at the team. Jim handed Susan a slate showing Mike Hawthorne.

"Hello, Director Hawthorne. Thank you for sending help. I'm not sure how much longer I could have taken this."

"No problem, Susan. I'm glad you're in one piece. Which brings up the point... I hear you've refused treatment?"

"Just for tonight sir. I have a favor to ask before I take a shot of PhageB." She paused and pointed the slate at Lizzie. "This is my cousin, Elizabeth. She has been through this abuse much longer than I have and will need treatment as well."

Mike smiled at the scared girl. "It's good to meet you, Elizabeth. Thank you very much for taking care of Susan. Don't worry about the cost. All of your medical expenses will be addressed."

Susan turned the slate back on herself. "One more thing, sir. I want to bring Lizzie with me. Can you arrange passage? I'll delay my trip home if we can travel together. I'll even pay her way from my credit balance."

"Elizabeth? Do you wish to accompany your cousin back to the moon? You are welcome, of course, but I need to hear if from you."

Nervous and shaking from the tension, Lizzie nodded, then answered. "Yes, sir. I would like that very much. If I stay here, I'm sure Uncle Howard will blame me for all this as well."

"I thought that might be your answer. As soon as I found out how you two had been treated, I arranged to clear a couple of seats on the next shuttle. As soon as the legal team takes your statements, I expect both of you to get a shot of PhageB. When you wake up, you'll have a day to relax at the spaceport before your flight."

Jerryville

Cheryl handed her husband her slate. It showed a 3D image of a small cage.

"What's this, hon?"

"It's a roly poly trap, Buster." I got the idea after looking at the video clips of the Chickmonks. I think it will be one way to establish relations with them. Right now, they use something similar made from woven fibers. They wear out fast, the critters chew out of them quickly if left too long, and they have to constantly make new ones."

"You're thinking of giving them metal ones?"

"Not right away, no. I want to use one of these to collect some roly polys of our own. Then, leave bags of them where the Chickmonks will find them. Eventually working our way to a face-to-face meeting and trading session." She pulled up some clips showing life in their village "In some ways, they are still in a hunter-gatherer stage of development. But there are signs of a sophisticated trading network. See the cooking area, next to that hut? There are several different sizes of glazed and fired pottery. That requires a kiln with nearby supplies of the proper clays. None of that sort of technology is apparent in the two Chickmonk camps we know about."

Buster looked at her notes. "It looks to me like they are in a transition society. Some things are more advanced than others. No metals that I can see though."

Cheryl continued. "So far, I've seen them collect and eat five different types of plants and six animals. The roly polys appear to be their favorite, but only two of the dozen males in this tribe seem to actively hunt them. Everyone else gathers plants."

Two days later, the couple had a thick canvas net sack full of displeased roly polys. With a skeeter as a watchdog, they hung the bag from a branch near the village.

DeeDee watched the video with them and everyone chuckled when they saw the hunter staring in amazement and suspicion. He poked the sack a couple of times and examined every inch of the immediate area, trying to figure out how the bugs got there. The hunter found a couple of their footprints and compared the boot-sole images to his own, much smaller foot. Finally, he untied the simple knot, took the net sack as well as the rope and hurried back to the village.

The colony leader turned to the researchers. "Okay, gang. Now that you've got their attention, what next?"

"We're going to repeat this every day for the next week. When he doesn't get nervous every time he hears the critters whistling and finds a bag, I'm going to let him see me hang a bag."

"Wear body armor and a helmet. Just in case he comes after you with that club."

Cheryl left the same sort of bag in the same place for the next few days. Under cover of darkness, they placed a couple of skeeters close enough to record the tribe's reaction to each of the gifts. The fifth day brought the first surprise.

"Hey boss, check this out." Buster wore a huge grin. "You're not going to believe it.

Curious, she watched the recording on his slate. It showed the Chickmonk hunter creeping silently through the woods well before dawn. He circled wide around the tree where they had been leaving the goody bags and settled under some bushes with a clear view of the trail.

DeeDee paused the clip. "He's smart enough to know someone is bringing it, and he wants a look."

"That's right. We expected that, but not what comes next. Advance it to the 04:38 mark."

She started the video and skipped ahead. The hunter was sitting still as a rock except for his head and eyes that slowly scanned everything within sight. Suddenly, his gaze locked on theirs. He was staring right at the skeeter, clinging to a branch, about three meters overhead. The Chickmonk watched for a few minutes, then slipped to the other side of the trail and a bit closer to the drop area. Every few moments his gaze would drift back to the skeeter and, from its slight movements, it was obvious he realized it was watching him, as well. His new location let him see the second skeeter, poised above the trail that led back to his village.

"That is when we decided it was time." Buster advanced the clip another few minutes. "My wife took the bag and made sure she was making noise as she approached. The moment she came into his view, she stopped. I flew one of the skeeters down the trail and had it land on her shoulder."

The hunter watched this, but didn't move. Cheryl waited a few more seconds, then looked away from him and slowly walked to the tree. She tossed the rope over the tree and quickly tied it off, as usual. As she passed, Buster flew the skeeter back up to the same place where it had a view of the village trail and the bag.

"Well, he didn't spook although I was surprised he noticed the skeeters. Those things blend in pretty well."

"Right boss, but don't forget this guy has been hunting these woods all his life. A skeeter is still larger than most of the insects we've seen around here and smaller than most of the birds."

"What's next?"

Buster shrugged. "That's Cheryl's call. This is her project, I'm just along for the heavy lifting."

The next morning brought another surprise. Both hunters showed up. One carried a sack full of the roots and vegetables gathered the day before. After hanging it up with the same sort of knot, they positioned themselves a few meters back, towards the village, but still in plain view.

Right at sunrise, Cheryl walked slowly into view. Buster flew one of the skeeters down to her shoulder. The Chickmonks showed no surprise, but only watched as she examined the bag. She replaced it with the roly polys, stepped back, faced the two hunters and gave a slow, half-bow.

As if on cue, the Chickmonks returned her bow but didn't try to follow her.

DeeDee looked at the tray of local produce. "I assume all of this has been tested?"

Cheryl replied. "Of course. Not only that, but we've been paying very close attention to how they prepare each item. It is possible to eat the roots raw, but not very tasty. Those long, stringy things that look like onions are way too tough without cooking."

Buster interrupted with a smile. "And you might find it interesting that roast roly poly wrapped in those large leaves tastes a lot like an herb-crusted lobster from Earth."

DeeDee gave him one of those looks. "And since when have you been sampling the local flora and fauna?"

He shrugged. "Sooner or later, we're going to have to try it all. Since the Chickmonks seem to have a similar metabolism to ours, I'm going with their staples for now." He paused and grimaced. "Although those red roots taste like shit."

"They are really bitter." Admitted Cheryl.

DeeDees slate rang. "Hold on. Lemme get this... Yes?"

"Boss, you gotta see this. Four Chickmonks are just outside the front gate."

The three of them exchanged a quick glance, then scrambled to see for themselves.

"Wear your helmet and armor, Cheryl. That's an order."

"Yes, ma'am." She understood DeeDee was just playing it safe as colony leader, but didn't look like she felt it would be needed.

They opened the gate and Cheryl stepped out. She whispered into her microphone. "The one in front is the one we first contacted. The other one is also a hunter and the two females on either side of them are, I believe, their wives."

She slowly walked over the bare, rocky ground that surrounded their colony. When she reached the halfway point, the Chickmonks started to walk towards her. Their clubs hung from their shoulders and each carried one of the net bags. Cheryl took a few more steps, then sat down, cross-legged. She held her hands open on her knees and waited for them to approach.

About two meters away, they stopped and said something.

"I'm afraid I don't speak your language, yet." She replied quietly.

The lead hunter said something else and three of them sat down in a semi-circle in front of her. The leader stepped forward and held out his bag. It held some more vegetables. She took it and gave a slight bow from the waist. He bowed as well, stepped back and took a bag from one of the females. It held a bundle of leaves that was still warm which he sat down between them. He unrolled the leaves to show a baked roly poly. The other female handed him her bag and the leaves cushioned a pair of colorful, glazed ceramic mugs. He set them next to the steaming roly poly and the other hunter handed him a matching ceramic jug with a stopper.

"Buster? I think he's preparing a picnic for us. Will you bring an analyzer with you? I've never seen this jug before. Also, bring out a clear glass pitcher of water and a couple of matching tumblers. I'm going to try and work a trade."

"You got it. Be right there."

The Chickmonks looked up when Buster walked out, but didn't appear concerned. He bowed towards them when he approached, then sat next to his wife. She took the small, pen-shaped device and dipped the end in the mug and waited.

Ten seconds later, DeeDee's voice came from her slate. "It's some sort of alcoholic drink. There are some trace elements that are similar to canibinoids, but we don't see anything really toxic. No telling what it will taste like, though."

"Thanks, boss." Cheryl picked up the mug with both hands and took a sip. Then, she handed it to her husband and he took a sip.

The Chickmonk leader did the same and passed it around to the others.

Cheryl carefully poured the water into the tumblers, placed them in front of the hunters, along with the pitcher. The four of them took a sip of the water, while staring at obvious amazement at the clear glass.

Over the next few minutes, little was said as they took a bite of each item. Finally, Cheryl pointed at herself with both hands and stated her name, three times, slowly. Then, she pointed at her husband and stated "Buster" three times slowly.

The lead hunter stared at her for a moment, digesting this information, then pointed at her and said, "SheeRel".

Cheryl nodded once, smiling with her lips closed.

He looked at her husband and said, "Buzzzterrr", then pointed both hands at himself and intoned, "CheeYok".

Over the next few minutes, everyone exchanged names, then, without warning, CheeYok and his family stood up. When they reached for the ceramic jug and cups, Cheryl placed her hand on top of the jug. She pointed at the clear glass items and then at CheeYok and then at the ceramic items and back at herself, indicating a trade.

There was almost no hesitation. CheeYok picked up the glass pitcher and the other hunter took the tumblers. They bowed from the waist, turned and marched back into the forest.

Buster gave a soft sigh of relief. "That was intense. I'm glad we don't have to drink too much of their booze though. I've got a helluva buzz on just a couple of swallows. Damn stuff tastes like raw corn liquor and packs a punch."

Empire City

Victor stood on the balcony and scanned the vacant city. It had been a very hard couple of months, but it was now finished and he felt incredible pride. "Too bad no one seems to have noticed." He muttered to himself.

He heard a gong sounding from inside his penthouse. "What th' hell? I didn't create a gong?"

Inside his entrance hall, he saw a full-length mirror with an ornate frame and realized it was a mirrorgate that wasn't there a few minutes earlier. It gave off a gong sound and he realized it was the doorbell. "Enter!"

The gate cleared and Roger stepped through, followed by about a dozen others. Each was carrying something.

"Roger! It's good to see you. I was beginning to think my little project had been forgotten.

They exchanged a hug and Roger started to introduce the others. He stopped when Victor's eyes grew wide as a saber-tooth tiger and black panther walked through the gate, flanked by Mark and Wendy.

Everyone shared a chuckle at his expression and Roger reassured him. "Don't worry, Victor. They're harmless." He introduced Wendy Mathias, and her familiar, Lady, as well as Mark Chambers, and his familiar, Hairball. "Which brings us to the main point of this organized home invasion." He handed Victor a fluted crystal glass that matched one held by all the rest, then lifted it in toast. "You have passed your final exam. Empire City is beautiful. Welcome to the family, Mage!"

"Thank you. Thank you." He took a sip of his own drink, then shook his head. "Somehow, I don't feel different. What's next?"

Wendy answered him. "I would recommend you return to the Creche and request a familiar like Lady. They are very helpful."

"Return? But I thought that was only for newbies?"

She answered. "That is what we tell everyone. But one of the advantages of becoming a mage is that you are able to return when you wish as well as take others back."

"What about bringing my people here?"

Roger shrugged. "Why ask us? You're a damn mage now. If you think about it, you can create your own mirrorgates and place them where you want. I would suggest a couple in the town square and one in each of the major building lobbies. After that, you can start selling..."

Victor interrupted him. "Leasing, my friend. Not selling anything."

Mark laughed. "I see what you mean, Roger. He is always a businessman. So tell me, Victor, what is the lease on that penthouse over there?"

Spaceport

Susan blinked several times and stretched, shaking off the lingering coma effect.

"How do you feel?" Lizzie stood on one side of her bed.

"Much better, thanks. How about you?"

"Wonderful. They told me I woke before you since your body had more damage to repair. I can't believe all the scars are gone."

"Yeah. Omniphage is good stuff. How long have I been out? What did I miss?"

"Just a little over a day. Here; I was asked to give you this as soon as you woke." She handed Susan a slate.

As soon as Susan turned it on, there was a simple message from the Director. "Call me." She did.

After they exchanged greetings, Mike informed her. "Our attorneys have filed briefs stating the fact that you and your cousin were in an abusive situation. Therefore, the court has the right to assign a guardian until you reach legal age. I have been assigned that role and you will be returning to Port Heinlein on the next shuttle. Even if the Childers are foolish enough to dispute this, I've been assured we can tie them up in a costly court battle for more than enough time."

"That is good news, sir. Thank you."

"You're very welcome. I must admit, I was surprised at how, during the scuffle in the barn, your Uncle managed to interrupt your attempt at self-first-aid and 'accidentally' injected himself with your dose of PhageB."

Susan grinned. "I do hope he's doing okay."

"She's doing just fine. Looks amazingly like your twin sister and has been extremely agitated. The local authorities are willing to hold her until the two of you were awake, so you can press charges."

Lizzie was staring, open-mouthed at her cousin. "She? Uncle Howard? What happened?"

"I'll explain in a few moments, cousin. In the meantime," She turned her attention back to Mike. "Tell me, please. Are there any of Uncle Howard's DNA samples stored in town?"

Mike shook his head. "Nope. That was one of the first things we checked. He didn't believe in all the modern medicine and just trusted in the Lord. As far as we can tell, he never even had a blood sample taken. We might be able to find some hairs on his comb back at the farmhouse."

Susan gave it a moment's thought before continuing. "This is my dilemma. She can attempt another shot of PhageB, with DNA extracted from her original hair, and I'll press charges. That means Howard will spend at least a few years in prison, right?" Before he could answer, she continued. "Or we can just forget to tell her of that option and let her return to High Valley without charges, but wearing the body she has now. I'm sure Sam and some of the Deputies will love having her around. What do you think, Uncle Mike?"

He looked at the two girls for a moment, then let a wide smile grow. "I think it is awfully nice of you to forego pressing charges as long as she agrees not to ask for custody. She will want to return to High Valley as soon as possible."

After Susan signed off and explained, Lizzie laughed until she was out of breath at the idea of their misogynistic Uncle Howard returning to the farm, looking just like the teenage Susan. When she caught her breath, she asked, "What now?"

Susan looked at her cousin in the plain white robe and then down at her hospital gown. "I'm ready for a shopping trip. There are probably some sweats around here and the next stop is the spaceport shopping mall."

Lizzie lost the smile. "But, we have no money."

"Don't worry, cousin. I've got more than enough to cover a shopping expedition. We need clothing, shoes, and a good meal. I also need to get us both fitted for skinsuits since we're going on a really long trip soon."

Less than an hour later, they stood in a small room inside the clothing shop. Susan closed and locked the door. "Okay. This is how it works. Watch me." She kicked off the hospital thongs and slithered out of the sweats while her cousin just stared. "See the ring marked in the floor? That shows the sensor array. Just do like I do." She stood with her feet about shoulder width apart and her hands spread out from her side. She addressed the computer with her name and for a few seconds, a series of bright lights flashed in a circle, around her. She stepped aside. "Now. Your turn."

Nervous at the unaccustomed nudity, Lizzie complied, then immediately replaced the sweats. "What now?"

Susan just smiled and put her sweats back on as well. "Watch this." She addressed the store's computer and told it to display both of them in skinsuits. Immediately, life-size holographs of each of them appeared. Each one wore a perfectly-fitted skinsuit. "I like white, but just about any light shade can be done. What color do you want yours to be?"

Lizzie thought about it for a moment. "How about pink?" As soon as she said it, her image wore a shades-of-pink skinsuit with deeper, maroon piping.

Susan changed hers to ivory white with shades of blue piping, then ordered two of each. "There. The travel garb is done. Now for something to wear for the rest of the day." She asked the store system to display a catalog of current popular spaceport styles. Their figures shrank to about four hundred millimeters tall and a dozen of each figure lined up, in front of them. Each doll-sized girl modeled a different outfit.

"My goodness! I don't think I should wear anything so

scandalous."

"Lizzie. You're not going back to High Valley and these are normal outfits for most of the civilized places. If you wear a long dress in this nice weather, people are going to stare and you will feel very uncomfortable. Take my word for it."

"Are these available in all sizes? They must have a huge storeroom."

"They will be custom-fitted to our measurements and will be ready any moment now." At that precise moment, a wall panel slid open and two fitted mini dresses hung on hangers with short, zippered boots sitting on the floor. "See? Let's get dressed and go find something to eat."

Jerryville

All of the colonists had finally been decanted. On the outside, the ship looked much the same as the day it landed. The inside was another matter entirely. Almost all of the interior panels, major support items, and CryoDox had been re-purposed to make homes and work spaces between the ship and the circular barrier wall.

Director Wendy "DeeDee" Miller stood in what used to be the cockpit of the colony ship and gazed out the wide, newly-exposed windows. A couple of robot tractors were preparing a nearby field for planting. Some colonists had setup a lumber yard on the edge of the forest, away from the Chickmonks, and had already started experimenting with timbers from some of the local trees.

"Skipper?" Igor's voice came from the stairwell.

"Up here." She answered.

He joined her at the window for a moment before speaking. "It's kind of hard to believe, isn't it? After all the dreams, science fiction stories, hard work, and now... here we are. The first human colony in another solar system." Paused, then pointed at where some Chickmonks were talking with their new-found friends. "And we've even got some for real aliens, to boot. Can't get much better than this, eh?"

She nodded, then shook herself from reverie. "You wanted me for something, Igor?"

"Yes, ma'am. I have been keeping a couple of buzzards busy the last week or so, developing some high-resolution topographic maps of the area. There is an interesting plateau about twenty-five clicks from here that would work out well for a rectenna farm. We have enough supplies to set it up and have enough space-based electrical power for some light industry."

"What's the hold up then?" She asked.

"It's covered with some really dense foliage and there doesn't appear to be an easy way up to it. I want to purpose one of our fabbers to making the parts for a heavy-lift blimp so we can put a tractor up there to clear the area."

"I hate to take a fabricator away from making tractors and home building components right now. We arrived in late spring. I want everyone to have a private home capable of withstanding heavy weather before the first snowfall. Why don't you just send one of the tractors to cut and clear a trail to it?"

"Because my best guess is that will take too long. It won't finish before winter and we wouldn't get the rectenna farm up before next spring."

She shook her head. "Sorry, Igor. But food and shelter are more important at this stage, than light industry. It will have to wait until next year."

He started to object, then stopped and shrugged. "Your call, skipper."

"Yeah. It is. But don't take it too hard. I know digging septic systems, drilling wells, and building our single-family cabins is boring, but you'll get to play with the big toys next year."

"You're only partly right. The cabins are turning out to be more challenging than I thought at first."

"Why's that?"

"The few trees you guys examined on the first landing were very similar to Earth conifers. They were a rather brittle, medium-density wood. That is what we used to design our basic cabins. This area around us has more than a dozen other species of large tree. See the ones they are feeding into the lumber mill, right now?"

She nodded.

"Those logs come from trees which are twenty to thirty meters tall and fairly straight. They are very common and have an extremely dense grain, similar to mahogany or fine oak. I ran some tests and modified the mill to produce timber frames using them, instead of the conifers. All the leaves, branches and other products from a full tree go into the chopper and the resultant slurry is used by one of the fabbers to make SIPs."

"Structural Insulated Panels." She acknowledged. "One meter wide, three meters long, and fifteen centimeters thick. The fabber creates a pair of eight millimeter plywood sheets with closed-cell expanded foam insulation between them. I'm familiar with it. So, you're saying the local hardwood trees are making structures that are stronger than the original plans?"

He nodded. "And I'm sure there are many other pleasant surprises waiting to be unveiled here on Micasa." Then, he excused himself and left, passing Cheryl Mathias on the stairs.

"Hi Cheryl. What sort of good news do you bring me, today?"

"Our knowledge of the Chickmonk language is growing daily. It seems a couple of the colonists are really good linguists and they are hard at work, developing a dictionary. We've also established a daily flea market where a lot of trading is going on. So far, I've got several complete sets of their pottery."

"Why several sets? Don't tell me you're turning into an art collector."

"I'm seeing different designs and CheeYok has told me they come from different places. He's also warned us of winter and how his people move south with the seasons. That is why they have such simple homes. They build new ones each year. I've also seen some very small, patch gardens."

"Sounds like you're making a lot of progress."

"I am a bit concerned, however." She glanced outside before continuing. "Even though their tribes are normally pretty small and move from year to year, CheeYok has told me that they do have well-defined territories and that there are areas where we shouldn't build."

"Sacred places? Have you reached the point where you are discussing theology now?"

"I wish I knew. He has invited Buster and me to travel south for the winter and will show us the forbidden areas on the way."

"Are you thinking about it?"

The teacher and researcher paused and shook her head. "I don't know. On one hand, it's an excellent chance to travel and study a fascinating primitive tribe. On the other hand, we would be on foot and living off the land for at least four months. I'm almost ashamed to say I'm feeling a bit spoiled with warm baths each day."

The Director gave her a wry smile. "You know we only have one six-place helicopter for emergencies right now. I can't allow it to stray too far from here. How long before CheeYok wants to leave?"

"Less than a month. I don't know exactly. Why? You have an idea?"

"I'll see about unpacking our backup helicopter. It will take at least a couple of days to make sure it is ready to go. After that, if you want, go walkabout with your aboriginal friends. I'll expect you to check in at least twice a day. If we don't hear from you or you report a serious problem, I'll send help."

"Thanks, DeeDee."

"Don't thank me just yet. I'll wait until you've been hiking for a week or so. And before you ask, a hot bath is not an emergency item."

Mage Council

Victor was happy.

For the first time in many years, he was doing something he really enjoyed, was proud of his work and had time to relax without pressing obligations. He knew it wouldn't last.

The doorbell gonged. "Enter!"

Mark Chambers and Hairball strode through the mirrorgate.

"Welcome, Mark. To what do I owe the pleasure of a surprise visit?"

He handed Victor a tightly-rolled scroll with a wax seal.

"This is rather archaic. I don't recall seeing one before. What is it?"

"It is a private message from the Mage Council. The wax seal will only open upon your touch."

When the Mage leader of Empire City touched the wax, it immediately dissolved into a red smoke and faded to nothing. He unrolled the scroll and read.

Mage Victor Charles Adams III

The Mage Council requests your presence for the purpose of discussing matters critical to Beta.

The Council member who delivered this scroll has been tasked with opening a gate that will bring you to the Council chambers.

We await your kind attention.

The Domain Lord, speaking for the Beta Domain Council.

Victor read the document twice, then turned his attention to Mark. "I must admit I'm a bit confused here. What the hell does the Domain

Lord and Mage Council want with someone who hasn't left their city in months? I thought we mages had exclusive control over our own domains?"

Mark answered. "There are things that effect all of Beta and they are what the Council must deal with on an infrequent basis. Any further information will be up to the full Council. Are you ready to go?"

"Now?"

"If you don't mind, sir. It is never a good idea to keep the Council waiting."

"Very well, but just give me a minute." He tapped a button on his slate. "Jack? I'm going to a meeting with Mark Chambers and some others."

"Want me to join you?" His friend and bodyguard asked.

Victor looked at Mark, who frowned and shook his head. "No. That's okay. I don't think I'll be too long. Keep an eye on things while I'm gone."

"No problem, boss. Have fun."

He slid the slate back into his shoulder pocket and gestured towards the mirrorgate. "After you, sir."

They emerged in a large hallway with benches and a dozen other mirrorgates on both sides. The end of the hall featured an impressive, deeply-carved double door. Hairball sat down next to the doors and Mark placed his hand on a polished brass globe of Beta. A soft gong sounded and he announced. "Mark Chambers, accompanied by Victor Charles Adams the Third, as requested by the Council."

"Enter!" A voice boomed as the doors slowly swung open.

The Council Chamber was round with a high, domed ceiling. The entrance doors opened on a passage between several rows of bleacher-like seats. Facing them, a curved dais held twenty-four seats, arranged like judges in a courtroom. It was obvious that only about half of them were filled.

Mark led him to the center of the room. "Please stand here for a moment, Victor." Then, he stepped up on the platform and took his place in one of the seats.

Angela Veski spoke. "Victor. It has come to the Council's attention that you have been experimenting. Would you be kind enough to share the results?"

Now he knew what this was about. "I assume you mean my double, back on Earth?"

She nodded gravely.

"When I heard about Mike Hawthorne's death and resurrection, I decided to investigate for myself. I had no desire to die, but thought there might be other applications and perhaps a more efficient way than sending warp-drive ships scampering about the solar system."

Mike Hawthorne asked, "So you decided to create clones of yourself. Is that it?"

"Before we go any further, I want to know if this is a trial and, if so, what are the charges and where is my attorney?"

The council members glanced at each other, some chuckled, some just smiled before Angela waved her hand. "Please. Some decorum, everyone. I think we've had enough fun at Victor's expense." She turned her attention his way, once more. "Please sit down and relax, Victor. There are no charges, you are not under arrest and even if you were, this council wouldn't be trying the case."

He glanced back and saw the comfortable armchair behind him that hadn't been there a moment before. "Then why am I here and why the third-degree?"

"You're here for two reasons. The first is that we only know part of the story on your research and want to know the rest. You aren't the only inquisitive one among us, you know."

"And the second reason?"

"The members of this council are impressed with what you have accomplished in the relatively short time you have been building Empire City. Because of that and your recent research, we are offering you a seat on this council."

The Mage of Empire City thought about that for a moment, then sat down in the armchair. A few more moments elapsed while he considered it some more. "Just what does being a member of this council involve? I'm already pretty busy, running and expanding Empire City."

Angela glanced to either side. "You see there are twenty-four seats here. They correspond to the twenty-four hourly timezones on Beta, same as on Earth. If you recall, when you were offered the raw land where you built Empire City, it was some distance away from the other communities. That is because we wanted it in a timezone by itself for now. If you take the seat, you will be a Master Mage and in charge of everything that happens within that zone. Additionally, from time to time, you will have to sit in on a council meeting, such as this, and help us with things that effect all of Beta."

"Sounds like an awful lot of responsibility. What's in it for me?"

"You will have access to our entire knowledge database. It is already far advanced from what is available either on Earth or the moon. And of course, there is the power. You have proven yourself a skilled leader who is loved and respected by those who work under you. As a council member, you will have an equal share in not only building Beta, but many other worlds."

Victor looked down and saw illuminated names of their home cities on the face of the step in front of each seat. Wendy Mathias had Contraridance. Buster and Cheryl Mathias had Morepork at their feet. The next available seat had been dark, but now lit up with Empire City. "What the hell." Victor muttered. Then, a bit louder. "You folks sure drive a hard bargain." He rose and took his place. The seat felt comfortable.

As soon as he was seated, the whole room started to shrink. The bleachers withdrew, into the walls. The empty council seats vanished and the seated ones closed up, to form a circle. A section of floor rose to become a round table. When everything stopped, Victor realized there was a small viewscreen set into the table in front of each of them.

A crystal goblet of wine appeared next to his view screen. Everyone lifted theirs while Angela made the toast. "Ladies and Gentlemen, let us welcome the newest member of this council. From now on, he wears the title of Master Mage and is trusted with all our resources. Welcome to the family, Victor!"

After the round of drinks and congratulations wound down, Mike Hawthorne spoke up. "Now will you satisfy our curiosity, Victor? We know all the research you've done here on Beta, but what has been going on back on Earth?"

"Fair enough. After I heard how you were resurrected, I asked a team of my engineers to look into the warp-drive system. At the same time, I arranged for a brick and helmet so we could join the Beta experiment. Since we are on a twenty-four to one time compression, I've now experienced more than fifteen years learning to become a mage and building Empire City. I've never lost track of the original plan, to provide an alternate body for myself, should my original one be destroyed, back on Earth."

Wendy Mathias asked. "And have you been successful?"

"The tools are in place. Now, I'm working on some logistics."

"Just what do you mean by tools? Warp-drive spacecraft don't grow on trees."

"Did I mention I have some really smart engineering researchers? Once they looked over the designs, they constructed a stationary chamber the duplicates the nervous system reset and mind-wipe of a warp drive. The same facility contains a Beta Brick and several helmets."

She continued. "And what about spare bodies? There aren't that many convicted murderers willing to take a risk."

Victor waved away her concern. "I wouldn't want the associated legal paperwork anyway. I've found a better option. When the unfortunate event occurs, I'm leasing."

A muttered chorus of "Leasing?" rose from around the table.

Victor smiled. "Yes. Leasing. Let me ask all of you a question. Since Beta has come into existence, do you occasionally find it much more comfortable and interesting than the so-called real world?"

His question was met with nods and mutters of agreement.

"If I may be perfectly honest, if something drastic happens to me back on Earth, I may not even choose to be resurrected. But if I do, then I've arranged with several of my senior researchers, to lease their bodies on a rotational basis. The lease contracts are for two years and when they get the old bodies back, there are considerable sums of money in their accounts. At the same time, they spend the forty-eight years here on Beta in a luxury apartment in Empire City and with enough coins in their purse to do pretty much anything they want."

Mike Hawthorne stood, stretched and addressed their newest council member. "You've done some good work there, Victor. Now it's time for us to reveal some things that are not well known. Once we had established the first little community on Beta, it became obvious that some of the warnings penned about the singularity, also known as the rapture of the nerds, posed a very real danger. We knew that once people got used to living someplace where there was no pollution, plenty of room to explore and incredibly tasty food and drink, there would be a rush to join. And when they found out their so-called souls remained here when they died back on Earth, nobody would want to leave. That is when we decided to limit Beta in many ways and to use it as a training ground for colonists."

"Training ground?" Victor's turn to echo a statement.

"Yes. Up until recently, there were any number of major

catastrophes that might wipe out the entirety of humankind. I assume you've heard of the first colony on Micasa?"

"Yes. Of course. But that is a very small effort. You can only send about a hundred colonists at a time and there is a long turnaround because the warp-tug is a kluge of left over parts and needs to be rebuilt after every usage."

Several of the members chuckled and Mike continued. "That is what we want most people to think. As a matter of fact, we now have two deep-space industrial fabrication facilities. They are turning out colonial drop ships and all their required supplies at the rate of two a year, Earth time. In addition, we have another couple of warp-tugs to deliver them to Micasa. Within the next year, another fabrication plant will come online. Our goal is to spread human colonies to at least three other solar systems within the next ten Earth years."

"Three others? I hadn't heard of any further expeditions."

"One of the first projects to leave our fabrication plant was a transhumanist brick assembly, wrapped in many layers of shielding . That was mounted in a frame with a nuclear reactor in one end and a huge battery of cameras and remote sensing equipment on the other end. Finally, the whole thing was wrapped in a set of warp-drive coils. There is no life support and no cargo area. We have three volunteer teams that are dedicated deep-space explorers. Each team serves a week at a time, warping to one solar system after another. When they return, all the data and images are analyzed. We have already found three more unoccupied planets similar to Micasa."

"Unoccupied?"

Port Heinlein

"Susan?" Lizzie sounded frustrated. Her cousin was already dressed and applying lipstick.

"Uhm?" She answered through pursed lips.

"What is it that you really want to do?"

"Enjoy my eighteenth birthday bash, eat some cake and ice cream, and generally have a good time. I assumed that is why we're dressing up. Why?"

"That isn't what I meant. Never mind." She shrugged. "Let's just go and have a good time."

Susan finished and turned away from the mirror. "Something is bothering you. What is it?"

"I dunno... I just..." She paused, as if trying to frame her concerns. "It's been almost a month and I still don't feel as if I belong here. I mean... You have a career planned already. You love your studies and know more or less what sort of research you're going to be doing over the next ten years or so. I can't help but feel like a third wheel."

"I thought you were just taking time while getting used to our culture. Have you been going to classes, too?"

She shook her head. "No. I dropped all of them a few days ago."

"Why?"

Lizzie gave a wry smile. "I asked myself that same question. Then, I went to the counselor and she asked the same question. She then referred me to a therapist who also asked the same question. It's taken some time, but I think I've finally come up with some answers."

Susan grabbed a comfy chair, facing her cousin. "The party doesn't start for another hour. Talk to me."

Lizzie took a deep breath. "At first, the therapist and I thought it was just a severe case of homesickness."

Susan gave a rueful smile. "You're might find this funny, cousin. But now that I'm back in Port Heinlein, I've occasionally found myself missing the wide-open blue skies. Is that part of it?"

"Yeah. But there is much more than just that. It's a cultural thing. I'm starting to think it doesn't matter how many millions of miles you get from home, you can't escape your upbringing. Look at us, for example. You're perfectly comfortable wearing those super high heels and spandex minidress that shows your body to perfection. I've tried these styles and just can't get past the feeling that I'm dressed like a slut. It's just not me."

"I've noticed you're dressing more in slacks or longer, fuller skirts. It's not that uncommon. We both see a lot of fashion variation. It's okay to be a bit... conservative."

"You were going to say 'prude', but I know what you mean. There is more to it than just clothing design. I dunno. It will probably just take some time." She shook herself and forced a smile. "Come on. I need to help you celebrate a birthday."

Three hours later, the band finished the last tune and started packing. Most of their friends had already called it a night.

Susan took a sip from her drink, then asked. "Who was that guy you were just dancing with?"

"Dunno. I thought he was one of your friends."

"Not mine. He's kinda cute though."

Lizzie shrugged. "If you like them pale and scrawny, then you're welcome to him."

Susan chuckled. "We've been here more than three months and I've introduced you to several nice guys. This is only the second time I've seen you dance. So, tell me cousin. What is your type?"

"If I had to choose based only upon appearance, it might be that drummer." She nodded towards the guy breaking down the drum kit. He was tall, square-jawed, broad-shouldered, and had dark red hair that framed his face in short, tight curls.

Susan glanced, then shook her head. "Lizzie, you sure know how to pick 'em."

"Why? You know him?"

"Oh yeah. He and I had some classes the year before my folks died. He can be a bit rude, but smarter than he looks. Too bad he dropped out to join the forestry team."

"What's his name?"

Susan took another sip, then stood up. "I'll probably regret this." She waved towards the small stage and hollered. "Hey! Varlon!"

The drummer looked up, scanned the remaining tables and saw Susan's arm waving. He waved back, stood up and strolled over.

"Hey there, Sue. Didn't think you remembered me. Was that party for you?"

"That's right. I'm eighteen and back in port for awhile." She gestured to her cousin. "Lizzie, this strapping lad is Varlon Smythe, with a "y" and an "e", and he's not really housebroken. Varlon, this lovely lady is Elizabeth Roberts. She's new around here. So play nice."

"Since I seldom play, that should be no problem. It's good to meet you, Elizabeth. Welcome to Port Heinlein."

"Thank you, sir. May I say I enjoyed the music. That was a very impressive drum solo at the end of the first set. May I ask the name of the tune?"

He paused and gave her a half-smile, "Pretty; good manners; great taste in music... My goodness, Susan. Where did you encounter this fine lady?"

"She's my cousin from Earth."

"Pardon me, Liz. To answer your question, that is a very old piece of music from California back in the late nineteen sixties. It's called "In-A-Gadda-Da-Vida" I'm glad you enjoyed it." He glanced towards the stage. "Liz, I have to finish breaking down my kit and get home. Tomorrow is an early shift. May I trade contact info with you?"

She nodded and their slates swapped the data in a couple of seconds. He put it back in its holster. "Thanks for the introduction, Susan. Happy birthday and I'm sure we'll catch up again, soon."

After he was out of earshot, Susan whispered. "I thought you didn't like to be called 'Liz", what's with that?"

"That's okay. He can call me anything he wants."

Susan just shook her head.

The next afternoon, Lizzie's slate held a message.

Liz,

It was nice meeting you last night and I'm sorry I was in such a rush. Would you like to grab a bite this evening? I can pick you up about seven.

Varlon

At precisely seven oh one, the door chimed and Liz opened it. Varlon said "Hello" then paused to let his eyes slowly sweep from her face, down to her heels and back again. "My goodness, Liz. You look lovely this evening."

She had opted for a compromise with black high heeled calf boots, matching tights and a thin, woven sweater dress in a pale gray. Her blonde hair fell in waves about her shoulders. "Thank you, Varlon. You look nice, too."

He wore black boots under deep forest green tailored slacks and a double-breasted sea-foam green shirt. "Thanks. Ready for dinner?" At her nodded assent, they started walking up the passage towards the main thoroughfare. "How adventuresome are you?"

"Adventuresome? I'm not sure how to answer that. What do you have in mind?"

"I'll be honest with you. I knew Sue had been to visit her relatives on Earth and there were rumors it hadn't gone well. When she said you were her cousin and new around here, I figured you might be used to somewhat more robust foods than we normally prepare. Since one of my jobs is in hydroponics, I thought you might like to try some alternate cuisine."

"That sounds good. I'm game."

The meal caught Lizzie by surprise. Since all of the fruits, vegetables and meats consumed in Port Heinlein were locally grown, she was used to fresh. This meal took it a step further with subtle flavors she had never tasted before. "This is great." She complimented after a few mouthfuls. "Just what is it?"

"The hydroponic gardens and orchards are restricted to a few hundred proven species. That is what shows up in our grocery stores and most restaurants. On the other hand, many of us have acquired packets of seed or cuttings of alternate species from Earth. We grow these in limited quantities in our own apartments and patios."

She nodded and swallowed another mouthful. "Yeah. I've seen more than a few herb gardens. Susan even has some unusual tropical flowers on her patio. But this is a restaurant..."

"It's not your average restaurant. Those of us that are actively involved in cultivating unusual plants banded together to form a co-op. Those that like to cook sign up for a rotating schedule where we play chef for an evening. The rest donate all the extra fruits and veggies. All the profits are used to pay our expenses. Any extra goes into a trust fund to purchase additional seeds and cuttings from Earth."

"Well, this is really great. My compliments to the chef."

He raised his glass and gave a slight bow. "Thank you. It is a pleasure to see you enjoy it."

She froze, startled. "You cooked this?"

"What? Did you think I was just some stupid jock that dropped out of school because I couldn't hack it? At least that is the rumor I've heard."

Lizzie opened her mouth, then closed it.

He chuckled. "The fact is, I did drop out of school. One day, I realized there were things I liked and wanted to do and things that just did not interest me in the least. So, I decided not to waste any more time with the stuff I didn't like."

"I guess you must like cooking then."

"That is just a hobby. I'm going to be a colonist."

Once more, she paused between bites. "Colonist? What do you mean?"

"Have you heard of Micasa?"

She shook her head.

"It's not real common knowledge yet. The powers-that-be down on Earth are not real happy about it and much of the technology involved is transhumanist."

She put down her fork. "Okay, Varlon. That is another word I've heard from time to time. I thought it was just a bunch of geeks playing some sort of super-realistic video game."

"It's much more than that, Liz. It's also the only way we can travel to other solar systems these days."

"Now you're just humoring me. I may not have had the education of most folks in Port Heinlein, but I did learn that nothing can travel faster than the speed of light."

"I am not the person to talk to about the physics of it all, but we do have a warp-drive and although it is nothing like all those science fiction movies, it is possible to leave our solar system. We already have one colony on an Earth-like world called Micasa. And at least another half-dozen colony ships are planned. I'm doing all I can to develop skills that will allow me to have my own farm and room for a family to grow."

"I must admit, I do miss the open skies of Earth. Port Heinlein is amazing and doesn't feel claustrophobic, but it is only about thirty kilometers wide."

Varlon stared at her for a few moments, as if making up his mind.

"What?" She complained and blushed. "What are you staring at? Is the Earth farmer's daughter really so weird?"

He reached over and took her hand. "Will you trust me for a little while, Elizabeth Roberts?"

His face bore a serious look she hadn't noticed before so she took a moment to answer. "Okay. What should I trust you about?"

He dropped her hand, tossed his napkin on the table, stood up, and told her. "Let' go back to your place. You can put on your skinsuit and then we're off to the hydroponics office."

On the way to his office, her curiosity got the best of her. "Okay, Mr. Varlon, Sir. You've got to see me in a skinsuit. But why?"

"I keep several spare skinsuits in my office. It was faster to take you home first. It will only take a minute for me to change." He took his eyes off the roadway long enough to smile at her. "I'm going to show you the ultimate horizon."

In what looked to Lizzie like a fancy locker room, he laid out a pair of stark white suits. They looked like much thicker versions of the skinsuits, with separate gloves and boots. They also sported hard collar assemblies and helmets. Her eyes grew wide when she realized what he was doing. "Oh no. No way, mister. Those are space suits. We had to wear them in the shuttle and that was scary enough."

"Don't worry, Liz. We're not going for a shuttle ride. I just want to take you on a short walk. You said you would trust me." He stopped and gave her a puppy-dog face. "Please?"

A few minutes later, they were in an airlock. "Part of my job is to make sure all the passive solar collectors are clean and providing enough full-spectrum sunlight. That means I have to come out here once in a while for a hands-on inspection."

The outer hatch swung silently open and he led her out from the shadow of an overhanging ledge and onto a platform. His arm around her shoulder was comforting, even through the thick material of the suit. He said nothing as she stared at the millions of stars, scattered from horizon to horizon.

They stood there for perhaps two minutes before she turned to look at him. "Pictures just aren't the same. This is incredible. Thank you."

Lizzie was smiling as she closed the apartment door. Then, she jumped at the voice behind her. "Hey there, cousin. What's with the skinsuit? I thought you didn't like showing all your goodies as you so aptly put it."

She spun around and hugged Susan. "I don't, silly. But as you've told me, they do serve a purpose. I was outside."

Susan stepped back in surprise. "Outside? As in putting on a spacesuit and walking out on the surface?"

Lizzie nodded, still smiling.

"Well, it doesn't appear to have produced any ill effects. Or is that smile just from the company?"

Journey

Cheryl shook herself, adjusting the tall backpack. "Damn! I forgot how much stuff you have to carry for a long hike."

Buster gave her a wry smile as he went through the same ritual. "Need I remind you that the last time we went backpacking, was in college."

It was just past dawn and CheeYok's tribe stood impatiently waiting. His high-pitched voice had acquired a substantial English vocabulary. "We must go." He announced, then turned and marched northward.

Marching slowly, but steadily, a couple of dozen Chickmonks, with CheeYok and his wife in the lead, followed the fertile valley. Although there were no noticeable trail markers, Buster noticed they always seemed to be fairly close to the edge of the deep forest. He mentioned this to his wife.

"You think the forest is their guide?" She asked.

"I'm not sure. It just seems odd at times. This veldt we're following is fairly easy walking, so that might just be reason enough. But have you noticed how really smooth and free of roly poly burrows our path has been?" He shook his head at the memory. "I damn near broke an ankle several times around our landing zone, until I learned to watch out for them."

The sun was low in the sky when CheeYok called a halt. The tribe formed a protective circle and someone started arranging stones in a loose firepit. The Chickmonk leader approached his human friends. "We stay here. Eat. Sleep." He announced. "You sleep good, here." He pointed to a spot inside their circle. Then, he looked up at the pale shadow-form circling high, overhead. "Buzzard sleep?"

"No, CheeYok. The buzzard has eaten enough to stay up for a few more days. It will watch for large animals, tonight."

The Chickmonk dismissed it. "Not needed here. No bad animals. In two days, we will go through bad place. Then, we must move very fast. There are many big, bad animals."

While their meal was cooking, Cheryl checked in. "DeeDee? We're camped for the night."

"So I see. The buzzard's view has become popular entertainment. It seems like a lot of folks are looking forward to homesteading some of the little side valleys you've passed. I do have a favor to ask, however."

"What's that?"

The colony director showed a buzzard's-eye view of a wide, flat ridge. "It looks like the valley you're following will pass by that plateau. Ask CheeYok if he can tell us anything about it. The geologists are in agreement that it looks weird."

The next day, the tribe came close to a series of tall, sheer cliffs and Cheryl asked their guide what was up there.

He pointed out a gash in the cliff, framed by two beautiful waterfalls. "If you go to that side of the falling water..." He pointed to the closest waterfall. "You will find a path. But it is not for this time. When we return, if you wish to see, I will show you the Last Place."

"Last place?" Cheryl wasn't sure she understood. "What do you mean by Last Place?"

He waved away her question. "It is just the Last Place. No time now."

A few hour's later, they came to their next campsite. This one overlooked a deeper valley with a wide, deep river and dense forest on all sides.

CheeYok pointed upstream. "Look. See other side?"

He was pointing at another open bluff about their same level, but about ten kilometers upstream. Their path led along the riverbank, with a narrow strip of the forest between the river and a rugged rock wall. He continued. "We leave at sun up. Walk very fast, all day. We have to be up there before dark. Many, many bad animals near river. No stopping. Sheeril, Buzzter, you understand?"

Buster agreed. "Yes, CheeYok. We understand. No stopping and walk fast all day."

"I sure hope we don't have to use these." Cheryl tapped the semi-auto pistol on her hip. "Target shooting was fun, but I hate the idea of killing some poor beastie just because we're invading its territory."

"Look at the bright side, hon."

"What's that?"

"Maybe they're really good to eat."

She rolled her eyes, shook her head, then punched him on the shoulder.

Unlike the seemingly random trail through the veldt, the path along the river was clearly marked by the passage of many feet over many years. It was not quite a road, but there were no big trees close to the river's edge and one flat rock shelf led to another, with occasional small sandy coves.

True to his word, CheeYok maintained a brutal fast walk for several hours. Their first break came on a wide, flat rock shelf the overhung the river and gave a clear view for perhaps a hundred meters or more, in any direction. Everyone sat down, sipped water from skin bags and snacked on some dried trail rations.

Buster whispered. "Hon. Notice how CheeYok has two of the men on watch? He's nervous as hell." He took another sip of water, then stood. "I'm going to take a turn at watch." He marched over to the guard on point, who was staring intently at the trail ahead.

Nothing was said. The guard just gave him a glance of acknowledgment, then concentrated on the way ahead.

Buster heard a sound, like something moving through the thick brush. Since everyone was keeping quiet, he tapped his earpiece and whispered. "Cheryl. Can you get a video feed from the buzzard and see what is moving, up around the bend?"

He only had to wait a minute or so before her whispered reply. "Got it! But I'm not happy, Buster. There are three gators the size of minivans sunning themselves on a wide strip of the trail. From the looks of the vegetation, there might be more hidden in the trees."

Buster tried to be a quiet as possible when he walked over to CheeYok. He knelt, pulled his slate and showed the aerial shots of the gators. CheeYok stared, obviously distressed, then stood, gripped his spear and motioned for the other hunter to join him. They exchanged a few words, then marched towards the giant predators. The human wasn't going to let his friends die just to clear the way. He made sure of the two extra magazines, then hurried to catch up.

CheeYok stopped and motioned for him to go back and stay with the rest of the tribe. Buster drew his gun, shook his head and continued. CheeYok caught up and pointed at the gun. Buster tapped the gun, then tapped his companion's spear. The Chickmonk leader gave a confused look, but shrugged and took the lead, once more.

At a narrow bend in the river, the trail lay very close to the water's edge. They peeked around the base of a huge tree and Buster got his first look at a Micassian predator. There were three on the bank and one guarding a jungle path. Two of them were a couple of meters in length while the third appeared almost double that size. It was farthest from them.

Buster saw his friend brace himself for a charge and placed a hand on his shoulder. "Stay!" He whispered. The man knew he only had limited ammunition and didn't think the small-caliber rounds would kill with a single shot. He took careful aim and fired.

The first shot hit the head of the closest gator. He had been trying for the eye, but instead took a chunk from a brow ridge. The beast roared in pain, rolling over several times and clawing at its face. The others froze, attention fixed on the source of the sound. The human didn't wait for them to sort it out. He fired again and this time, hit the next beast in the eye. It too, rolled over, only this time, it started to convulse. The largest one made a mad dash for the water and it looked like a submarine, sliding out of drydock.

The third gator roared a challenge and came at them. Buster had never seen anything so terrifying in his life. It went from standing still to race horse speed and he had no time to properly aim. He fired as fast as he could draw the trigger. It seemed like forever, but was only a few seconds before the monster stumbled and fell, bleeding from a half-dozen wounds. It twitched a few times, then all was quiet.

"Reload, damnit!" Cheryl's whisper sounded harsh in his ear.

He dropped the magazine, stuffed a new one in his weapon, then grabbed the fallen clip and checked. It only had two rounds left. He noticed his hands were shaking.

CheeYok and the other hunter had spread apart from them and were staring in amazement.

His wife touched his arm. "What's with that one?" She pointed at the gator half-hidden between the trees. It was obviously agitated, but holding its ground.

They both jumped at DeeDee's voice in their earpieces. "I think I know why it's there. I had the buzzard deploy a skeeter for a closer look. There's a nest in a small clearing about ten meters behind that one. I'm thinking there might be baby gators someplace close."

Buster glanced over his shoulder and saw the rest of the tribe was lined up, behind them. He exchanged a look with CheeYok and the leader barked an order to the other hunter. Spear held ready, the two of them marched down the trail. CheeYok stopped between the momma gator and the water and his companion paused a few feet further on, staring intently at the river.

Cheryl and the rest of the tribe rushed past the still-twitching gator bodies and nervously made it around the far curve. As one of the Chickmonk males passed, he jumped on the first gator and shoved his spear through its eye, deep into the brain. It immediately stopped twitching. He then turned and darted between a couple of trees and disappeared into the jungle.

Since everyone else had ignored him, Buster and Cheryl did the same.

The tribe maintained a grueling pace for the next hour, until the path led away from the river and up, towards a gap in the nearby cliffs. The final spurt of energy took them to an overhanging ledge and the first permanent structures they had seen.

"Now that is beautiful. It reminds me of an ancient cliff village from Earth." Cheryl's whispered comment garnered an appreciative nod from her husband.

There were no ladders, just narrow, hand-carved steps in stone. It was designed to keep out animals, not other Chickmonks. It was also obvious that it wasn't a permanent dwelling.

While some of the tribe built a fire, CheeYok asked his human friends to follow. He was obviously proud of the cistern, fed by a clear trickle from a spring. On the other side of the wide rock ledge, a deep crack in the rocks was the communal privy and waste disposal.

They heard cries of joy and rushed back to find the young male that had slipped away, was back. He carried the carcasses of a pair of baby gators. Each one was less than a meter long. They had both been killed with a single spear thrust through the eye socket.

CheeYok spoke. "Thank you for my life, Buzzter."

"There is no need for thanks. I did what I could to help."

"Every year, when we pass this way, at least one of us is lost. This is the first time all have passed without harm." He paused before asking. "Will you show me how to use that noise spear?"

Sadly, Buster shook his head. "I'm afraid not, CheeYok." He drew the gun, dropped the magazine and showed him the cartridges. "These are what make it work and I used almost a third of them. It will be a long time before I can get any more."

The Chickmonk leader nodded understanding. "One day, my friend, I will find something valuable enough to trade for one of them."

Everyone feasted on roast gator tail while the hides were rolled in something akin to salt.

Another week's march and they found another cliff city. This one was obviously a year around village. The overhanging rock sheltered several wide ledges in a curve more than a half kilometer long.

"This is why the original surveys reported no intelligent life forms. All their permanent structures appear to be hidden from satellite view." Buster's voice held admiration.

"Yeah, but they should have noticed that." She pointed down the valley, towards a series of what were obviously planted fields. "That sort of agriculture doesn't occur naturally. Also, look at the smoke plumes. It's still warm and I count more than a dozen."

He agreed. "I think this is the source of their ceramics, as well. Look over there." Her husband pointed towards a low adobe structure with a wide window. Various jugs and other brightly-colored containers lined the window ledge.

Suddenly, there was a commotion ahead. CheeYok was shouting at a group of Chickmonks blocking their path.

The leader of their adversaries was dressed like an ancient Roman centurion. Some sort of deep rose colored cloth formed a short tunic.

Over that, smooth leather straps held armor with the distinctive texture of gator hide. He held his spear in both hands and made it obvious he didn't want these strange, new beings to enter their encampment.

Buster put a hand on CheeYok's shoulder. "That's fine, my friend. We will make camp out here. We don't want to cause you any trouble."

"It is not your battle, Buzzter. He has called me a liar when I say you are a great hunter that kills with thunder."

"Do you want me to make thunder again, my friend?"

CheeYok froze and a smile spread over his face. "It will not kill?"

Buster drew his weapon, aimed at a rock ledge about a hundred meters away and fired. The boom echoed down the canyon, some rock chips flew in a cloud of dust and Buster put it back in its holster. The silence was deafening.

After a few moments, the centurion guard took a step back and to one side so that they could pass.

Cheryl whispered. "Somehow, husband of mine, I don't think you made a friend just then."

Buster nodded. "I will have to figure some way to make up for that guard losing face."

Port Heinlein

Lizzie stared at her closet, then pulled down the little black dress that she had already told Susan she wouldn't be caught dead wearing. She slithered into the stretchy wisp of fabric, shook everything into place, put on heels and posed in front of the mirror. The conservative farm girl cringed, but had to admit she looked just as sexy as any of the other women. Except for that bra. The light lunar gravity and once-a-decade Omniphage treatments meant most women didn't wear them. She realized it was a bit of a security blanket on her part. It landed on the bed a moment later. Swallowing nervously, she made an effort to stand up straight and strut around the room, as her cousin had demonstrated.

Her slate chimed. It was Varlon, so she restricted the view to her face. No sense in spoiling the surprise. "Yes?" She could tell from the background, that he was still in the hydroponic warehouse.

"Hi Liz." He paused. "I... I hate to do this to you. I know I promised to cook tonight. But there has been an emergency and I'm running late."

She frowned. "No. I understand. If you want to cancel..."

"No! Not cancel. Just a bit of a delay is all. If you don't mind, head over to my place. I've already keyed the door for you. I should get there about the same time you arrive."

"Are you sure?"

He made a puppy-dog face. "Please? I'll try to wrap this up as quickly as I can."

A half-hour later, she stepped out of the pedicab, paid the driver and tapped his doorbell. After no response on the third ring, she placed her palm on the keypanel. It blinked green and the outer hatch slid open. She quickly passed both doors and froze.

His man-cave was a dump! Okay, she thought to herself. Maybe not a dump, but he was a bit messy. Like most of the apartments she had seen, the kitchen, dining, and living areas were an open-concept space. A wide window looked out on his private balcony and the now-familiar panorama of the thirty kilometer wide Port Heinlein crater. The few sections of comfortable furniture had towels and various pieces of clothing scattered about. A half-completed model of some sort of aircraft and related bits and pieces covered most of the desktop.

She walked into the kitchen and noticed a couple of baskets of fresh vegetables on the counter. The fridge was sparsely populated with a whole chicken, a half-dozen bottles of lunar beer, and a few packs of cheese. The cupboards held plates, glassware, and an unexpectedly nice collection of spices and teas.

The back bedroom was immaculate. She immediately tagged it as the guest room. The master bedroom was much like the living area. The bed was rumpled, one dresser drawer was half-open, and a few articles of clothing were scattered about.

Lizzie's snooping was interrupted when her slate dinged. It was Varlon again.

"Hey there! Listen. I'm really, really sorry, but I'm going to be about an hour longer. I was hoping to get home and clean up a bit."

She interrupted his apology. "Don't worry. I'm a big girl and more than capable of amusing myself for an hour or so. But don't make me wait much longer than that."

He looked relieved. "Great! Sorry for the mess. I'll be there as soon as possible."

Almost exactly an hour later, the door opened and he strode in. Then, he froze and looked slowly around the room. It was immaculate.

"I'm glad you could make it. I was just about to feed dinner to the cat and leave."

She was wearing a white apron and standing behind the kitchen counter.

He lifted his chin and obviously sniffed the air. "Uuhmmm. Something smells good."

She removed the apron and hung it on a wall hook, then stepped from behind the counter.

His eyes snapped first to her unconfined breasts, then traveled down her legs and slowly back up. A smile creased his face and he stepped forward.

Lizzie held up her hands, palms facing him. "Stop right there, mister. You are still wearing jeans and teeshirt while I took the time to dress up. I'm sure you need a shower and that will give me time to get dinner on the table.

Ten minutes later, he was back, hair wet and combed, dark leather deck shoes, pressed khaki slacks, and a blood-red button-down shirt with a wide collar.

"Sit!" She ordered and he obeyed.

A pair of sealed beer bottles stood next to glasses rimed with frost. He opened and poured both while she place a salad at each setting. She finally sat down and flipped back a dishtowel to reveal warm dinner rolls.

"Well don't just sit there, Varlon." She was waiting for him to start.

He picked up a roll, then paused and set it back. "Do you... Do you want to say grace?"

"I thought you were one of the atheists that seem to be the norm around here?"

His face was serious. "I am. But I also have a deep respect for other cultures and history. If it makes you feel better, please go ahead."

She reached over, took his hand, and bowed her head. "Dear Lord. We thank you for these gifts which we are about to receive from your bounty. Amen."

He echoed. "Amen." And looked up to see her smile.

Dinner progressed with small talk, interspersed with her smiles at his un-subtle attempts to stare at her breasts.

Finally, she raised her half-empty glass. "A toast, my good man."

His thick eyebrows rose at the same time he lifted his glass.

"To tests and passing grades."

He responded and drank, then asked. "Dare I ask what that was all about?"

She sipped her beer and laughed. "Why don't you tell me if I've passed?"

A smile played at the corners of his mouth. "Passed?"

"Time to stop the charade, Mr. Smythe. This whole evening has been a test. I just want to know if I've passed."

His smile was open, then. "What makes you think it was a test?"

"I've seen your workspace. It's very clean and neat. Although you dress roughly most of the time, it's always clean. When I looked around, I realized that all the clothing scattered on the furniture and floor was clean. It looked like a movie set that had been purposely designed to be messy." She pointed towards the kitchen. "All the stuff needed to cook a tasty meal was waiting for me. And to top it off, you stayed away exactly long enough. So, I ask again. Did I pass?"

He stood, wiped his mouth with the napkin, and held out his hand. She took it and stood up, to meet him. He gently pulled her close and put his hands on her hips. She put hers on his broad shoulders.

"Yes. Ms. Roberts. You most certainly did pass with flying colors. Although I was pleasantly surprised at your lovely attire. One would think you were trying to seduce me."

She chuckled and reminded him. "My face is up here, Mr. Smythe. You've been staring at my breasts way too much this evening."

His eyes met hers and a long moment later, their lips met.

After a few minutes, she pulled back with a small gasp. "Are you sure, Varlon?"

"Sure about what, Liz?"

"I don't want to be just another of those girls."

He placed a finger on her lips. "The last woman I was with was more than six month's ago. And before that was almost a year. I have been looking for a woman like you for a long time. If you want to take it easy, I understand. But I'm not going anywhere."

She shook her head and leaned in closer. "I'm tired of taking it easy."

He took her hands from his shoulders and lifted them over her head, pushing her back against the wall. His body pressed against hers and the thin khaki fabric did nothing to hide his arousal. His husky whisper sent chills down her spine. "I noticed you made the bed as well."

She gave him a quick kiss on the cheek, then nibbled at his ear.

"Besides good housekeeping, that is called good planning."

Winter Camp

"CheeYok. Do you know the guard who met us at the gate?"

"His name is BaYok and he is one who protects the market."

"I noticed he was wearing a large knife on his belt. Do you know what it is made of?"

"In the far north, there is a type of tree that grows slowly and the wood is very hard. Such knives as his are difficult to make and very valuable. They are not as hard and sharp as your metal knives, but it can be made as long as your arm."

Buster nodded, thoughtfully. "You have taught us a great deal, my friend. Now it is time for us to pass on some knowledge. But first, I want to meet BaYok once more. Will you take me to him?"

A few minutes later, they found BaYok sitting on a wooden bench and eating a bowl of stew. When they approached, he put it down, carefully wiped his beak, and stood to meet them.

BaYok was tall for a Chickmonk. His eyes were almost on a level with the human before him. He folded his arms and glared at Buster.

"BaYok. I am told you are the protector of the market. I wish to trade with you."

CheeYok translated and the guard in centurion garb stared for a moment before barking an answer. "What do you want to trade?"

Buster unclipped the stainless steel machete from his belt, then offered it, hilt-first, to the guard. It was only slightly longer than the guard's short-sword.

BaYok took it and slowly pulled it from the sheath. His eyes widened when he saw the polished silver blade. When he turned it, the sunlight glistened off the razor edge.

Buster touched CheeYok on the shoulder. "Please tell him it needs sharpening and is very strong. Like a sharp rock, it can be broken, but that is very hard to do."

BaYok spoke a few words and CheeYok translated. "He asks what do you want in trade?"

Buster slowly pointed to the wooden blade hanging from BaYok's belt.

The guard didn't waste time. He stuck the steel blade and sheath into his belt and quickly untied the thongs lacing the wooden knife's sheath. Once free, he held it in both hands and let his eyes rove over it.

Then, he offered it, hilt-first, to the human.

With a half-bow, Buster accepted the leather-sheathed blade and took a step back.

BaYok rattled on for a moment and CheeYok passed it on. "He wants to know what you will trade for the gun on your hip."

"Tell him I'm sorry, but my Director has given strict orders that we are not going to sell or trade any guns." He offered an option. "We can get more knives of different shapes and sizes. Tell him to use it for awhile, then we can discuss what other types he would like."

The two Chickmonks spoke for another couple of minutes, and then BaYok surprised the human. He stepped forward and held out his hand. Buster shook it and the guard turned his back and walked away.

CheeYok quickly explained. "I told him about the human custom of shaking hands to seal a business deal. He just offered you a great compliment as well. For a hunter to turn his back, means that he trusts you to stand behind him. You have found a great friend, Buzzter."

"It is always good to have friends." He turned back to CheeYok. "I saw you showing off the clear glassware we traded for when we first met. Do you think that will be valuable?"

"Oh yes, my friend. We have already been offered a lot for them, but I do not wish to trade."

Buster nodded. "We can get more of them. Who owns the land and buildings of the market?"

"There are only a few families that live in the market all year. They own all the land and buildings. Why?"

"I notice there are some fairly large buildings around the market, but none of them are more than two stories. Also, they all seem to have almost flat roofs. Why is that?"

"I don't know. That is how they have always been made. You must ask a builder."

"It is almost sundown. Tomorrow, will you take us to meet a land owner who creates pottery?"

Like all the others, the store was another flattened mushroom of a building with doors and windows on all sides. The largest window faced the street, opened and with a shelf full of sample ceramics.

CheeYok introduced the two humans to a Master Potter named CherrunNor. After his initial shock, the potter was pleased to hear they were interested in trading for some of his wares.

They showed some samples of trade glassware that had been

designed to be especially sturdy and would travel well in backpacks or sledges. Each cup fit inside another with a simple grass packing. Four stacked cups fit inside the serving pitcher.

CherrunNor studied the pieces for awhile, then spoke to CheeYok.

"He is interested in trading some of his wares for these, but wants to know how they are made."

Buster smiled at the anticipated question. "Ask him if he will show me his workshop and ovens."

The potter heard the request, barked some instructions to his assistant to keep an eye on the shop and led the visitors out the back door of his shop. Another, similar structure sat in the middle of a large lot. Protected on all sides by a high wall, piles of various types of clay, rocks, and other building materials were neatly stored against the outer sides.

Buster gestured towards the roof. "From all the vari-colored smoke stains, I would guess he's taking us to his kiln."

Inside, the stifling heat was almost too much for the humans. Several kilns were in operation and racks of various goods stood ready for the ovens.

CherrunNor motioned for them to look around, but cautioned them not to touch, since many items might burn them.

Cheryl asked if they could examine one of the racks out in the daylight. CheeYok translated and the potter took them back outside, to where some apprentices were working at wheels. He picked up an empty rack and handed it to her.

"Buster? Take a look. I think this is bronze."

Her husband hefted the wire frame, scratched it with his fingernail and nodded. "I think you're right. In that case, he has all the technology needed for a step up to blown glass." He turned to their translator. "CheeYok. Please ask him if he knows how to make a long tube out of this metal." He held his hands about five foot apart. "It needs to be this long and about as big around as my finger."

After a long discussion, it was decided that such a thing was possible.

This had been discussed back at Jerryville, so Buster asked, "We are willing to teach CherrunNor how to create glass. But it may require some travel for supplies. Ask him if he owns any land with a house that he is willing to trade for this knowledge?"

After a quick exchange, CheeYok translated. "He has no land with houses that are not already in use by others in his clan. He does own some land nearby that he has not built on yet. If you will teach at the same time he is building a new house, he will trade the land and the finished house for the knowledge of how to make glass. He does want to protect his investment and you must not teach it to any other potter."

"Tell him he is wise, but we will only promise not to teach it for five years after he makes his first glass. After that, others will need to know as well."

"He says to make it ten years and your home will be constructed by the finest builder in Winter Camp."

Buster thought about it for a moment, before answering. "Tell Master CherrunNor that he honors me with the offer, but I would rather deal with the Master Builder myself. We will make it tens years in exchange for two good plots of land that are high and dry. Nothing down by the river."

Later that afternoon, CherrunNor showed them a couple of lots on the outskirts of Winter Camp. They were marked by low walls. One had the crumbling remains of a previous dwelling, while the other had a few small trees and brush.

Nashville

"Hey, Chuck!"

Victor Charles Adams the Third stifled an annoyed expression at the hated contraction of his middle name before he looked up. "Yes, James? What can I do for you?"

The city councilman had his usual all-too-perfect smile spread on a twenty-something face. Since the acceptance of Omniphage, most successful politicians tried for a slightly older and more experienced visage, but this old man had been playing the game so long that he could afford the movie star appearance. "Word has it that you're onto something big. What's this off-world city you're supposed to be running by remote control?"

Victor sighed. "As usual, the gossip channels are much like the coconut telegraph of the islands. I've been very stressed recently and decided I needed a bit of rest and relaxation. A few of my employees introduced me to an amusing video game. That's all."

"You know, that is exactly what I was told you were going to say." The friendly smile vanished and was replaced with a cold stare that was at least more honest. "Don't forget who runs this town, Chuck. The council has been a good friend to your business. I'd hate to see all that goodwill evaporate."

Victor sat back, elbows on the arms of the chair and fingers steepled. "Oh believe me, I know very well where a large chunk of our corporate profits disappear. The fact is, I'm getting rather bored with this town. Since you're here, you might as well be the first to know. I'm moving my trustworthy people to another headquarters and before the year is out, this building and many related structures will be vacant. Think of all the prime real estate you'll have available for new tenants."

"But... But! Nashville has been your corporate headquarters since before the Phage wars. We've stood shoulder-to-shoulder and rebuilt this place."

It was Victor's turn to return the cold stare. "You mean you've been taking payola since before the wars. I've just grown tired of dealing with you and your cronies. My new project is taking much of my time and the rest of it, I intend to spend on a tropical beach. Now get out of my office, you parasite."

The faux smile was back. "I'm rather sad to hear you feel that way, Chuck. Perhaps in a day or so, you'll reconsider."

The office door opened and two security guards appeared in response to Victor's hidden summons.

James glared at each, then back at his host. "Security? Surely you're joking, Chuck."

Victor looked at his chief security officer. "Jack, this gentleman was just leaving. He is not to be allowed past the lobby desk from now on."

After seeing their guest to the front door, the security chief returned. "Are you sure that was wise, Victor?"

"Probably not, Jack. But my patience has grown way too thin the last few months. We're only a week away from closing this place down. Now that he's taken the bait, we know which of our staff have been feeding him information."

Jack waved aside the follow up question. "Don't worry. I was listening and as soon as I heard the key phrases, I fired both of the traitors. The guards are helping them clean their desks right now. Within the hour, they will be on the street."

Victor nodded. "Most of the loyal staff are already working in Empire City. The few that live downtown in Nashville are scattered and we'll make sure that the councilman thinks they have retired. He's going to go nuts trying to figure out where we've moved our offices."

"I notice you didn't enlighten him on Beta or offer him a helmet."

The magnate stood with his hands clasped behind him and looked out, over the city skyline. "There are more than enough lazy, corrupt, nasty people already there. If I can keep his level of experience out of the melting pot for even a few days longer, I will. This way, when he does surface, he'll be dealing on my turf." He gave a tired sigh, then turned back. "Have you heard the good news from our research team?"

"No, sir. What's the latest"

"They have been able to build a stationary warp system that is just strong enough to wipe the nervous system. With a volunteer body, we can duplicate the Hawthorne effect. I've made sure the lab has current samples of all our genetic material as well as a couple of Beta bricks."

Jack smiled. "That is good news, Victor. Speaking of Beta, you've not shared much of the mage council stuff. I know it's been keeping you busy."

"I'm not going to discuss it here. Tonight, back in Empire City, I'll fill you in on some of it."

An hour later, the two men drove out of the office building and headed for their homes. As each one pulled into their driveways, they were met with a hail of automatic weapons fire.

Bode'

As pilot of a totally new spacecraft design, Steve Saunders was in his element. He handed his co-pilot a squeeze-bulb of orange juice, then fastened himself into the command chair. "Status, Dawn?"

His blonde co-pilot took a sip before answering. "All ship's systems are green. I just finished reviewing some close up images of our landing site from the buzzard Jerryville sent over."

"Anything change?"

She shook her head. "Nope. Since they reported the Chickmonks, I was worried we might have chosen the wrong beachfront. Now, it looks like all them critters prefer the deep woods and temperate mountain regions. As soon as you finish your review, I think we're go for the de-orbit burn."

He chuckled. "Better not let Buster and Cheryl hear you call them critters. Those two have grown quite attached to our new planetary neighbors."

"I know. I'm just waiting to meet some of them, first. I can't help but think they are going to take offense at all these foreign invaders taking over their planet."

The two old friends continued chatting while the other two crew members shook off the CryoDox effects. When everyone was secure and and all ship's systems were still green, it was time.

A pair of solid rockets were fired and, after they had killed much of the colony ship's orbital velocity, they fell away, to burn up on reentry.

The first whispers of atmosphere illuminated the magnetoshell braking field as Steve and Dawn guided the large ship through the most hazardous part of their voyage.

After discovering the Chickmonks, transhumanist engineering teams developed a new colonial vessel for landing on large bodies of water. This would eliminate the need to clear a landing area with a fuel-air explosive. The first Type Two colony ship was given the colony name Bode' and carried one hundred CryoDox as well as all of the same equipment and supplies needed to jump start a human presence.

The fuselage was shaped like the old NASA shuttles only with a much sturdier biplane wing arrangement with dual vertical stabilizers. Since it was only to be used once, for an unpowered flight, there were no giant engines nor fuel tanks. Small thrusters were used in space, while the magentoshell field controlled upper level atmospheric flight. Slower, low-level flight was with the usual control surfaces built into the wings.

Steve's voice was all business. "I have us at ten thousand meters and on a nominal glide path."

"I concur, Sir. My board shows sea-state at one meter or less with a moderate ten kilometer per hour westerly breeze. Our touchdown is on-course for eight to five kilometers from the beach."

Over the next few minutes they passed through a few wispy clouds on a smooth glide. Just as he had practiced for hundreds of hours in the simulator, Steve flared at the last moment and the huge craft shook as it slid onto the deep blue waters of the open sea. A thin line composed of brilliant shades of green was visible on the horizon.

Dawn's voice held a slight tremble of emotion as she reported. "Captain, all sensors are nominal and further environmental reports will deal with depth rather than altitude." She paused before adding. "Welcome to Micasa, Sir."

He smiled as he chided. "Save it for the beach, Dawn. We still have to get this thing high and dry." He glanced once more at his instruments, then ordered. "Deploy the outboards."

"Aye, Sir. Deploying outboards now."

Moments later, four water jet-drive units, driven by powerful electric motors, folded down from the lower wing surface. They pushed the seaplane that had been a spacecraft towards the distant shoreline.

Steve Saunders, wealthy entrepreneur from before the Phage wars, one of the founders of Alice Island, and later lunar mission pilot, now enjoyed the role of sea captain as he guided the huge vessel towards the wide inlet. The other three crew members had already started the decanting sequence for the first half-dozen that would help establish their new home. Each of them were monitoring video and environmental feeds from a pair of buzzards they had launched from a hatch on the back of the Bode'.

"Sir? I have a good visual on our primary landing site."

Steven glanced at her monitor. "Now that we're up close, I don't see any reason why we shouldn't go ahead as planned. Anyone have an objection?"

A chorus of agreements followed and the Bode' continued cruising up the center of the wide river mouth as it met the sea. Their goal was just past a slight bend in the river with a wide sand beach on the inside of the curve. The jungle terrain hid a slight upward slope to level ground protected by a promontory rock ridge line.

"Captain? I count three large gators on the beach, about three hundred meters east of our target site."

"I see 'em, Dawn. I hope you all realize that until future notice, there will be no skinny dipping in the river."

The other three chuckled as the pilot turned their craft to face directly at their chosen landing spot. "Going to engines at maximum now." He intoned as the sounds of the jet drives increased and the huge craft picked up momentum.

Moment later, the hardened hull of the Bode' touched the sandy bottom and the combination of engines and mass slid them up the beach. As soon as there was no water for the jet intakes, all engines cut off. With a dry crunching sound, the seaplane slid to a stop with only the last third of its hull still lapped by the small waves.

Steve quickly scanned his board. "I see all green still here."

"I concur, Captain. No damage and just for the record, those gators must have thought we were the biggest gator on the beach. They're all in the water and swimming upstream like their tails were on fire."

"Good. One less thing to worry about for now. Let's turn this baby around so we can unpack the tractors."

Dawn popped a side hatch and a ladder fell down to the sand. Assisted by Samuel, they carried tools to open a small hatch on a wingtip. They pulled a cable from a reel and walked it up the beach and into the edge of the jungle.

"Captain? I see plenty of trees, but most of them look like some sort of palm. There are no real root systems, so they won't work for anchor points."

"Understood, Dawn. You and Sam will have to make your own. You know the drill."

With a resigned sigh, she agreed. "Come on, Sam. We need one of the drill anchors."

They returned to the Bode' and came back with a spiral hole-digging tool. After a half hour of motor buzzing and struggling to keep it vertical, the auger was buried more than a meter deep. The connected the cable and got out of the way.

The Bode' slowly reeled in the cable and over another half hour, managed to turn itself more than halfway around. The stern was now up on dry sand.

Although superficially similar to the NASA space shuttle, the fact that Type Two landers like the Bode', had no main engines meant the stern portion was actually a wide cargo door that folded down to provide an unloading ramp. Two tractors quickly rolled out and, attached to cables from the stern, headed into the jungle. Each of the tractors had a power drill attachment and were soon locked into the ground, slowly pulling the huge craft the rest of the way around and inexorably uphill.

Two days passed and the drills reset themselves more than a dozen times each, but in the end, the Bode' sat on a small rise, ten meters above the flood-tide line.

Port Heinlein

"My goodness, Lizzie. I'm guessing you and that lumberjack are getting along well. I've hardly seen you the last couple of weeks."

"You are only partly right, cousin. Varlon and I are getting along quite well. But he has his work and I have mine."

"Work? You haven't said anything about that. Tell me."

"I'm back in school, now. It's part of my apprenticeship program.

I've decided to go back to what I know. Since I'm already familiar with most domestic animals and basic farming principles, I've already skipped over that part of the training. Right now, I'm learning basic mechanical engineering so I can work on tractors and similar equipment."

"I'm not sure I follow. What sort of apprenticeship program is this?"

"It's the same one Varlon has been following." She paused and looked sheepish for a moment. "I know you dream of flying to the stars and a life of research and labs and such... But that just isn't for me. You've heard of Micasa, right?"

"Yes. Of course. We have a small research colony there."

"That is what most folks believe and what they have been telling the news media. The fact is, we have already sent two colony ships and more are being planned. The apprentice program is for potential colonists."

Susan sat back, stunned. "That sounds like it will be a lot of hard work in pretty primitive conditions. I can't imagine dealing with all of the unknown insects and animals. How do you know what is venomous or might just eat you?"

Lizzie took both of her cousin's hands in hers. "Most of your life has been spent in the pursuit of science and living in these picture-perfect surroundings. Mine has been spent in the open air, surrounded by blue skies, mountains, forests, and all sorts of animals, both wild and domestic. For a long time, my dream was to marry a good man and help run a small farm of our own. You've helped me not only to feel free to be myself, but to dream big. And that is exactly what Micasa means to me. The only limitation there is the size of the land we can take and mold."

Susan smiled. "With lumberjack Varlon at your side, right?"

Her cousin shrugged and grinned. "Why do you think I've been wearing such provocative clothing? He's already invited me to move in with him."

Susan sat back. "Move in? When?"

"Not just yet, silly. I'm going to hold out for a bit longer. Besides, I enjoy having him court me."

"Who would have thought it?" Susan muttered.

"Oh! I almost forgot the other interesting news. I've been chatting with Aunt Martha."

That statement wiped the smile off Susan's face. "What? What does she want?"

"Relax, cousin. I actually called her. She sent me an email last week from the town library, asking how we were doing. It seems things were a little rough around the farm for a couple of weeks, until she got sick of listening to Aunt Howard ranting about the devil's work. She told her to shut up and start doing her share of the farm work, just like every other woman. A horrendous fight ensued and I guess Martha won. Since Uncle Howard is no longer a legal entity in the valley, Martha has inherited the farm. She asked the sheriff to come out and help her chastise a nasty-mouthed girl that didn't know her place."

At this point, Susan was grinning from ear to ear. "I'll bet that was awkward. What did they do?"

"Aunt Howard was told by the Sheriff that she had a choice. Either submit to Aunt Martha's house rules and behave in a proper, God-fearing ladylike manner, or they would escort her out of the valley."

"And? What did she do?"

Lizzie grinned widely. "She actually tried to attack the sheriff in front of his deputies. They locked her up for several days. The judge ordered her to leave the valley and not return. So, they escorted Aunt Howard to the mountain pass, gave her some cash and a backpack with some clothing and sent her on her way."

"What is on the other side of that pass?"

Lizzie shrugged. "Only a long downhill desert road that splits in two. Part of it goes south, towards some small, mostly Latino towns. The other road leads to the spaceport. But you haven't heard the best part."

Susan couldn't help the glee in her voice. "What? It gets better than that?"

"Oh yes. Martha heard from the Sheriff, that Aunt Howard, now called Harriet, ended up at the spaceport. She tried to beg some of the medics to use the devil's brew to change her back to a real man. They said no one would volunteer a DNA sample since they had all heard the story. She was informed the only place that sort of research might be done was at Alice Island or Port Heinlein and since she had only a small amount of cash, both of them were out of her reach. She went looking for work and the only place that would hire her is one of the local pubs. She's a tavern waitress and part of her salary is a small room in the back."

They sat silent for a few minutes before Susan spoke. "You know I have no sympathy for Harriet. But I do feel bad about Aunt Martha having to run the farm all by herself, now."

"That's okay. She has been doing most of it for years. Uncle Howard spent the majority of his time in town, drinking with his cronies and sleeping around. She's happy to be rid of him, I think. We're going to stay in touch now that she has a slate."

"Aunt Martha has a slate?" Susan was incredulous.

"I've saved a little bit of money from my job and paid one of the wolfmen that rescued us to take one out to her and spend a little time teaching her how to use it."

Susan grimaced. "My goodness. I'll bet she wasn't happy to see one of them on her doorstep again."

"Actually, there was no problem at all. I sent her a letter beforehand, warning her to expect him and that he had a present for her. What really surprised me was that he said she ended up inviting him to stay for dinner."

Consulate

"Well, I must admit, that was an interesting ceremony." Buster stood next to his wife as they watched their new neighbors return home.

"In a primitive society, the concepts of land ownership can be pretty tenuous. All they really needed was for Master CherrunNor to call a gathering of all the locals and announce he was turning this land over to you."

"I guess. And now, he's waiting for me to show him how to make glass. I'm not sure he realizes how much work he's taking on." He kissed Cheryl, shouldered his backpack and joined the ceramic Master and CheeYok. Accompanied by two apprentice potters, Buster led them back up the trail, towards the jungle river banks.

It didn't take too long to find a bank of fine, white sand that glistened in the sunlight.

"CheeYok, please tell Master CherrunNor that this is some of what we will require." He scooped up a handful and let it sift through is fingers. "Tell him, the lighter the color and smaller the particles, the better it will be."

Back at the pottery shop, another craftsman had already delivered a long, bronze tube and a cup-shaped ladle with a long handle, both to Buster's specifications. Hours later, the first crude glass bowl was blown and set aside, to cool. All three of the potters were amazed and by dark, each had a small bowl of their own.

Two days later, Master CherrunNor introduced them to Master PakkatNor, the builder. As in all the other shops they had visited, the builder lived in back of the same structure that housed his office. Instead of drawings or paintings, he showcased his work with a shelf full of simple clay models. The mushroom-shaped roofs lifted off to reveal interior variations.

Buster had come prepared. He showed PakkatNor his slate, then used a blank wall surface as a projection screen. He showed 3D images of the sort simple, of two-story, rectangular building he wanted on one of their new properties.

The master builder stared at the images for a few minutes, with a strange expression. He barked something at CheeYok, then got up and stomped from the room.

Buster was perplexed. "What is wrong? What did he say, CheeYok?"

Their guide shook his head. "He says that what you propose is forbidden. He will have nothing to do with it and neither will any builder in Winter Camp."

"But, why is it forbidden? I don't understand. Please tell him that I apologize, but we need to know why."

CheeYok got up and followed the builder from the room. A few minutes later, CherrunNor returned and told the humans, through their translator, that if they would tell him how many rooms they wanted and for what purposes, he would design a proper dwelling. If they agreed not to build their design, he would take them on a long journey to show them why such ugly structures were forbidden.

Angel Heights

Susan was tired of the party. Lizzie and Varlon were having a ball, celebrating the end of their classes and she felt like a third wheel. The back patio of the club looked out over the bay and the jungle-covered mountain loomed behind. She followed the boardwalk to the jogging trail and in a few minutes, turned the corner. The party sounds were gone now, overshadowed by the rushing water pouring off of Angel Heights, more than a kilometer above.

Since the whole island was a tourist resort for both Earthers and Selenaphiles, there was always someone walking on the scenic trails day or night. It was no surprise to see a handsome Latino standing with his hands clasped behind him and gazing up, into the mist-shrouded heights.

He glanced around as she approached. "Hi. Had enough of the party?"

She nodded. "Oh yeah. Just thought I'd take a look at the falls before heading home. Sorry to intrude on your thoughts."

"No problem. Please, join me." He waved her up to join him.

Susan only looked up a minute before she caught him staring. "Excuse me. Looking for something?"

His eyes snapped up to meet hers. "Sorry. But I'm sure I know you from somewhere."

She started to say that was an old line, when he snapped his fingers. "You're Susan Childers, right?"

"Yes." She held out her hand. "And you're...?"

He shook. "Excuse me. I'm Antonio Garcia. Pleased to meet you, Susan. I must admit, I've been a fan ever since I heard of your dive."

"My dive? Oh my goodness. That's been more than four years ago, now. Seems like forever."

"You're a legend in some circles. That took balls, lady."

She stared at him for a moment, recognition dawning on her face. "Now I know who you are." She deepened her voice and intoned, "And so it begins." Then continued in her normal tone. "And you have a nerve, calling me a legend when you landed the first ship and helped build Port Heinlein. Chukkers, isn't it?"

He shook his head, ruefully. "That was a lot longer than four years ago. So tell me, Miss Childers, I assume you were part of that graduation party back there, what is your next project?"

"Call me, Susan, please." She leaned on the railing and looked out, over the bay. "I'm going to take a break, work on my physical training to clear my head for a week or so, and then join one of the Micasa colony teams."

"I thought you were a born and raised Selenaphile? Aren't you afraid of all those wide-open spaces?"

Her face grew serious. "I used to be. Then I spent over a year on Earth. Now, although I love it, Port Heinlein is too small."

Nothing was said for several minutes while they were both lost in their memories. Then Chukkers broke the silence. "I know you had some rough times. But you're a real strong lady. You're gonna do okay on a new world."

She turned to face him, arms folded under her breasts. "Coming from someone who knows rough times, that's a compliment. Thank you, Antonio."

"You're welcome, Susan. And feel free to call me Chukkers."

"Your turn, Chukkers. What are you doing, these days?"

"I think this is the part where we can agree that great minds think alike. I'm training in the new colonial lander simulators and am going to be a colonist, myself."

"Oh really? Any idea where you're going to end up?"

He smiled and nodded. "Yep. I am going for the tropics. I was born and raised in Tampa, so it will be fun to settle for a few years someplace where there are nice beaches."

"You survived the Phage wars, didn't you?"

He lost most of the smile. "Oh yeah. That was one of those rough times we've been talking about. Probably a lot like your farming experiences." He glanced out, over the water, then back at her. "I'll tell you what, Susan. Let me take you to dinner and we'll both trade war stories. Fair enough?"

Heavy Industry

Victor was pissed! "Jack. That bastard killed both of us. I was willing to just walk away politely and let him have his damn city and that fucking bastard had us shot."

Jack poured a couple of shots and handed one to his boss and old friend. "So, what now?"

The Master Mage tossed back the whiskey and glared out the window at the Empire City skyline. "First off, I have setup a little warning system. We will know the instant he gets a helmet and joins Beta. Every time that pissant reincarnates, I want one of our people to hunt him down and gut him like a fish. He is never going to have any sort of life here."

"Consider it done, boss. I might just take care of it once in a while, myself. That getting shot stuff really hurts."

"I'm going to have our desert team prepare a couple of the lease bodies for us. We should be able to rise from the dead in a week or so, Earth-time."

"You going after him on Earth, too?"

Victor started to answer, then seemed to think it over a bit. "No. It's just not worth it. Let him have his two-bit kingdom. We've too much other work to take care of both here and back in Earth space."

"What's next on the agenda, then?"

"You know how some Betans built those fabrication facilities for warp ships?"

Jack nodded and poured another shot for each of them.

"I've volunteered to ramrod something similar in the Micasian system. Only there, we're not only going to be fabricating warp ships. Instead, we're going to setup a steel mill as well as some other heavy industries to supply the colonists."

"If we do all the heavy industries off-planet, that will save a lot of pollution and habitat destruction. Good plan."

The Last Place

PakkatNor proved a gracious host once they got past his total horror of building a rectangular structure in the open. He arranged with CheeYok to take them back along the way they had come and visit the Last Place. None of the Chickmonks would say anything more about it until after the humans had seen it for themselves.

Cheryl, Buster and CheeYok sat around a small table in PakkatNor's office and the master builder excused himself. One of his apprentices opened and held the door for him a few minutes later. The humans were a little surprised to see both the apprentice and their hunter friend bow towards the cloth-draped tray their host placed on the table.

PakkatNor took a moment to look at each of his guests. "This has been part of our history for a long time. It shows us the only safe way to build." He gently lifted the concealing cloth.

Buster's eyes grew wide and his wife gasped at what lay before them. It was a model of one of the mushroom-shaped structures. About a half-meter wide and perhaps half that tall, it glistened in the light. It was made of some sort of clear, crystaline material. Rooms full of furnishings appeared inside. The foundation was some sort of smooth, dark granite, while the roof appeared to be a type of sandstone.

Cheryl reached out, but PakkatNor grabbed her wrist and pushed it back. "No! Only a Master Builder may touch something of our ancestors. You may only look."

"Hon?" Buster was down on one knee, arms on the edge of the table, staring at it from a lower angle. "I'm trying to get a handle on how this was made. It looks like the roof lifts off, but all that glass looks like it is one-piece." He looked up at their host. "PakkatNor, can you lift the top off so we can see inside?"

Without replying, the master builder lifted the roof and set in on the soft cloth that had covered the model.

Cheryl leaned over to peer closely at the interior and furnishings. "Is that table molded into place or can it be moved?"

Their host seemed to be enjoying their wonderment as he waved his fingers through each of the rooms and as his fingers passed, each piece of furniture vanished, to reappear once his hand left the room.

"Holograms." Buster's voice held a note of awe. "The walls contain holograms of the furnishings."

"But how?" Cheryl wondered. "That requires very sophisticated photography and lasers and..."

"PakkatNor. Please tell me who made this and where did it come from?"

He replaced the roof and covered the model once more with the ceremonial cloth. "Tomorrow, we will journey two day's south and you will see for yourselves." He gave the humans a polite bow and left with the treasure.

As soon as they were back in their camp, Buster called Jerryville. "DeeDee, back before we left Port Heinlein, did anyone do an analysis of Micasa near space?"

"Of course. It was one of the things the initial survey team did even prior to their landing. Why?"

"Anything at all anomalous?"

The colony leader shook her head. "Not that I recall. This appears to be a much older solar system than Sol. Micasa is very stable. Two small moons and a few Trojan asteroids that pose no threat for the next few thousand years. I ask again. Why?"

"Because Cheryl and I just saw proof of a high-technology industrial base. And I know damn well that there is nothing like it on the surface right now."

He went on to describe the holographic model and DeeDee said she would task some of the orbital resources to take a closer look at their neighbors.

Two days later, the two humans, CheeYok, and the two craftsman from Winter Camp stood at the base of the odd plateau that their friend had promised to bring them to in the spring. A drizzling rain that verged on sleet hampered their trek. They were only partly sheltered by a wide overhang of rock.

Buster asked CheeYok, "How much farther, my friend?"

"It is too late today. The trail ahead can be bad. We must go all the way to the top of the mountain."

Cheryl finished setting up their small tent and motioned for Buster to join her. Once inside, she zipped it shut. "I just finished talking with one of the buzzard techs. He says that before the storm hit, they managed to get some pretty good close-up images of the trail head on top of the waterfall."

"They see anything interesting?"

Nothing obvious except for the fact the terrain is not natural. One of the geologists says this plateau looks like karst topography, but it is the only one like it in the area and none of the rest of the landscape supports the idea." She paused. "One other thing. The background radiation is more than six times higher than the valley or the surrounding mountain slopes."

Leftovers

Victor waited until the Master Mages were all seated in the council chambers. "Thanks for coming, everyone. I wanted you together for the news. As you know, one of my teams has been planning a steel mill and industrial fabrication facility in orbit around the gas giant in the Micasa system. Our first warp tug arrived at the small moon we had chosen for our base and had quite a shock. It seems we were not the first to consider it. We found the remains of a huge industrial complex. Most all of the machinery has long been reduced to junk by meteor impacts. Some very smart folks are looking at the images and data feeds right now, but the current guess seems to point at the facility being at least ten thousand years old."

Mark Chambers questioned. "Any idea who built it?"

"Once we got past some of the exposed ruins, we found both painted art and statues. It looks like the Chickmonks were once a space-fairing species."

He waited for the hubbub to die down before continuing. "We don't know much more at this point. Now that you have been informed, I'm going to ask for archaeological volunteers to help sort it out. Unless there are objections, I don't plan on looking a gift horse in the mouth. There are several subterranean areas that we can easily clean up and use for our own facilities. We'll leave any art of course, but the debris can be removed and the rooms resealed."

Wendy spoke. "Now things are starting to make sense." She paused as Victor and some of the others looked her way. "I was just chatting with the leader of the Jerryville colony and they told me Buster and Cheryl had seen a high-technology artifact in the Chickmonk's Winter Camp. Supposedly, they are going to be taken to an area where it was found." She went on to describe the holographic model house.

"It looks like we might get some answers soon. In the meantime, my teams will continue work on the new fabrication facility."

As this meeting was taking place, Buster, Cheryl, CheeYok, and PakkatNor followed a narrow footpath that wound up and through a narrow gap in the cliffs. The opening was close to the base of the waterfall and hidden from the rest of the valley. Although not a difficult climb, it followed a long, winding path between granite cliffs.

Finally, the trail leveled off and they found themselves in a dense forest. The trail seemed well-defined and easy walking. "Buster? Notice how smooth this path is? Underneath the coating of dead leaves, the rock is polished."

"I would guess it's been in use for many, many years. Even granite wears down if you walk on it enough."

"That's another thing the bothers me. This is not the sort of rock one would expect to find as karst topography. It seems way too hard."

PakkatNor paused on a small rise and beckoned the rest to join him. When they lined up, he pointed at obvious door frame, set into a smooth, dark gray surface, hidden by an overhanging rock ledge. "That is the entrance to the Last Place." When no one said anything, he walked forward and through the opening.

Buster followed, glancing from side to side as he entered. "Hon? Be sure to get some shots of that doorway. See those damaged sections on the side? I'll bet there were hinges and a locking door at one time."

"I'm more interested in the lights." Cheryl point at their guide. As PakkatNor walked up the gently sloping corridor, the top third glowed with a golden light. It wasn't terribly bright, but more than enough to see the way. The master builder paid it no mind, but just continued.

They passed two more ruined door frames and several side doors that were still sealed. There appeared to be no visible gap between the frames and the door panels. At the third opening, PakkatNor led them into a large hall. It was about fifty meters wide, several hundred meters long and had a domed ceiling more than twenty-five meters over their heads. The light seemed to have no single source, but emanated from a meter-wide band around the hall and slightly over their heads.

Starting about a half meter from the floor and ending at the light band, the walls were covered in a continuous mural.

Their guide gave them only a few moments to take it all in, then impatiently motioned for them to follow. He led them down the center of the hall, turned and faced a dramatic section of the mural. "Here! Look, but do not touch. That is why we do not build houses like yours."

Cheryl held her slate in front of her. The camera grabbing extremely high-resolution images as she spoke to the colony leader. "DeeDee, are you seeing what we're seeing?"

"Yes. Just keep scanning. We can take time for deep analysis later. How do you interpret the scene he is showing you?"

"It looks like some scene from an old Hollywood alien invasion movie. I see a couple of aircraft and what looks like laser beams, destroying other aircraft and buildings."

Their host motioned them closer and pointed to a detail to one side of the scene. "Look! Only these buildings survive." He pointed towards a cluster of round, mushroom-shaped buildings, sheltered against a rock wall, nestled among giant trees.

The Chickmonks were very fast language students. In only a few weeks, both CheeYok and PakkatNor had improved to the point of being able to hold real conversations.

"PakkatNor, please tell me who is doing this." Buster pointed towards one of the flying craft with a deep red straight line connecting it to a burning and half-destroyed building.

He gave a very human shrug and grimace. "We did. Brothers, sisters, mothers, fathers, friends became enemies. It happened long ago and once started, could not be stopped."

Cheryl asked the obvious question. "Why? Why did you fight and destroy all you had built?"

PakkatNor shook his head in obvious sorrow. "No one knows. It was a very long time ago."

Party Town

Something about his Latino upbringing was making it difficult for the one-time macho Tampa gang-member Chukkers, to admit he was nervous about picking up a girl for a date. Granted, the now-legendary pilot, Antonio Garcia could afford to be cool. Heaven knows, he had no lack of pretty things throwing him the come-hither eye, but Susan was different.

He paused in front of her door and adjusted his formal suit. The only consideration he had given his ego was the gold and silver badge on his lapel. As he was reaching for the doorbell, he was caught by surprise when the door swung wide.

Susan Childers was radiant in a dark maroon off-the-shoulder gown that showed her figure to perfection. She smiled at his startled expression. "I got tired of watching you primp in front of my door, Mr. Garcia. Are you ready to go?"

His eyes took in everything from her heels to the luxurious mane of blonde hair. "My goodness, but you are stunning, Ms. Childers. And yes, I am ready." He held up his crooked arm and she took it.

"I'm glad you like it. Now, how about telling me a bit more about what to expect, this evening."

"First, a couple of drinks to help us handle some boring speeches by director-types, then a more relaxed dinner, and finally, some more drinks and dancing. How does that sound, to you?"

She smiled up at him. "Pretty good, actually. It's been awhile since I've had an excuse to dress up and this should be just what the doctor ordered."

Neither of them were prepared for the scene in front of the convention center. Port Heinlein Security personnel were scattered all around the entrance courtyard and in the lobby. They were watching everyone, very closely. It was a very obvious and unusual show of force.

They stopped next to one of the uniformed cops and he smiled as one recognized them. "Hi there, Chukkers. Who's the pretty lady and what is she doing with you?"

"Watch it, Charlie. This is Susan Childers and she obviously has very good taste to be seen with me. Susan, this is Charlie Scopes, an old friend that helped build this place."

Susan stifled a chuckle and held out her hand. "Good to meet you, Charlie."

He shook it and used a stage-whisper. "Be careful with this fellow. He has a suspicious look about him."

Chukkers lowered his voice to a conspiratorial whisper. "What's going on, Charlie? Why all the heat? I thought this was just a pat-on-the-back meeting for some director types."

Charlie glanced around before answering. "We've gotten word from several sources that some Earthers are pretty pissed about the colonizing efforts. They seem to think we should continue paying them exorbitant prices for things we can't grow here. Supposedly, some hotheads want to disrupt the conference." He glanced down at Chukkers' lapel. "You might want to hide that badge, too."

Susan interrupted. "I was going to ask, what is that?"

Her date answered. "It's a badge that Mike Hawthorne's original Alice Island team came up with at a reunion, awhile back. It is only supposed to be worn by those of us who survived the Phage war." He turned his attention back to the cop. "What do these folks have against this badge?"

"Part of their core group thinks Omniphage is an evil thing that destroys souls. Real religious nutcases, if you ask me. But supposedly, they have managed to sneak a few of their people up here and want to protest anything that keeps humans away from their home planet."

They thanked him for the warning and continued into the dining hall.

An hour and a half later, they had survived the boring speeches and equally boring dinner and escaped to the dance floor. A couple of fairly fast dances had segued into a slow number.

"You dance well, Mr. Garcia."

"As do you, Ms. Childers." He held her close, enjoying the soft feel of her hair against his face.

"Chukkers?" Her voice was a whisper.

"Yes?" His voice matched hers and his eyes were half-closed.

"Do you see that woman in the baggy, dark blue dress and long, black hair? She's standing by herself, next to the service door."

He slowly danced them around so he could see over her shoulder. "Yeah. I see her. She does look familiar. Why? Do you know her? Is she a relative?"

"She looks a lot like me, wouldn't you say?"

"Yeah, now that you mention it, why?"

"Where is your friend, the cop? We need to warn someone. I can't be sure, but I think I know who that..."

She was interrupted by a couple of explosions. Both security guards in the room collapsed and the band stopped playing. There were a couple of screams as people ducked to the floor, some trying to hide behind flimsy tables.

"Everyone stay were you are. If you move, I will shoot you." The voice belonged to the black-haired woman. She was holding an Earth-style handgun.

Chukkers whispered. "You know her? How the hell did she get a gun?"

They were crouched behind a table, only partially hidden by the tablecloth. Susan removed her shoes and slipped the dress straps off her shoulders.

"What are you doing?" Her date was torn between staring at the person with the weapon and his date's partial nudity.

Her voice was a harsh whisper. "I can't fight in that damn gown. If he sees me..."

The shooter's voice rang out, once more. "I know that there are multiple cameras recording this. I just want you all to know that your deaths will not be for nothing. I'm are here to put a final end to this palace of perversion and ungodly deeds."

"What do you want?" Someone towards the back of the room asked.

"Want? What I want is just two simple things. You see, I know I'm probably going to die here. But that is okay, as long as two things happen. You see, I'm looking for a slut by the name of Susan Childers. She is going to pay for destroying me. I know she's here, someplace. After I watch her suffer, I'm going to let the rest of you go, before I blow this whole place right back to dust."

Chukkers whispered. "What the hell did you do to her?"

"That only looks like a her. That used to be my Uncle Howard."

Another shot rang out, tearing a chunk out of the wall behind them. The shooter's mouth was pulled back in an insane grin as she stared at the Susan. "There you are, you little cunt! I've been waiting a long time for this." She aimed at Susan's head, peeking from behind the table. "Come out so we can get a good look at you."

"Stop!" The commanding voice came from the doorway. Two security team members stood by the door. They were pointing stunners.

The woman who used to be Howard turned and let her dress slip open. "Better not shoot me, boys. If you do, things will get messy." Under the loose dress, she was wearing a corset covered with blocks of what looked like plastic explosive. "I'm wired so that if I get hit with those tasers, then this will go off. There is enough here so I'll never notice it. But the corner of this building will come down."

They security men froze. Nobody in Port Heinlein had seen such explosives other than in movies.

Susan jumped. She had been working out, trying to keep the Earth-toned muscles in shape so she might apply for the colony. In the light lunar gravity, she sailed more than three meters high and landed in front of her enemy. One arm came down hard on the forearm holding the gun and her momentum carried her forward, tumbling the two of them in a roll.

Despite the numbing blow, the woman kept hold of the weapon and was trying to roll away from Susan's attack. Fueled by fear and fury, Susan grabbed the wrist with the gun and held it away from her. The weapon went off once more and someone else screamed.

"You bastard!" Susan yelled. "I should have finished you back on that damn farm!" Both hands were holding the gun hand to the ground while Harriet's other hand was clawing at the side of Susan's face. People were screaming and stampeding around them, trying to escape. The security team was shoved back out the door. Susan let go with her right hand and snapped her elbow back as hard as she could. It hit Harriet on the cheek, stunning her for a moment. Susan repeated the move several more times until she saw more of an opening when her opponent leaned back, trying to avoid the blows. She let her elbow miss the next pass and instead, used the edge of her open hand to chop with all her strength at her opponents unprotected neck. There was a sickly crunch sound and Harriet lurched back, mouth wide and gasping.

One of the security guards finally fought past the crowd and he stomped on the gun, pinning it to the ground. The other one stood, white and shaking with fear, but brandishing his taser. "What about the explosives?"

Susan rolled to one side, watching Harriet's face as she clawed at her throat, trying desperately to breath past a crushed larynx. It only took a few moments before she stopped moving.

"Don't move, miss. They still might go off." The guard was obviously terrified, but doing his duty, nonetheless.

"Don't worry, officer. This stuff can't hurt anyone. I recognized it the moment I saw it. It's just plasticine modeling clay with some wires and stuff. I've used it for some sculptures in art class."

That's when she remembered her date. "Chukker's? Where... Oh my god!"

The pale beiges and browns of his formal outfit had been forever spoiled with the bright patches of bright red blood.

Artsie Fartsie

Victor looked up as from the slate when his security chief walked into the room.

"You have a guest, sir. A Dr. Sara Evans said she would like a few minutes of your time."

"Of course, Jack. Send her in."

Dr. Sara Evans strode through the door a moment later. She was preceded by a reputation as a petite, yet well-proportioned bundle of blonde dynamite.

The multi-billionaire met her halfway and held out his hand. "Dr. Evans. Welcome to the ranch."

"Sara, please. I try not to use the fancy titles except for bureaucratic missions."

"Agreed. And please call me Victor. I understand Jack and I have you to thank for the wonderful new bodies."

"It was a very interesting project to make an Earth-bound warp drive into a reincarnation machine."

Victor offered something to drink and she asked for a simple cola. He poured two from the wetbar and handed one to her. "I don't recall hearing anything of you in Beta. Have you stopped by the corporate offices in Empire City?"

She took a sip and gave an appreciative smile. "It's been hard to find a decent cola since the phage wars." She took another sip before answering. "Actually, that is part of what I wish to speak with you about. Some friends and I have been transhumanists for the last few months and we've spent a great deal of time in deep forest areas of Beta."

He took a sip, then nodded. "Getting back to nature as an escape from the bright lights and laboratory. Sounds like a good way to decompress."

"It's actually more than that, Victor. We've been training. Learning some new skills as well as honing some we had neglected. We have put together a group of artisans and we want to immigrate."

This caught the industrialist off-guard. "Immigrate? To where?"

"Micasa, of course. We have been looking at maps and have chosen this location for an artist's colony." She handed him her slate and he took a moment to look over their suggested site.

"This is in an upland region, far from the coast. Since we've discovered the Chickmonks, we're not going to use modified Type One landers any more. The explosive used to clear the landing site is way too disruptive and we still haven't mapped all the Chickmonk areas."

"We can use a Type One lander as long as the site is pre-cleared. And we've come up with an idea on how to handle that. Also, since you're a businessman, we have already prepared a business plan that shows a net profit within a couple of years."

"Profit? From Micasa? Now you do have my attention. Please go on."

"Some of my friends have been doing research on wood samples brought back on the few trips using Type One landers. Not only are there several species of trees in the upland forests that are very dense, but they contain trace elements that Earth insects find distasteful."

"I understand. That means they would take a very long time to degrade, here on Earth. But the cost of bringing industrial quantities of this lumber would be incredible."

"We aren't talking about building materials, Victor. What we propose is an artisan colony. We want to build three major industries. The first would be lumbering. This will supply materials for our own projects as well as building supplies for other settlements on Micasa. The second thing is fine art projects. We already have several galleries here on Earth that would love to display and sell original colonial art."

Victor finished off his cola, placed the glass on the coffee table, then sat back, hands folded in his lap. "And the third item?"

"Custom furnishings created from this wood. We can ship them in flat packs, ready for assembly and once again, there are galleries frothing at the mouth for examples of alien wood products for their sales floors."

"You said you had a solution for the Type One landing problem?"

"Yes, Victor. My colleagues and I want to ship a couple of heavy-lift blimps to Bode'. Once there, they will be assembled and used to transport robot tractors to the area we want to settle. They will clear a section of ground suitable for our colony. After we are established, we can ship finished products via blimp, to the spaceport."

"Sara, it sounds to me like you've put a lot of work into this project already. What do you need from me?"

"Neither myself, nor any of my team members are wealthy. A few of us work for you and we have no complaints about our wages, but we can't really afford to pay for an entire colonial effort. We know you support some of the warp-drive teams and all we're asking is for you to look at our business plan and if you agree, invest in our venture by building us a ship."

He considered her request for a moment, before answering. "Let me look over these notes." He gestured at his slate. "If they play out as you say, then I'll have one of the deep-space fabricators build and ship a robot cargo craft with your blimps, tractors, sawmill, and other colonial necessities."

"Thank you, Victor. If you've any questions..."

He waved her to stop. "Have you picked your team, yet?"

"About a third of them, yes. You will be happy to know we're not going to strip all your top scientists from your Earth operations. Most of the ones so far are sculptors, potters, painters, blacksmiths, carpenters, hot-rod mechanics, and other folks that like to build things. I've even picked my landing crew."

"Experienced pilots?"

"Only recently. Brenda Yellowfeather and her husband Matt, have been spending days on end in the simulators. When you get right down to it, there really isn't too much piloting required of a Type Two. I want them with me since they are fellow artists and dedicated to this project."

"What about Chickmonks in your proposed settlement area?"

Her expression lost some enthusiasm. "We've been in communication with Buster and Cheryl as well as the Bode' settlement. The Chickmonk population appears to be must smaller than first thought. Steve Saunders loaned us a couple of buzzards to do a detailed survey of our selected area. There are no Chickmonks, nor any visible signs they have been anywhere within a hundred kilometers of the area."

After Sara left, Victor contacted the director their deep-space fabricator.

"Warp World Fabricators, Director Vance, speaking." He was looking away from the camera, then turned to see who was calling. "Oh! Victor. What can I do for you?"

"You recall the Starliner plans we had shelved until Micasa finally had enough commerce to warrant a regular trading run? Well, they are shelved no more. Start building one. I'm also sending you an order for some heavy-lift blimps and tractors equipped to clear deep forest areas."

Vance thought a moment. "I believe we only have the second Bode' Type Two colony ship getting finishing touches right now. Once it is delivered to L5, we'll get on the new orders."

Two months later, an unmanned spacecraft splashed down and was towed upriver to Bode'. Less than a week passed before the first blimp, accompanied by a flight of buzzards, headed for a high mountain valley.

Colonials

"Hijole!" Chukkers muttered as he woke up. "Damn! That hurt!"

"I've been told that getting shot usually does hurt. But you're all better now, Mr. Garcia."

His eyes popped wide open. "Susan! What happened?"

She handed him a chilled glass. "Here. You're probably thirsty."

He sat up against the pillows and took a drink. "Thanks. Now, I take it I was hurt pretty bad?"

She nodded, face serious. "You gave me a helluva scare. Try not to get yourself killed around me, okay?"

"I'll try. What happened?"

She filled him in on where Harriet had come from and her demise. "And now, Mr. Garcia, you need to get your butt into the shower. I'm cooking something special, to celebrate."

"You're celebrating surviving that maniac?"

"Nope. I'm celebrating a decision."

He said nothing. Just stared at her, waiting for the rest.

"Into the shower, now." She quietly ordered.

She avoided his question until they were more than halfway through the meal.

"Susan, that was delicious. You really know how to cook."

"Thank you, Mr. Garcia. It is one of the good things from my time on the farm."

"What's with the Mr. Garcia, bit. Why don't you call me Chukkers, like everyone else."

"I kind of like Tony or Mr. Garcia from now on. Chukkers doesn't seem to fit. At least for me. Don't you think it is time for you to outgrow the rowdy gang-member image? Somehow, I just don't picture you as a gang member."

"Susan, I will admit, I did hear some of what you went through after your folks died. But it is nothing to compare with how I grew up."

"So tell me. I'm all ears." She leaned back in her seat, one hand holding a wineglass, the other folded under her breasts, fingers resting on her other elbow.

His eyes glanced down, then back up to meet her soft smile. "Are you sure? It's a long story."

"I've all night. Stop stalling." Her face grew serious. "I really do want to know. You tell me your story and I'll fill you in on the details of mine."

He took another sip of wine and leaned back. "My great-grandfather was a rancher in Michuacan, Mexico. That was back, before the revolution. He was un caballero, feo, fuerte, y formal." He intoned the statement with a grand flourish of his arms.

"What's that mean?"

"It is an old Mexican saying that states he was ugly, strong and a fine gentleman in the old ways. During la revolucion' the federales killed many of our family, stole much of our livestock, and burnt many of the ranch buildings. When it was over, the family was pretty much broke and barely able to make a living. My grandfather had no future there, so he moved to the United States along with many other braceros during World War II. After the war, he married a beautiful woman and settled in Ybor City, where he opened a garage." He paused, eyes focused out the window, at the cheery lights ringing the Port Heinlein crater wall.

She watched him as he was lost in memories for a moment, then prompted. "Don't stop now, Mr. Garcia. This is interesting."

He gave her a half-smile of embarrassment before continuing. "The garage did okay until my dad got sick. He died when I was fourteen. Mom lost the garage to some creditors and things kinda went downhill. You see, Poison was more than a gang to me. It was my support system; mi familia. I don't think I would have survived high school if it hadn't been for them. We took care of our own, ya know?"

"I can understand suddenly not having parents. But how did you get from there to being a legendary pilot and Selenaphile? The only real trace of your past that I've noticed is when you get excited, you have a Spanish accent. If you were raised in Florida, where did that come from?"

"In Ybor City, all the old Latino families spoke Spanish at home and English in school or at work. It was a vibrant and exciting culture. We took what we liked from both worlds and made something new that was ours." He put the empty wineglass on the table, set his elbows and steepled his fingers. "When Omniphage hit, things went bad pretty fast. The entire Tampa metro area was falling into chaos. Some friends turned an old parking garage into a flea market and later, into a community center for art, music, and education. They called it the Lazy Fair." He chuckled. "It wasn't until I was in Officer's School that I found out that was a play on words for an old free-enterprise term. Anyway, when the shit hit the fan, I was suddenly promoted from being just another punk with an attitude and a gun, into part of a security team, protecting the Lazy Fair. The whole thing grew bigger than anyone thought and within a few months, I was a team leader, working with regular police and military officers. That is when I learned a lot about responsibility."

Susan started clearing the table. "Keep going. I'm just going to put these in the washer."

His eyes watched with appreciation as she left the table. "Want another drink?"

"No, sir. I'm thinking enough for now. What about you?"

He stood up and shook his head. "None for me, thanks. Anyway, when things finally calmed down, the Lazy Fair had become the new center of Ybor City. Some of us that were tired of it all were offered military slots. I took one. During boot camp, they discovered that all those hours I had wasted playing video games might be useful. I had a knack for flight simulators. Based on recommendations from some good friends, they marched me off to Officers Candidate School and then to flight training."

She sat on the couch and tapped the space next to her. He sat and put his arm on the back, around her shoulders. "I know how the rest goes, sir." She smiled up and him. "A wise guy riding a rocketship lands nearby and tells the world that it's time to grow up."

He chuckled. "I'm never going to live that down, am I?"

"No. And you shouldn't try. It was the truth then and still is."

His free hand tentatively touched her chin.

She lifted her face and their lips met.

When they pulled apart, she asked. "You like this dress I'm wearing, Mr. Garcia?"

"Uh huh. Oh yes. Very much."

"It has something in common with the one I wore a few nights back, when we were so rudely interrupted."

"What's that, Ms. Childers?"

"It slips off very easily."

***

The Port Heinlein dawn lighting gave a golden glow to the bedroom. Chukkers woke to a soft puff of air on his cheek. He opened his eyes to find Susan's smiling face. She was laying on her side, one arm supporting her head while the other rested along her flank. The sheet was crumpled at the foot of the bed.

"Good morning, Ms. Childers."

"Yes, it is, Mr. Garcia. Did you sleep well?"

"Oh yes. Very well indeed. What about you?"

"I was up awfully late last night, but did manage a few winks." She chided.

Her hand moved from her side and traced up his stomach to his chest. The stomach muscles twitched at the soft touch. "That is something else that had never occurred to me. The handsome and muy macho Latino pilot is ticklish."

"Let's keep that our little secret, shall we?" He elbowed himself up and placed a hand on her shoulder, slowing caressing her side and finally cupping her hip. "You're not going to call me Chukkers, are you?"

She shook her head. "Nope. It's just not how I see you. Sorry."

"What about Tony, then?"

She shrugged. "I dunno. Maybe. Mr. Garcia will just have to do for now."

"What sort of image do you think I should project, Susan?"

"You're going to pilot a colonial lander, right?"

He nodded.

"The way I see it, that is a one-way trip. At least for another few years, you will be stuck at the colony. The only things you'll pilot will be blimps or SAR helicopters. Am I right?"

"Actually, I'm a lousy helicopter pilot. They won't let me near those things. I'm firmly convinced that they don't really fly. They just create so much noise and stench that the planet rejects them."

She grinned at the humor, then continued. "So what are you going to do, Mr. Garcia?"

"I'm going to build a Lazy Fair."

She stared, eyebrows raised, waiting for him to explain.

"I think you missed out on what kept us together during the Phage War. It was a rather simple free market and community center brought about by necessity. Poison became a defacto police force. That is when I learned to be more than just a teenage gangster."

"You're planning on becoming a community organizer?"

His turn to nod. "In a way, yeah. Someone's got to do it and in between times, I'm going to explore a whole new planet. That should keep me amused for another few decades." His gaze came back to her. "What about you, Ms. Childers? What are you planning on doing from now on?"

"Awhile back, I thought I wanted to be an astrophysicist." She paused. "You're going to laugh, but after my time on in High Valley, I found out that I actually enjoyed caring for the animals and riding horses. I've been taking some courses on animal husbandry and farm management."

"Don't worry. I'm not laughing. I am a bit surprised, that you would even consider going back to Earth after your experiences."

"I'm not. I'm going with you."

His brow wrinkled. "What? Where?"

"To Micasa, silly. We're going to be colonists. While you were sleeping, I pulled in some favors and have been signed up for the next flight to Bode'."

"That's the one I'm scheduled to pilot."

"I know. Just make sure you don't kill us, understand?"

Vinge'

Elizabeth Roberts felt heavy. She blinked several times and finally focused on the big man, learning over her.

"Here. Drink this. You'll feel better."

"Valon? Are we there?"

His voice held amusement. "Yes, ma'am. We are on the ground, surrounded by mountains and a forest filled with huge trees." He helped her up and out of the CryoDox. "Wait until you see it, love. It's magnificent."

After a few swallows, the liquid seemed to re-energize her and she looked both ways. "I see most of the CryoDox are still closed. How long have you been up?"

"A couple of days. As we planned, the bridge crew only woke up about a dozen of us after landing. Our job was to finish unloading the tractors and set up the first shelters. It's late spring here. Some snow still on the ground and we might still get another blizzard before things start to warm up. You feel up to stretching your legs a bit?"

"Oh yes. I'm well rested and fully awake. Let's see our new home."

Sara Evans met them on the machinery deck. "Lizzie! Good to see you up and about. Brenda and I are about to die from testosterone poisoning."

"Hi captain, or should I call you governor, now?"

The researcher and now colony leader rolled her eyes. "Please. Let's leave the fancy titles for when politics becomes important. Right now, your man has been busting to show you something. Bundle up warm and don't keep him waiting." She didn't wait for a reply before heading upstairs, towards the command deck.

"Here. Put these on, darlin'." Varlon handed Lizzie a pair of long, black boots and a dark brown coat.

She sat on the preparation bench, put on the boots, and sealed them. "I guess the skinsuit is normal wear for now?"

"Until we get our own places ready, yeah. Skinsuits inside, boots and cold weather gear over them for outside. It's been pretty chilly the past couple of days."

She slipped into the jacket and took time to check it out in the full-length mirror. "This looks like one of those old western dusters. Some of the cowhands wore them in winter. And what is the long tail on this hood?"

"That is actually a medieval invention that I've applied to the more modern trail duster. You can leave the hood back in nice weather. If things get uncomfortable, you pull the hood forward, down to your eyes. The long tail is called a liripipe and wraps around your head twice and tucks in to itself. That provides a weatherproof seal to help keep the warmth."

They stepped out, on to the loading ramp and Lizzie took her first look at their new home. The robot tractors that had been sent early had cleared and leveled a circular field more than five hundred meters in diameter. The broad base of the cone-shaped lander filled the center spot and a dirt and rock embankment circled the outside edge. A couple of dozen inflatable habitats filled about half of the remaining space. Varlon pointed to one of them, near the outside wall.

"Just for now, we're sharing that one with three other couples. It's warm and dry, but more than a little too cozy for my taste."

She glanced up and saw the sun was just peeking over a nearby mountain range. "What time is it, Varlon?"

"Only about nine in the morning. That ridge runs north south." He turned the other way and pointed. "Downslope, about two kilometers, is a river. A couple of small streams on either side of us, feed into it."

"Just like the maps we saw right before we left. Any surprises? What about Chickmonks?"

"None whatsoever. Want to see what we've been working on the last couple of days?"

She grinned and nodded.

They walked about six hundred meters until they came to another clearing. This one had a long, open machinery shed setup as a sawmill. A six-legged tractor that looked like a giant insect was holding a tall, straight tree with one monster claw, while the other arm held a power saw. The tree had already been stripped of branches and the driver guided it on to a pile of similar logs. Lizzie looked down towards the other end of the mill and a wide shed held neatly stacked piles of cut lumber.

"When the robots started clearing our landing zone, they stacked the larger trees here. Waste not, want not, you see."

Lizzie added. "Once they were through with the landing zone, they got busy and built the mill. When you guys woke up, you started collecting more timber and have been turning it into lumber." She turned to look at him. "I'm right, aren't I?"

"Yes, ma'am. Right on the money. We already have enough finished lumber to build at least a couple of homes. We do have to wait until we unload the rest of the tractors, however."

"Why? What's the holdup?"

"There are two things to consider. One is the most obvious. Location. Each family is going to claim an area, not to exceed twenty-five acres. I'm not going to build anything until we both agree on the location."

"Thank you, dear. That is appreciated. And what's the other holdup?"

"There are a couple of specialized well-drilling tractors in storage. Once we decide on a location, we will dig a well, then install a septic system. When those two items are in place, I'll build you a house like you won't believe."

"How long do you think?"

He shrugged. "Hard to tell. The local timber is tough stuff. It is very hard to cut. The good side is that it will last a long time. The bad part is that it is taking us longer than we had planned. Once we decide on a spot, I'm guessing a couple of weeks before we can move in."

"In that case, Varlon, where is this spot you said you thought I might like?"

True to his word, her husband had chosen a beautiful spot. Less than two kilometers from the landing zone that was destined to become downtown Vinge', there was a small box canyon. A waterfall near the back of the canyon filled a pond and small stream, exiting to one side of the canyon opening.

They stood on a rocky ledge, several meters above the stream while Varlon pointed at various items on the landscape. "I'm thinking we can easily build a stone wall between these two ridges. That high ground about two thirds of the way back, on the other side of the stream will be a nice place for our home. It's big enough for the main house, two barns, and later on, a bunkhouse for temporary hands." He point to the other side of the stream. "The lower part of the valley looks like it is part of the flood plain during the spring thaw. That means it should be pretty fertile. I'd like to plant some crops there."

"You're right, Mr. Smythe. I do like it here. I have a suggestion though."

"Yes, Mrs. Smythe?"

"Let's build the stables first. Then work on the house."

"You want to thaw out those two horses you've got packed in CryoDox, don't you?"

She nodded. "The sooner we get them out, the sooner we can use them to explore. Also, I want the stable so we can decant the foals as well. In a couple of years, I want to have a dozen quarter horses, ready to sell, rent or trade. If that means we spend an extra couple of months living in a tent, then so be it."

Jerryville

All the human slates beeped at the same time and when they checked, a male face filled the screen. "This is Steve Saunders, Governor of Bode' settlement. I have good news to share. As many of you know, a transhumanist team has build a heavy-industry fabrication plant in orbit around our gas giant."

The screen cleared to show images of the facility and his voice continued. "Part of their mandate is to supply us with high-grade steel and other metals which don't appear to be too common here on Micasa. The good news is that the first shipment has already arrived at Bode'. We are due to get another unmanned lander in less than a month. In the near future, there will be plenty of building materials."

Buster and Cheryl broke out into huge grins. Her enthusiasm was evident. "Want to give our friends the good news?"

That evening, the ambassadors sat down to dinner with their closest Chickmonk friends.

Buster tapped his glass for attention and three humans along with eight Chickmonks turned their attention his way. "Good friends. As you know, my wife and I started these weekly dinners so that we would all get a chance to learn more about each culture. Well, there has been another motive, which we've not needed until now." He paused and realized that after the months in Winter Camp, he was able to discern detailed emotions from each of the once-alien faces. "Among my people, there have been concerns about giving your people too much technology, too fast. I've shared some of our own history with you so that you can understand our concerns. I'm happy to report that we've been given permission to start teaching you some of the skills your ancestors once had."

BaYok, the Guardian of the Market asked the obvious. "What exactly are you offering, Buzzter?"

"Many of the things we use are made from metals which are in very short supply here on Micasa. They are common in other parts of your solar system, however. We have a factory that will produce and deliver them. The first shipment just arrived in our seaport town of Bode'. We are going to get some of those supplies very soon." He paused to place some tools on the table. "BaYok, when we first arrived in Winter Camp, you and I exchanged blades. It was the start of our friendship."

The guard nodded agreement.

"At that time, you asked if you might have a gun. I'm still not willing to give you one. I will, however, start you down the road to making your own."

Startled sounds of surprise came from several of their guests, but BaYok merely watched his host, waiting for the rest.

Buster picked up a steel hunting knife and a short, Japanese-style saw. "These are just two of thousands of useful tools that can be made with steel. We are going to help you to build a school to teach those who wish to learn, how to be a blacksmith."

"Black... smith..?" The guard was turning the word over in his mouth.

Buster repeated the term twice, until the alien pronounced it correctly. "That is what we call a person who works iron and steel to create tools. It is a first step that can be taught to others and help increase your people. It will be a few years, but as each step is learned, we will teach the next." He turned to CheeYok. "Old friend, you told us on the trail to Winter Camp that it was the first time you have ever passed those beasts without losing at least one of your tribe."

"That is true, Buzzter. I did not think I would live to see Winter Camp once more."

"That should not happen again. We are going to help your people to grow healthier, live longer, and not be so dependent on the forest."

BaYok interrupted. "There is something that does concern me, my friend." He gave himself a moment to frame his words. "I have heard there are some among us that do not trust this new way of doing things. They are worried that you will destroy us so that you will have all the good land for yourselves."

Cheryl spoke. "Believe it or not, BaYok, that has been a concern among my people as well. Our own history tells us of great wars that came when two groups of people tried to live in the same area. Let me show you something." She fiddled with her slate a moment and then pointed it at a clear spot on the wall. It projected and image of Micasa as seen from orbit. "All of you have seen this image of our world, before. Now let me show you what we have only recently discovered." The image changed to a topographic map of the globe, with their continent centered on the screen. She zoomed in until only about a quarter of it was visible. "See those three bright blue dots? Those are our three settlements of Jerryville, Bode', and Vinge. This bright red dot is Winter Camp, where we are right now. Since we first discovered your people, we have modified our buzzards with instructions to look for other tribes. Just this past week, we finished the survey of this entire continent." She tapped the slate and a single, bright-green dot appeared. "That dot is the current population of Winter Camp. Currently, there are approximately twelve thousand of your people living here. We have found three other camps and only one is larger, with about twenty thousand. Scattered around these camps, within a two-week walk, there are very small tribes. We have determined that over this entire continent, there are less than two hundred thousand of your people."

The Master Potter, CherrunNor inquired, "That seems like a great many of us. Are you saying there is plenty of land for all?"

"In part, yes. But we do not want to repeat the mistakes of our past. With our help, your people are going to become much more numerous and eventually attain our level of technology. We want to plan ahead so we can avoid conflicts over land."

Buster interrupted. "That is one reason why I was so careful about following your customs of purchasing the land for our embassy and hiring your people to build this fine home. We want to live in peace and that is best accomplished among equals. We plan on teaching how to read our maps and examine some of the land. Eventually, we will divide the continent into territories and certain ones, such as Winter Camp and the Last Place will be protected and cherished as part of your cultural heritage. Our satellites have already located many other ruined areas. When the time comes, we will form joint teams to study them and perhaps find out more about what happened to your people, so long ago."

OhSheetz

Mike Hawthorne appreciated the beautiful shades of blue, green, brown, and white of the planet rotating below. "She is lovely, isn't she, Chukkers?"

The pilot stopped his nervous scanning of the entire instrument panel and glanced at the other seat. "Yes, she is, sir. I must admit, I'll miss this sort of view."

The ex-director smiled at that comment. "I wouldn't worry if I were you, Captain. I think it won't be too many decades before Micasa has a thriving space-based economy and you'll get bored with ranching."

"Maybe. A lot depends on how horses take to Micasa foliage and terrain. Susan seems to think they will be very popular, even after we build some roads."

"The highway infrastructure to support cars and trucks is still many years away. I think she has a good plan."

"May I ask you something, sir?"

"Knock off the sir bit, Chukkers. I am tired of being the one in charge. This is your bird. I'm just an old man that pulled strings to get a front-seat ride with the best damn pilot I know." He glanced over, before continuing. "What is it you want to know?"

"What are you and Angela going to be doing after we land?"

"About twenty kilometers south of Bode' Beach, there is a barrier island that protects a marine estuary. On the mainland side, there is a relatively high ridge of land that we're going to homestead. I want to build a marina and boatyard while my wife is planning on an small resort."

"That sounds nice. You like to fish?"

Mike laughed. "Hah! You might find this hard to believe, son. But I was raised on the water and helped my dad run a head boat during high school. Back then, I got sick of salt water and fish and when the time came to leave home, I enrolled in the ROTC program at our local college. The Army kept me on the go for the next thirty some years. I was just about to retire and spend my days fly-fishing when Omniphage came along."

One of the screens blinked and revealed their warp tug pilot. She glanced up and spoke. "Bode' Three, that ocean storm has moved well to the west. Your next entry window will take you over it at more than twenty-five thousand meters."

"Thank you, Warp Two. That will give us plenty of headroom. We are ready to go."

"Very well, Bode' Three. Initialize your magnetoshell field. We are standing away now. You are go for de-orbit burn in four minutes and twenty seconds... mark."

"Thank you for the ride, Warp Two."

Chukkers and Mike went through the checklist one last time and finished with a minute to spare.

"You look like you're in a hurry, Chukkers."

"I'm just being overly cautious, Mike. I made a promise I intend to keep."

"Promise?"

"I promised my wife I would not get us killed in the landing."

Mike smiled and nodded. "Now that is a promise I will keep you to as well."

Chukkers keyed his microphone once more. "Warp Two, we are go for de-orbit burn in twenty seconds..."

The solid boosters shook the delta-winged biplane as they dragged it slower and slower, finally falling away just as the first whisps of atmosphere illuminated the magnetoshell.

Mike said nothing but just watched as his pilot monitored the automatic re-entry sequence. Everything was executing perfectly. The view screen lit up with the warp tug pilot once more.

"Bode' Three, we have you over that hurricane in about a minute. It looks like it has developed a wider trailing cell over the last hour. Your course will take you right over it. You might see some flashes from lower-level lightening."

"No problem, Warp Two. We'll just consider it a welcoming fireworks display. Thanks for the heads up."

True to her prediction, a few moments later, they noticed colored flashes from below.

"What the hell?" Mike exclaimed, while looking out his side window.

Before the pilot could answer, there was a series of blinding, brilliant blue and white flashes. The spacecraft shuddered and the magneto field flared out to half again its normal radius, then disappeared. Immediately, they heard the atmosphere screaming by as the poor craft was buffeted.

The outside noise was no match for several howling alarms from the instruments.

"Chukkers! That flash got me. I can't see shit!"

"Don't feel bad. I'm blind too... And I don't have flight controls!"

"What?"

"There is no feedback to the stick. We're just gliding and... whoa!"

The craft bucked hard to one side, then rolled over and started to spiral, out of control.

Chukkers' voice was harsh. "All the damn systems are off-line. I'm going for a hard reset now!"

Purely by touch, his experienced hands found the hard reset switches. The ten seconds it took to reset everything seemed like hours to the men. The first thing they noticed was the spiraling barrel roll stopped and the craft leveled off. Then, Chukkers killed the alarms.

"No sense listening to that racket. I know damn well we're in trouble. Can you see anything, Mike?"

"Some hazy stuff is coming back. The flash is wearing off. I still can't make out the instruments, though."

"Bode' Three, this is Warp Two. Acknowledge."

"Warp Two, we are still here, but are trying to regain control. What happened?"

"We're not sure, but we saw a blue sprite lightening bolt follow the ionized trail from your magnetoshell field. We lost all telemetry until just a moment ago."

"We lost all flight systems here and I had to do a hard reset. The craft is responding now, but I'm trying to clear my vision. We were flash-blinded."

"Well, you better get it back fast, Chukkers. You are way off-course."

Mike was leaning forward, blinking rapidly and adjusting the size of the map display. "I can barely read the map, but none of that coastline looks like anything around Bode'."

The warp tug pilot agreed. "It's not. The coastline ahead of you is about four hundred kilometers south of Bode'. It's some pretty rough mountains near the ocean and you're way too low and way too fast right now. You cannot make it to Bode'!"

"Give me a beach then!"

"No beaches wide enough for you to fit even if you made it down. All we see are cliffs. You better set it down out to sea and Bode' can send someone to help tow you in."

Chukkers shook his head. "At our speed, two hundred kilometers will take way too long. We also have no idea if there was any hull damage from that strike. I'm not prepared to bail water with buckets. Give me another choice, fast!"

"Can you see your maps, yet?"

"Yeah. The bright flashes are fading and I can see around them now. Where am I looking?"

"You are still going too fast. Execute some lazy-eights to scrub speed before you pass over the coastline."

"Roger that." He pulled the lumbering spacecraft into a series of tight turns, first one way, then another, slowly working their way closer to land.

"Looks like some thick cloud cover ahead." Mike stated the obvious.

"Those are really low-lying clouds, Mike. We can't be sure, but it is pretty cold weather down there and I think you're flying into fog. Chukkers, use your instruments for final approach."

"I think some of them didn't recover. She's handling well now, but

I still have no idea where we're going. We can't keep gliding up here forever."

Mike was studying the map display. "There!" He pointed. "There is a wide mouth to a river and it makes a gentle curve. The inside of the curve looks like a sand beach. We should be able to put down just outside the inlet and cruise into that beach."

The pilot scanned the map and decided. "We are almost on top of it. I'm going to try one more pass, then land outside."

"Chukkers, no!" The tug pilot warned. "I have a detailed map here and there are several rows of barrier reefs and rocky ledges curving out from that point of land. If you try to land at sea, those rocks will eat you."

"Where then, damnit! I need a solution, now!"

"Fly just over the entrance and set her down in that wide bay, just past the two ridges. The river curves a bit, but if you get her in the water, you'll be slow enough to motor around to the beach."

"We're in the clouds. I can't see shit."

Mike's voice was calm. "You're doing fine, Chukkers. We are at three hundred meters and dropping."

"There! We are under the fog. There's the inlet... Shit! Hang on!" The pilot pulled back on the stick and the huge craft sluggishly rose just a bit, barely missing a line of giant rocks, scattered at the entrance to the bay.

The bay was much narrower than it appeared on the map and they were still hurtling along, only a dozen meters off the water. A huge rooster tail of spray marked their passage. Chukkers was tight-jawed, his fingers were white on the controls. What looked like a solid, dark gray wall of rock was coming up at them, fast. The gentle curve of the river was much tighter when traveling at their speed.

"Turn, Chukkers, Turn!" Mike shouted as the mountain face loomed ahead.

At the last second, they banked hard, the wingtip raising its own tail of spray as it barely glazed the water. A narrow, but smooth section of water lined up with their nose and they finally touched down. At their speed even water is hard and their teeth were jarred while bouncing off the light chop.

"The beach!" Mike shouted.

"I see it." The thin white line was off-center from their course and rapidly approaching. "Sheet!" His Latino accent was evident at his voiced frustration. "We're too damn fast."

He turned towards the narrow strip of white.

"Damn, more rocks!"

The Bode' Three shook and bounced as it skipped over a large, flat rock shelf. Ripping and grinding sounds gave voice to the destruction of their hull. As a wingtip was ripped off by an outcropping, the craft veered towards the cliff.

"Sheet! Sheet! Sheet!" Chukkers' accent was the least of his worries as he fought the controls, feeling his ship being worn down as it slid up the snow-covered gravel of the beach. The nose crumpled against a vertical wall of rock and they came to a jarring stop.

Mike looked at the pilot. "Chukkers?"

White faced, jaw clenched, he just stared at the crumpled metal and cracked windshield.

"Chukkers! Sit back. Let go of the controls. We're down."

Slowly, he sat back in his seat and unclenched his fingers from the joystick. Almost from reflex, he glanced at the console, with its mix of multi-colored lights. They were mostly red and yellow. He killed power to all the flight systems and finally took a long shuddering breath.

"Bode' Three? Chukkers! What is your status?"

"We are down and on the beach, Warp Two. At this point, I have no idea how much damage has been done."

Another voice and image showed on the communications screen. It was Bode' settlement director, Steve Saunders. "Congratulations, Captain Garcia. That was some landing. I'm glad you're down in one piece."

Chukkers gave him a half-smile. "Anything you can walk away from, is that your criteria, Mr. Saunders?"

"According to tradition, the pilot who lands at a new settlement gets to name it. I don't think we will be seeing you and your flight down here, so what are you going to call your new home?"

"I really don't care at this point. I will differ to the senior member of the flight crew. Mike? What is this place going to be called?"

"Are you sure about that, Captain Garcia?"

The pilot waved his hand in dismissal. "Yes. Just give it a name and then I'm going to take a walk below to see what sort of damage we have incurred."

"In that case, just for the record, I tend to agree with the name our intrepid pilot gave us during the last few seconds of our landing."

Brows furrowed, Chukkers turned to his copilot. "What are you talking about?"

Mike ignored him. "I hereby dub this place the new community of OhSheetz." He took time to spell it amid laughter from the Bode' communication team.

Ports of Entry

After the laughter died, Mr. Saunders suggested, "Why don't you two stretch your legs and get a quick visual inventory of your ship. Do you have any cold weather gear?"

Mike shook his head. "I'm afraid not. Everything we have readily available is for a semi-tropical climate. If you check the video feeds, we're looking at about thirty centimeters of snow on the beach and maybe a meter on higher ground, around us."

"In that case, don't go outside, just yet. You have plenty of power and supplies to stay warm and dry until we can sort out a plan of action."

Both Chukkers and Mike nodded agreement, then unstrapped and went back, into the bowels of their ship.

Two hours later, they were back on the command deck, taking part in a conference with the other three settlements. Steve Saunders asked, "Mike? You look a bit bedraggled there. Are you cold?"

"Yeah. After we did an internal tour, we are satisfied that there is no serious damage. Captain Garcia and I launched a pair of skeeters for an external survey. The images are on our shared space, now."

Chukkers added. "I also launched a buzzard and gave it a local, terrain mapping chore. It started flying a tight grid pattern, using all on-board sensors, at the mouth of the inlet. It will stop and return to recharge when it gets about a kilometer upstream from us."

Valon Smythe wanted to know, "Are you going to decant anyone?"

Mike shook his head. "Not right now. All the CryoDox are in good shape and we've power enough to keep everyone on ice for the next year if needed. I've got a more pressing concern at the moment." He pointed at a video feed, panning around the immediate area of the Bode' Three. "See that line of debris? Right now, we're high and dry. Since Micasa has a pair of very small moons, there are no major tidal forces. This beach we are sitting on, has little sand. It's mostly small, water-worn pebbles. From the shape, and all the driftwood debris, I'm thinking that as soon as we get a good thaw, this river is going to flood."

Everyone was quiet for a few moments, while they switched their attention from the satellite topographic maps to the various video cameras.

Varlon stated the obvious. "Since there are only some pretty steep and rugged-looking rock walls ahead of you. It's a cinch you are not going to haul the lander up there. I don't see more than a few square meters of level ground anywhere nearby."

Chukkers added, "I don't think we should make any decisions until we get the detailed topographic data from the buzzard. It's using a FLIR to give us down to less than twenty centimeter resolution for the maps." He changed the topic. "Which reminds me. Steve? Has anyone been able to come up with a long-term weather forecast?"

"Yes, Chukkers. You might see some more snow and a overcast with morning fog for the next day or so. Then, it should clear up for at least a few days. Long-term, we expect warmer weather is not going to happen for at least another couple of months."

Mike smiled. "That is actually good news. We won't have to worry about a flood tearing us to scrap metal anytime soon. Although the cold weather might be a problem while we are looking for a high-ground parking place."

Lizzie Roberts spoke up. "I think we're going to be able to help with that, sir. As soon as Varlon and I heard where you had landed, we realized you would need some of the same cold weather gear that we have been using. I've asked our friends and everyone has tossed in some heavy coats, boots, and gauntlets."

"If I recall..." Mike checked his map. "You are still more than a hundred kilometers away, over some pretty rough mountains. How are you going to get them to us?"

Steve interrupted. "Actually, it is closer to two hundred kilometers. But, delivery is no problem. I've already had the flight crews prepare one of our heavy-lift blimps. It will leave here with some supplies we had already planned on sending to Vinge. It will unload there, load your cold weather gear, and meet you. They probably won't be able to land, but will hold station over you, to unload."

Lizzie pointed to a satellite map. "There are three mountain passes between us. Two of them are pretty rough, but the northern one cuts over to a small lake at the headwaters of your river. Which reminds me... What are we calling the river?"

Mike clapped Chukkers on the shoulder. "You gave me the honor of naming OhSheetz. You better leave your mark on the river."

The captain thought a moment before answering. "Upstream, call it Crystal River and from that mountain ridge where it curves around, out to the inlet, we'll call it Tampa Bay."

"Memories of home, right?" Steve smiled. "That is how it will be then." He drew a line on the map from Vinge, over a mountain pass and down the crooked Crystal River gorge, until it arrived at OhSheetz.

Chukkers agreed and added. "I think we should go ahead and decant the preliminary post-landing team so that we have enough extra hands to help unload and also to help us move the ship somehow."

Everyone agreed and the meeting ended.

Naturally, Mike decanted Angela and Chukkers decanted Susan. Two other couples followed and the Bode' Three command deck felt crowded.

Two days later, the City of Bode' heavy-lift blimp floated gracefully between the mountains framing Crystal River and Tampa Bay. Dawn Smith was the pilot. "Bode' Three, this is City of Bode', Captain Dawn, commanding. Are you ready to receive guests, bearing gifts?"

Chukkers had to smile. "Hello Dawn and of course we're ready. The prevailing wind has been steady, flowing down the fjord. I would suggest you fly past us, turn around in the wide curve of the bay and then drop mooring lines as you approach from our stern. As soon as you approach, we'll head out to meet and tie you down."

As soon as the lines were secure, a hatch opened and familiar faces appeared.

Susan shouted a greeting. "Lizzie! Good to see you, girlfriend."

Varlon stood with one hand on the hatch frame and the other wrapped around a bundle. He waved it and shouted, "Catch!"

Susan caught it and it unrolled to show one of Varlon's custom foul weather dusters. She gave the hood a quizzical look, then shrugged into it. "Thanks!"

In quick order, other dusters were distributed. The side pockets held warm gloves and soon everyone was dressed for the weather. Dawn shut down the engines and followed the rest into the Bode' Three.

Amid handshakes and hugs, the blimp pilot said, "We have some fresh veggies and frozen meat on board to help brighten your diet. I'm sure you are already sick of the basic nuke-a-ration." She continued. "Since you guys weren't in any immediate danger, we took a slow trip over here. I kept our speed down to what the buzzards could manage at cruise and while they ran mapping sensors. We now have much more detailed information on Crystal River."

Mike added. "Our buzzards just finished mapping from a kilometer each way, up the coast to about two kilometers upriver. I think we may have a solution." He pointed to the topographic map on the large display. "This whole area looks a lot like northern European fjords. We just don't have the ability to drag this poor old bird up those rock faces. But, if you look just around that bend, about a kilometer from here, the other side of the river meets a gently-sloping alpine meadow. There is not much of a beach, just lots of trees and underbrush, but it does have a gentle slope that our winches should be able to haul us up and out of the flood plain."

Varlon asked. "Lizzie and I were commenting on that area when we passed it. Those trees are all pretty hardwood. You will have to clear a passage first."

Dawn added. "That is why we brought those two extra tractors, Varlon. I made sure they had timbering attachments. We'll fly them up first light, tomorrow and put them to work." She turned to Chukkers and Mike. "What kind of condition is your lower hull in? The trail you left in the beach gravel shows some metallic debris. Are you still waterproof for the trip up river?"

Mike shook his head. "The nose nacelle has been torn up pretty badly, but we have no way of knowing what is underneath. From inside, it all looks sound, but only an outside inspection is going to tell us for sure. I don't think there is anything we can do about it, one way or another. We have no choice but to make the trip. I checked our stern drive units and they are intact and we have plenty of power since the reactor was undamaged. The hardest part I think will be dragging ourselves off this gravel beach without causing more damage."

Varlon waved his hand. "I think I can help with that. While the tractors are clearing our new parking lot, we can jack up the back of the lander, then put one of your tractors to work, bulldozing snow into the trench you left. We can use packed snow to lubricate your way back off this sandbar."

"Good idea. Also, the City of Bode' can't lift this monster lander, but we can provide some lift and a lot of pull. Even if you have some leakage, we should be able to keep you afloat long enough to get upriver. Once on dry ground, the tractors and winches will have no problem getting you out of harm's way."

Mike spoke up. "It seems to me that we shouldn't waste valuable real-time discussing this here. Let's grab a good meal, then some sleep. While we are in Beta, we can take several days to look over the detailed maps and make sure of how we want to approach this. Agreed?"

That suggestion brought a smile to everyone's face.

Steel Rails

Victor stood on a balcony, high above the city he had created, staring off, into the distance.

"You're looking pensive today. That worries me."

Victor knew his best friend's voice. "And well it should, Jack. Much as I love what we have here, I'm about convinced that it was too easy."

The security chief put both hands on the rail and glanced at the glistening diorama of Empire City. "Too easy? I don't think I'm following you."

"Empire city and all the rest of the physical stuff around us was created with magic. I merely did the design work, willed it into existence, and the Beta operating system, which no one really pays any attention to, made it happen."

Jack shrugged. "Yeah. But that is the way things happen here in Beta and isn't that why you are a Master Mage?"

"Mike Hawthorne and several others warned me this would happen. The human race is dividing... or perhaps I should say, has already divided into two, distinct cultures."

"I take it you are referring to the transhumanists who spend as much time in Beta as possible and those folks that either reject it entirely or only drop in once in a while, for parties and planning sessions?"

Victor nodded, then continued. "It's more than that, actually. You and I died in that drive-by, back in Nashville. And yet within a week, we were reincarnated in our new lease bodies. Tell me. What percentage of Betans do you think are permanent residents; ghosts as it were?"

"I have no idea. Haven't paid any attention. I take it you have?"

"Right now, more than twenty percent. And the number grows

daily. Some of the folks on my team have been offered lease bodies and they have rejected the idea." He turned away from the railing, folded his hands behind him and strode back into the lush office. "Many of our best technicians have volunteered to be warp-ship pilots and there are some that want to form their own, permanent warp-ship crew and take a few thousand year jaunt around our galaxy, exploring in the best Star Trek tradition."

Jack slid the glass door closed, accepted a drink from his boss, then sat on the couch. "That sounds like fun, actually. What's the problem?"

"Logistically, no problem. I added their ship request to the que and the Saturn yards should have one ready in another six months or so. I did make them promise to make regular return visits to drop data packets with their discoveries. What concerns me is the fact that the more time passes, we are going to see a total division between the transhumanist cultures and physical humans."

"Isn't that part of the idea of the Singularity as proposed by Vernor Vinge and Ray Kurzweil?"

"You're partly right, Jack. Except he envisioned everyone joining the party. We're not seeing that. Take, for example, Susan Childers and her cousin, Lizzie. They have Beta personalities, but they don't care for Empire City. They spend their time riding horses and exploring, much the same thing they are doing in real life, back on Micasa. I've spoken with them about it and they treat Beta as a sort of virtual reality training system. They do party here, but spend minimal time. They are devoted to building their real settlements." He paused and took a drink before continuing. "I think that what we are seeing is not so much the Singularity as a Multiplarity. A wide range of options open to humans as a species and that fragmentation is going to continue until there are parts we won't even recognize."

Jack appeared to think about it while sipping his drink. After a few minutes of companionable silence, Victor asked his opinion.

The security chief gave his friend a wry smile. "I keep coming around to the same thing. So? So what if we spread through the cosmos as both biological humans, transhumans, or something totally different? All of our eggs are no longer in one basket. Did you know there have already been some babies born on Micasa? If a rogue asteroid blasted into Earth, we still have one large and several smaller lunar colonies. There are now four settlements on Micasa and the last report I saw, a robot warp-drive found two more solar systems with planets similar to

Micasa and Earth. I count that as a win."

"I'm starting to think Empire City has been a wonderful virtual reality trainer for me, as well. Now, I need to apply what I've learned to a real world project."

Jack put the glass down with a click and a huge smile spread over his face. "Good! I've been bored too. When and where, boss?"

"I've been talking to some of those folks that want to become galaxy explorers. They are happy to give up their biological bodies. Our new ones back on Earth are permanent. If you want to come along, I'm going to contract a few dozen CryoDox to ship us to Micasa."

"Somehow, I don't imagine you as a rancher or dirt farmer."

Victor laughed. "You're right, Jack. I'm going to take the long, slow road to build an empire this time. What do you think of the idea of a railroad?"

Jack gave him a surprised look. "I have no idea at all. Never even considered it."

The Master Mage waved his hand and a Micasa topographic map appeared. "Those glowing dots are the four existing settlements. The closest ones are about twenty-five kilometers apart. The new one, OhSheetz, is almost three hundred kilometers from the others. Small quantities of trade goods can travel via ocean-going ship or blimp, but I want to plan for the future."

"Sounds good, boss. But right now, all their high-technology stuff has to be dropped from one of our off-planet fabricators. Trains run on steel rails and that takes a mature industrial infrastructure."

"Or course, Jack. And everyone I've spoken with on Micasa agrees that they don't want to pollute the planet the way we've screwed up Earth. They want to keep most heavy-industry off-planet. I'm going to have a series of drone landers built. Each one will be packed full of rail and the hardware needed to build rolling stock. The dense forests will provide ties and timbers for trestles. All the preliminary design work is part of historical records from the late nineteenth and early twentieth centuries on Earth. The first line will connect Bode' and Jerryville. That will help us sort out any bugs. The next line will connect Jerryville and Vinge. That will have to follow a whole bunch of rivers gorges and over a couple of mountains."

"What sort of traffic do you see on these, Victor?"

"Initially, timber from the cold southern mountain regions, fresh fruits and vegetables from the Bode' and Jerryville plains, and fresh seafood from OhSheetz, Bode' and Rutan."

"Rutan? Where's that?"

Victor pointed to a delta plain southwest of Bode'. "I'm going to fund a new settlement there. It will be a commercial fishing hub and new arrival port of entry for colonists and tourists."

"I think it might be a bit premature to consider tourists. Aren't all colony ships one-way?"

Victor shrugged. "They are now, but I've commissioned a Starliner program. They are much smaller and are designed for a monthly transit between L5 and Micasa Low Orbit. They will only handle twenty-four CryoDox and a couple of ton of cargo. The big selling point is that they will transit both ways, once a month. Two weeks at L5 and two weeks at Micasa. I've already had inquiries about tickets."

His desktop slate rang and he tapped it. "Yes?"

It was Wendy Mathias. "Hey there! You wanted to be kept in the loop about OhSheetz?"

"That's right. How are they doing?"

"They found a very nice piece of high ground and have successfully moved the lander. There was some damage to the bottom and it leaked like a sieve once it hit the water, but with the blimp providing an extra tow, they made it up river. I just heard a few minutes ago, that they have already setup the first few inflatables and the blimp is headed back to Vinge'."

"That is good news. I'll have to send my congratulations. When are you and Mark going to immigrate?"

She laughed. "Hell no! We have a wonderful life in Port Heinlein and are having a ball with our domains here on Beta. I have no desire to plow a field or get eaten by some gator on another mudball."

"I understand. Give my regards to Mark."

She nodded and the screen went blank.

"See what I mean, Jack? Just more fragmentation. Those two are happy in their roles."

"Different strokes for different folks. I can see that, Victor. But I can't help but wonder how long it will be before they get bored and follow us."

New Neighbors

After a very wet spring, CheeYok led the tribe back to Jerryville. With the help of some humans, the Chickmonks planted much larger gardens. They were promised trade goods for their extra fresh crops.

Cheryl's slate rang and she saw the Master Potter from Winter Camp. "CherrunNor. How nice to see you."

"I wish this were a social visit, Cheeral. But I have a favor to ask."

"What is it? Is something wrong? You look worried."

"It's one of my pupils in the new glass-blowing shop. There was an accident and he has been badly burnt. Our healers say he won't last more than a few days."

Cheryl's face echoed her concern. "I'm so sorry to hear that, CherrunNor, but what can we do to help?"

He paused, and nervously looked around before continuing. "I have heard your people speak of something called ohmnee?"

"It is called Omniphage and it works for us, but we have never tried it on any of your people. I don't know if it would work or if it would just kill you faster. I know some of our healers have been investigating it. Let me call you back in a little while."

"Call quickly, Cheeral. He is in a great deal of pain and may not be with us much longer."

As soon as the screen cleared, Cheryl called one of the research team to explain the situation.

He nodded understanding. "We have been thinking much the same thing. Their biology is similar to ours in that they use something like DNA/RNA, but we really don't have enough time to be sure. We have a modified version of Omniphage we are calling Chickphage, but it is strictly a laboratory sample now. You were right to warn him it might cause instant death. We just don't have enough data."

"This student is going to die anyway. If he will agree, it will be a first case."

"Okay. Let me know and I'll prime a CryoDox with the new stuff and have it out at the helo pad in an hour."

She called CherrunNor and gave him the option.

"How long before you can get this to us?"

"We will fly it down in a helicopter and you can meet us with your student. If all goes well, we should be there by dawn."

Three days later, a healthy Chickmonk climbed out of a CryoDox. He immediately asked to be taught the human language.

CherrunNor waited until Cheryl and Buster were alone before asking. "What is going to happen next, my friends?"

"What do you mean?" Buster replied.

"You have this power of life and death and are already more numerous than my people. I have been studying the history of your people on the slate and see you have a fascination with war and conflicts over territory. If you continue coming to our planet, what is to become of us?"

Buster keyed up a map on his own slate. "I was wondering when you would ask that. The question has occurred to us as well and we do not want to have any trouble with your people. Take a look at this map we have been working on."

He pointed to highlighted areas that formed three narrow strips, following valleys and one irregular blob that covered most of a wide plain near the equator. "We have been searching for more of your people and these are the only areas we have found them. You are right in that there are very few of you left. Now that we have a working version of Chickphage, you should be able to increase your numbers. In the meantime, our leaders have established rules stating that any of you are welcome in our communities as if you were one of us. That includes following our laws when applicable. You may attend our schools, work with us, and establish your own businesses. We are going to set aside those highlighted areas as well as other, similar ones as nature preserves. We are not going to establish settlements in them. Those of your people that wish to maintain your existing traditions may do so there. We are looking forward to living in peace."

The elderly Chickmonk smiled. "It appears as if you have been practicing that speech for some time." Before they could answer, he went on. "I am glad to see you have planned ahead for this. We too, want to live in peace."

Celebration

Victor wore a soft smile as he watched Paulette shooting pictures in almost a continuous stream. She was an excellent photographer with an eye for things that many people would miss. Their blimp was cruising sedately down the Crystal River gorge, and only an occasional bump from a gust of wind disturbed their ride.

She paused and took several shots at the same section of rock wall. "Victor? How far away is the end of the railroad?"

He glanced at the map. "They should be cutting through this part of the line in week or two, why?"

She sent her images to his slate. "Take a look and tell me that isn't another ruin, back under that ledge."

He glanced back, but it was already out of sight. Her photos were enough to show a polished rock wall, hidden from aerial view. Deep in the shadows, there appeared to be a door frame. "I will have the survey crew check it out. I'm sure the Mathias and their Chickmonk friends want to add it to their future archaeological digs. It looks like it is much higher than where we will put the roadbed."

She continued shooting while Victor considered his good fortune. After doing the initial reconnaissance on Beta, she had kept a low-profile in his company. Only after he had commissioned a large oil painting from some of her original sketches did she agree to visit Empire City. She was pleasurable company for dinner, but had been forthright in stating she just didn't like cities. The wild mountains held an appeal she couldn't deny. It took several years of occasional dinners both on Earth and Beta, before she allowed them to be anything more than friends. When he had told her he was going to become a colonist, she asked if she could go along. He agreed on one condition, that she marry him.

As they passed OhSheetz, getting ready to make the standard airship turn over Tampa Bay, prior to landing, he asked, "Are you going to print some of those shots to share with us poor mortals, love?"

She put down the camera and gave him a quick kiss. "Of course I will. But only a few and in small format. I am still trying to find the proper natural replacements so I can make my own oil paints here on Micasa."

"I guess it is time to tell you about your Landing Day present." His eyes held a hint of mischief.

"Oh? I know that with all your money, you could easily have more Earth paints sent. But I want to use local, natural materials."

"I know. And I approve. After you master the local stuff, you will be able to start your own art school. That is why I asked the Mathias' if they would hire Chickmonks to help you out."

She looked at him. "But I thought they didn't have any tradition of painting, except for those ancient murals, that is."

"That's right. But they do have a diverse ceramics community. You've seen some of their colored pottery. I know they have someone with the skills needed to mix those colors. I've commissioned them to be your studio assistants for one year. They will be living with us as soon as we return from this little vacation."

She hugged and soundly kissed her husband. "Thank you! I'm sure that will speed the search and who knows, we might just start a Chickmonk school of art."

The blimp dropped the landing lines and ground crews secured them. The dozen lines pulled them snug against the landing pad and the huge airship's engines spooled down and then grew silent.

The pilot's voice sang out from the intercom. "OhSheetz City! All ashore what's goin' ashore!"

The still air held a biting cold sting after the warmth of the blimp. An early-season blizzard had dumped about a foot of snow two days earlier. This left any somewhat level surface covered with glistening white. A few of the remaining inflatable shelters had been covered with soil to create additional insulation. More than two dozen new structures surrounded the shell of the unfortunate lost lander. It would be used for storage and emergency shelter for a few more years, and then relegated to being a combination of school and museum exhibit.

When he stepped down from the ladder, Victor turned to see a large man with close-cropped hair and military bearing.

"Happy Landings and welcome to OhSheetz. You must be Victor Adams." He held out his hand.

"I'm Victor Charles Adams the Third and I'm glad to meet the famous General Michael Hawthorne face-to-face." They shook. Mike introduced his wife, Angela and Victor introduced Paulette.

Angela too, gave the now common holiday greeting. "Happy Landings! You two are lucky. We just finished our community center and this will be the very first Landing Day celebration to be held in it. Most of OhSheetz is planning on attending the party."

The closer they got to the largest of the new buildings, the more Victor was impressed. "Who is your architect? That is an impressive piece of work."

Angela answered. "Thank you. Actually, it has been a joint effort. Since none of us had really been prepared for settling in this climate, we knew we had to get some advice. Varlon Smythe suggested some old Earth books on building design and we realized that there is a huge amount of extremely dense hardwood timber around us. Since it will last a very long time if properly maintained, we looked at some classic construction techniques from both Europe and Japan. The only metal parts are hinges, locks, and electrical components. The main structure is interlocked timber framing. We don't make screws or nails. The walls are packed adobe sandwiched between three centimeter thick planks."

Paulette wore a huge smile. "The brilliant blue of that roof is amazing. It looks like Spanish tile."

Angela nodded. "Good eye, there. Once we showed some Chickmonk potters how to make barrel tiles, they have been turning them out in an amazing array of colors. I think it is going to be their first heavy industry."

Mike looked at Victor. "Speaking of heavy industry, when are we going to see that railroad?"

"We just flew over the work camp. It's only about twenty kilometers up river. We are way ahead of schedule. It should be here before spring. The survey team should be here by now."

"They arrived a couple of days ago. We fed 'em, put 'em up overnight, and they headed back upstream the next day. You have some dedicated workers, Victor."

The industrialist smiled at the compliment. "All of my employees are dedicated because I believe in giving them achievable goals, reasonable pay, and real bonuses for a job well done. That survey team, for example... They have already picked out a couple of areas along the track where they are going to homestead their own small towns. Each whistle stop community is a seed planted that we hope will grow into a thriving network of communities to fit all tastes."

Once inside, the lobby glowed with warm colors that belied the bleak gray and white of winter among the southern fjords. Everyone shed their gloves, dusters, and greatcoats. Toe-tapping fiddle music wafted past the inner doors and when they were opened, the visitors saw the party was already well under way.

"Victor!" The shout came from one side and Chuckers, Susan in tow, came into view. "Happy Landings!"

This started another chorus of Happy Landings and a round of raised glasses.

"Mr. Garcia! Happy Landings to you as well. I understand this beautiful place is all your fault."

The Latino slapped him on the back and retorted. "Only because that deathtrap you sold us was no match for my superior flying skills." He grabbed Victor's hand and in both of his and shook it. "Seriously, my friend. That colonial lander is one sturdy bird. If you're interested, I'll show you the pictures from our crash site and the damage she sustained. I'm really surprised we all didn't end up scattered among the rocks of Tampa Bay."

"Nobody could be happier that things worked out. And from the looks of this magnificent community center, your settlement is thriving. Jerryville is almost two years older than OhSheetz and they have nothing like this. What else have you been up to that we don't know about?"

Susan shared a smile with her husband. "We all wanted to finish our in-town duties fast so we could focus on the ranch. By the time spring arrives, we expect to have our first foals. Three of our mares survived the CryoDox and are pregnant. We are looking forward to your railroad allowing us to trade breeding stock with Jerryville and Vinge'. In another five years, there will be a large enough herd that we'll be able to open a quarter horse riding academy."

    ***

The party went on and it was after midnight before Victor and Paulette went to bed. While their bodies repaired themselves, they woke in Beta.

"My goodness, love. That was a lovely gathering. And that building. We just have to do something similar for our corporate headquarters, down in Bode'."

"Agreed, darlin'. I've already requested a copy of the plans and building techniques."

She watched as he got dressed. "Something troubling you, Victor?"

"Not so much troubled as surprised. Did you notice the small contingent of Chickmonks at the party?"

"Of course. While you were trading engineering secrets, Lizzie introduced me. They are from the first apprentice class that CherrunNor took on to learn both pottery and glass-blowing skills. They have taken on a small compound just upriver where they constructed a kiln to supply us with locally-made barrel tiles and window glass. That is where they got the tiles for that fancy roof on the community center."

He nodded his appreciation. "I'm amazed at how fast the Chickmonks seem to be taking to modern technologies. I was seriously concerned for their future as a species when I saw the first hunter-gatherer video clips. Fortunately, that appears to be only a few scattered groups. And they all learn English and new skills in very short order."

She slipped into a thin dress and heels, suitable for the warm climate of Empire City and followed her husband out to the deck. "What is on the agenda for today, Victor?"

"I think we should let Empire City run itself for a few days while we visit our neighbors in other domains."

Archeology

The last kilometer of track into OhSheetz seemed to happen almost overnight. A loading dock platform had already been constructed and when the last section of track was stable, the town erupted in celebration. The following day a blizzard hit and kept most everyone snowed in for the next three days.

Paulette inspected the railroad cars in preparation for their ride back, through Vinge' and then to Bode'. Victor stood on a corner of the platform, out of the way and enjoyed the incredible scenery offered by the sloping alpine valley and curving fjord.

"Master Victor? May I have a moment of your time?" The slight buzzing accent came from a Chickmonk bundled against the winter chill. "I am DorratNor, Master Potter and Glassmaker."

"Of course, DorratNor. I must admit, I'm very impressed with the fruits of your labor that I've seen around town."

The Chickmonk gave a little bow. "You are too kind. But I bring a small gift and a request. Is your wife able to join us for a few minutes?"

"Certainly, come. Let's get inside where it is warmer. I know your people are not as fond of the cold as we are."

They met Paullete in the dining car and she recognized their guest. "DorratNor! It is good to see you again. What has pulled you from your beloved kiln?"

"It is good to see you as well, Mrs. Adams. As I told your husband, I have a request and a small gift." He placed a polished wooden case, slightly larger than a briefcase, on the table and opened it. Inside, it had padded cells with a dozen blown glass jars. Each clear jar contained a brilliantly colored powder. "When you told me about this painting you wished to do, I had my apprentices assemble these samples. They are the basic powders that we use to give color to our products."

"Oh my goodness!" Paulette gushed. "This is exactly what I have been looking for to make some paints." She lifted one of the jars and looked at the symbol molded into the side. "What is this?"

The Master Potter spoke a word in his language, then repeated it a couple of times until she pronounced it correctly. "That is what we call the source of that powder. I will be happy to teach you the other names as well."

"I don't know what to say. Thank you, of course." She was entranced as she let her fingers caress each small bottle.

Victor knew his wife would be lost with her new toy, so he interrupted. "Excuse me, DorratNor, but you mentioned a request?"

"Yes. Master Adams..."

Victor held up his hand to stop his guest. "Please, DorratNor, call me Victor. It seems we are to be both friends and business associates. I know my wife will want to purchase more of those powders from you in the future."

"Certainly, Victor. And you may call me Dorrat. There is no need for formality among us." He paused. "I have heard that you discovered another of the old places of my people and that it is near here. Is that true?"

Victor turned on his slate and showed the potter the few images that his wife had taken from the blimp.

"That does indeed look like the entrance to the Last Place near Winter Camp. Does the train go near it?"

"Yes, Dorrat. The tracks pass below it. Let me look at the topographic maps to see how accessible it is." A few moment later, they determined there was a zig-zag trail that rose from a nearby outcropping of river rock.

"Those slates are very useful, Victor. Can you perhaps print out a map so that I might show my students and we can arrange to visit when the spring arrives?"

Victor only took a second to decide. "Wait here, my friend. I'll just be a moment." He returned a couple of minutes later with a pair of new slates. "I have kept some spare slates in case one of ours gets damaged. It would please me greatly if you would accept these two as our gifts. I will key one of them to you and you may keep the other in your shop for your students."

DorratNor took his and bowed deeply. "Thank you! You have no idea what this means to us."

Victor returned the bow and continued. "Our new railroad is not on a fixed schedule yet. I have a proposal. Paulette expressed an interest in those ruins and I'm curious as well. The train can have us at the base of the trail in less than an hour. It shouldn't take more than a couple of hours to walk up the mountain, examine the area and take some pictures. We can make a day trip of it if we leave early."

"That would be wonderful. When would you like to leave?"

The industrialist looked at his wife and she replied. "We shall have to ask some of our friends to join us. How about the day after tomorrow?"

Two days later, the small train headed back up the gorge, pulling a consist of five enclosed cars and four empty flat cars. The Childers and the Hawthornes joined their little expedition. DorratNor brought his first apprentice.

"Excuse me, Victor. But I notice there is a metal plate set into the center floor of each of these cars. What is it for?"

Tell me, Dorrat. Has you heard that most of us consider ourselves as transhumanists?"

"I've heard the term before. It means you consider yourselves more than human. You believe in some sort of other world. Beta, I think it is called."

"Yes. You are correct. In order for us to visit Beta in our sleep, we must have a very complex device we call simply a brick. Each of the railroad cars, our blimps and our homes have a brick buried in them someplace."

His guest just nodded and said nothing more.

In some ways, their expedition was a bit of a disappointment. In others, it was exciting. After a two hour climb, following the ancient trail, they found the doorway was still tightly sealed.

Victor clapped a hand on DorratNor's shoulder. "Actually, my friend. This is very good news indeed. It means that when we return in the spring, we will have tools with which to open the door and everything inside should still be in perfect condition. We may learn a great deal more about your history."

"Victor?" Paulette's voice expressed concern. "What's happened to my slate? It seems to have died."

He checked his with a baffled expression. "Same here. That is weird. I've never seen two fail at the same time."

The Chickmonk's face showed extreme dismay as his was blank as well.

"Wait a minute." Victor thought furiously. "I just checked my map before we arrived and it was working perfectly." He turned and jogged back down the path. As soon as he turned the corner and was out of sight, he hollered for them to follow.

Less than a hundred meters away from the door, all of their slates reset and were working perfectly.

Victor and Mike looked at each other and ever the military man, Mike suggested they return to the train. "There is some sort of electronic damping field active near that door. I think we should be very careful how we proceed at this point."

Everyone was lost in their own thoughts as they left the mountain. The train ride back gave the colonists time to report their findings and share all the photos up to the point where their slates and cameras had stopped working.

Mike approached Victor after the Chickmonks headed back to their shop. "I think we should all get some sleep. A few days in Beta will give us time to analyze what we have so far. In the meantime, I think that mountain bears closer observation."

"I think you're right, Mike. Let's sleep on it. I'll call a Mage Council meeting in three days, Beta time."

After the initial greetings, Mike Hawthorne called the full council to order. "You've all seen the data we've gathered so far. The floor is open to suggestions."

Before he could continue, the sound of a gong chimed through the hall. Everyone looked around. But no one seemed to know what was happening.

Mike's authoritative voice filled the room. "Did any of you invite a guest to this meeting?" He was met with blank stares and shaking heads.

The gong sounded once more.

"Someone has been invited. Either way, I don't think we should be bad hosts. Enter!"

The massive double doors swung wide and a single Chickmonk entered. He wore something that resembled a black skinsuit, red trimmed, with matching boots and gauntlets. A full cape in bright red flowed from his shoulders. He strode into the center of the room bowed deeply to Mike, then turned and repeated the bow to each of the four corners.

When he faced Mike once more, he spoke with a perfect English accent. "Please forgive the theatrical nature of my arrival. It somehow seemed the easiest way to meet and address you all at once. My name is BeeRatYok and I am the last Master of the species you refer to as Chickmonks.

Mike stood up and returned the bow. "It is a pleasure to meet you, BeeRatYok. I was totally unaware that any of your race had either the ability nor been given the chance to use one of our helms. May I ask how you found these council chambers?"

Their unexpected guest smiled. "Believe it or not, humans are not the first race to have developed a virtual world such as Beta. There are an unknown number of such worlds. My people developed one right before the Ending, almost thirty thousand years ago." He waited a moment for his words to sink in, then went on. "When your train passed below our keep, the bricks came into range and we knew someone still lived on our planet. We examined your Beta system and realized it was a much more primitive version of our own. I'll have some of my people get with yours to update. In the meantime, you are as much a surprise to us as I am to you."

Angela found her voice. "BeeRatYok. Your title suggests you are a hunter. Are there many more of your people in the mountain?"

"The title is a vestige of what once was. Let me fill you in on a little history." He paused to collect his thoughts before continuing. "My people had developed much as yours. About thirty thousand years ago, we had space travel and several colonies scattered around our solar system. We were experimenting with the warp-drive but had only explored a few, nearby worlds when the Ending arrived. It came in the form of a massive shower of asteroids. They were the result of some cosmological event. We detected the first ones just months before the main body arrived. Many of us escaped into Alan, our version of Beta. We created bricks as fast as possible and scattered them all over our planet and solar system. Hundreds were packed into our only two warp-drive capable ships and sent to orbit a nearby red dwarf." He paused once more, obviously unhappy to be recalling the horror. "The first few asteroids to arrive were devastating, killing millions. Within a week, several had the same impact as the single event that killed the dinosaurs in your history. Of more than ten thousand bricks scattered around our planet, only three survived, buried in deep shelter. The surface of our world was a turmoil of winter and the few records we have show less than a thousand of our people actually survived, on the world you call Micasa. Fewer than a million escaped in our virtual forms and less than two dozen in our physical bodies, on the warp ships."

Mike Hawthorne asked softly, "BeeRatYok, may I ask your age?"

The Chickmonk smiled. "I was one of the fortunate few to escape on a warp ship. I gave up my physical body once we arrived in orbit around the red dwarf. We returned to Micasa about a thousand years after the Ending and found nothing but a narrow band of tropical jungle and the rest of the planet locked in an ice age. Only one of the brick installations was still working. We linked up with it and the inhabitants said that none of our people had survived on the surface. Another visit, five thousand years later and we decided the memories were too raw. We left the planet to heal itself. We had no idea that any of our people had survived on the surface. When you parked your train and visited the entrance to the mountain, it was an easy matter for us to scan your systems and learn about humans. That is where I learned to speak English. Imagine our intense surprise when we realized you were accompanied by some of our people that had no idea of our existence."

"What are your plans now?" Victor asked.

"All of our people are now what you call transhumanists. We have a million year old culture among billions of bricks scattered around the red dwarf. We are in constant communication with other species that have followed similar paths. You are welcome to this world, Victor. We are pleased to see physical members of our species survive and will be happy to assist you in uplifting them to your technology level. We will also assist your transhumanist teams in updating your bricks and hardening Beta so other races can't just drop in, as I just did."

Victor appeared skeptical. "And what do you ask in return, BeeRatYok?"

"Only your friendship, Victor. You see, the universe is populated with many different species and most of them arrive at our level sooner or later. Some of these species are truly alien and are not at all friendly. The sociable societies such as ours value friendship as it helps us all to prosper." He waved his hand and a star map appeared to float before him. "Each of the blinking dots is another civilization. You may examine each one in detail. There are more than a million showing in this small segment of our galactic map. I'm leaving you with this and an invitation to visit my domain. We have much to learn from each other and another few billion years to enjoy the journey."

Mike stared at the map for a moment, then his gaze went up to their guest. "Thank you, BeeRatYok and the invitation is mutual."

BeeRatYok, smiled acknowledgment, bowed once more, and disappeared in a blink of light.

###

Author Notes

This book has been in development for more than fifteen years. It started as a few quickly-typed notes on a future history idea and grew sporadically as concepts and situations occurred to me.

Most of the photography and artwork is mine, however I must credit the fabulous cover art image of a Colonial Lander Type II, to my friend John Picha. He's a gifted illustrator, graphic artist, animator, and author in his own right. Thank you Sir!

http://www.takejohn.com/

Genetic Science

No one will ever accuse me of being a genetic scientist. While developing this story, I gathered a great deal of data. Despite that, I've been informed by at least two people who should know, that Omniphage, as I describe it, won't work. While they agree that some form of genetic manipulation to cure any disease and even to rebuild us, will one day be possible, we are nowhere near this level of breakthrough. That's why it's called science fiction.

Hot Rods

AMX

I had the privilege of owning a 1969 AMX for several years. Wish I still had it. With a 390 cubic inch V8, four-speed transmission, and limited-slip rear end, it was a powerful beast that could go from zero to sixty and back to zero in eleven seconds flat. For the time it handled well, although these days it might best be described as "squirrelly". https://en.wikipedia.org/wiki/AMC_AMX

El Camino

I've also owned a 1972 Chevy El Camino. It was a fun ride to haul stuff around. My wife, myself, one dog, two cats, and our possessions used it to escape Port Isabel, Texas, back in 1973. https://en.wikipedia.org/wiki/Chevrolet_El_Camino

Spacecraft

The Multiplarity trilogy mentions several different spacecraft. It might be interesting to see the real-world examples that inspired these craft.

The first is, of course, the US Space Shuttle. While there are many good reasons why it never fully achieved its potential, the fundamental shape was the result of more than twenty-five years of airframe development. The Shuttle was such a good basic shape that the USSR copied it with their Buran Shuttle. A great deal has been written on both designs.

https://www.nasa.gov/externalflash/the_shuttle/

https://en.wikipedia.org/wiki/Buran_(spacecraft)

Project Black Horse

The US Air Force commissioned a study in 1993 to 1994 that was published as Spacecast 2020. So far, only about a third of it has been declassified., It makes for some fascinating reading. One of the requirements discussed was the ability to deliver warfighters or equipment anyplace on the globe within a couple of hours. The link is to an excerpt from Spacecast 2020 that describes a rocketplane.

http://csat.au.af.mil/2020/papers/app-h.pdf

From the document:

"The description above is not science fiction. It is an entirely plausible outcome of the development program described in this paper. The initial reaction of many readers to the assertions above and the Black Horse TAV concept in general is that it is too good to be true, and that the claims are reminiscent of Shuttle or NASP promises. In fact, Black Horse is substantially different in concept from either of those systems, and the numbers and assertions in this paper are based on a preliminary but iterated design (i.e., several steps beyond a point design) performed by technically credible engineers."

One of the primary designers involved in Project Black Horse was Mitchell Burnside Clapp. In 1995 he left military service and founded a company called Pioneer Rocketplane.

https://en.wikipedia.org/wiki/Pioneer_Rocketplane

Mr. Clapp is a true renaissance man. Besides being a gifted engineer, he's also a songwriter, musician, and currently is in charge of a DARPA program.

http://www.ovff.org/pegasus/people/mitchell-burnside-clapp.html

"Mitchell Burnside Clapp is the founder of Pioneer Rocketplane, which begat Rocketplane Limited. He graduated from MIT in 1984 with two degrees in Aerospace Engineering, one in Physics, and another in Russian, establishing the trend of being constitutionally unable to limit himself to just one field of endeavor. During 1988 he attended the USAF Test Pilot School (pretty much forcing him to gafiate for a while), from where he graduated in that year to work on the YA-7F program, serve as an instructor on the school's staff, and later as the Air Force's flight test person on the DC-X program. It was this experience that led to his initial involvement with the alt.space community, and indirectly to his development of aerial propellant transfer technology to enable horizontal takeoff, horizontal landing spaceplanes."

Falcon9

The world's most powerful rocket!

Warp Explorer

Single-Stage-To-Orbit (SSTO) has been the dream of every rocket scientist since Wernher Von Braun. This fictional spacecraft is designed to carry four crew members on short, exploratory trips.

Warp Tug

Essentially a framework to hold a warp-drive system, three "Bricks", and a team of transhumanists that will not suffer from the extreme conditions of deep space and warp-drive travel. The tug is designed to carry a Colonial Lander from an assembly point to another planet.

Colonial Lander Type I

Shaped like an early NASA Mercury capsule, this series of landers is much larger. They are designed to use a large ablative heat-shield, parachute, and final retro-rockets to soft-land a large number of colonists and their supplies. The landing area is cleared by a large fuel-air bomb prior to the main craft leaving orbit. Once down and unloaded, the lander becomes an emergency shelter, colonial meeting area, and eventually, a museum.

Type II Colonial Lander
Designed for open water landing
96 Colonial CryoDox plus 4 crew CryoDox
12 Buzzards and 144 Skeeters
stored in upper wing

Colonial Lander Type II

This spacecraft borrows from the original lifting-body, space shuttle design. There are two primary differences. One is there is no landing gear. The hull is designed for water landings. The second difference is the biplane (dual wing) design. The upper wing serves as storage and deployment for skeeters and buzzards, while the lower wing carries batteries and outboard jet drive motors for seaborne travel.

Super-heating on reentry will not be a problem since these ships will use a magnetoshell system that has been described and tested by NASA.

https://www.nasa.gov/feature/magnetoshell-aerocapture-for-manned-missions-and-planetary-deep-space-orbiters

https://www.nasa.gov/offices/oct/early_stage_innovation/niac/2012_phase_I_fellows_kirtley.html

Lunar Colony

As I envision it, the colony would be established with a series of robots to move lunar soil (regolith and dust) to prepare an area for a fabrication plant that used local materials to create solar panels. A massive solar panel array would provide power for boring machines that used both physical digging and laser-sintering to create and seal tunnels.

http://www.spacesafetymagazine.com/space-exploration/moon-landing/sinterhab-3d-printed-moon-base-concept-lunar-dust/

The first humans would setup inflatable habitats like those from Bigelow Aerospace. Once deployed and connected, the robot tractors would bury them under several meters of regolith to provide radiation and micro-meteor protection.

https://bigelowaerospace.com/

The desciption of cables, struts, and dome material to cover a massive crater are being developed now with 3D graphene.

https://futurism.com/mit-unveils-new-material-thats-strongest-and-

Micasa Map

While writing about the new planet Micasa, I knew I needed some sort of map to help me place the various colony locations. My first few attempts at cartography were an ugly failure. Apparently, that is one skill I'm not going to develop any time soon.

That is when I remembered the beautiful NASA/JPL images of Earth. The images are free for the downloading. I grabbed some that depicted terrain as I envisioned it on Micasa, then cut and pasted sections from various images to create an image of this fictional world.

Software Tools

Other than the physical hardware of my desktop computer system, I have no financial investment. All of my software is Free and Open Source. The following is a list of what I used to create this book.

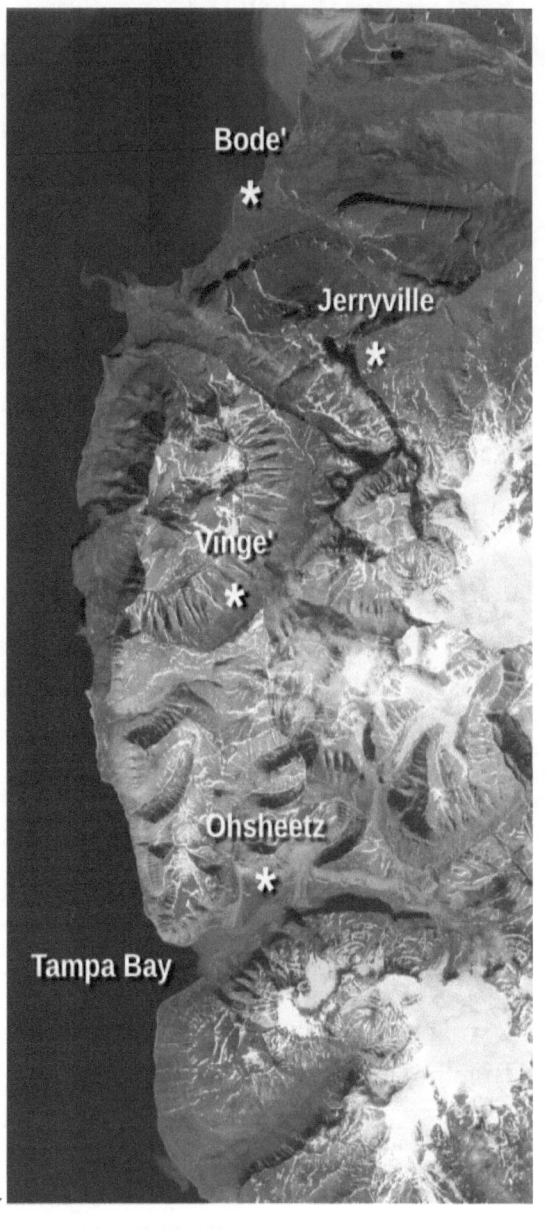

Kubuntu Linux

Kubuntu is an operating system built by a worldwide community of developers, testers, supporters and translators.

Kubuntu is a free, complete, and open-source alternative to Windows and Mac OS X which contains everything you need to work, play or share.

http://kubuntu.org/

Libre Office

LibreOffice is a powerful office suite – its clean interface and feature-rich tools help you unleash your creativity and enhance your productivity.

LibreOffice includes several applications that make it the most powerful Free and Open Source office suite on the market.

http://www.libreoffice.org/

GIMP

The GNU Image Manipulation Program (GIMP) is a cross-platform image editor available for GNU/Linux, OS X, Windows and more operating systems. It is free software, you can change its source code and distribute your changes.

Whether you are a graphic designer, photographer, illustrator, or scientist, GIMP provides you with sophisticated tools to get your job done. You can further enhance your productivity with GIMP thanks to many customization options and 3rd party plugins.

https://www.gimp.org/

Inkscape

Inkscape is a professional vector graphics editor for Windows, Mac OS X and Linux. It's free and open source.

https://inkscape.org/en/

Other Resources

Google Earth

https://www.google.com/earth/

NASA/JPL

There are thousands of public-domain images available.

http://www.jpl.nasa.gov/spaceimages/

Wikipedia

It should be noted that Wikipedia is ONLY useful for tertiary research. I use it for quick-reference, but any serious researcher should dig much deeper.

https://www.wikipedia.org/

###

About the Author

Anthony Stevens, aka E.C. Field, is an Olde Pharte Technogeek,
Author, Photographer, Leathercrafter, Gearhead, SCAdian, History
Freak, Cosplayer, and Graphics enthusiast.
He has written more than a dozen novels, some lyrics, doggerel
poetry, and more than a few short stories.
He's a cat lover (seems to be a writer thing, eh?) and although born
in Florida, has traveled a great deal. He and his wife are currently
enjoying life in south Florida.

Discover other titles by Anthony Stevens at:
http://postorbitallibrary.com
Facebook: https://www.facebook.com/masteranthonystevens
Smashwords: https://www.smashwords.com/profile/view/ecfield
Ello: https://ello.co/anthonystevens
MeWe: https://mewe.com/i/anthony.stevens2

www.ingramcontent.com/pod-product-compliance
Lightning Source LLC
Chambersburg PA
CBHW020503020726
47493CB00001B/158